NIGHTFALL

BOOK THREE OF BLACK EARTH

M.S. VERISH

NIGHTFALL

nightapplecreations.com

Written by M.S. Verish
Edited by *Night Apple Creations*, Carolyn Dubiel, and Richard Moore
Cover concept and map design by Stefanie Verish
Cover artwork by *Deranged Doctor Design*
(e)Book layout by *Night Apple Creations*
Author photo by Denise Costanzo
First published: 12/25/2013

~WORLD OF SECRAMORE~

Legend of the Ravenstone - *Ravenstone*

Curse of the Ravenstone - *Ravenstone*

(**The Hawk's Shadow** - *Short Story*)

Dawning - *Black Earth*

Meridian - *Black Earth*

Nightfall - *Black Earth*

The Silver Sigil - *Origins*

* *The Dark Tide - Origins* *

* *Forthcoming* *

CONTENTS

Northern Secramore
Mordrin Varg
The Northern Kingdoms
Markanturos
Veloria
Mystland
The Southern Kingdoms
Falquirian Territory
Karistell Ocean
The Freelands
Shadowblaze Coast
Nemeloreah
Secrailoss
Draebongaunt Ocean
Blackdust Islands
Amber Coast
Firethorne Shore
The Dragon's Garden
Acaroth
N
W
E
S
Jornoa
Southern Secramore
Cornabaez

The Edge
Mordrin Varg
Northern Secramore
Cardigus
Markanturos
Mystland
The Southern Kingdoms
Desert
Falquirian Territory
Belorn
Nemeloreah
Nemeloreah

The Northern Kingdoms
Traders' Ring
Veloria
Iliantheria
Thieldrerin Mountains
Jumull
Cornam
Grevlow
Valesage
The Freelands
Nightwind Mountains
Shadowblaze Coast
Haloan Mountains
Tauman

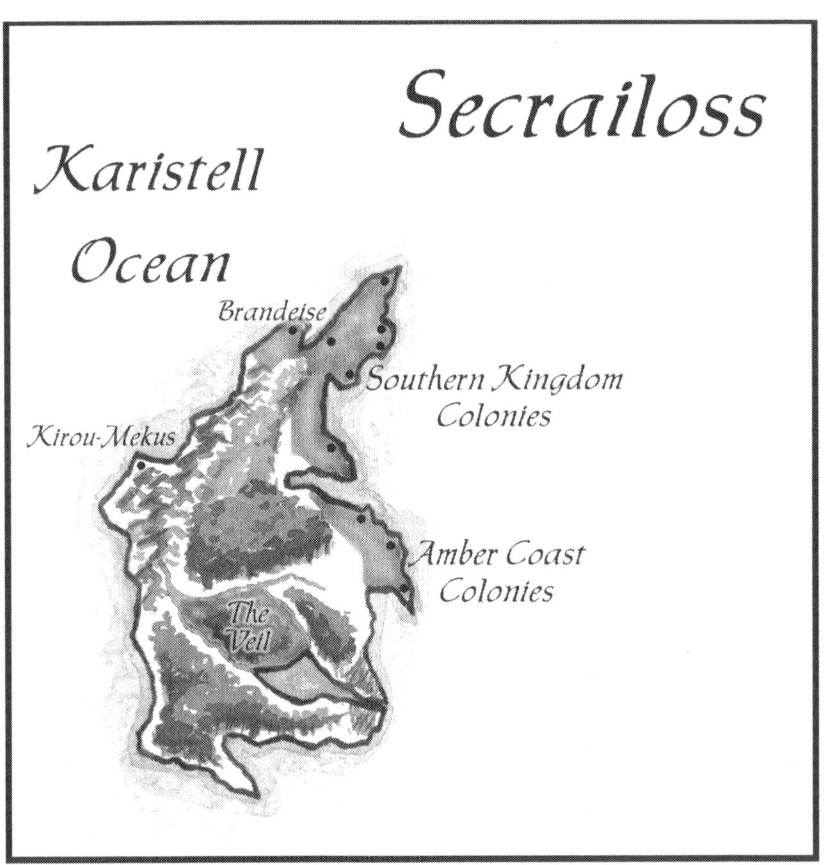
Secrailoss
Karistell
Ocean
Brandeise
Southern Kingdom
Colonies
Kirou-Mekus
Amber Coast
Colonies
The
Veil

Southern Secramore

Blackdust Islands
Crimson Mountains
Firethorne Shore
The
gon's Garden
Acaroth
Androth
Norzom
Orenza
Syuna Desert
Cornabaez
Cornabaez

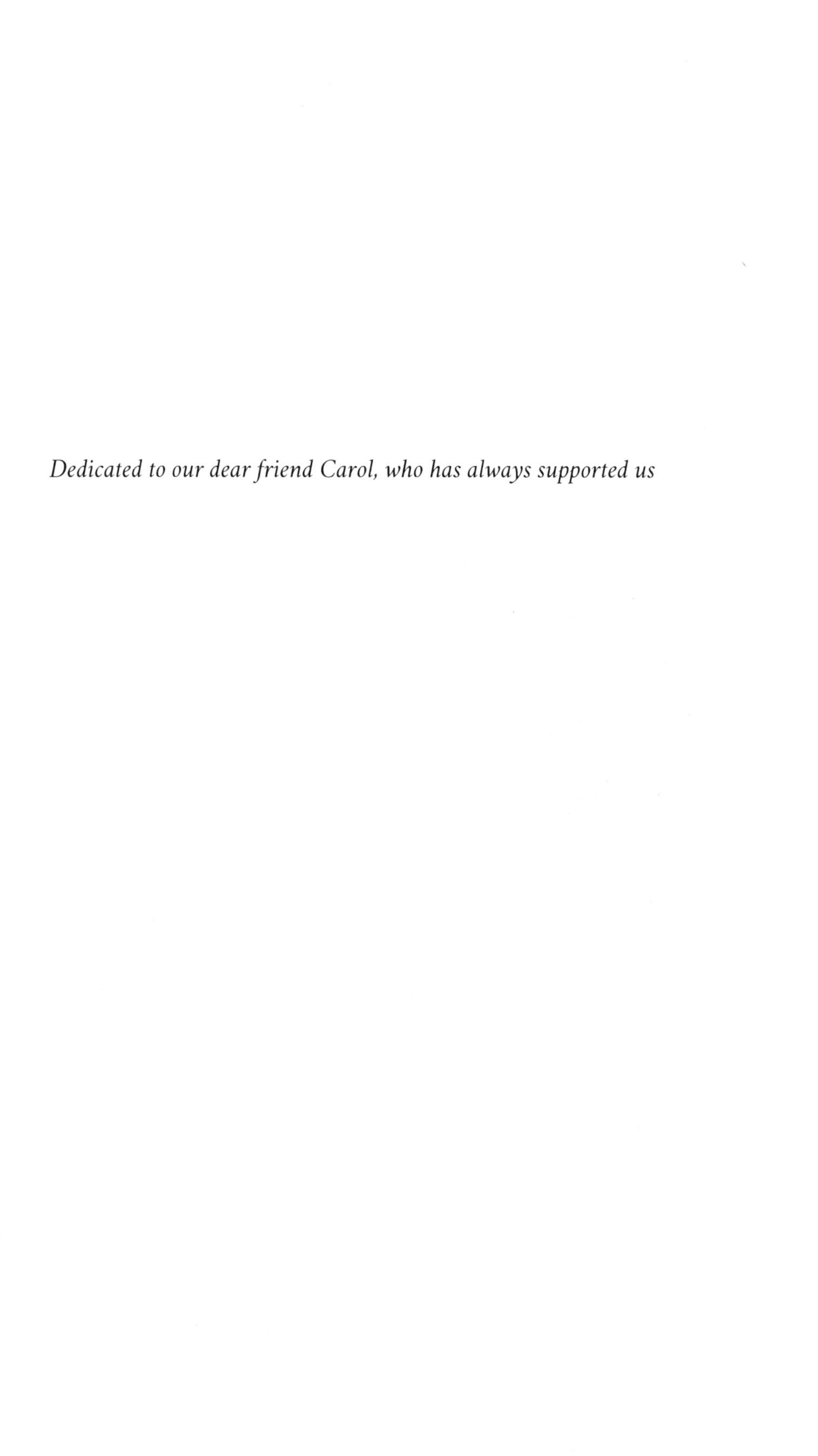

Dedicated to our dear friend Carol, who has always supported us

NIGHTFALL

BOOK THREE OF BLACK EARTH

M.S. VERISH

1

CAUSE FOR CONCERN

"*The rose, it has faded*
Like the hours, petals fall
One by one
'Til there are none left at all.
The birds have gone silent
Beneath the darkening pall
No sound is uttered,
There is no sound at all.
The cold, it holds fast
To the trees great and tall
The chill fog, it settles
Amongst one, amongst all.
Moonrise and starshine
That great pale ball
So distant and lonely
Watches over us all.
All days have an ending
As do we all
Give way to the shadows

That bring us Nightfall."

His soft words trailed like smoke, giving way to the splashing of the waves as they lapped against the ship. The poem was, in fact, a song—the words to which Catherine had believed forgotten, though she often hummed the melody. It could have been a lullaby, and the Draebongaunt Ocean a cradle. A dark blanket patterned with scattered stars spread wide above them as they stood at the bow, gazing at the horizon. Catherine slipped her hand into the Ilangien's. It felt cool and papery, like an autumn leaf from a season past. His fingers clasped hers, and she moved closer to feel his warmth. A trace of a breeze skirted the ship and lifted his moon-white hair, reminding her of the gulls they had seen drifting upon the wind. Then he turned to her, his silver-blue eyes filled with questions. Only one escaped his lips. "Who are you?"

CATHERINE WOKE NAUSEATED, a tempest brewing inside her. The blanket had been kicked away save for the corner she clutched in her hands. She shivered and stared into the darkness, hearing the ship creak, and feeling the vessel breathe with the waves. She turned to the pallet next to hers to find it empty. Her stomach turned, and she shuddered with a sudden chill. *Do not let this dream come true,* she thought, and she wrapped the blanket around her and went in search of her companion.

ERAEKRYST LOOKED at the Demon and smiled. "I knew you would regain your senses, given enough time."

The white-skinned creature shrugged and continued to swing his legs from where he sat atop the bulwark. "Or maybe y' lost all sense, mate."

"For all that I have lost, my sight has never been so clear." Eraekryst lifted his head into the wind. "All will be righted, *Durmorth*, as you will see."

The Demon turned to look at him with fox-like, violet eyes. "Then stop fooling around. There isn't much time—not for y', an' not for me."

Eraekryst shivered and wrapped his cloak tighter around his shoulders. "What is it that you believe I am about?" he asked, irritated. "I am headed for the Veil. They will know how I must defeat Seranonde—"

"'S not about 'er, Olde Man," the Demon said, standing to balance on the rail—just as he had done when they had first met. "This is bigger than 'er." He walked along the edge, and Eraekryst followed on the deck.

"To what do you allude?"

"Y're the Mentrailyic. Y' should know." The Demon paused to study him. "The future."

"Ah," Eraekryst said, raising a finger. "The future you do not believe can be predicted. Fickle creature, have you changed your opinion?"

"'S nothing to do with my opinion."

"Then speak plainly," the Ilangien said with a twist of his hand. "And explain to me how it is you appear thus, pale-skinned and feral as you once were."

The Demon grinned his sharp-toothed grin. "Same as y'appear 'thus.'"

"The Shadow was your plague," Eraekryst said seriously. "It will be your end."

The Demon held wide his hands. "Do y' see me shaking?"

Eraekryst stared, confounded.

"I'm 'ere because o' y'."

"Then I must be successful," Eraekryst murmured. "I must defeat her."

His friend shrugged. "Depends."

"By all means, elaborate," Eraekryst demanded, his arms folded.

"Y'ave to pull y'self together, mate," the Demon said, just as serious. "Y're a fat olde man 'oo talks to 'imself. What do y' think y'ave to do?"

"Must I repeat myself, *Durmorth?* The Veil—"

"No. Y'ave other idears—the ones y' don' share with y'r lady."

Eraekryst turned away. "'Tis my concern, not hers."

The violet eyes bore into him. "Yeah, an' what do y' plan to do? Bring the 'ole bloody mountain down? Not really a small thing, as I see it."

"I—"

"Don't be stupid. Don't waste y'r time. Don't waste y'self. Y' need y'r strength for the Veil...and for *'er.*"

Eraekryst turned on him sharply. "You have no conception of what Kirou-Mekus is, for what it is responsible. If I do not destroy it, who will? How many more will suffer as I suffered?" His brittle voice gained strength. "You cannot ask me to ignore that prison!"

"Sounds like vengeance, Erik. 'S not always the same as justice. Is it really worth it?" The Demon's expression softened. "We 'ave work to do, mate. An' we don't 'ave much time." He spread his wings and faced the ocean.

The Ilangien's anger turned to concern. "Where are you going?"

The Demon glanced back at him. "Why? Will y' follow?"

Eraekryst hesitated, then moved up to the bulwark. "Do not leave, *Durmorth.*"

A clawed white hand extended toward him. "Are y' ready for this?"

Eraekryst's frown deepened, but he started to climb the bulwark. He reached for his friend's hand.

"Can y' save us?"

Eraekryst stood precariously on the railing, biting his lip as his balance shifted. "I am ready," he said.

"Bonzer," the Demon said with a nod. "I'll be waiting." He jumped, his wings angled back so that he plummeted straight for the water.

"No!" Eraekryst cried, reaching for empty air. But then he started to fall.

There was a shout from behind him, and strong arms pulled him back on deck. He landed on his side, becoming aware of a circle of men around him.

"Crazy old man! What were you thinking?"

"We should tie him down," another said.

"He's not in his right mind. We should leave him at the next port."

Murmurs in favor of this decision grew until they were interrupted by a woman's voice. "Enough. He is my charge, and you will not decide his fate."

Catherine appeared, wrapped in a blanket. Her face was pale but hard, and she stared at each of the sailors as if daring them to dispute her.

"But milady, we just watched him have a conversation with himself," one said.

Catherine ignored him and knelt beside Eraekryst. "Lady, he was here. The *durmorth* was my vision," he assured her.

"Erik," she said in a grave tone, "Medoriate Crow is in Cerborath. He could not have been here."

"Not 'Medoriate Crow.' The *durmorth.* He does have wings," Eraekryst said.

More murmurs amongst the sailors drew their attention.

"Please," Catherine said to them. "Leave us alone."

The crew slowly dispersed, but their presence lingered in the form of watchful eyes.

"What happened?" Catherine asked him. Concern and fatigue had deepened the lines upon her face.

"He was here," Eraekryst repeated. "If not as himself, then as some possible future version of himself." He sat up with her assistance. "Lady Catherine, this was a promising vision. I know now that he survives and that his Shadow is returned to him. He had implied that my endeavor to save him will be successful."

The doubt did not leave her expression. She reached to touch his face. "I am afraid for you," she said softly.

Eraekryst pulled back. "What I divulged to you is no cause for fear," he insisted. "Do not regard me as though I am afflicted by some incurable illness. Visions have ever been a trait of my abilities."

"Yes, but this vision nearly drowned you," Catherine said.

"I admit 'twas a strong lure," he said, "but no harm had come to pass."

"This time," she whispered, looking away.

"We are nearly at our destination," Eraekryst said, resolute. "The opportunity for mishap is waning." He gripped the bulwark to help him to his feet. "Do not submit to fear, Lady. I need your confidence." He gave her a smile.

She nodded, but she did not smile back. As she stood with him, her focus turned to the horizon. "Erik…the melody you play for me—my song, as you call it… Do you know the lyrics to it?"

His brow furrowed. "You know that I do not."

She sighed and took his hand. "Yes. Yes, you are right. Never mind."

THE SUN WAS BREAKING, bloodshot and weary in its attempt to rise above the mountains. The sky was tinted like blood-stained snow —pale and ill-boding—with thin slivers of clouds imbedded like splinters beneath the skin. Arythan felt much the same way: aching, worn, and heading into a foul humor. He had been climbing for hours in the frigid cold and encompassing darkness, hoping to cut away his infected thoughts with the sharp mountain air.

But sharp as the air was, sharper still was the pain in his chest. He had already cycled through the excuses most convenient to believe. The arrow-wound from Desnera had been mostly self-healing, and already a couple months had passed since that adventure. He would have argued that the near return of his Shadow had hurt him more, leaving a larger hole that would never completely heal. That, however, was a different sort of pain. What he felt now was undeniably physical: the tingling in his limbs, the pounding in his head, his winded lungs, and, of course, the protesting of a weak heart. It did not pound against his chest with the fury of a galloping horse, and it did not burn like warm water upon frost-bitten hands. That would have been respectable pain. No, his heart skipped and fluttered like a drunken butterfly, and occasionally that butterfly would stab him like a maddened hornet. It was shameful.

More shameful was the truth behind this frailty. He was born weak—a mixed-blood freak who somehow survived a childhood of unending illness. But it was a jealous, vengeful wizard—Cyrul Frostmeyer—who had taken him by surprise and nearly caused his heart to explode. Arythan had felt the pain then, just as he had felt it in every welling he had had since then. And Eraekryst, that traitorous, pointy-eared ass, had purposely made light of his folly, this permanent consequence.

He is learning his own lesson now, the old fool, Arythan thought bitterly. He did not easily award others his trust, and the Ilangien had betrayed him in a most deliberate and selfish abuse of his godlike abilities. *Whatever Catherine Lorrel has seen in you, I don't know, but if she is my replacement, then she has my sympathy.*

Light-headed, Arythan sank to his knees, closed his eyes, and took a few deep breaths. In the brief time he rested, the cold huddled around him, trying to permeate the few layers of clothing around his lean frame. Though he hated to be chilled, he hated more to be constricted and smothered. The wind dried the sweat on his brow, and he would not have been surprised if it had turned to ice. With a shiver, he opened his eyes and stood. A rocky ledge drew his attention for some limited shelter. Once he reached it, he plucked the large, mottled feather from his scarf and planted it in a snowy mound.

It's too much, he thought, prying an icy lock of hair from his face. *All of it. Too much.* Once he had been a vagabond with nothing on his mind but survival. Now, however, his life had become a labyrinth of paths, all tight-walled and twisting. Was this really his life he was living, or did it belong to someone else?

A force stirred inside him, and Arythan tried to ignore it. There was a darkness filling the void where his Shadow had been. Unlike his Shadow, this darkness was nothing of substance. It was cold, hollow, and devouring, and it made him feel like a monster. The day the Desneran queen died, it had nearly consumed him. He was almost responsible for her demise, and at the time, he had not cared.

Arythan stared at the distant mountains, but his attention remained upon his rising anger and frustration. *Too much. Too much at once.* He began to tremble, and magical energy raced for him without his summoning.

Calm down. You came here for peace of mind, not to destroy the mountains. He took a breath. Then another. His breathing came faster, harder, his world was a teeming mass of energy buzzing around him. There was so much power, so much raw potential that circled him, looking for a way inside—looking for a channel, a direction.

Let it go.

Arythan did not. He could not. For as much control as he believed he had learned over the elements, they held sway over him, too. His heart faltered in a moment of weakness, and his walls crumbled. Like a torrent of floodwater, the magic poured through him, inundating him in a violent welling. Black and boiling clouds formed in seconds, and lightning gnashed like jagged teeth. The wind contorted around him, a partner daring him to duel. He always let it take him. He always became the vessel.

Not this time, he vowed, and he began to take control. The wind fought him as he tried to seize it. To grab it would have it slip through his fingers; he had to shape it without force. He loosened his grip, and the battle turned. His opponent became his partner in an elemental dance. The lightning and the thunder became a beat, steady and reliable, and the clouds were their stage. It was a moment of harmony so completely new to him, that he nearly lost his focus. When everything else in his life was chaos, he had found the eye of his storm.

He glimpsed a shape—a figure—in the periphery of his vision. Arythan would swear the tall and motionless man was his brother. *Em'ri. Do you see it? Do you?* He calmed the winds and assuaged the churning clouds, but he did not move for fear of falling over. The figure approached him, and he came to recognize the lean and bearded face of Othenis Strix.

Though the leader of the Ice Flies was smiling, his gray eyes searched Arythan suspiciously. "Medoriate Crow, I would say you seem curiously disappointed to see me." He held up the feather the mage had planted. "You did wish a meeting?"

Arythan nodded. "Sorry. Y' looked like...someone else." He swayed unsteadily on his feet, and Othenis gripped his arm. "Just need a spit," he murmured, and sank to the ground.

Othenis crouched beside him. "I am starting to see how a mage is so very different from a wizard," he said. "It was like you had a bear eating from your hand."

"'S not normally like this," Arythan admitted. "I didn't know I was a mage 'til I came to Northern Secramore. I still 'ave a lot to learn."

"This is where you come to practice?"

Arythan frowned and brushed the snow from his coat. "No. This is where I come t'escape."

"I must say," Othenis began, "that I thought I would see you sooner. I'm sure my alliance with Garriker had you surprised."

It was not the only surprise. Arythan shrugged. "Sorry. I got shot."

Othenis smoothed his beard. "I had heard. But you have made a recovery."

"Traded one problem for another," the mage muttered. He drew a jack from his pocket and lit it between his lips. "'S bloody cold. The cave's close by."

Othenis nodded and helped Arythan to his feet. The mage melted the snow from his clothes, and he led the way to the shelter.

"What troubles you, Arythan? I would think you are headed for brighter days, what with the Merchants' Guild soon to vacate Cerborath."

The mage shook his head. "Three-part problem. Tha's the first one."

Othenis frowned but waited.

"Garriker is the second." He presented the dark crevice that was the entry to the cave. Inside a ring of Wizard's Fire ignited, casting the shelter in a soft, blue glow. Once they had both settled upon the blankets, Arythan continued. "The third—" He took a puff from the jack. "Is that I'm going to be a father."

Othenis blinked. A smile stretched his beard, and he patted the mage on the shoulder. "Congratulations…though I do not see how that is a problem."

"Y' will," he promised, running a hand through his hair. "I'm going to be married. Three people: makes it a family."

Othenis looked at him, his brow furrowed. "I think most people want a family."

Arythan took a deep hit from the jack. "I never planned this. I can't be a father. I don' know a bloody thing about caring for a family."

"Valid concerns," Othenis said, "but you need to trust more in your instincts. Your wife and child will need you, but they will also support you."

"Maybe it works that way for others, but not for me. Not now."

"You refer to problems one and two."

"The Merchants' Guild isn't leaving," Arythan asserted. "They'll scale back, work in secret. I'm 'elping them with the Ice."

"The king has made a pact with me," Othenis said. "And while Garriker does not hold the most favored reputation, I believe he is a fair man—a man of his word. He said his relations with the Guild were at an end; he intends to see them gone."

"That's the king," Arythan said, his gaze leveling upon the other. "The king is in Desnera with 'is wife. Prince Michael will take the throne of Cerborath. Mikey's made 'is own pact—with the Guild. 'E thought 'e'd write me into it." He took a few more puffs on the jack, trying to keep calm.

"The king is not aware of this."

Arythan shook his head. "Y' asked me to poke around—to learn 'oo I work for. Y' knew 'twas the Seroko. Y' knew 'twas the bastards 'oo killed my brother."

"I'm sorry," Othenis said. "I felt it was something you best learn for yourself. I am disappointed to learn that the prince has initiated this conspiracy. I'm not in the habit of making enemies."

"Try being a traitor to y'r king. Try being a traitor to y'r brother an' y'r family," Arythan said, his voice rising. The fire also rose. "My oath is to Garriker, but 'is son will be the one on the throne." He crushed the burning jack in his trembling hand. "I watched my brother die," he seethed.

"You are in a hard situation," Othenis said, his voice even. "There is one question that will make all the difference to me helping you."

Arythan looked up at him expectantly.

"The Seroko only know you as Arythan Crow, correct?"

The mage narrowed his eyes and nodded.

"They will try to learn more about you. You must remain a mystery. They can never know that you are Hawkwing's brother."

"What does it matter?" Arythan snapped. "I want them to know. I want to tell them jus' before I burn out their 'earts."

"And you will negate all that Hawkwing strove to keep sacred," Othenis said. "You can have your revenge, but there is a better way —a way that will not jeopardize your family. I know you want them to be safe."

The mage threw the ashes of the jack in the fire and slumped forward with a sigh. "I don' know what to do. 'S all too much."

Othenis placed a hand on Arythan's shoulder. "You brought me here for a reason. Let me help you."

"I'm listening," he said, though he did not look up.

"This is my situation. The Seroko-Merchants' Guild cannot be allowed to mine the Black Ice—"

"Why?" Arythan interrupted sharply. "What's so important about the bloody Ice?"

Othenis smiled grimly. "Ah, so that secret is yet a mystery for you. Do you truly believe that so successful a force as the Merchants' Guild needs ground crystals to maintain their empire?"

Arythan remained expressionless. "I wouldn't know."

"There isn't much repute in addicting the aristocracy to a euphoric Enhancement," Othenis said. "The Enhancement is a front. It's an excuse to be here and mine the Black Ice. You know what the Ice is. You know it comes from the remains of immortals. While the rest of Secramore believes immortals are creatures of fantasy and folklore, the Seroko know—somehow—of their existence. They know where the Ice is to be found, and they intend to exploit it—as a means to immortality."

Arythan stared at him.

"Do not seem so surprised. If anyone will find the key to life eternal, it's the Seroko, and I do not want to consider what they will do with that sort of power." Othenis smoothed his beard. "They must have some sort of map to guide them," he mused.

"'S a book," Arythan said quietly. "A book about the Ilangiel."

"Have you seen it?" Othenis asked, his eyes wide.

The mage nodded slightly. "I stole it for them, from a mountain." He dug his fingers into his hair. "I didn't know it then. I didn't know Safir-Tamik was with them."

"But you might be able to recover the book," Othenis said.

Arythan shrugged. "Maybe. But they'd still dig up the Plains."

"If we knew the locations of the Ice, we could take this one step further," Othenis said, strength feeding his words. "We could destroy it."

"It can't be destroyed," Arythan said immediately.

"How do you know?" Othenis challenged. "Because Seroko wizards have been unable to do so? We know the limitations of wizards."

"I can't burn it," Arythan said with a shake of his head. "All I can do is dissolve it in water—reform it."

"We have to try. If there is a way to destroy it, we'll find it," he said, determined.

"'We' or *me*?" Arythan muttered.

Othenis held out his hands. "But would that not be the perfect revenge? Thwart the Seroko and their greatest ambition?"

"Y're forgetting problems two an' three," Arythan said, irritated. He stood and began to pace. "What 'appens to m' family when I'm 'anged for treason?"

Othenis stood to face him. "We would have to be very careful about our correspondence, but I could have some of my people watch over your wife and child until the Black Ice is destroyed. I can give them sanctuary, and I can see that you and your family disappear after this plan is executed. You can join us, Arythan.

Fight for a worthy cause, as your brother did. You will not be risking anything more than you already are. You need only keep me informed of your situation, work with the Ice in secret to test its weaknesses, and keep your identity hidden from the Seroko. You are capable of all this."

Arythan held his gaze. "Y' swear y' will help protect m' family."

Othenis clasped his hand. "I will. I promise."

The mage did not smile as Othenis handed him back the feather.

"This is the right choice, Arythan. You know that it is." The tall man headed for the entrance of the shelter. He turned. "Again, congratulations, Medoriate." And then he left, though the mage had more than enough on his mind to keep him company.

2

THE FAMILY NAME

"Pregnant!"

The word echoed in the dining hall as Prince Michael Garriker III responded to the letter in his hand.

Victoria could feel her cheeks redden, and she looked at Arythan across the table, giving a slight shake of her head. She had not told anyone, save the father of the child and the healer, Diana Sherralin. She noticed Arythan had only picked at his food—a sure sign he was troubled. He could devour more food than anyone at the table and have nothing to show for it. She wished it was a gift she had, for soon she would outgrow her clothes, and the secret child would no longer be a secret.

"Father wastes no time," Michael said snidely. "And as for that Desneran whore—"

"Michael," Ladonna warned, placing her hand on her husband's arm. "Our children are present."

"What's a 'hore'?" Mira asked, trying to sound mature for her eleven-or-so years of age.

"Enough, Mira," Michael said. "Do not repeat anything I say."

"HORE," Riley announced proudly, and Ladonna squeezed his mouth.

"Well, children, you will soon have a new aunt or uncle. How does that sound?" Michael asked.

"I don't care," Mira said, and Riley nodded in agreement.

"Do not bring them into this," Ladonna said to her husband. "They are too young to understand."

"Are they?" Michael turned to Banen and waved the letter at him. "What do you think of this, dear brother?"

"I side with Mira," Banen said, emotionless.

"You don't care? Not at all?" Michael asked.

"I was never in line for the throne," Banen snipped.

Victoria could not help but study him. He was always so cold, so distant. But there was a hint of color in Banen's tone; she could not interpret it if she tried.

"Crow," Michael said, and Arythan froze. "How is your wound?"

The mage's deep blue eyes flicked in Victoria's direction before he faced the prince. "Bonzer."

Banen scowled and shoveled another spoonful in his mouth. Arythan picked at the venison. Awkward silence ensued.

"Family is important," Michael announced. "I value that we are all here to share in this meal. We will need to keep our ties strong when Father permanently relocates to Desnera." He took a sip of wine and pointed his knife at Arythan. "And speaking of relocation… I have found the perfect country setting for you, Crow. There is a manor beside a lake, perhaps two hours by carriage south of the castle. The old woman who lives there is a relative—I won't bore you with the family connection—and she has several attendants who upkeep the grounds. She is delighted at the possibility that you should bring Victoria for an extended stay."

Victoria looked at Arythan questioningly, and it was his turn to redden.

"I thought 'twould be nice," he said quietly, "for us to be away for a while."

There was always more to his ideas than what he said aloud. They would have much to discuss after dinner. "Yes, that would be nice," Victoria said. As she motioned the server for another portion of meat, she caught Banen staring at her.

"Hungry?" he asked.

"It *is* dinner," she said.

"Perhaps you missed lunch," Banen said.

Arythan glared at him. "She did."

"Why not give her your portion? It grows cold on your plate."

Arythan stabbed the meat with his knife, and it began to sizzle. "Better?"

"Enough, children," Michael said with a wave of his hand. "You should know that I have arranged for entertainment this evening."

Banen scowled. "Father would never—"

"*I* like entertainment, Brother. And I think it would do all of us good to relax and enjoy the actors." Michael brought his cup to his lips and paused. "I trust there are no objections."

No one said a word.

"Excellent," Michael said and took a sip. "We will move to the solar where it is more comfortable. I have invited some friends to join us. I doubt the performers will show the caliber of entertainment our Dark Wizard once provided, but this should be a nice diversion."

The meal ended, and the occupants of the table slowly migrated to the solar. Victoria lingered toward the back of the procession so that she might have a word or two with her betrothed. Arythan gave her a wary smile, and she felt her stomach twist—just a little.

"A manor in the countryside?" she asked, slipping her hand into his.

"Why not?"

Victoria shrugged. "When would we leave?"

"In a week," he said, and she raised her eyebrows.

"Oh. You've had this planned, then."

He nodded.

"When were you going to tell me?"

"Soon. Michael likes to spoil surprises."

"Ah." She searched his face, first looking for a hint of emotion, then admiring his features. "He is going to be very handsome."

Arythan turned to her in surprise; she had achieved her goal. "What?"

"You know," she said smoothly. "We have yet to choose a name."

"Could be a girl," he whispered in her ear.

"I don't think so."

He gave her a funny look, and she swatted his arm. "Anyway, we have time. Why are we leaving so soon?"

"Later, Tori." And she watched his expression fade to empty as they entered the solar.

They sat amongst a group of twenty—a small crowd for one of Michael's famed events—and waited for the performance to begin. A man in flamboyant dress appeared to read a poem titled, "The Golden Rose." Victoria found it hard to pay attention, and it did not help that her bladder was full. She squirmed and shifted, feigning laughter at the humorous moments when all she wanted to do was use the garderobe.

"What's the matter?" Arythan asked at last.

"I need to go," she said flatly.

A couple heads turned in their direction, Banen's one of them.

"Come with me," she insisted.

"Alright."

They stood and excused themselves, not meeting any of the curious eyes that followed them. Once they were in the hall, Arythan kissed her hand. "Nice idear, Tori."

Victoria frowned and quickened her pace. "No. I really do need to take care of something."

"Oh."

When she had finished, she found Arythan pacing the hall. "So… Is there more to this restless mood than the countryside manor?" she asked.

It took him a moment to answer as he ran a hand through his hair. "I don' think I'll make a good father," he said at last.

Victoria laughed at him. "How can you say that? You are ridiculous."

"'S not ridiculous," he said, stopping to face her.

She could see in his eyes that he was anxious, and that unnerved her. She took a breath and took his arm. "Talk to me, Medoriate."

"I 'ate m' father," he said. "I wasn't what 'e wanted. I couldn't please 'im if I tried. I don' want to be like 'im."

"Then don't be," Victoria said simply. "Be everything he wasn't."

"Easy to say," Arythan muttered. "'E's still inside o' me. I feel 'im when I'm angry. I always thought I was diff'rent, but I can't escape what—'oo I am."

"I think I understand," she said, considering his words. "But there is one thing you're not considering, my love." She squeezed his hand and smiled. "That's why I am here. You will tell me if I am acting ridiculous, and I will tell you if you are being absurd. We need to have faith in each other."

"Y' don' seem afraid at all," Arythan said, his expression softening.

"You mean that this little piece of both of us is growing inside me and will split me open like an overripe fruit?" she asked. "You might say I am a little concerned, but truly, we can only move forward. I will love our little family."

"What if it 'as white skin, claws, and wings? Or 'as enough magic to burn down the castle?"

"Yes, you are being absurd right now." She pulled on his beard to bring him closer. "He will be a handsome baby boy." Victoria stared into his eyes before their lips met.

THE SHORT SEASON of summer had asserted itself in Cerborath. All trees were green, and one could conceivably venture outdoors without a coat or hat. Even so, it took much coaxing for Victoria to pry Arythan from his dark, concealing attire. "It's *summer,* Arythan. You can wear your coat and scarf the other ten months of the year."

"This isn't summer. In summer y' can fry a fish on a rock. Y' grow blisters from walking barefoot on the sand. The birds stop singing midday because 'tis so bloody 'ot." He folded his arms, which were only concealed by the sleeves of his linen shirt. "'S like I'm naked."

"Do you want to be?" Victoria asked coyly. She had abandoned her gown for a peasant's simple dress.

He smiled but did not reply as he helped her into the carriage.

"You packed light," she commented.

"I don't own anything," he said honestly. "Except the clothes y' won't let me wear."

The sun was bright in the sky, and greenery seemed to glow beneath it. The rhythm of the carriage wheels and hoof beats carried the couple along the road, and their spirits were high. Victoria chatted along the way, filling the silence. Now and again Arythan would glance out the window to see Narga trotting contently behind them.

"So tell me," Victoria asked, a hint of suspicion in her voice, "if this is meant to be time away from the castle, why did you bring your horse?"

"She's the other lady in m' life," Arythan said.

"You can tell me the truth," Victoria said, lifting her chin. "I heard it on the wind that His Majesty has sent the B.E.S.T. to kindly remove the Merchants' Guild from the Ice Plains. I would think they would need your help—especially if you are to take over production of the Enhancement."

"The wind is a bit noisy," Arythan said, indifferent. "Truth is, Garriker didn't want me there—in case the Guild got nasty about it. 'E didn't tell me to take y' into the country. 'Twas *my* idear."

"Very romantic. But that still doesn't answer my question."

"What question?" He glanced out the window to check on Narga.

"Never mind."

On they rolled through open fields dotted with summer wildflowers. The leaves of the trees rustled in the wind, and butterflies bounced amidst the blooms. A sturdy stone building arose before them, dressed in moss and ivy. A rough wooden fence guarded a menagerie of sheep, goats, ducks, and chickens. "Reminds me of where I grew up," Victoria murmured, allowing Arythan to help her from the carriage.

A footman appeared at the door and hurried toward them with a warm greeting and introduction. Arythan turned Narga loose, and he and Victoria were escorted inside. A plump old woman as old as time itself waddled toward them, embracing each of them as if she was their grandmother.

"Lady Carilynda Thornbrush," the footman said, embarrassed.

"Lyndi," the old woman said, waving away the attendant. "I didn't realize I would share my home with such a handsome young couple." She winked at Arythan and took Victoria's hand, dragging her away. "This is so very exciting. We have much to prepare, my dear."

Victoria glanced back at Arythan, who merely shrugged. He looked at the footman, and the footman looked back at him. "How can I be of assistance, milord?"

Arythan fished in his pocket and pulled out two jacks. "I need a lil' reassurance, mate."

The man smiled and accepted the small red stick. "Absolutely, milord."

They headed outside to smoke and talk, and the better part of an hour went by before they were joined by a third gentleman. Then, at last, the front door to the manor opened, and Victoria and Lyndi came out.

Arythan was speechless. Nothing had physically changed about Victoria: not her dress, not her hair…nothing to speak for the time the women had spent "preparing." But her eyes glistened with tears, and her lips were strung in a joyous smile that made her glow with life. The jack fell from his fingers as he went to meet the most beautiful woman he had ever seen.

He searched her eyes, and very slowly, his own smile grew. "'Ello, Lovely."

"Arythan," she whispered, her voice choked. "You didn't tell me—"

"'Twas a surprise." He took her hand and pressed something into it.

"No, no! You put it *on* her finger!" cried a voice from behind them.

Arythan felt his face heat, but Victoria was already staring at the ring, slipping it on her own finger.

"I don' know 'ow 'tis done," he confessed, "but that bloke's 'ere to marry us." He gestured to the Keeper of the House of Jedinom watching them.

"You are such a foreigner," Victoria said, flinging her arms around him.

"Not even 'Uman," he said, and she laughed.

The Keeper rushed up to them, clearly disconcerted. "No kissing! You may not kiss until you take your vows."

"What about all the times we kissed before?" Arythan protested.

"Don't give him trouble, Medoriate," Victoria warned. "I do not want any trouble on my wedding day."

"Y'll be stuck with it every day after," he returned.

"I know." And they parted for the Keeper to make their union official.

THAT AFTERNOON ARYTHAN and Victoria celebrated their marriage amongst amiable strangers. The feast was not kingly, but it was a fair bounty for a modest wedding. Once they were finally able to break free of Lyndi's hospitality, they retreated to their room to enjoy each other's company. The hearth burned brightly, and the shutters were left open to the sounds of crickets and toads and the occasional meandering breeze.

"I never thought it would be someone like you," Victoria said, tracing the mark of the black sun on Arythan's arm. "As a little girl, I always envisioned some high-born noble or prince—handsome, of course—and disgustingly rich."

"'Ow do y' know I'm not 'igh-born?" Arythan asked from beside her. "An' I can't 'elp it that I'm ugly. Y'll just 'ave to live with a beast."

"Stop, now. You didn't let me finish," Victoria said. "You may fulfill some of my childhood dreams, but you are so much more. You are mysterious and magical. You're pretty good with a sword—"

Arythan propped his head on his hand. "Pretty good?"

"And you're strong, and smart…."

"Pretty good?"

She pointed a finger at him. "Now it's your turn. Talk about me."

"Y've 'eard everything I can say about y'. If I say all that again, y'll just roll y'r eyes."

"Tell me how beautiful I am," she insisted.

"Y're very beautiful."

"A poet you are not." Victoria said with a wry smile. "I think that is another trait I love about you, Arythan. You never let words get in the way."

"Hm." He began to smooth out her hair.

"Soon you won't find me beautiful," she said, eyeing him. "I'm going to get round and irritable."

"That's why I brought Narga."

Victoria punched his arm. "I've thought a lot about the baby," she said, growing serious. "I want you to name him."

Arythan made a face. "I'm not the best bloke to—"

"I'm serious, Arythan. I want you to name our son."

"What if—"

"I'll name her if she's a girl," Victoria interrupted.

"The names I know aren't like the names y' know," he said.

"I've considered that," she confessed. "I want something different. A name like no other. A name with meaning."

He lay back on the pillow and gazed at the ceiling. "Reiqo," he murmured.

"Rye-ko?"

"Y' don' like it," he said.

"No, actually…" She turned to look at him. "I like it a lot." She sighed. "I just don't know where you're from."

"'S a southern name. An island name," he said, distant.

"Does it have a meaning?"

"'Alone,'" he said. When he saw her expression, he amended, "Alone in a good way. Like a—"

"Leader," Victoria supplied.

"Rebel."

"I see. You came up with that rather quickly. Is there a story I'm missing?"

Arythan blushed. "Reiqo would've been my name, if I'd chosen it."

"How do you choose your own name?" Victoria asked, intrigued. "Does that mean you're nameless until you are old enough to speak?"

The sarcasm was lost with his response. "Er…in a way. There are family names passed down to the children. When y're olde enough, y' get to choose y'r name." *If you survive….*

"So instead of 'Reiqo', you chose 'Arythan.'"

"No."

She snapped her fingers. "Right, because you have an alias! I can't believe I didn't consider it sooner." She moved closer to him. "So what is your name, my husband?"

"I don' 'ave one." Arythan saw her eyes narrow. "I don't. 'S complicated."

"I think I'm fairly intelligent."

He gave her a half-smile. "When I was olde enough to choose m' name, I ran away. So I didn't 'ave m' birth name, an' I didn't earn a new one."

"Jedinom's Sword, Arythan. Just pick a name," she said.

"'S not like that. 'Tis an important tradition, to earn a name." He stretched and closed his eyes. "I didn't earn one, so I don't want one."

"Our child will call you by a name that isn't even yours," Victoria objected.

"'E can call me 'father.'"

"That's not what I mean."

"'Dad,' then."

Victoria tried to tickle his ribs. "Now you're just being difficult."

He opened his eyes. "What's a name unless it means something to y'?"

She sighed. "So if you can't have the name you want, you will give it to our son."

"Y' said I could."

Victoria rolled onto her back. "You are fortunate I like the name you chose." She smirked. "You rebel, you."

3

THE GUIDE

"We need a guide," Catherine said, taking in the whole of the marketplace. Colonists bustled by in bright, colorful clothing, carrying baskets of fruit and boxes of provisions from the docked ships. There were merchants and parrots and monkeys, rustling palms, trampled sand, sweet-smelling flowers, and the cheery sound of a flute. Gulls cried, waves lapped at the shore, and the breeze mingled with chatter from the people around them. It was a kaleidoscope of activity and color—so very different from the Northern Kingdoms. She was overwhelmed by her surroundings, lost like a child who had wandered from her parents' sides. "Erik...."

Catherine turned to her companion, but he was not there. "Please do not wander now," she said under her breath. She searched the faces around her; he had vanished. "Erik?" she tried, knowing it would be a useless effort.

"Are you lost, milady?" asked a gentleman from behind her.

"I have lost my companion," she admitted, embarrassed.

"Just off the boat, are you?" He winked at her. "I am from Brigram. I shared the same look when I first arrived at Brandeise."

Catherine studied him, thinking he was probably her age, if not older. His hair and beard were more gray than brown, but he carried himself like a noble. He was barely taller than her, but he was broad-shouldered and fit. He took her hand and bowed. "Halgon Thayliss at your service."

"Catherine Lorrel," she told him, knowing she was blushing. How long had it been since anyone had bowed to her?

"You are not from the Southern Kingdoms, are you, Lady Catherine?" Halgon asked. "I can read it in your accent, in your manner."

"No. I am a long way from home." She glanced at the crowd again. "Cerborath, actually."

"That is a distance," he marveled. "And if you have just arrived, I would imagine you are famished. I would be honored to treat you to a fresh meal—your first in the colonies."

Catherine noticed he had not released her hand. She frowned and took a step away. "I am afraid I must find my companion first."

"Do not fret," Halgon assured her. "There is nowhere for him to go. Brandeise is a peninsula, surrounded on three sides by water and a jungle on the fourth. I promise I will help you find your friend, but I must not neglect the needs of a lady." He gently pulled her hand, and Catherine hesitated. "I mean no harm, Lady Catherine."

"Of course not, but..." Another quick look around revealed... nothing. Eraekryst was still missing. Catherine turned back to Halgon with a slight smile. "Very well. I accept your offer."

CATHERINE COULD TASTE the rum in her drink, but the juice was sweet and delicious—a welcome change from the stale wine she had consumed at every meal aboard the ship. There was some sort of unleavened bread with jelly, seasoned fish, and a small cake made of exotic fruit. "Thank you for this," she said, feeling more relaxed.

"It is my pleasure," Halgon returned, touching his cup to hers. "Welcome to the colonies." They sipped their drinks. "What is it that brings you here, if I might ask?"

"My companion," Catherine said. "He wishes to...visit his friends."

"And he decided to see them in your absence," Halgon said.

She shook her head. "No. He merely has the tendency to become distracted. I know he will be wondering where I am."

"Describe him to me, so that I might help you find him."

"Well, he is tall—six feet with some to spare," Catherine started. "He has fine, white hair that has grown a bit these last few months." She drew a line to her chin. "His eyes are silvery-blue—like the winter sky at dawn. He is fair-skinned, with a delicate nose, thin lips, and a pointed chin... Though not as pointed as when we first met." She felt her cheeks heat. "He is rather fond of Hu—good food, and we both have indulged a bit in our travels. He gained a fair bit of weight, some of which he has since lost." She gave a vague gesture to indicate his girth and smiled absently when she pictured the Ilangien in her mind. "Still very handsome—even if he is older than he should be."

"Milady."

Catherine surfaced from her thoughts, finding Halgon's face before her instead. "My apologies," she murmured. "I—I rambled on, didn't I?"

"Do not apologize," he said. "I am, however, a bit confused. You refer to this man as your companion, but you describe him as one would a husband."

She gave a nod. "Sometimes I forget that he is not."

"You intrigue me, Lady Catherine," Halgon said. "I hope your visit here is one of intended duration."

Catherine could feel her ears burning. Then she heard a sound

—a melody. It came from behind her, and her face was aflame with color. Her head bent low as the tune of the violin grew closer. She stared at the table, waiting. When the music ceased, she heard a whisper in her ear. "What song would delight the lady as she dines?"

"'The Wanderer,'" she replied, at last looking up to see Halgon's suspicious expression. He nodded to the one behind her, and Catherine dipped her head in confirmation.

"Aye, 'tis the Minstrel," the voice announced to the rest of the tavern. "And the lady wishes to hear 'The Wanderer,' who, we may note, was not aimlessly meandering but *searching* at the lady's request."

Catherine turned around. Eraekryst stood with his shoulders squared, his chin lifted in defiance. His hair had partially fallen into his eyes, which were affixed upon her. He did not acknowledge Halgon at all; rather, he gestured grandly—violin in-hand—to the confused-looking man a few paces from him.

The stranger was short and stocky, with curly blond hair and a scruffy beard. He was likely in his thirties, strong, and...one-handed. He glanced at the Ilangien, then at Catherine, then at Halgon. Before he could speak, however, Eraekryst introduced him.

"I present to you our guide, Master Jaice Ginmon."

"'Ow do y' know me name?" Jaice demanded.

"Because we have met before," Eraekryst said, and he closed his eyes and began to play Catherine's song. No one interrupted him; no one said a word until he had finished the tune, bowed, and taken his place beside Catherine.

"Master Ginmon, please join us," Eraekryst invited, and a chair slid itself up to the table. Everyone stared at him. The Ilangien, however, kept his sharp eyes upon Jaice until he sat down.

"This is an interesting gathering," Halgon said.

Catherine took Eraekryst's hand. "Lord Halgon Thayliss assisted me with our belongings. He has been most kind to me."

"Milady, I am no 'lord' of standing, though you might find I am of notable reputation in this community." Halgon waved a hand. "As for your belongings, I could not allow a lady to carry such a load. When I saw her alone, I thought I might be of some use."

"And here they are," Eraekryst said, looking at the few bags beside the table. "Thus we will require no further assistance with our burdens."

Halgon frowned. "A lady should never shoulder any burden."

"Lady Catherine is capable of carrying such a minimal load," Eraekryst said.

"Sir, this is not about her capabilities. It is about respect," Halgon insisted, his face coloring.

"I respect her capabilities," Eraekryst said easily.

"I believe the situation is manageable," Catherine said, feeling the tension rise. "No one need express any concern."

Jaice raised his hand.

"Not yet, Master Ginmon," Eraekryst said. "Ours is a party of three; we are surplus one."

Halgon's face tensed, and his hands clenched. "You are arrogant for a newcomer, and I find you insulting. You would be wise to guard your manners, for I have the power to make this venture of yours most uncomfortable."

Eraekryst sat forward. "'Tis already uncomfortable without your interference. There is a moth caught in a web at the melon vendor's stand. What will you do about it?"

The lines in the older man's face smoothed, his jaw relaxed, and his hands opened. He stood and bowed. "It has been my pleasure, Lady Catherine. I am sure we will meet again."

She nodded but could not manage a smile.

Halgon walked away, and Jaice gawked after him. "What'd y' do to the mayor, mate?" he whispered. "Y' some kind o' wizard?"

Catherine interrupted before Eraekryst could say a word. "That was blatantly wrong." She stared at the Ilangien in disappointment. "How could you do that to him?"

Eraekryst pulled the hair back from his face and bound it with a string. "I have purpose here," he said softly. "I will not be deterred."

"But you—"

"Did he suffer?" Eraekryst asked, meeting her gaze.

Catherine turned away. "No, but that is not the point."

"I cannot bother with fools while my companion waits in peril," Eraekryst said, his voice hardening. "This, this was a trifle, the bat of an eye, the passing of the slightest breeze. Think not upon it."

Catherine said nothing in the following silence, and the Ilangien turned to the expectant man in their company. "Master Ginmon, the spirits of the ocean have spared you," he said. "Despite your injury, I trust that you have maintained your profession as an adventurous guide."

Jaice looked down at the arm that bore no hand. "'Oo are y', an' 'ow do y' know me?" he asked, just above a whisper.

"Obviously I was aboard the same ship that fateful night. You would not recognize me now, for I have had my own ill fortune with which I contend."

Jaice looked up and studied him carefully. "Y're talkin' a few years ago now. The Kirou-Mekus blunder."

"'Twas my liberation from the mountain," Eraekryst said.

Jaice looked at him harder. "Nah, can't be... Pale Bloke?"

"Adventurer," he returned.

"Jedinom's Co—" Jaice glanced at Catherine—"Sword. Y've changed a bit. An' y' talk now."

"I have always spoken," Eraekryst said stiffly. "My appearance now is the result of a spell—a spell I must break to save the life of another. You recall the Demon."

Jaice broke into a grin. "Oi, that lil' bloke! 'Awkshadow, yeah. 'E was a good mate. Wish 'e'd 'ave been 'ere. Where's 'e now?"

"He is the royal medoriate for King Garriker II of Cerborath," Catherine said, trying to infiltrate the conversation.

"'Struth?" Jaice asked, slapping the flat of his hand upon the table. "Goodon'im!"

"He is being hunted," Eraekryst continued, without emotion.

"By Lorth, mate!"

"I aim to help him."

"Alright."

"As my lady asserted, we have need of a guide."

Jaice scratched his head. "Y' need a ship if y're traveling the colonies. They're scattered—"

"'Tis not my purpose," Eraekryst said immediately.

"We are searching for a place known as the Veil." Catherine's eyes moved from the Ilangien to Jaice. "It is a place where the immortals dwell."

Jaice had visibly paled. "What makes y' think I know such a place?" He laughed. "It's like a child's story. A fairytale. Immortals? Yeah, an' flying 'orses and dragons. Right-o."

Eraekryst rested his chin on his palm. "Your hand was severed by mermaids."

"Yeah, well, *they're* real. Sea bitches," Jaice spat. Then he apologized to Catherine.

"Do not lie to me, Human," Eraekryst said, a slight edge to his voice. "I will know it."

"An' then y'll make me free a moth?" Jaice asked, folding his arms. "Look, mate, I'm sorry, but I can't 'elp y'." He stood and pushed in his chair. "Sorry."

Eraekryst frowned, and Catherine touched his shoulder.

"Wait," she told the retreating guide. "Please, hear what I have to say."

Jaice turned and sighed. "'Twon't change me mind."

"Perhaps not," Catherine said, "but it is clear you have been to this place. You know what it is, and you fear it. We do not ask you to risk anything in this venture. Take us as far as you will, and instruct us as to the rest of the way."

"No one should go there. I'll be leading y' to y'r deaths," Jaice said. "Can't 'ave that on me conscience."

"'Tis my death if I do not go," Eraekryst said. "And 'twould be the death of your companion, Hawkshadow."

Jaice turned away and scratched his head.

"Please, Mr. Ginmon," Catherine begged. "It is a matter of urgency. The risk will be ours, and we understand this well."

Jaice's arm dropped to his side. "'Twill cost y'."

Eraekryst produced a weighty bag and passed it to Catherine. "We are willing to generously compensate you for your time and effort," she said. She held the bag out to him, and he took it with a grim expression.

"When do y' want to leave?"

LITTLE TIME WAS WASTED in acquiring the proper attire and provisions needed for a five-day journey through the jungle. Eraekryst and Catherine finished a light meal while Jaice browsed the market. He returned with two shoulder bags that might have equaled his weight, but he seemed to have no trouble managing them despite his missing appendage.

"Feel better that y've shed those 'eavy northern frocks?" Jaice asked. He pulled three palm-woven hats from his supplies and divided them accordingly.

"The fragrance is most repelling," Eraekryst said, wrinkling his nose and holding the hat in his hands.

"Yeah. 'S what keeps the bugs away. Lil' bastards bite, sting, and crawl all over y'."

Catherine made a face and immediately set her hat in place. Eraekryst sighed and did the same.

"Well, then," Jaice said, tipping the brim of his own hat, "let's be off."

The sun was almost at its peak in the sky when they ventured into the verdant and shadowed depths of the jungle. While the light was scarce and dappled, the heat of the day was trapped beneath the broad and fleshy leaves.

"We are perpetually damp," Eraekryst complained, lifting his hat to push his sweat-soaked hair from his face. He wiped his hand on his shirt and scowled.

"'S a jungle, mate. We'll be a ripe mess a'fore night falls," Jaice said. He hacked at some thick stalks in their way.

"Must we massacre the vegetation?"

Jaice chopped a vine hanging in front of his eyes. "Plants don' cry."

"Aye, but they do, Master Ginmon. You are but deaf and blind to their plight."

"Y' do want to get to this Veil place, right?"

Eraekryst said nothing, and Catherine eased the tension. "I am certain Mr. Ginmon will have us tread as lightly as we can." She winced when another vine was slashed, its sticky fluid spattering the air.

The afternoon wore on in the green tunnel that was their world. Loud and random cries from the wildlife were just as surprising as snakes they thought to be vines. The insects were large enough that they generated a breeze when they buzzed by the travelers' faces. There were also exotic flowers and tiny, colorful frogs tucked away in niches and pockets that only the wary eye would spy. By the time the sun's hidden light had shifted to waning gold, Eraekryst was leaning heavily upon his cane, and Catherine was stumbling over roots—too weary to lift her feet any higher. Jaice had seemingly limitless energy, and he looked back upon his followers with a hint of sympathy.

"Alright. We'll quit for dinner," he said.

Costrels were raided for water, and sweet bread, fresh fruit, and goat cheese were passed around. Jaice had started a small and smoky fire, and then he pulled three neatly folded linen sheets from his bag. "For sleeping," he said brightly. "I won't tell y' why we won't sleep on the ground." He enlisted Eraekryst's help in tying the material to the trees to serve as hammocks. "We'll 'ave to sleep with our faces a'neath the blanket."

"You are strangely quiet," Catherine said to the Ilangien. "Are you all right?"

"Aye, Lady," he said simply.

She reached to tuck a lock of hair behind his ear. "All will be well. This is what we have intended to do. You will be yourself again."

He nodded. "Forgive me. I am weary, and my own odor disgusts me," he said and awkwardly climbed into his hammock.

"Sleep well, Erik," Catherine said. She nestled into her own hammock but found Jaice was still seated on a log beside the fire. "Are you not tired?"

"Nah," he said, stirring embers with a stick. "'Struth, I won't sleep well 'til this is over. But if it means I can 'elp 'Awkshadow out, I'll lose a few winks."

Catherine regarded him thoughtfully. "So you were there when Eraekryst was liberated from Kirou-Mekus."

"Oi. Can't forget it." Jaice grinned at her. "Y' fishin' for a story, luv?"

"Only if you are willing to tell one."

"Well, I tend to get mixed up in bad business. Not me fault, 'struth. I signed on to steer the lil' ship off the coast 'ere. Bunch o' wizards wanted treasure from the Black Mountain. Thought 'twould be best to come from the sea—even with the rocks in the way." He took a sip from his costrel and wiped his mouth on his sleeve.

"Kinda surprised me to find the kid they 'ired as their thief wasn't 'Uman. 'E was this scrawny, white bloke 'oo sometimes looked like a normal kid, an' sometimes looked like a pointy-eared, shark-toothed monster. 'Is eyes were purple and glowy-like—the eyes of an animal. Guess tha's why 'e stayed under that cloak. Didn't talk much, either, but we became fair mates. We were both in on the job for the money, an' we weren't gonna get paid 'til the end.

"So we set out on the ship, an' when we reached the coast, I take out the dingy, and this lil' bloke dives right in. Waves are crashin', an' current's pullin'. All I can see is the tip of 'is white nose. Thought for sure 'e'd drown, and for awhile, I lost sight of 'im. But then I spy 'im on the rocks, climbing up like a lil' white spider. 'E gets inside the mountain, and Lorth can say what 'appened in there. 'E never spoke of it."

Jaice rubbed his chin. "All I knew was when 'e came out, 'e wasn't alone. This pale bloke with long 'air was with 'im. They were bein' chased by the Jornoans, an' they took another swim to escape. I 'elped them into the boat, an' we sailed off fast as we were able." He sighed. "I tried to get 'Awkshadow to join me. I know 'e thought about it. Could've been good business. But there was somethin' stopping 'im, an' then the storm came. Poor bloke got blamed, an' the crew tried to shove us overboard."

He looked at Catherine and held up his truncated arm. "Mermaids. They caused the storm, an' they tipped the bloody ship. Took me 'and, and I thought they'd take me life too. Must've blacked out, because all I can remember is waking up on the shore." He shook his head. "Never got paid. Never learned what became of anyone. So I came back to Secrailoss."

"That is quite a tale," Catherine said, awed. "I am sorry about your loss, but Erik and I are fortunate that you were here to guide us."

Jaice shrugged. "Can't seem to escape this place. Maybe one day I'll 'ead south an' try my luck as a prospector."

"You are young yet," she said. "And you have time. I believe this will be my last adventure."

"Aw, y'ain't through yet, luv. M' father sailed 'til 'e was nearly blind an' deaf."

Catherine tried, unsuccessfully, to stifle a yawn. "I believe there are those who are always moving, always searching. I would rather be the one to settle somewhere quiet, where I can live contentedly the rest of my days."

"Y're from up north, right?"

"Yes," Catherine said with a hint of sadness. "I was the Countess of Silvarn, and I lived in my father's manor—a place called Lorrelwood—where the forest grew wild, and the animals would venture near. It was beautiful." She closed her eyes and tried to picture her home. "Even now it seems like another lifetime since I left."

"Sounds like y'ad everything y' wanted. Why'd y' leave?"

"I was in a position to help someone," she said. "Someone I had come to care about deeply."

"Y'ad to choose," Jaice said, nodding. "Will y'ever go back?"

Catherine opened her eyes partway. "No. That is the past, and it is gone. I can accept leaving the past behind so long as the future holds promise."

"Seems like words to live by." Jaice said. "I'll 'ave to remember them."

Catherine smiled and drifted to sleep.

4

ABANDONED

"Ah, me, I am both cruel and heartless," Eraekryst murmured, wiping the sweat from his brow.

"Yes, you are."

"How could you leave her a second time?"

"She will not come looking for him."

"I wish that she would not, for her life would be safer beyond my presence," Eraekryst admitted. He pushed deeper into the vegetation. "Alas, she will come, for I am the reason she is here. But neither she nor Master Ginmon will awaken 'til late in the day. I have deepened their sleep so that these weary limbs might carry me a fair lead."

"Still they will catch you, and she is not likely to forgive you."

"I do not seek forgiveness." Eraekryst nearly tripped over a root. He took a moment to catch his breath before moving onward into the darkness.

"You seek revenge."

"You—all of you—should appreciate my effort. That no one else be harmed by the hands of so cruel a society—'tis an act of justice."

"Justification, rather."

"Let him raze the mountain. Let him avenge us!"

"And then let him perish in the avalanche of his own creation."

"You are not so kind. You never were," Eraekryst said. "But then again, neither am I."

"This is what the counselor predicted. The one who watched over you—he knew you would return."

"He also said you would remain here."

"The terms of my return are not to submit to servitude," the Ilangien snapped. "The *koncarys* did not understand. He was one victim among the many. He was poisoned by his own kind, and he perished because of their obsession. The infection must be cleansed." Eraekryst poked blindly before him with his cane. "I will see it done."

"Do you even have the strength? Or will you be imprisoned again?"

"I cannot be bound! Even the Nightwind Queen was swept away by my power—sent to Meridian by my design."

"Madman. You still run. You run from Seranonde."

"She can wait. I will deal with my foes in the order they have wronged me." He felt something sharp snare his leg, and he kicked at it. "This mortal weakness is a trifle, and it has not clouded my mind to madness."

"So you say. What of the Light you crave? What of the longing stirred within you?"

"Also soon to be remedied," Eraekryst said, unconcerned. "For now the Black Mountain calls, and I pity those who will be there when I answer."

"OI, NEVER SLEPT SO LATE BEFORE," Jaice said, still somewhat groggy. "Sun's 'igh already." He rubbed his eyes and focused upon the woman sitting in the cot. "Don' fret, luv. 'E can't 'ave gone far, eh?"

Catherine said nothing, staring at the violin case Eraekryst had left behind.

"'Ey, s'alright," Jaice said, patting her arm. "'E's not exactly in the best o' shape. We'll catch up to 'im easy."

"He planned this," Catherine said, her voice hollow. "It was always his intention to go to the mountain."

"Kirou-Mekus? Why'd 'e do a mad stunt like that?"

She looked at him. "Because he is sick. I have turned my sight from it time and time again because I did not want to believe it. I am always the fool," she whispered.

"Don' talk like that. Le's just focus on finding 'im. If 'e's 'eading for the mountain, 'e'll be going that way." Jaice pointed.

"Are you certain?" Catherine asked. "He could have planted an idea to misdirect you."

Jaice assured her with a smile and a wink. "'E can't be that clever, luv."

"You do not know him."

The guide's smile faded. "Well, le's just 'ope he didn't do that."

Catherine nodded, and they gathered their belongings before setting forth in the direction Jaice had indicated.

"Foul fortune," Eraekryst spat, sitting down heavily beside the stream. He rolled up the leg of his trousers to find a swollen red mass the size of a fist. Pus oozed from two small holes at the center of the wound, and when he reached to touch it, the skin was hot and sticky.

"I have not the time for this inconvenience." He scooted closer to the stream and allowed the cold water to wash over his leg.

"If only you could heal yourself, Ilangien," a voice taunted. *"If only the power of the* Ilán *was within you."*

How he longed for the warmth of the Light. The lack of it was like an unquenchable thirst that burned in his stomach and left his mouth parched. "There are other ways," he said aloud. "I have read about them." He perched his spectacles upon his nose for a better view. Then he tore a strip from the linen hammock and tied it tightly above the wound.

He pulled his supply bag closer and sifted through it, pulling free a small knife. "The *durmorth* would not so much as flinch," he said. "And neither will I." Taking a breath, he drew the blade across his skin.

He bit down on his lip as the knife cut deep, and a welling of blood ran down his pale leg and into the water. He let the stream flow over the wound, watching in fascination as the scarlet trails snaked down the creek.

Blood. He was surrounded by blood. Slick and warm upon his hands, wet and fresh upon his clothes. His breathing quickened as he dared lift his eyes. A body. *His* body. The wizard. Face-down a few feet before him, like a priest prostrate before an idol. He began to shake.

"No. No—I did not—" He looked at his stained hands. "I am not responsible," he whispered. "I did not do this!"

"You did. You murdered me. You murdered all of us. And you will pay for it."

Eraekryst gave a cry. The memory faded, and he saw the thick canopy of leaves above him. "Where—?" He lifted himself up, and the spectacles fell from his face. He saw the knife and the bag beside him. His leg was numb in the creek, but the bleeding had stopped. The swelling of his wound had diminished only a little. "Time wasted," he muttered, and undid the tourniquet.

He attempted to stand and found his leg did not seem a part of him. "Better that I had severed it," he said. All he could do, it seemed, was wait.

~

"THAT BASTARD!" Jaice cursed, then apologized to Catherine. "'S bloody nightfall, an' we've been traveling in circles all day."

"The suggestions are strong," she said, "but we have to overcome them."

"Not sure 'ow we'll do that." Jaice kicked at a root. "We'll 'ave to make camp again. What is 'e? 'Ow can 'e do this to us?"

"He is a Mentrailyic. He can alter perceptions with his mind... among other abilities." Catherine sighed and began tying her hammock.

"For a sick bloke, 'e 'as all 'is thoughts in order. Tomorrow could be the same as today."

"It could be, but he would not want us lost here. This was a delay," she said.

"Y' sound pretty sure o' y'self," Jaice said, preparing a fresh fire where the old one had been the night before.

"I have journeyed with him from my home," Catherine said. "And for all his misdirection and trickery, he would never intend us harm."

"Y' sure y're not married to 'im?" Jaice asked, mock suspicion in his voice.

Catherine said nothing.

"'Y really care about 'im—more than care. To leave behind y'r 'ome...."

"Yes." She brushed her fingertips across the violin case. "I want to save him, and I do not know if I can."

"Tha's 'ow it usually works," Jaice said. He had sparked a flame and was gently tending it.

"Your pardon?"

"In any good story, the bloke with all the magic an' power always 'as a weakness. 'Is weakness is always something simple—something 'e overlooked."

"I am the weakness he has overlooked?" Catherine asked.

Jaice smiled. "Well, I wouldn't phrase it like that. I'd say y'r what 'e's missing. The one 'oo 'as to balance 'im out a bit."

"I hope this is a good story, then," Catherine said. "I want your theory proven true."

"Yeah, an' I'd like y'r theory to be true too. I don't want to be 'ere another day, let alone the rest o' me life."

Catherine, resigned, climbed into the hammock. "Then our best solution could be sleep. Maybe dawn will bring with it certain clarity."

"So we'll see, luv."

HE WAS BLINDFOLDED, but his surroundings were shaded. He could hear the birds, he could feel the damp and sticky air. He jolted along on some sort of cot, and the voices of those who bore him spoke in a tongue he did not know. He was not gagged, but he was bound—tightly, too, by thick ropes around arms and legs. And there was something rigid—something wrought from metal around his neck. It was this object, this collar, that kept him weak. He could feel it pulling at his energy; he could barely lift his head, let alone draw from the *Ilán*.

"Naeva," he said in a fragile voice, *"what have you done with me?"*

Of course, there was no response.

"Naeva," Eraekryst said. "You abandoned me."

"That was one hundred and three years ago, Ilangien," said a voice. *"Open your eyes."*

He opened his eyes. He did not know how much time had passed, and he did not recall how he had come to be laying face-down in the dirt, surrounded by dark and craggy mountains. Eraekryst struggled to push himself upright on weakened arms. His bag of provisions was next to him, as was his cane, and his leg pulsed with its own heartbeat. He did not bother to look at it.

Kirou-Mekus commanded his attention, rising from the rest of the peaks like a malevolent deity, shrouded by a dark and jagged cape.

"You have come home."

"This is not my home," he croaked. His throat was raw, dry. When had he last eaten? Drank? Did it matter? He had arrived. On some reserve of strength he stood, unsteady as a newborn fawn. He staggered to the base of the mountain, where the rocky façade of a door had been left open, a dark and waiting hole behind it.

"The silence—this is not right," he whispered. "It cannot be right. They would see me. They would come to seize me." He lifted his hands before the mountain, trying to sense any form of life. But the Light was no longer with him. He lowered his hands and stared. "I am here."

Minutes passed, but there was no one to be seen.

"The Stone of Prophecy has returned to you!" Eraekryst cried.

Nothing.

"You see I am not broken!" he shouted, flinging wide his arms. Then he began to laugh. "You are prudent in your trepidation. This day will be your end."

He moved to the door and peered inside. There was only obscurity beyond, and so he entered the passage with his hand upon the wall for support. He shuffled along blindly until his fingers collided with an object not made of stone. He felt its form and pried it from the wall with the power of his will. The Jornoan word for "fire" dropped from his lips, and the torch blazed, washing the corridor in green light.

Eraekryst continued down the passage, the sound of his footsteps his only company. "Hiding in this mountain will not save you," he murmured in his withered voice, "for 'tis only earth and stone. I have seen all things, and I will find you."

He went to the temple, where the Demon had waited for him. Like the passage, it too, was dark and empty. He pulled at the rope in the lift, careful to keep the torch away from it. It opened to the kitchen, where pots and utensils had been overturned and scattered. Instead of the scent of fire, there was only rotting food. From the kitchen, he went into the divination chamber, from the chamber to the stairwell, and through more passages. All of them were empty.

"Trickery!" he cried. "Show yourselves, lest I hunt you from each crevice and every shadow!"

"They are gone, Ilangien."

"No," he snapped. "The Jornoan zealots would not abandon their stronghold. This place is built upon blood and delusions. Both stain too deeply to disappear."

Eraekryst knelt upon the ground and pressed the flat of his free hand to the floor. He closed his eyes and searched for answers. He could envision the quick steps of running feet, nervous cries and angry shouts, shadows and faceless forms. But that was all. "Tell me your story," he demanded. His sight remained dark.

"You see that they have gone," the voice insisted.

"Gone where? For what purpose?"

The blindfold was removed, the cot was set upon the floor. The Jornoans lifted him from it, loosened the ropes. "You are home," one said in a heavy accent, cackling.

Eraekryst opened his eyes and shook his head, ridding himself of the memory. He stood and pressed onward to a secluded corridor, the light of his torch his sole source of illumination in the darkness. Before him was a door. His door.

"Shall I walk into your trap?" he asked aloud. "You had sent the *koncarys* after me, to bring me here. Now that I am here, shall I complete his mission? Shall I step inside my former prison?" Shadows swallowed his words and nothing more.

He gripped the handle of the door. "See that I do not fear you!" He flung it open.

Inside was his chamber, just as it had been the day the Demon freed him. The chalk drawings were still upon the walls, the cot still in place. And next to it....

A lithe form sat upon the ground, its head bent to face the folded hands resting in its lap. A soft, golden aura streamed around it.

Eraekryst's breath caught in this throat.

The figure slowly lifted its head to regard him through loosened locks of long, golden hair. Its eyes were brighter than the moon, and they met him with such sorrow that Eraekryst subconsciously took a step forward. "You," he breathed.

Blood was spattered upon the white of the prisoner's clothes. *"You are too late,"* the younger version of himself said in a voice bereft of hope.

Eraekryst took another step closer. "No."

The youthful Ilangien held up his blood-soaked hands. *"They are gone."*

"Where? To where have they gone?" Eraekryst asked, moving toward himself. The youth stood, but stared past him.

"We are here, Ilangien."

Eraekryst spun to see them. *All* of them, standing in a crowd, watching him with empty eyes. The Lost Ones. He knew every one of their faces; he had seen them die. He had been the one who killed them. "I came for justice," he said, raising the torch.

"So did we."

"I am not responsible for your deaths," Eraekryst voiced. "Done by my hand and not my will, you are free to leave me in peace!"

The specters did not move.

"Where are the ones who guard this mountain?" he demanded. "They are to blame. I am here for them."

"They are gone," said the voice of the wizard. *"Only you remain."*

"Koncarys!" Eraekryst shouted. "You knew! Why lead me to an empty mountain?"

The wizard laughed. *"To die, Ilangien. You must die as we have died."*

Eraekryst frowned but stood his ground, bearing the torch like a weapon. "I have not suffered to die in this prison," he said.

"You have been abandoned, Eraekryst of Celaedrion. First by your own people, then by the Durangien queen. Even your own counselor has left you. You are naught but a remnant, a piece of this mountain...as are we."

There was a sound—a sound Eraekryst knew well. The sound of moving stone. The sound of the door closing. It disappeared into the surface of the stone wall, marked only by his chalk drawing. He trembled in growing rage. *"You will not keep me here!"* he shrilled, and the stone prison shuddered.

The spectral form of the wizard stepped forward. *"We will not abandon you. Not ever."*

Eraekryst flung the torch at them, and it skittered across the floor before the flames sputtered and died. The ghosts, too, vanished from his sight. "I came here for peace!" he cried. "I came here for justice!"

"And you will have it," the wizard's voice echoed. *"At last you will embrace the truth."*

In the darkness Eraekryst tore at his hair and dropped to his knees. "I will not be bound!"

"This is where you belong. The Stone has been broken."

Those lasting words burned into the air, pounded in his brain. He slammed his fists into the ground, and the mountain trembled. His scream loosened traces of rock and earth from the ceiling and walls.

"I am not broken!"

~

Catherine gave a cry as the ground trembled beneath her. She fell to her knees, her bag slipping from her shoulders.

"By Lorth!" Jaice cursed, bracing himself as the tremor continued. Leaves and fruit tumbled to the ground, and birds fled with a clamor as the scattered trees around them swayed and creaked. There was a roar unlike the sound of thunder, though pending rain was the only threat promised by the overcast sky.

All motion then ceased, leaving an aftermath of eerie silence.

Jaice set his own load down in order to help Catherine to her feet. "It was him," she said, unnerved. "We may be too late." She quickly gathered her bag.

"'Ow strong is 'e?" Jaice murmured.

"I do not know," she confessed, "but I fear he will test his limitations. We have to hurry."

"I'd 'ate to be one o' those Jornoans right now."

They broke from the forest for a clear view of the mountains. There was a rising cloud of black debris where the peak of one had collapsed.

"Jedinom's Sword!" Jaice marveled, squinting at the sight. He nearly tripped over an obstruction on the ground. "'Ey, luv," he said, drawing her attention from the landscape. He tapped the cane and bag with his boot.

Catherine looked gravely at Eraekryst's belongings, her own bag gripped tightly in her hand. "Jaice, I have to go to him."

"Not if 'e's tearin' down a mountain," the adventurer said. "I can't let y' do that."

"I must." She knelt down and pulled a bundle from her pack, staring at it as though she could look nowhere else. "I have to save him, or he will destroy himself. I know he will."

The ground shook again, and both of them jerked their attention to the mountain. A fresh cloud rose like smoke, obscuring the damage done.

"Y' may be right," Jaice agreed. "But I won't let y' go alone." He looked at the bundle. "Just 'ow do y' plan to stop 'im?"

"I...am not sure," she said, hesitant. "I will know when he sees me." She did not look back at her burden. "Maybe it will be enough that he sees me."

"'Ope so, luv."

They picked their way across the rocky terrain, following the Ilangien's staggered footprints. As they neared Kirou-Mekus, however, there was no sign of him. There was crumbled rock, and there was ruination—exposed fragments of an inner-mountain society that would soon be buried again—beyond anyone's reach.

They stopped a fair distance from the mountain when another tremor began. Catherine took hold of Jaice's arm. "This is not your risk to take," she said. "From this point I should go alone."

The adventurer nodded and helped strap the bundle to her back. He did not ask her what it was, and for that she was grateful. "I'll be 'ere waiting," he promised. "Watch y'self."

Catherine found she needed both her hands to scale what was left of the Black Mountain. Her arms and legs throbbed from the effort, and several times she nearly fell when loose debris tumbled away beneath her grasp. The earth had not ceased rumbling, as though it was growling in warning, and eventually it would snap. Her greatest consolation was that she had not encountered any bodies...yet.

She tried not to consider her fears. She tried not to think of anything at all but climbing the rocks before her. The mountain breathed beneath her, and suddenly it heaved upward. Catherine was thrown a short distance, the wind knocked from her when she landed on her belly. As she gasped for air, her first concern was the burden she bore. Her fingers stretched to her back to ensure the bundle was still there. Her breathing steadied as her eyes focused upon what lay ahead.

She was at the top of the collapsed peak, and the view was

humbling. The Draebongaunt Ocean stretched in front of her, massive waves gnashing the rocks with foamy teeth where the fallen mountain had been ingested. All at once she felt so very small and insignificant.

But then she saw him, and her eyes filled. Eraekryst was on his knees, his clothes filthy and ragged, his hair in disarray. He was sickly pale, with streams of blood still damp—trailing from his nose, his ears, and even the corners of his sunken, bloodshot eyes. But his lips were spread in a thin smile as he regarded her.

Catherine struggled to sit upright. "Erik."

"You see, Lady," he said, his voice hoarse almost beyond recognition. "No more. There will be no more." He succumbed to a grating cough, spitting a mouthful of blood upon the rock. "All will be laid to rest, and then—then peace. For them and for me. I have waited so long..." He closed his eyes and lifted his hands.

The mountain shuddered.

"Erik," she said gently, crawling toward him, "you must stop. You will not survive this."

He did not seem to hear her, nor did he open his eyes.

"Please," she coaxed. "We can leave this. We can go to the Veil and see you healed." She paused to smear the tears from her eyes. "Erik."

"Soon, Lady," he promised. "When I have finished." He tensed, the veins prominent on his furrowed brow, his posture rigid, his fists clenched. He was perfectly still as the mountain buckled. A huge piece broke away and slumped into the ocean, the sound like an explosion.

"Please, stop!" Catherine cried, unable to contain her emotions. "You will die. I cannot watch you die."

He said nothing—did not move at all. But the mountain continued to relinquish pieces of itself to a watery demise. Their own vantage point was in jeopardy as the mountain's base crumbled away. When she felt their base shift and begin to slide toward the ocean, her heart leapt to her throat.

"Erik, this is madness," Catherine cried, looking for something to hold on to. There was nothing, and even if there was, it would do no good.

Eraekryst's eyes opened. "Madness," he echoed, staring at the distant horizon. "No one can understand. I am what they made me. I am alone."

"No, you are not." Catherine held out her hand, straining to reach him.

He looked at her, now cold and distant. He lifted his hand and pushed her away with the force of his will.

She was stunned. Stunned by the emotionless eyes, stunned by the unseen blow that cast her away from him. As she lay there, she realized her mistake. She had used the one word to describe him that others dropped so carelessly—the one word of cruel judgment that undermined all that he had endured, suffered. She had become like *them*, unraveling in one moment the bond that had taken months to forge.

Catherine's eyes watered as she watched him orchestrate his own destruction. He would not listen to her now; he was beyond her reach. With numb fingers she undid the strap that held the bundle to her back. She held the item in her hands, scarcely able to see through her tears. There was only one way to save him; she had never wanted to make this decision. Her fingers pulled away at the bindings and linens until the golden, sparkling form of the crystal rose appeared before her eyes.

She knew Baliden would have used it for love. He was strong enough to make such a decision. The decision literally rested in her hands now. Did she love Eraekryst enough to use so terrible a charm? There was no doubt to the answer, for she had proven her feelings time and time again as they journeyed. This would be a permanent solution—a burden she would bear the rest of her existence. She drew her sleeve across her eyes and stood.

Catherine started to approach the Ilangien's kneeling form, the rose cradled in her grasp. Her strides were determined; she could not hesitate, for she would only have one opportunity, if that. She was a few yards away when he turned to look at her.

No words were spoken, no gesture made. The ground shifted, and she was caught off-balance. She began to fall, and the rose flew from her hands. It landed in the rocks near the Ilangien; Catherine could not say if it was still intact. She knew only that her one hope of saving him was gone.

The earth quivered beneath her, and she did not care. How could it matter now? This was the ending that mattered to him. If "peace" meant death, then so be it. She could not fault him for his logic, not after all he had endured. That was a dark piece of his life she could not touch, would never know. If she knew nothing else, it was that she would be here with him when the last of the mountain fell.

A startled cry forced her to lift her head. Eraekryst had turned from the ocean, facing a crystalline vine that crept toward him along the ground. Like a golden serpent, the vine pulled itself along the rocks, spiraling around his foot. He tried to move, brush it away, but it circled tighter.

Catherine gasped and scrambled toward him. The rose had taken root as though it had a mind of its own. It had assumed her mission, but as she watched, her heart pounded with uncertainty. The panic in his eyes—the desperation to escape... He knew what it was. *He knew.*

By now the vine had moved up to his torso, and he had not the strength to resist it. The thorns tore at his clothes, bit into his skin. More vines emerged, ensnaring him in a matter of seconds.

"No," Catherine gasped. She held herself back, willing herself not to touch the shimmering stems that laced over the rocks like pulsing veins. She was beside him now. The vines had brought him to the ground, and as he lay there, his eyes met hers. She could only see betrayal in them.

"What have...you done to me?" he mouthed. He gave a final strain as the light left his eyes. Then his lids closed, and his body slackened.

Catherine cried aloud, in grief. Her trembling hands stopped just short of his face. "I am sorry. I am sorry. Please—please come back!" She did not know what to do; there was nothing she could do. The vines began to retreat back to the source, where the rose had fallen. His body was left torn and bloody, and she sought to wipe the stains from his face. A face that was yet warm.

He still breathed, if shallowly. He was alive, though she felt little relief. She took his hand and held it to her lips. *Just what had she done?*

5

SANCTUARY

The afternoon was golden, swathed in light and warmth from a benevolent sun. Scattered strands of broken fire rippled upon the water, and she stood there like an immortal, gleaming and beautiful. Victoria's back was toward him, her long, chestnut hair unbound and cascading over her shoulders. Her robe lay abandoned upon the bank, while she tiptoed daintily into the water.

Arythan smiled when she hopped back a step, daunted by the difference in temperature. She clasped her arms to her chest but did not retreat further. Rather, she took a bold stride forward, emitting a small yelp as she did so. She did not know he was there, watching her from behind the trunk of a burly oak; she certainly did not expect the water to retreat from her. It ebbed from her ankles, and she stared at her muddied feet, unmoving.

After a moment, Victoria took another step forward, and the water withdrew again. She held her left foot just above the surface, and the water filled in the distance between her and the shore, leaving her on her own island of mud. She stomped her foot down and lifted her head. "Arythan!"

The water moved back in, spiraling around her and lapping at her legs in frisky little waves. Victoria turned back toward the shore, searching for the hidden culprit. "I know you're there, you coward. Show yourself."

Arythan stepped out from behind the tree, lifted his hat, and bowed.

"Get over here," she demanded.

He set his hat upon the ground and strode forward to meet her, wading straight into the lake until he had come face-to-face with her. "Yes, milady?"

Her attempt at restraining a smile was failing. "Your clothes are wet." She lifted a sopping sleeve between her thumb and forefinger.

"Y're very perceptive," Arythan returned, and he swooped her up in his arms and carried her deeper into the lake.

"Jedinom's Grace, that's cold!" she cried, pretending to fight him.

He dumped her into the water, and she gasped, her green eyes a mirror of betrayal. Retaliation came a blink later, when she assailed him with relentless splashing. A giant wave rose from behind him, and she stopped, gaping at the suspended wall of water.

"You wouldn't...."

"I might."

"But I'm a defenseless woman. You're supposed to be my hero."

"Alas, luv, I 'ave only ever played the role of a villain."

Victoria closed her eyes and braced herself for the inevitable, but Arythan cast his arm back, and the wave split and sank back into the lake. She opened her eyes and smiled at him. "I knew you wouldn't do it."

"Right."

They gazed at each other a moment, hair plastered to their heads, lips purple, shoulders trembling.

"I'm cold," Victoria admitted.

"'Struth," he agreed and took her hand. They trudged to the shore, teeth chattering.

"So are you going to warm me with some of that magic?"

Arythan left her side and disappeared behind the oak. He emerged with a blanket and wrapped it gently around her shoulders.

"That will do," she said, smiling as he moved her hair aside to kiss her neck. They sat down together, and her hand emerged from the blanket to grasp his. He drew upon the heat of the sun, and Victoria nestled against him. "This has been the best week of my life. Now if only you could make the summer last forever..." she murmured, closing her eyes.

"Y' like it 'ere."

"It is peaceful." Victoria sighed. "But there is more than this place, more than the season. And I have a feeling the one reason for my happiness is about to tell me that our time here is over." Her fingers reached up and rubbed at his beard.

At first Arythan did not respond. He looked out at the lake and tightened his arms around her. "Y' don' 'ave to go. I don't want y' to go."

She wrenched away to turn and look at him. "I don't understand."

"'S good that y're away from the castle. Away from the rumours, the people... I want y' to be 'ere when the time comes."

Her eyes widened. "You want me to stay here until the baby is born? All those months?" Victoria pulled away to better assess his expression.

"They'll take care of y' 'ere." He did not meet her gaze. "I 'ave to go back. Michael needs me at the castle."

"I want to go back with you," Victoria protested. "I am your wife now. I should be at your side."

"I'll come back to see y'," Arythan promised. "Then we can spend time alone."

"Arythan, you're keeping a secret." There was hurt in her voice.

"'S no secret the prince will 'ave me busy," he said. "Y'll give me a reason to escape." Finally he looked at her and managed a fleeting smile. "'S a time o' change—with the king an' Desnera… A lot will 'appen, an' I don't want—I don't need—"

Victoria put a finger to his lips. "It's all right," she said. "I can see it now. You are concerned for us." Her smile was much more convincing. "And it is sweet that you are so protective."

Arythan's cheeks reddened.

"I will do as you ask. I will stay here," Victoria said. "But there is one condition: you must visit me as often as you are able. I expect poetic letters, small gifts, and most importantly, you must fetch me in time for Summerfall."

"Y' want to go to Summerfall?" he asked, surprised.

"It would be wise to enlighten others of the pregnancy *before* the baby is born, no?"

He shrugged, and she poked his chest. "Promise me, Medoriate."

"I promise."

She turned back around and leaned against him. "So…when do you leave?"

"In the morning."

Victoria stiffened and clutched his hands. "I didn't think it would be that soon."

"I didn't want it to be. Michael sent a letter."

"Yes, well, he has his wife with him. If he thinks he can just pull you away, he will have to face me first," she said with an air of defiance.

"I love y'." Arythan had uttered the words quietly. He had never said them before, and until this point, they had never suited him. But now they felt right, and he meant them as sure as he guarded the truth in his heart. He wondered if she had heard him, for she did not utter a sound, did not so much as twitch.

A pair of ducks lighted on the water, their splashes interrupting the moment of silence.

"Tori...."

She shook her head. "Just be still," she whispered. Though he could not see her tears, he sensed them in her voice. "You said all I needed to hear. This moment—right now—this is mine."

He nodded, and they sat in silence together, beneath the golden afternoon.

"GOOD AFTERNOON, LADY CATHERINE."

Catherine spun to find Halgon Thayliss in the doorway of the cottage. Embarrassed, she wiped the sweat from her brow and removed the stray and plastered locks of hair from her face. "Good afternoon, sir," she said, straightening. "I apologize—I did not see you."

The mayor waved a hand. "Please, call me Halgon. You are part of our community now. It is my responsibility to see how you are faring." He stepped inside, assessing the interior of the dwelling.

Catherine's blush deepened. The cottage was still a mess, with debris upon the floor and dust upon the furniture. She had only begun to determine any repairs needed for the structure, for the week had come and gone in a whirlwind of time. "A little work will do wonders," she said. "There is nothing I cannot manage."

Halgon shook his head in sympathy. "This is not work fitting for a lady. I would not see you shoulder this task alone." He stepped around a pile of dirt she had swept. "I am rather surprised that Mr. Ginmon did not stay to help you with this mess."

"I told him not to," Catherine answered immediately. "He was kind enough to offer his home to us." *More than kind,* she thought.

None of this was his burden to bear. Jaice had helped her bring Eraekryst back, saw to it that they were settled in his cottage. In return she had funded his journey to Southern Secramore to try his fortune as a prospector. Most of Eraekryst's money was gone now, but she was not afraid of work. In fact, she had welcomed the disrepair of the cottage as a distraction from the matters pressing at her heart.

"You are quite an independent woman," Halgon said with a smile. "Still, I would hope that you will accept my assistance." He glanced at the adjoining room, and Catherine subconsciously moved before the doorway. "How is your companion?"

She upheld her smile as best she could. "There is yet no change in his condition."

Halgon took her hand and patted it. "I am so sorry to hear it. But you must keep your hope. I have seen others suffer through worse than a snakebite."

There was a moment of awkward silence where she hoped he would take his leave. But the mayor of Brandeise lingered, a thoughtful look upon his face. "I am worried for you," he confessed. "What with this shamble of a cottage and the stress over your friend… You need a moment to breathe." He still held her hand. "If you recall our first outing…I would like to have another."

"No," Catherine said immediately. "I am sorry to decline, but there is so much to do, and I cannot leave Erik alone."

Halgon smiled again. "I had anticipated this response from you. I took the liberty of bringing my servant along; Brenna waits outside. She is quite capable of looking after your friend, given his stable condition. She can tidy the room the short while we are away."

Catherine started to protest, but he stopped her with a look. "You can spare just a short while for an old man like me, no? Humor me, if you will not allow yourself a moment to relax."

"You make it difficult to refuse," she said, uncomfortable. The truth was, she was famished and exhausted, and she doubted she could convince him otherwise.

"Then do not refuse. Please, Catherine."

She wavered.

"I am certain there will be plenty of food to bring back for him." Halgon nodded toward the Ilangien's room.

"Very well," Catherine said. "Though I am a bit of a mess. If I could have just a moment...."

Halgon nodded, and she dashed into the room behind her. It was the only room that had been cleaned, and meticulously so. The window was open so sunshine and fresh air could reach the lone occupant. Catherine moved to the bed where Eraekryst lay and placed a hand upon his ashen brow. It was cool, like marble—as it had been since they brought him back. His chest rose and fell shallowly but steadily beneath the light blanket.

No change, she thought with a sigh. *What I would not give that you open your eyes this moment.* Catherine smoothed the hair from his forehead. "I will be back soon," she promised. "I will try to bring something new for you to drink." She was grateful that she had been able to provide him with some nourishment—even if it was a liquid diet. He had lost a bit of weight in his state, and whether he had heard her or not, she had told him that this was not the way to rid himself of his "excess." Catherine gave him a lasting look. "Do not cause the servant trouble."

Then she turned away, unwilling to shed tears before facing the mayor. Once she had rejoined Halgon, she found Brenna, the plump, middle-aged servant, already studying the room in dismay. Catherine made it a point to address her. "Thank you for watching over him. He will be no trouble, but if you could just make certain the wind does not move the blanket... He needs the fresh air, but I would hate for him to catch a chill."

Brenna nodded without expression, and Halgon reclaimed

Catherine's hand. "She is quite diligent, I assure you. Now, take your breath of fresh air as we step outside...."

Catherine managed a final glance behind her before she was escorted from the cottage.

~

IT HAD BEEN A LONG NIGHT—A night without the moon or the stars, without sky or ground...a night of wandering without thought or purpose. Words without shape slipped through his fingers, evaded him like birds made of wind. There was nothing to which he could cling: not an image, not a sound. He wondered if he existed at all except for some vague but constant awareness that promised something more.

The "something more" came to him slowly—a sensation pressing against him, an even permeation of a condition he could not escape. Cold. Yes, it was *cold,* and the coldness connected him to another realm, a realm since lost to him. The physical realm.

The darkness abated when he stirred, opening his eyes to a tangible place of *things.* There was cold, but there was light, and there were walls. Names of surrounding objects came to him, though he did not know how. *Window, table...* On the table: *violin, spectacles...* He saw them like words in a book, but they were random and out of context.

There was a sound, and his eyes flicked toward the window. With the light came the sound of the wind. The unseen breeze found him, and he felt his body tremble. *Shiver. Cold.* The sentences were slowly forming. But then... His body? It occurred to him that of all the objects he could name, he did not have a name for himself. He simply *was.* And just what was he?

I am cold. A fact attributed to the wind that had lifted the blanket from his chest. *I am without a shirt.* Pale flesh dotted with goose bumps and a multitude of small red scabs met his eyes. He lifted an arm and discovered he was very weak. Attached to the arm was a hand with thin, aged skin and bulging veins. He gripped the edge of the blanket and peeled it away. *I am without clothes entirely.* He studied his body, desperate for more clues. *Well-fed. Clean. Intact but for small scratches and fading bruises everywhere. How did I earn them?* He moved his legs, his toes. *Wait....*

His right leg was bandaged. Would he be able to sit upright? Did he have the strength? On his first attempt his arms buckled. He tried again and propped his back against the wall. Not only was he weak, but he was sore in his muscles and joints. Gingerly he drew his leg toward him and lightly touched the linen wrappings that surrounded his calf. The concealed skin was tender to the touch. He debated whether or not to remove the bandage to see the wound, but then decided against it. There was nothing else about his body—that he could see—that warranted concern. But there was also nothing that had inspired his identity to return to him.

The table beside the bed was his best resource. He donned the spectacles and found they helped him see better in close proximity. *My eyes are flawed.* He picked up the violin and found his fingers wanted to hold it a particular way. *I am a musician.* He plucked a few strings and set it down. Now that he was upright, he could see that there was a cane propped against one of the table legs. It was adorned with botanical carvings. *I am not steady on my feet.*

Well, he would test that theory. Before he could shift himself from the bed, he paused. A new sound reached his ears: a vocal sound. The sound of a woman. *Humming.* It was distant enough that he deduced it had carried from outside. *Someone had tended to me. Perhaps it was her. She will know me.* He moved his legs from the bed, snared the cane, and pushed himself to his feet. There he stood, swaying awkwardly until he could determine his balance and find a reserve of strength.

His feet were cold upon the dirty floor, and a random breeze reminded him that he was naked. A glance around the room did not reveal any articles of clothing. *At least I have the blanket...* He shrouded himself with the material and took a step forward. And another. And another. It was more of a shuffle toward the doorway, but at least he was upright and moving despite his stiff and strengthless limbs. Cane gripped tightly in one hand, blanket held fast in the other, he moved from the bedroom into a....

"Mess" was the word that came to mind. *Dirt, debris, litter. Mess.* Now he had to pick his bare feet a little higher, lest he impale them on some random object. The door to the outside was open, just across the room. He merely had to—

He did not have a chance to cry out, even if he had been able. His feet were no longer beneath him; the floor was. All he could do was sit there, his bottom throbbing, his ears ringing. He fixed the spectacles upon his face, though they were not necessary to see the object to blame. A long stick with stiff grasses at its end was at his feet. *Broom.*

A shadow fell upon him, and there was a gasp and a scream. The woman outside had found him, but her reaction was not one of familiarity. Though she was much better fed than he was, she moved much faster, bolting out the door with a look of panic upon her face. He was, again, without a lead to follow. He gathered up his blanket and struggled to his feet with the assistance of the cane. Woman or no woman, there could be more people outside. Someone would know him.

The sunlight hit him, and he manipulated the blanket to form a hood. There were more words swirling in his mind. *Trees. Ground. Earth. Sky, sun, clouds.* The structure from which he had come was isolated. There were no others in sight, and thus there were no other people. Above him a mass of sound caught his attention. *Birds.* They lighted in a nearby patch of greenery with bright spots of color. *Plants, flowers...water.* The water was in the form of a pool, shimmering beneath a stand of palms. It reflected the brightness of the sun; it would reflect him, too.

Eagerly he approached it, though he took more care than he had inside the building. Frogs yelped and leapt from his path, and a little spectrum of finger-sized fish scattered as he knelt beside the water's edge. Beneath the bed-linen cowl was a stranger's face. He pushed the material away to rid himself of its shadows. Short, white locks of hair hung above the water; they had fallen away from a pair of delicately tapered ears. He brought his hand up to touch them, as though he had never seen such ears before. If he had, he certainly could not remember.

The ears were attached to an old man's face. How old was old? He was not certain, but his skin sagged and creased around his eyes, mouth, nose, and chin. Even his forehead had contours—like someone had crinkled paper and tried to smooth it out again. The eyes staring back at him from behind the spectacles were a pale sort of blue, but they were not knowing eyes; they did not share any secrets.

This is me, he thought, in shock. *This is me, and I have no notion of who I am.* This thought inspired his delayed panic. He dropped the cane into the water with a splash but scarcely noticed. His other hand released the blanket, and both hands rose to his face to touch it, to pull at the flesh, to test just how real it was. *Who am I?* His hands dropped to claw at and shatter the reflection. *Who am I?* The ripples settled again, and the same face watched him; it shared his distraught expression, mocked him. He cried aloud and smashed the image, pulling back so he would not have to see it again.

A shout came from behind him, and he turned. There was a woman with long, black hair fastened behind her head. She was fuller in build, older in appearance—streaks of silver in her hair, a worn look upon her pale face. Her gray, wide-set eyes were glistening with tears as she hurried toward him. She knew him, and he should likely know her, though he did not.

She came within a few yards of him, and he could not contain his anxiety. *"Who am I? Who are you? Where are we?"*

She stopped and searched him with her eyes. "Erik." She took another step forward, and he could tell she was gauging him. "Erik, what are you doing? Are you all right?"

Her words... They were not the same as the words in his head, but he understood her. Whatever language in which she spoke, he knew it too. "Who am I?" he repeated in her tongue. "Do you know me?"

He watched her bring her hands to her lips, watched the tears roll faster down her face. She slowly nodded, and he clutched at the blanket as he turned to face her completely. "Please...help me," he begged. "I need to know...."

She completed her course and knelt beside him, wrapping her arms around him. He stiffened, unsure how to react to the sobbing woman. Was she sad? Joyous? And what was he supposed to feel? After a moment, she drew back, swallowing her emotions and drying her tears. "I'm sorry," she said. "You must forgive me, but I...I'm grateful to see you. It had been a week since...."

It seemed to him that she was having great difficulty composing her thoughts. He looked at her expectantly, held her gaze.

"Do you...remember anything at all?" she asked, slight hope in her voice.

He shook his head and glanced back at the water, at his reflection. "I do not know who I am, how I came here, where I am... Who you are... Nothing." His voice fell flat.

The woman swallowed what promised to be another round of tears, and he suspected there was more to them than gratitude for his presence. "I will tell you all I can," she said, rising. She extended her hand toward him. "But first let me see you inside and...cared for." Her eyes returned to the blanket.

He retrieved the cane and handed it to her, and then she helped support him on her shoulder. She walked him back to the bed, where she pulled some clothes from beneath it. "They are new. I was saving them for when you awakened, and I do hope they fit." She held up a shirt in front of him. "You did lose a bit of weight, so I hope...."

"Did I?" he asked, looking at himself. "All of this is new, clothes aside."

She handed him the bundle and turned away as he traded the blanket for the attire.

"Is there modesty between us?" he asked.

"We are close," she said. "I have had to care for you. I just...want to give you a little space, a little privacy."

"I would rather nothing left to question," he said softly. "And it seems I am already indebted to you."

Her reaction was unexpected. "Do not say such a thing," she whispered, and he just barely heard her.

"I do not understand."

She turned around and looked at him, her eyes glassy. "We are lovers. We have been for a long time. There is no debt to be paid."

He blinked, unsure what to say. What did it mean to be a "lover"? There was no inherent concept to this word. It was not like a "table" or a "window." He understood "love" as a higher level of care. There must be some underlying importance to their relationship that would cause her to be so upset.

She straightened his shirt, smoothing a few wrinkles, before taking his hand and sitting with him on the bed. "My name is Catherine Lorrel, and you are Erik Sparrow, a famous musician."

"Erik Sparrow," he repeated. "'Sparrow' as in 'bird?'"

She nodded.

"A strange name." He looked at the violin on the table. "I had gathered as much about my vocation."

"You play beautifully," Catherine said, but he had already turned away from the instrument.

"Why do I not remember this? Why do I not remember you, my name, or anything prior to waking in this bed?"

Catherine did not look at him. "There was an accident. We were venturing in the jungle, and you were bitten by a snake." She gestured to his leg. "The poison overwhelmed you, and you became very sick. I did not know if you would ever wake up."

Erik gazed at the leg in question. "But you have new clothes for me."

"I kept hope, Erik. You seemed to improve, but nothing was certain."

"Why was I exploring a jungle?"

"You have a fascination with birds. You were hoping to spot a rare hummingbird."

"A bird that hums?" he asked, trying to envision such a creature. "I would imagine such a bird *would* be rare."

Catherine looked at him, and he could tell she wanted to smile, but she would not allow herself to do so. "It does not actually sing. It is a small bird with a long bill, and it beats its wings so quickly that they make a humming sound."

"I would hope, at the very least, that I had spotted it. Did I?"

She turned away and shook her head. "I am afraid not."

He began a secondary assessment of the room in which he had awoken. "What is this place, Catherine? How am I here?" He pulled away from her to stand, and he felt her hand grip his arm to steady him while he retrieved the cane. Then she released him as he shuffled around the bed, heading toward the window to gaze at the landscape.

Catherine's voice found him as he admired the flawless sky, breathed in the freshness of the air that was no longer quite so cold. "This is the colony of Brandeise, on the continent of Secrailoss. We traveled here a couple weeks ago from Northern Secramore. We wanted to be somewhere different—somewhere without kingdoms and roads. The monarchy was encouraging people to come here to establish a firm foothold in this land."

"These names of which you speak," he murmured. "They hold no meaning to me. Places that exist by the sound of your voice alone. They could belong to another world—a distant and fantastical place. Names of importance, but names I find utterly useless."

"They may come to mean more to you in time."

He turned to her, hopeful. "You imply that I might remember all that I have lost?"

Catherine bit her lip. "I am not a medic, Erik, but I have the same hope as you."

Erik gave a nod. "And what of this dwelling? Is it a temporary refuge?"

"It belonged to the guide we hired for our venture into the jungle. He had helped me bring you here. As a traveler himself, he has allowed us to reside here in his absence."

She stirred beneath his steady gaze, but something had caught his attention. He returned to her side and brushed aside a lock of her hair, tucking it behind her ear.

"Erik..." Catherine's face was a mix of surprise and uncertainty.

"Your ears," he said, "are not like mine."

She gave a half-hearted laugh. "You would notice such a trait," she said.

"Why?" he asked immediately.

"Well, because you are very observant—more so than most people. I had trimmed your hair, to help keep the fever down." She stood and exposed one of his ears, touching it lightly with her finger. "Your ears are one of your most endearing features. They are unique—a family trait passed on to you."

Erik found her gaze had shifted from his ears to his eyes. Her fingers slid softly across his cheek and to his lips. For a single gesture, it seemed to hold meaning, though he did not know what. And the intensity of her stare....

She leaned closer to him, reached up as if to whisper, though she did not move toward his ears. Her lips nearly touched his, and his brow furrowed in confusion. His change in expression caused her to withdraw immediately. "I'm sorry," she blurted. "I do not know what I was thinking. I have been alone, and I just... I am so happy you...."

He saw her shatter, tears falling like broken glass. She crumpled upon the bed, her face buried in her hands as the sound of her grief filled the room.

"Catherine," he said. "Do not cry. You are not alone now." He joined her, unsure what to do. Whatever course of action he had interrupted—should he complete it? Would it ease her emotions? Cautiously, he touched her shaking shoulder. Her trembling diminished, and she slowly lowered her hands to reveal her reddened eyes, her damp cheeks. Awkwardly, he touched her chin and gently lifted it. Her gray eyes were upon him again as he drew nearer. Then he pressed his lips to hers.

Erik did not know what was to follow, but it did not matter. She did not move away this time but fortified their contact. He saw her eyes close, and he closed his too, wondering how long they would remain thus. But a moment later, Catherine pulled away, still reddened but bearing a slight smile.

She gave a laugh and brought her hand to her cheek, as if to conceal her face again. "I...I am willing to believe you had no notion what that was about."

"My notions are few at present," Erik admitted.

"That was a kiss," Catherine said shyly. "It is a gesture of intimacy between lovers."

"Have we not had a 'kiss' before?" he asked, still confused by her embarrassment.

"No. No, we have not." She smoothed her skirt. "And I would not have tried to kiss you, but my feelings got the better of me."

"Why decline the gesture, if we are lovers?"

Catherine turned to him abruptly. "Because it is wrong—wrong for me to be so intimate when you have scarcely come to understand...when I..." She could not complete her words, and he feared she would upset herself again.

"Catherine," Erik said gently. "I will come to understand. The fragments of my world will become one, but not without your assistance." He smiled for her. "I am not afraid of this challenge, and I am eager to rediscover myself and the life we shared." He purposely collected her hands and held them. "I beg you not hold back from me."

She nodded and rested her head against his shoulder, and they sat together for a long while, listening to the birds and feeling the ocean breeze against their backs.

6

PLAINS AND LABOR

"Crow, over here."

Arythan lifted his head, rain sluicing off his hood and into his face as he spied Brann Alwin motioning him over. He sighed and tried to lift his foot—only to find it held fast by mud thicker than the pottage he had for last night's dinner. In fact, pottage was every night's dinner, and unlike wine, age did not improve its quality. He pulled harder, and found himself liberated —nearly toppling into the viscous pit. When he set his foot down again, he could feel the cold, damp muck oozing between his toes. He stared at his empty boot and swore.

"We are waiting for you, Crow."

Nigqor-slet. He tugged at the boot, and after a loud sucking sound, pulled it from the mud. He did not bother putting it back on before he trudged to where the wizard stood expectantly.

"Is that your—"

"Yes," Arythan snapped, dropping the boot. His patience was shorter than a Cerborathian summer. He was soaked and chilled to the bone, and the mining had begun at dawn, when it was barely light enough to see. The rain had started hours prior to the excavation, rendering the Ice Plains a gooey mud flat. He could have worked his magic to see fairer weather or at least solidify the substrate, but it took most of his energy to focus on the task at hand: uncovering the crystals. In the past few weeks, the crew in the Plains had been reduced to a third of what it had been. All Merchants' Guild wizards had been dismissed except for Brann Alwin, and most of the laborers were gone as well. Garriker had expected Arythan to continue production of the Enhancement on a smaller scale, but the presence of the Guild—even reduced—was a dangerous little secret the mage had been forced to keep.

"You are rather testy today," Alwin said, eyeing Arythan warily.

The mage merely stared at him.

"Anyway, I think we should try this section. The last pit seems empty." He gestured to an untouched quadrant of mud.

"Fine." Arythan looked up to see the handful of laborers heading toward them with their tools. *Could be worse. I could be one of them.* He turned toward the mud and concentrated, forcing the rain down harder so that the mud would thin. Then, like an artificial tide, he would draw the dirty water away from the exposed crystals long enough for the laborers to extract them. It took upwards of an hour to fill a cart with raw Ice, and for the entire duration, he had to keep the water from doing what it would naturally do: fill in all holes. Though it seemed a menial task, he could not allow his focus to slip, could not allow his thoughts to drift.

The laborers descended the pit, some with buckets, some with shovels and picks. They did not look Human, covered from head to toe in thick, brown-black sludge. Michael had once told him that they were recruited criminals, and Arythan wondered if, on days like these, they would prefer a jail or the stockade. He felt his stomach gurgle and wondered just how many hours they had been working. The sky had not changed from its dismal, gray pall. For all he knew, they had missed their midday meal.

"Last one," he told the wizard.

"Watching them does make one tired," Alwin said, and Arythan fought the urge to slug him. "Join me for midday meal?"

You join me every day. You're not that lonely. He forced a nod. What choice did he have?

"I hear the cook will treat us to fruit pudding," the wizard said with a grin.

"Bonzer." *If it looks remotely like mud, I'll pass. Not that I can taste it anyway. A real treat would be honey-almonds. They are Tori's favorite. She might be eating them right now, enjoying a hot cup of cider, sitting by a window and watching the ducks on the lake—*

"Crow!"

Several shouts from the pit accompanied the wizard's voice. Muddy water had started to rush back into the depression, whirling around the men's legs. "Sorry," Arythan muttered. He had slipped. If he was not careful, he could drown all the laborers in a matter of seconds.

"Perhaps you're right. We should break soon." Alwin patted him on the shoulder. "At least you will be dry this afternoon."

I don't think I will ever be dry again, the mage thought gloomily, returning his attention to the mud.

THE DINING HALL was dark and quiet, a lonely fire crackling in the hearth as the rain pattered down on the roof and against the windows. Arythan and Brann Alwin sat closest to the heat, while the laborers kept their own company at the opposite end of the long table. The clatter of spoons and bowls replaced most conversation, though Alwin found no need to preserve the relative silence.

"I know what you're thinking about," the wizard said, pointing his spoon at the mage from across the table.

Arythan stopped stabbing at his pudding long enough to lift his gaze to Brann Alwin's amber eyes.

"The big Cerborathian festival is at hand, isn't it?" he asked with a smile. "'Summer's End', is it?"

"Summerfall," Arythan muttered, and went back to torturing his dessert.

"Ah, yes, Summerfall. I can only imagine that in so cold and desolate a place, every occasion is made to be a grand one. The other medori and I had our own celebration last year. The hall is quiet now, and I will have to find a way to keep myself entertained."

"Yeah, about that…" Arythan began, and he imagined he saw a shadow cross the wizard's face. "Seems like we're missing a couple figures of authority." He had, before leaving Victoria's side, prepared himself to endure the presence of Safir-Tamik and Sulinda Patrice. Time and time again he had told himself that he must wear a veneer of respect, lest he draw unwanted attention from his enemies. Since he had arrived at the Ice Plains, however, he had scarcely glimpsed the pair. Arythan was certain they were lodging in one of the adjacent buildings, but with Alwin constantly at his side, he had not had the opportunity to investigate.

The wizard's smile nearly faded. "Yes, I believe Lord Tamik and Lady Patrice had some business to attend to."

"A visit to Michael?" Arythan pried.

"I did not question them," Alwin said with finality. "But it is the silence of which I speak. Come the holiday, I will have to find a suitable diversion here."

Erik always spoke of the silence, Arythan thought absently. He regarded the wizard and forced a smile. "'S a masquerade," he said. "No one would know the difference if y' came."

Alwin shrugged. "Perhaps not. I'm not certain it's a chance I am willing to take. I do not know how my employers would gauge taking such a risk, that the king might recognize me."

Or that someone might just tell him who you are, Arythan thought malevolently. *That could solve many of my problems.*

"Still, I appreciate your optimism, Arythan. I can assume you will be attending?"

The mage nodded and watched Alwin eat another bite of pudding. For some reason, it made him squeamish. He purposely turned his thoughts to Victoria. He would need to bring her back to the castle. She would likely want him to find her a costume, and then she would undoubtedly insist that he find a new one for himself. Preparations were always tedious, but in a strange sort of way, he looked forward to being at her side when the great straw bear was torched, when the feasting began, and when they would dance before the unmasking. And he would be there beside her when it came time to announce the child....

"...would change when Prince Michael becomes Cerborath's king?" Alwin asked.

Arythan did not have to hear the entire question to know its content. The wizard was trying to talk politics as subtly as he could. "Nothing will change, mate. Michael loves a social scene."

"He certainly does," Alwin reflected. "Let us hope he will not indulge too liberally. That you saved his life once, he should know better."

Arythan pushed the bowl aside and leaned forward, his elbows on the table. "Y' said y' couldn't 'elp 'im because y're a wizard."

"Right."

"So if both wizards and mages 'ave different talents, why do wizards think they're better?"

Alwin seemed surprised by the pointed question. He dabbed at his mouth with a napkin. "First of all, Arythan, I wouldn't want you believing that I see myself as superior."

"I was speaking generally," Arythan clarified with a smirk.

"Then generally speaking, you and I both know that you cannot fairly compare wizards and mages."

"Y' can't? 'S not what I learned in Mystland," he challenged.

Brann Alwin studied him a moment. "Are you trying to coax some sort of confession out of me? Do you want me to tell you that Mystland wizards are jealous of mages? Or that wizards have more versatility?"

"They do, though."

Alwin scraped his bowl for another spoonful. "Do you intend to eat yours? If not, I will lighten you of that burden, though you are missing a delicious dessert."

Arythan pushed the bowl toward him.

"Thank you kindly. When it comes to Old Magic, there is beauty in simplicity. All that you need is there before you, and you have only to shape the elements to your command. It takes but a thought, or maybe even instinct."

The mage nodded.

"For working with a natural substance like Black Ice, mage magic is perfect," Alwin said. "A wizard's magic is more complex. Some would say it takes more skill—"

"Why?" Arythan interrupted.

Alwin blinked. "Well, because it is a synthesis of magics."

"'M a foreigner. I don' know what that means."

"A synthesis—a combining—to make something new. I could make a potion that will cause a woman to fall in love. It would involve many steps, and the process would create something that had not existed prior."

"So I can't create anything new, 's what y're saying," Arythan summarized.

"Well, no. You cannot."

"'S impossible," he pressed, staring at the wizard.

Alwin's mouth twisted. "Yes, Arythan. It would be impossible unless you could freeze lightning or create fire-rocks. The elements cannot be combined. They oppose each other. That is why you must contend with them as they are."

"Making a mage inferior, generally speaking."

Alwin smiled. "I will make no such judgment. You want me to make an excuse for the attitudes of other wizards, and I won't. I can't." He began the second bowl of pudding. "Mm. Is this why you left Mystland?"

Arythan smirked again but said nothing.

"Well, my friend, without you, the production of the Enhancement would be a long and tedious process for me. I am glad you are here." Alwin glanced out the window. "And I see that our weather has not improved much. Fortunately, you need not worry about that this afternoon."

"'Oo's worried?"

THE LARGE, wooden tub was full of melting snow and not warm bathwater. It was a fact Arythan lamented, for though he had traded his soaked and muddy attire for clean, dry clothes, he was unable to shake the chill that had permeated the whole of him that morning. He shivered and tossed a chunk of crystal into the tub.

"Would it not dissolve faster if you pulverized it first?"

Arythan tried not to flinch. The wizard was always there. He was like a third arm—an arm without a hand—useless and in his way. "I thought y'ad a letter to write," he said, trying not to sound snippy. When they had parted ways after the midday meal, Arythan had hoped Alwin would busy himself for the remainder of the day, but the wizard must have nothing better to do than watch him work.

"I wanted to make certain you had everything you needed," Alwin said, moving up beside him to peer in the tub. "And here I thought the snow was already melted."

Arythan folded his arms and stared at him.

Oblivious, the wizard turned to the small mountain of black crystals behind them. "I can help you crush these. Then you could focus on heating the water and dissolving the particles."

"I don't need 'elp."

"But look at all this—"

"No. Really. Y' should finish y'r letter. Call it an early night."

"Arythan, if I did not know better, I would say you wanted me leave you alone."

The mage clenched his fists and then forcibly changed his expression to one of mild amusement. "No, maybe 's just me 'oo wants an early evening. Been kind o' tired."

Alwin smiled and patted him on the shoulder. "I should say so. You always turn in late." He glanced at the pile of Ice. "What if I helped you make one batch, and then we call it a day. We are our own authority for now, so I think we would be within our rights."

"Bonzer." Arythan turned his attention to the tub. "I was thinking of leaving in the morning. I need time at the castle before the festival."

"Of course."

"Y' sure y're staying 'ere?" He heard the sound of the mallet, the crunch and clatter of crystals upon the floor.

"Yes, regretfully. I will likely continue our progress and wait for my employers to return."

"'S not all on y', y' know."

"Thank you, but you have done the majority of the work. And you are the prince's medoriate; he will expect you to attend."

No, I'm the king's *medoriate. And I wish he would be there to sort this mess.* He concentrated on the snow and watched as it turned transparent, slipping down the sides of the tub to add to the accumulating liquid at the bottom. *Michael said his father won't be back until after the festival. Knowing the king and his love for celebrations, it is purely intentional.*

Alwin came up with a small bucket. "Mind yourself, Arythan. Do not breathe this in." He waited for the mage to turn away before he dumped the black powder into the tub.

Why not? Arythan wanted to ask, though he knew the question would remain unanswered. He had spent three years in Cerborath, and still no one would disclose the danger the Ice posed to medori should it be consumed. The darker side of himself, in fleeting moments of passive aggression, considered adding the Enhancement to Alwin's drink—just to learn the truth. Then he would think of Cyrul Frostmeyer and how the wizard had mistakenly poisoned the Ilangien. *Alwin is definitely not an immortal, and I'm not a murderer.*

Arythan gave a nod as the wizard dumped another bucket into the tub. By now he could feel heat radiating from the water, and a few wisps of steam escaped into the air. He stepped away to wrap his scarf around his nose and mouth, then stirred the mixture with a broad plank. The shimmering black liquid lapped at the sides, and he had to be careful not to stir it too forcefully.

A couple more buckets of Ice, and the water began to simmer. He signaled to Alwin that the solution was ready, and together they moved a broad, shallow tray beneath the spigot at the bottom of the tub. Alwin stood back and waved him on, and Arythan slowly opened the valve. A cloud of steam rose as the hot liquid poured from the tap, flowing over and covering the surface of the tray. Arythan closed the valve and focused upon the tray, drawing the cold to the liquid as quickly as he could. Geometric patterns crystallized in small, sparkling forms that encrusted the tray like black frost. Once the entire tray was covered in the solid, they chipped away at it and shoveled it into waiting bags.

Finally, Arythan pulled the scarf from his face and used it to dab the sweat upon his brow. "I'm done."

Alwin nodded. "That was more than I could do in several days. Go and try to get some rest. I still have a letter to write."

Arythan did go, but there was no time for rest. He returned to his cell and withdrew the chunk of crystal he had slipped into his coat pocket. He wrapped it in a linen cloth and added it to the bag he would take with him to the cave. Insomnia was a terrible condition to waste, and he had plenty to accomplish. He tucked the bag under the desk and left the hall.

Which one would it be? he wondered, gazing into the cloudy night at the silhouetted structures adjacent to his own. The largest building was the laborers' quarters, and the one next to that was the mess hall and kitchen. The only remaining structures belonged to the blacksmith and the medic—neither of whom resided any longer at the Ice Plains.

He headed for the medic's ward, reasoning it would be a much more habitable place for his enemies of authority. Of course, the door was locked, but it was no more an obstacle for him than hopping stones to cross a creek. He picked the lock with a broken fork he had stolen from the mess hall and slipped inside.

I just need to see it—to know where they keep it, he thought. He remembered the book well from the first time he had stolen it, from Kirou-Mekus. He would not take it now, even if he found it. Its absence would raise suspicion and alarm, and the finger would inevitably be pointed at him. Arythan would have to exercise rare patience until he learned how to destroy the Ice. Only then would he strike, razing all the Seroko hoped to accomplish. The thought made him thirsty for vengeance, but timing was so very, very important.

The initial room held tables that had been converted to desks. Both were empty but for an inkwell and quill, a couple candles, and a wax seal. There were no papers, no books. The space was, in fact, immaculate. He moved to the shelves against the walls. As he read the titles there, however, he realized the books had belonged to the medic—left behind when the Merchants' Guild had been ordered to leave.

Of course it's clean, he thought. *If the king should visit by surprise, it would have to look abandoned.* Arythan smirked as he ran a finger along the desk top. *Garriker's not an idiot. There's not a trace of dust here.*

He proceeded to the back room, where there were several cots and a chest of drawers. There were a few articles of clothing in the drawers, but much like the front room, he found nothing of intrigue. Arythan started to wonder if maybe Safir-Tamik and Sulinda Patrice had chosen the blacksmith's shop for their quarters.

No, the desks are clean. They must work here. He returned to the front room and searched again: under the desks and chairs, by the window, along the wall. *What would Em'ri notice? What clues would he see?* He eyed the chair. *What else isn't dusty?* A new angle might reveal more. He was not short, but he was not tall, either—at least, not tall enough to see atop the shelves. Arythan dragged the chair to the wall and stood atop it for a better look at the books. Most of them were dusty, but there was one spot on the shelf where a book had been dragged across the surface.

Herbs of the Northern Mountains, the title read. It was a thick book, but when he carefully pulled it closer, it was not as heavy as it seemed. *Interesting.* He took it from the shelf and opened it, finding the pages had been cut away so that they concealed another book. *The* book—the journal about the immortals and their magic. This had been the book that brought him to Kirou-Mekus, where his life began to slip from his grasp and into a direction he never could have foreseen. He had once held it in demon hands, and now he held it again, a different man entirely. He had changed, but the book's promise had not. He once hoped it would be a means to his salvation, and now again, he would steal it with that promise in mind.

But I must wait. Arythan sighed. So minor an object, so important its meaning. *In theory it contains the locations of the Ice.* He stared at it. *How much more can there be? How much would I have to destroy—if I could destroy it?* His fingers pried at the edges of the journal, trying to free it from its cryptic cover. As he did, a fine, dusty soot rose from the pages like mist.

What—? His eyes began to burn. *Nigqora.* He shut the book and replaced it so that he could rub his eyes. Already they watered, and tears leaked down his face. He pressed his fingers over his eyelids and smeared the tears and soot away, but the burning did not cease, and when he opened his eyes again, his vision had started to blur.

Nigqora! He nearly fell off the chair. *I will not panic. I must not panic.* He looked around the room, but nothing had a solid edge to it. He covered one eye, then the other, but both were equally afflicted. Thoughts whirled in his mind, and he sought a fragment of logic that would guide him. *I have to get out of here.*

He took a deep breath and returned the chair to the desk, nearly impaling himself on the corner as he did so. He cursed and stumbled his way to the door, then outside. Arythan searched his pocket for the broken fork. He knew it by touch, but even as he brought it to his eyes, it was nothing more than a fuzzy shape. Close up, at arm's length—it did not matter; its image did not sharpen at all.

Arythan felt for the lock and hoped he would be able to blindly secure the door again. His first attempt failed, and he had to try again. He started at a sound from behind him, but he could not distinguish anything from the stillness of the blurry landscape. Turning back to the lock, he closed his searing eyes and heard a click. He tried the handle, and it held fast.

There was little cause for relief. He needed to make it back to his cell, and then... *Othenis. Othenis will be waiting by the cave.* His head was beginning to ache, but he tried to walk as quickly, quietly, and straight as he could back to the hall. He paused at the door, his ears straining for a sign that Brann Alwin was stirring close by. But only the sound of the fire in the hearth greeted his ears, and he made his way to his desk. The bag was where he had left it, though now it was a shapeless spot of brown. He felt for the strap and slung it over his shoulder. *The stable....*

Several times he nearly fell, and he wondered how so many large rocks ended up in his path. Inside the stable was nothing but darkness, and he stood there, reminding himself again that he could not panic—not yet. *"Narga,"* he said softly.

The mare nickered, and he slowly walked forward, his hand outstretched before him. He drew a small blue flame upon his palm, but it did nothing to clarify the darkness around him. *"Help me find you,"* he murmured to her, listening for the sounds of stirring in her stall.

At last she whinnied, and the blue flame caught her movement. He knew enough that horses and fire were not a good combination, so he extinguished the flame and tried to feel for her halter. Her soft muzzle shoved into his hand, and a whuff of warm air escaped her nostrils.

"Good girl." Arythan found the latch to the stall door, but he realized there was no way he would be able to saddle and bridle her—not in the dark, and certainly not with his eyes in the state they were in. He hoped that she would not test his authority today.

Arythan patted her nose and opened the door. He could feel the weight of her brush past him, hear her step into the aisle. His free hand gripped the halter. *"Veriq, Narga,"* he coaxed, walking back toward the dark blue patch that had to be the night sky. She clopped alongside him, and as they moved through the door, he could feel the coolness of the night air upon them. Then he stopped and stared at her shadowy form. *You are so damn tall.* He felt for the stringy strap to the bag and brought it over his head, securing it so it would not slip from him.

"Narga, des," he said. "Down. *Des."* She did not move immedi-

ately, and he imagined her ears flicking back and forth, deciding if she would obey or not. *"Please."*

And then, miraculously, the large black form lowered to the ground. He praised her and rubbed her neck. He slid his leg over her broad back and gripped her mane. *"Iat,"* he urged, and she rose like a mountain beneath him.

"All right. You know where to go. Same place we go every night." He nudged her with his heel, in what he believed was the right direction. She began slowly, uncertainly, for this was a new experience —to be saddle-less *and* bridle-less. Her master did little more than urge her forward. She did not know how fervently he hoped she would not take off to wherever she pleased. What she did seem to sense was that something was wrong, and that this was a matter of urgency. As if a decision had been made, she began to trot, carrying her master into the night, toward the mountain path she knew well.

Arythan was reminded of when he had been taken prisoner by the Ice Flies. Upon his release he had been blindfolded and bound atop Narga's back, left to wander. Again he was cold, again he was blind—listening to her hoof beats upon the trail. The difference now was whether or not he would ever regain his vision. He clutched her mane, his face against her neck, his eyes pressed shut as they yet burned in their sockets. His face was sticky with tears, his head throbbing from the pain. But there was only one thought worse than being blind for the rest of his life: how would he tell his wife?

While he was sightless on a mountain trail, she was waiting for him in the country manor, excited at the thought that he would soon be coming to whisk her away to the lively festival of color, music, and company. Summerfall was less than a week away.

Othenis will be able to help, Arythan assured himself. *He has a wizard—maybe several—and they will know what to do.* Over and over, he convinced himself that this would be his solution, until at last, Narga stopped.

Arythan opened his eyes and tried to determine where he was. Could this be the shelter where he left her when he proceeded to the cave? *"Narga, des."* The mare merely stood there. *"Des.* Down. *Des,"* he said more firmly. Still she did not move.

"Please?"

Arythan sighed. *She is waiting for her oats. I have none.* He braced himself and slid from her back. It would have been too much to ask that he land on his feet. The fall was much farther than seemed possible, and the impact of the frozen ground upon his belly almost took the wind from him.

The mare nudged him, and he groaned. *"No. Sorry."* He forced himself upright, and felt for the rocky wall that guided him along the narrow ledge. He dare not stand, and so he crawled, aware that his left leg and hand were not two inches from empty air and his final plummet. Arythan kept his useless eyes to the ground, and only when the substrate broadened did he look up to see the dark mass of the cave before him. In the midst of the dark mass was a horrible, blazing blue light. He drew a sharp breath and shielded his eyes.

"Arythan, is that you?"

He did not have a chance to respond as Othenis's form moved in front of him.

"Jedinom's Sword!" Othenis gasped. "Your eyes! What happened?"

"What? Are they melted?" Arythan asked, panic creeping into his voice.

"No, but... Can you see at all?"

"Barely."

"Let me help you." He guided Arythan into the cave.

"The light's too bright."

"I'll extinguish it." Moments later, all was dark.

"Arythan, I am going to get help."

The mage nodded. He sighed and closed his eyes, lying back against the blanket Othenis had bundled behind him. He tried to empty his mind, focusing upon the sound of the wind outside, the coolness of the air. He did not know for how long he lay there, but when he opened his eyes again, he could see nothing. Nothing at all.

7

GRATEFUL

"I am so very sorry, sir!" The girl glanced at the furry brown creature hiding behind her legs. "Henry almost never behaves in such a way."

"In a hungry way, you mean?" the tall, old man asked. He had crouched a little lower, trying to better see the animal that now feasted upon his banana. "What manner of creature is a 'Henry?'"

The girl laughed. "You must be one of the newcomers the villagers are talking about—the one from Cerborath."

"Cerborath?" The man looked confused and glanced over his shoulder at a woman across the road. She, however, was preoccupied at a market stand. He turned back to the girl. "Is Cerborath the same as Northern Secramore?"

The girl smiled. "I had heard you were very ill—that you had lost your memory. Such news travels fast around here." The creature at her feet suddenly scurried up her body and came to sit upon her shoulder, the banana still in its mouth. "I've never been north. I was born here." She gestured to the animal. "Henry is the name of my monkey. I don't believe monkeys live up north—or at least not where you're from. My name is Selmara."

The old man straightened. "My name is Erik." He gestured to the woman now approaching. "My friend is Catherine."

"It is nice to meet you," Selmara said. "And I can get you a new banana."

He smiled at her. "No, thank you, but you would do me a kindness to direct me to the medic."

"Follow the road past the dock. She lives on a hill with a little fence around her garden."

"Thank you, Selmara."

"Good luck to you, Mr. Erik."

Catherine joined him and took his hand. "I see you are the victim of theft."

"Henry was hungry," Erik said, and they strolled together down the road.

"You are fast to make friends," Catherine said. "I hope you will tell me if you become overwhelmed. This is your first trip into town, and there is much to take in."

"Yes," he admitted with a nod, "but I am ready."

"You seem much stronger, and I'm glad for it. A few more days, and you will be climbing trees and jumping in puddles."

Erik looked at her curiously. "Is that what I did before? I can't imagine it." His gaze fell to his cane.

"I exaggerate, of course, but your recovery has been quick. Though..." She paused and pulled him to a stop. "I admit that I have another reason for coming into town."

He waited for her to continue.

"I was told that the women here need the help of a seamstress. I intend to see if I can be of any use to them."

He nodded. "What is a seamstress?"

"One who sews material—fabric and linen."

She could see that he was still confused. "I would stitch cloth together."

"Ah."

They resumed walking, and Catherine continued to search him for a reaction. "You would not mind, then, if I took on work? It would earn us some money for a modest living."

"Why do you ask me about your decision?" He stopped again to watch a bird fly overhead.

Catherine shrugged. "I suppose it is my way of informing you of what I intend to do." She coaxed him along. "I need to stop at the tailor's shop, but I am sure you would like to continue exploring in my absence."

He looked at her, uncertain. "You wish for me to venture on without you?"

"It would be good for you," she assured him. "I will find you when I am finished."

"I doubt I shall get very far."

"Then I will find you faster," she said with a girlish grin.

He returned a smile of his own, and they made their way to the tailor's shop. Catherine had just gone inside when Erik poked his head in after her. "Catherine is a very good seamstress," he said to the women there, and then he disappeared.

He meandered along the road, his destination at the forefront of his mind. He passed the dock and found the hill with the cottage, the garden, and the fence. The door was open, and he peeked inside.

"Oh—come in," a woman said. She was young, dark-haired, and comely, and though Erik did not remember her, there was little doubt that she knew him. She set down the bouquet of flowers in her hand, and guided him into the room and to a chair.

"Ms. Lorrel was so worried about you, and now I see you are walking around."

"Currently I am sitting," he said, and the medic smiled.

Her smile faded, however, when she watched him a little longer. "It's true, then, that you have no memory of what happened to you."

"None at all," he said. "And so your name...."

"Orilian," she replied. "I wish I could have met you under better circumstances, Mr. Sparrow." She pulled a chair closer to sit across from him.

"It is my circumstance that led me here."

Orilian held up a hand. "Before you ask me, know that I cannot bring your memory back. I wish that I could, but my healing is not magic."

"I already know that my past recollections may or may not return as time progresses," Erik said softly. "I wish to know about poisonous snakes and how such wounds are treated."

Orilian nodded. "You are piecing together what happened to you." She stood and took a bottle of liquid from her cabinet. She handed it to him as she sat down again. "Adder's Blood. It's not actually blood but a mixture of healing herbs that seem to help stop the effects of the venom. Even after you were treated, I had my doubts that you would survive. You were already burning with fever when you were brought here, and the venom was working its way through your body."

Erik stared at the bottle a little longer before he handed it back to her.

"It was curious, though, all the cuts and scrapes...like you had gone through a patch of roses."

At the mention of roses, his eyes found her bouquet. "I was told I had been intent on spotting a hummingbird."

"I don't think any hummingbird is worth the risk of encountering all the venomous creatures of that jungle," Orilian said. "Every year I treat at least three snake bites, a dozen spider bites, and a few cases of children eating poisonous berries. You number among the fortunate who survived."

"I think often upon it," Erik said, and he gripped his cane to stand.

"Without any insult intended, Mr. Sparrow…but given your age, Jedinom must have been with you."

"Jedinom? Was that the name of the guide?" he asked.

She shook her head and gave him a sad smile. "Jedinom is our holy protector." She escorted him to the door. "I'm sorry I couldn't be of more help, but I will pray that your memory returns to you."

He paused at the threshold. "I could not help but notice that you try to sustain flowers indoors. Would they not survive longer reared by seed outside?"

Orilian blushed. "Northern customs must be quite different." She fetched the bouquet to show him. "These were a gift from my betrothed."

"A token of affection?"

"Yes, from the one who intends to marry me."

"A vow, then." His focus alternated between the blooms and her face. "I have so much to learn."

"You are a nice man, Mr. Sparrow. If I can ever help you, don't be afraid to call on me."

Erik thanked her and made his way down the hill. With the sun at its peak, he found it sapped his energy and made him tired and weary. He eased himself down on a large rock and watched the passersby. One older gentleman glanced at him twice before heading in his direction.

"Mr. Sparrow, are you all right?" he asked.

Erik held up a hand to shield his eyes from the sun as he tried to recall the stranger's face. "Just resting," he said. "We have met before, then."

A mixture of surprise and amusement crossed the stranger's face. He held out a hand. "Yes, we have, though I had forgotten—no insult intended—your condition. I am a friend of Lady Catherine. Halgon Thayliss, at your service."

"Ah—she has mentioned you," Erik said. "You have been kind to her through my illness." He extended his hand as well, and Halgon took it and gave it a shake. He did not seem to notice Erik's bemused expression.

"I have tried to lend my assistance as mayor of this community." Halgon's shoulders squared. "I am surprised to see you up and about."

"It was important to me that I rouse myself from this murky dream."

"Yes, well, it's good to see you better, but the sun seems to be taking a toll on you."

"I do feel quite warm," Erik admitted.

"Why don't you come with me, Mr. Sparrow? I live close by. You could stand some shade and a drink."

"Thank you," Erik said, and he rose and followed the man to a large home with a maze of different rooms. Servants bustled by, tending to this and that, and Halgon directed one of them to bring them drinks. Unlike the cottage Erik shared with Catherine, this one was furnished and immaculate. There were colorful woven rugs, cushioned chairs, and a hearth that did not look as though it had been destroyed in a bonfire.

Halgon gestured to one of the chairs, and Erik found—with some relief to his back—that he sank a little into the soft cushions. Halgon sat adjacent to him, and in another moment, the servant returned with their drinks—some sort of fruity concoction.

"It is a tragic situation you have, Mr. Sparrow," Halgon said. "To wake up with no memory of who you are."

"I hope to recover my memory in time," Erik said. He took a drink and marveled at the sweet flavor.

"I hope you do, too. I know this must be difficult for you as well as Catherine. She is a strong woman, and she has a valiant heart."

"She does," Erik agreed.

"Where is she, might I ask? I would think she would be at your side."

Erik took another drink. "She is at the tailor's shop, looking for work as a seamstress."

Halgon frowned. "She takes on many burdens. I suspect this is an effort to support the both of you."

"As she has told me."

"Do you...do you not think it fair that you shoulder some of her burden? When you're strong enough, of course."

"I am not sure I understand," Erik said, his brow furrowed.

"Of course," Halgon said with a wave of his hand. "I forget your condition. I will tell you this straightforward, and we will keep it between you and me."

Erik leaned forward to better hear him.

"A man must support his family. Catherine is your family. She is too proud to say it, but she has taken the responsibility for the both of you. You need to make money to survive, to buy your food, to earn a living. She wants to support you, but a seamstress can only earn so much. You need a vocation—a job. You have to help her, sir."

"I want to help her," Erik said, concerned. "Where would I find a vocation? What would I do?"

Halgon eased back in his chair and studied him. "I think I can be of assistance. We have a village farm in need of extra hands. Animals and crops need tending, and if you think yourself capable, I could find you work there."

"If this will help Catherine, I will do what you ask of me," Erik said.

"I'm glad to hear it, Mr. Sparrow. She must be a fine wife."

"Wife?"

"Oh, I've forgotten again. Catherine did say the two of you were not married," Halgon said.

"We are not," Erik confirmed, "though we are lovers."

Halgon's face reddened at the term. "Well, that is between the two of you. In any case, she is devoted to you." He stood.

Erik looked down in surprise to find he had consumed every drop in his cup. He handed it to the servant and stood. "Thank you for your kindness—to Catherine and to me."

"It is the least I can do," Halgon said. "Come and see me tomorrow morning, and I will show you the farm."

Erik nodded, and he was shown out. He had not ventured ten paces before Catherine appeared, hurrying toward him.

"I thought you had vanished," she said, flushed with worry.

"I was exploring, as you requested."

"Yes, but—"

"Are you now a seamstress?" he asked.

"It would seem I am." Her gray eyes roved over him suspiciously. "What have you been about?"

"I, too, have a vocation," he announced. "I will tend to crops and animals on the village farm."

Catherine's mouth fell open. "How did you manage such a feat? Are you certain you are capable of such work?"

"Halgon Thayliss believes that I am," he said with confidence. "What are 'crops'?"

"You foolish man," she murmured, then sighed. "You did this for me, didn't you?"

"I must support you," Erik said seriously. "I have been blind to your burdens."

She blushed. "Admittedly this life will demand a bit more effort from us, but there will be more to us than work." She took his hand and smiled up at him.

"Do you want me to kiss you?" he asked.

Her blush deepened. "Yes, Mr. Sparrow. I would like that."

CATHERINE HAD CHASED him away from the hearth. She knew that he meant well, but it had become clear that his desire to assist with all matters culinary would be to her detriment. She had, as an alternative, suggested that he play her a tune on the violin—to see if he could remember any melodies. So Erik had disappeared into his room, and she heard the resonance of a few notes before he appeared again, empty-handed.

"What is the matter?" she asked, her heart heavy.

"It does not entice me," he said. "I do not know what to do with it."

"You can just play random notes, glide the bow over the strings," she offered.

He shook his head.

But you played so beautifully.

"I only need a little more time, Erik. Why not take a walk along the shore?"

He seemed to brighten at this idea, and so he set out. When she was certain he was beyond the cottage, she wiped her brow and sat down in a chair beside the hearth. *So much of this new life is more difficult than I could have ever imagined. More than the weight of the labor is the weight on my heart. I lie to him at every turn, but every lie is backed by the hope that he will find new happiness here. I want to believe I can be his savior rather than the one who destroyed him.*

Catherine dabbed at her eyes with her apron. *I was told you would go mad without the Light. I was told you would fade. But you have awakened to a fresh life, and there is wonder in your eyes again. I could live with you like this until our end. It would be everything I have dreamed. Your pain is gone, your mind is free.* You *are free.*

She stood and stirred the bubbling pot. "Look at me," she murmured. "Sara would be laughing. How I miss them. I hope they are well." She ladled the stew into a couple bowls, placed them on a tray with some spoons, and headed outside to find her companion. She spied him on the shore, sitting in the sand with his cane beside him, facing the ocean and the setting sun.

The sky was flaunting evening hues of violet, crimson, and

rose, and the last of the sun kissed the waves farewell. She stood next to him, admiring the sight, until she looked down and found his silvery-blue eyes upon her.

"You should unbind your hair," he said. "It would be beautiful in the wind." He lifted his arms to take the tray from her.

"I always wondered what you found to be beautiful," she said, complying with his wish.

"Did I not tell you?"

She sat down beside him and dug her toes into the sand. "You were...more reserved, I suppose."

"Was I?" His eyes followed the locks of her hair as they played around her face. He smiled at her—how she had come to love the freedom with which he smiled. "I see no need to guard my tongue with such a sight."

"You speak like a poet trying to woo a young maiden," Catherine said. She handed him his bowl.

His smile slipped away with the wind. "Though I have failed you as a musician."

"Your heart has taken a different path," she said. "While I will miss your music, I have something much better: the source of inspiration." She set her bowl down to touch his hand.

"Tell me of how we met."

There was a moment of silence when she could only stare at the ocean. She had prepared for this—perhaps too well. The story was a grand variation of the truth, and the only cause for her hesitation was that she knew it was a lie. *But aren't all stories created in such a way? It is merely that: a story. A fanciful story.*

"It was the festival of Summerfall in Cerborath, where I grew up in the care of my father. He was of noble blood, and I enjoyed a wealthy life. But I was already sixteen and without any suitors—a fact that worried my father."

Erik finished a spoonful of soup and spoke. "I do not understand."

"A noble's daughter is usually married off before she is fourteen," Catherine said. "But I did not have the patience for young men—not then. My head was full of dreams and fanciful thoughts of the forest in which I lived and the tales that surrounded it. I loved to walk barefoot in the woods, call to the birds, sing beneath the sun when it so suited me. This was not behavior acceptable for an aristocrat's daughter. My father never discouraged me, but he did fear for my future."

Catherine sipped from her bowl. "And so I was sixteen, unspoken for, and required to attend the festival of Summerfall. The festival itself is so steeped in tradition that I knew exactly what to expect. There would be feasting, dancing, music, and socializing. None of it was of interest to me.

"The feast began as it always did, but when it came time for the musician to play, there was a twist in my fate. The king had found no ordinary minstrel, you see. This was some magical being who could charm a unicorn with the sound of his fiddle. And then I saw him, as radiant as his melody." Catherine closed her eyes, and her lips curved upward. "His hair was long and golden, and he was tall and slender with eyes the color of the spring rain. His fair skin betrayed his youth, though he was older than me.

"He played his magic, and when he was done, he vanished, and I thought my heart had vanished with him. I searched for him during the dances, but he was not there. And when the night was over, and guests took their leave, I rode with my father in the carriage back to our manor, tears in my eyes. I could not explain it to him, how I felt. He would not have understood if I could.

"The moon had been out in its entirety, and as we rode, I spied a traveler on foot. I had but glimpsed him in passing, but I knew it was him. I *knew* it, like one knows her own name. I begged my father to stop, and we invited the minstrel to ride with us. I can remember gazing at him, and he gazed back. If anything was said, I cannot recall, but he came to stay with us a while, and so he won my heart."

"And that eccentric musician stole you away from your home and father," Erik finished.

Catherine opened her eyes. "My father gave us his blessing, actually. It was my choice to leave, and he wanted to see me happy."

"Were we?"

"Very happy. We have been together a long time. Long enough to see the color in our hair fade. Long enough to watch the years add lines to our faces."

Erik set down his empty bowl and faced her. "Why did I not marry you?"

It was a question she had not expected; a question to which she had not an immediate response. She watched the waves roll in as she considered an answer. "I...I do not know that we ever made the time. We were always on the road, traveling from one town to another, seeing Secramore with the eyes of children."

"To see so much but not the one so often in one's sight," he mused.

"You are strangely sentimental this evening," Catherine teased, trying to lighten to mood.

"I merely wonder about the life I led—the life we shared."

"Time has slowed for us now," she said. "I have no regrets about the past, and I rather look forward to the days ahead."

"And now," he added. "Now is the best time of all." He set the bowls and tray aside and stood, offering his hand to her.

She took it, assuming he wanted to walk along the water's edge. He pulled her to where the waves fizzled into bubbles and pointed to the ground. "I have found the most amazing creatures," he said. "Watch." He scooped a handful of sand and lifted it for her to see. Fingernail-sized, wedge-shaped clams sat atop the sand and quickly began to disappear, burying themselves beneath the surface. Erik gave a laugh. "You can feel them against your palm, when they dig deeply enough."

Before she could speak, he dipped down again and retrieved a fresh handful. "You try, Catherine." Then the wet sand was in her hands, and the little creatures were tickling her skin. She gave a shout of surprise and looked up at him, incredulous.

His expression stole her breath away, and she knew that they had found happiness.

8

A SIGHT TO BEHOLD

The paper was starting to tear; Victoria could feel the softness of the crease as her fingertips smoothed it for the hundredth time. She glanced down at the letter that had become an item of comfort and consolation. The ink was smeared from her tears, the body was wrinkled, the corners were dog-eared. *I don't even know why I brought it. It's not his writing.* She drew a deep breath as the carriage rolled to a halt outside the keep. *Most importantly, it's not him.* She stuffed the letter away.

Her eyes fell upon the empty seat across from her. This was when he would open the door and help her down. This was when he would take her hand and escort her to the door. She would see his smile from beneath the mask, and then— *Oh, stop. You will make yourself cry, and that won't do anyone any good.*

The door opened from the outside, and the coachman helped her down. It was a fair night, and she could smell the smoke and char on the breeze from the burning of the Great Bear. Her tardiness was intentional; she meant to arrive just before the feast. Victoria looked up to see a figure in white waiting at the keep's entrance.

"Would you like me to escort you inside, milady?" the coachman asked.

"No, thank you."

The man in white came down the stairs to meet her. She knew his broad shoulders, his proud stance, his confident gait. She did not know what Michael was thinking when he kissed her hand, and his eyes swept over her discerningly.

"Lady Ambrin, it has been an eternity since I have seen you," the prince said. "I am delighted you are here, though I regret that your companion is not."

"Your Majesty," Victoria said, blushing, "I am here as Madame Crow, and I will do my best to represent my husband in his absence…so long as he does not expect me to perform feats of magic."

"Dear Victoria, there will be magic, I promise, but for you, I must extend my congratulations." He began to lead her up the stairs. "It would seem you have more than your marriage to celebrate."

Of course he noticed, she thought, her face afire behind the mask. *Everyone will notice. I was fitted for my costume a week ago, and now it's snug.* "Thank you for the carriage," she said awkwardly.

"My pleasure, Victoria. When Crow wrote to me about his illness, it was all I could do to comply with his request."

"He did not…" She sought the right words. "He did not elaborate upon his condition, did he?"

Michael turned to her, and she imagined his expression as one of surprise. "I meant to ask if you knew any details, but our Dark Wizard has a habit of being mysterious. I had hoped to pay him a visit, but preparations for the festival kept me from my goal."

They walked into the hall of costumed guests, and Victoria faltered in a world she once knew so well. Could it be that her quiet time away was the cause of her discomfort now? Or was it that she knew what to expect from such a setting—knew what awaited her this night? She kept close to Michael's side, relieved he had not yet relinquished her hand. "He told me not to see him," she admitted. "He did not want to risk my health."

"Ah, yes, he had a similar message for me. Far be it for me to undo a thoughtful gesture, but I am rather concerned." He patted her hand. "I will go the Ice Plains once all is settled here, and I will enlighten you to his condition."

"Thank you," Victoria said.

The prince smiled. "It is a night of merriment, Madame Crow. Go and be merry. I will not disclose your identity."

Victoria stood there a moment after he had gone, feeling abandoned and alone. She moved toward the tables that had been adorned with colorful fabrics for the feast. Her stomach growled, and she frowned. It seemed as though she was always hungry, always looking for something to eat. At the manor, the cook never ceased his efforts, and the meals had always been fair. Meals at the castle were meant to please the king, and she had nearly forgotten just how elaborate they could be. Of course, this was Summerfall, and the tables this night would contain the most abundant spread of all.

Gentle pressure fell upon her shoulder, and Victoria spun to see a woman in an elegant white gown and a mask of white roses. *Ladonna.*

"It *is* you!" Michael's wife exclaimed. "I did not recognize you at first." Ladonna embraced her. "You and Arythan must be so happy."

Some wine would make me happy right now. Victoria watched her glance around for a face that was not there. "Yes, though I assume Michael told you...."

Ladonna's smile faded. "Michael is not my most reliable source of information. Is something the matter?"

"Arythan is not here tonight. He has taken ill."

"I am sorry to hear that." Ladonna seemed genuinely disappointed. "Is it serious?"

"I cannot say. I have not seen him." Victoria wondered if it was suspicion, doubt, or concern that gazed back at her. "I hope to hear from him soon."

"With Jedinom's good graces," Ladonna said.

Victoria was grateful when the bell interrupted their conversation. Everyone migrated toward the tables to stand and await the prince's greeting.

"Will you not sit with us?" Ladonna asked.

Victoria hesitated. *I'm behaving like Arythan, avoiding all attention.* "Of course." She followed the noblewoman to the head table, trying to ignore the curious heads that turned in her direction. She might well have been naked for the way Banen regarded her. *You had your opportunity. Now I have started my own family.*

Michael raised his hands. "My good people," he began. "I have the honor of addressing you at this grand occasion tonight. This is more than Summerfall. This is the beginning of our golden era. In this time of change, when Desneran leadership rests precariously in my father's hands, Cerborath is the rock upon which we build our alliances. You may have questioned the decisions your king has made, but I can assure you that nothing is more secure than Cerborath's legacy—a legacy that will soon be mine to continue. Be at ease and rejoice! Tonight we look ahead with confidence and hope. Tonight we drink to success and unity. Tonight we celebrate together as a growing family."

As the people applauded, Victoria thought about her own "growing family." How would a change in leadership affect her, Arythan, and their child? She knew she had not been the only one surprised when the prince outright stated his pending coronation. Had the king been present, would Michael still have been so bold? They sat down to a dinner full of whispers and murmurs, and Victoria did her best to ignore them all. The wine never tasted so sweet, and every bite of every platter at every course was expounding with flavor. She cleared every helping without much thought, and when the meal was finished, she wondered where the time had fled.

All but the head table was cleared to make way for the dancing. When Victoria stood, she realized just how much wine she had consumed. The hall spun just a little, but her spirits had brightened, and a new goal was set before her. She had spied who she believed was Diana Sherralin lingering at the outskirts of the hall. *I don't know why I did not think of her sooner.*

Victoria took her cup and started for the healer, but a shadow blocked her path and refused to move.

"He wastes no time," Banen said, his tone scathing. "Nor do you."

Emboldened by the drink, she folded her arms, cup dangling from her fingers. "I was tired of waiting."

There was a moment of silence when he stared at her, and she stared back.

"So where is he? Did he decline an invitation to be social? Did he think he would send you in his place while he hides away with his secrets?"

"What are you talking about?" Victoria asked impatiently. "Are you drunk?"

"You are the one holding the cup, Victoria." He folded his arms.

"I do not have to answer to you. Neither does Arythan."

"I could not care less about anything he would say to me. Since the both of you are so terribly happy together, I was merely wondering why you're here alone." Banen shrugged. "But then again, it is not my business." He gave a nod and walked away without looking back.

He does this to me every time. Every time there is an event or occasion, he makes certain to pull his knife and dig into me—just enough to make me bleed. I hate you. I really do. She gulped her wine and waited for her eyes to stop watering. *Diana Sherralin. I need to find her.*

The healer had not moved from the wall, and she turned warily to Victoria as she drew nearer. "Good evening," Diana greeted in a monotone.

"And to you," Victoria said politely. She never knew the best way to approach Diana Sherralin. The woman was always cold and often abrasive, and Victoria had the distinct impression the healer did not much care for her. When she had first approached Diana about her suspicions of pregnancy, the healer had said, "Well, what did you expect?" Victoria had had no response then, just as she could think of no tactful way to ask a favor of the woman now. She was surprised when Diana prompted the conversation.

"Medoriate Crow has a way of avoiding social occasions. Unless, of course, he managed to injure himself or contract a malady of some sort."

Victoria nodded, her stomach sour. "It would seem to be the latter."

"My intention was a jest." Diana sighed. "But I see you are serious. What has he done now?"

"It's what he *hasn't* done." Victoria gestured to the empty place at her side. "He should be here, but he wrote—someone else wrote a letter for him—stating that he would be unable to attend the festival." Without knowing why, she retrieved the letter from the bosom of her dress and handed it to the healer. "He told me not to go to him because—-"

Diana held up a hand for silence while she read. When she had finished, she returned the paper. "You want me to see him."

Victoria nodded.

"If I have time, I will go." Diana gave her a nod. "You should not indulge so in the wine. Your child consumes all that you consume."

Victoria stared after her as she walked away, then looked at her empty cup. *She definitely does not like me.*

The sound of laughter nearby caught her attention. Victoria did not have to remove the womens' masks to know who they were. Their actual names were irrelevant; their role at such gatherings was what earned them their reputation. They were the wolves that circled the unsuspecting herd, looking for the weak to tear apart and devour. They could smell vulnerability a mile away, and it drew them in with their merciless passion to cause suffering. This evening they had found her.

"You seem unhappy, Victoria," one of them said. "What is the matter?"

"That's not her."

"Yes, yes it is," another insisted.

"Someone has been visiting the cook's pantry."

"Sampling the pastries."

I am not in the mood for this. "Or maybe I'm pregnant," Victoria snapped. "As in, starting a family with my husband. You've met him, I believe. He is the royal medoriate." She was awarded with a full ten seconds of stunned silence while the ladies worked up to a new attack.

"The Dark Wizard with his scary black mark. I hear he is a savage—one of the Torrgarrans."

"Can you imagine what his child will be like?"

"A little monster or demon, to be certain."

"It will tear right through her and eat her alive."

"Do you ever listen to yourselves?" Victoria asked, raising her voice. "You are so stupid, the things you say." She knew she was feeding the fire, even as she retaliated, but she could not keep silent.

"I think we are making her uncomfortable."

"Or we have struck a nerve. I think she is afraid—afraid of what's inside her."

"We should be careful, lest she begs Medoriate Crow to turn us into toads."

"I heard he is the one who killed Desnera's queen. Burned her alive in a burst of blue flame."

"I heard he is a demon in disguise, serving the king's every whim. His Majesty pays him in cursed gold."

Victoria snorted in disgust and started to walk away.

"Where is Medoriate Crow, Victoria? You seem a little lost without an arm to hang on."

Do not look back. Just keep walking.

"You rejected a prince for a bloodrot wizard." The comment followed her, as did several others. She headed for the one place they would not follow: the balcony. Outside the air was brisk but not too cold to bear.

I've thickened up. I can endure it, she assured herself. But even as she pulled a loose lock from her face, she could feel the dampness of her own cheek. *Dammit, Arythan. Where are you? If you can't be here for a silly festival, how will you be there when your child is born? Jedinom help you if you're lying....*

Victoria crossed her arms for warmth. *He doesn't lie. Something is wrong with him. I know it.*

She heard Banen's voice before she saw him. "I thought you were tougher than that."

"So did I. But I guess I was wrong." She did not bother to face the younger prince. "They know how to uproot the fears you bury. I should have been ready." She fought a shiver. "Anyway, you don't care. You said as much."

"I lied."

Victoria felt a cloak cover her shoulders, and she eagerly enveloped herself in it. "I don't claim to understand you, Banen. Every Summerfall I've spent with you has ended in a row. We fought all the time, and all I had to show were tears. Now some whores tease me, and you come to express your compassion?"

Banen moved up beside her to gaze across the courtyard. "I am not completely cold and heartless."

"I know," she said softly, "but you could never muster that warmth when I needed it. You were too damn afraid—of what, I can't say. But it's too late now."

"Yes," he said, glancing at her angrily. "Too late for me, though your hero should be the one at your side now. The actor. The one who pretends to be a part of this world. He is not what he seems, Victoria."

She stared at him, feeling tears drip down her cheeks again. "You forget I'm also an actor. I know what is inside him. He loves me, and he shows that he loves me. He doesn't care what anyone else thinks."

"That's because he hides himself. You just refuse to see it." Banen pounded his fist on the railing, and Victoria drew back, startled. "Victoria—"

"We're married." She held his gaze, saw the ice melt in his eyes —if just for a moment. "I am bound to him, and I'm going to have his child."

Banen turned away, and for a long while, there was nothing but silence between them. "You never did say where he is."

"The Ice Plains. He said he was too sick to come." How many more times would she have to explain Arythan's absence? Every time she did, she had to swallow the growing sense of unease in her heart. The temptation to head for the Plains herself was becoming difficult to ignore.

"I would have given you more," Banen said bitterly. "You know that I would. I brought you here—"

"Stop. Please." Victoria lifted the cloak and handed it back to him. "If you want to remind me of the life I led, if you want me to feel unending gratitude for all you've done, you should know that it haunts me every day. I wonder if you will grow so angry that you will expose me for what I am, have me removed from the kingdom...."

He lifted his mask to look at her, and she was immediately shamed by the hurt in his eyes. "Do you think so little of me?"

"Banen, I'm sorry, I—"

"I do not regret anything. And I am not so low." He pulled his mask back down and moved toward the door. "I have nothing to hide from you."

"Wait," she said, but a loud sound from inside snared both their attention. They entered the hall and found a cloud of red smoke was dissipating from around the high table. In its midst stood Michael, a radiant smile upon his face.

"My father is not one for frivolity," Michael said to his audience. "Tonight, however, we are in the midst of a festival, and I have arranged for a special display of magic." The rest of the smoke cleared to reveal three wizards dressed in bright, silken robes, standing behind him. Michael presented the medori to his guests. "I present to you: the Three Charmers."

A hesitant applause followed, and Victoria and Banen exchanged a glance. "My father will be livid," Banen said. "These wizards are from the Merchants' Guild. I had told him not to do this."

"I thought the Merchants' Guild was supposed to leave Cerborath," Victoria said. She watched as one wizard levitated above his companions.

"It was," Banen said darkly. "Michael gets what Michael wants."

"Keep your eyes closed, Medoriate. I'm going to remove the blindfold."

Arythan could feel Nistel's fingers pull free the material. He took an anxious breath, knowing what would be asked of him next.

"The blistering around his eyes is healing quickly," the Ice Fly wizard said. "The salve has definitely helped. I'm hoping that several days of complete darkness has given his vision a chance to return."

"I will extinguish the fire," Othenis said.

"No, actually, this will be a fitting test. Medoriate, slowly open your eyes."

Arythan did not want to open his eyes, because he had come to face the terrible truth of his condition. Day or night, it did not matter. His was a world of lasting darkness.

"Medoriate."

"I 'eard y'," Arythan muttered. He opened his eyes, and true enough, it did not matter. "Nothing."

"You're staring at the fire. Can you see any light at all?"

"I said 'nothing,'" the mage snapped.

"I don't understand," Nistel said to himself. "His eyes should have healed—at least shown some sign of improvement."

"Blisters aside, they look the same as when he first came here," Othenis said, craning over Nistel's shoulder. "The whites are blood-red, his pupils are cloudy. Well, maybe cloudi*er*."

Arythan turned away from their voices, but he could not shut them out. He felt as though he was in another world entirely, and sound was the only connection he had to the reality he had known. The one voice he longed to hear was far away, and the only way he would ever see Victoria again was to conjure images from his memory. And in time, as with all memories, those visions would fade.

"We need to face our options," Othenis said. "Regardless of any magic or medicine, Arythan's condition may be permanent. Already we risk that he has been missing for too long. Summerfall is over. Others will be searching for him. We cannot return him to the Ice Plains, because the Seroko will know what he has attempted."

"What do you suggest?" the wizard asked.

"We must be prepared to harbor him as one of our own. Relocate him if necessary."

"No." Arythan felt for the cave wall and eased himself down. "I won't abandon Tori."

"We can take her," Othenis said, "but if we do, you will not be the only one charged with treason. Is that a danger you are willing to place her in?"

The mage frowned. "Would've been the same if I 'ad stolen the book an' destroyed the Ice."

Othenis sighed. "Yes, but the difference is timing. We could have given you time to talk to her. As of now, we have run out of time."

Arythan ran a hand through his hair. His entire life had changed in the course of one night; all his plans had fallen to pieces. What would he be able to salvage, if anything? *I'd be better off if they killed me,* he thought. *Then no one would be in danger. Someone could find my body long after the vultures have picked clean the bones. Tori would hate me for abandoning her, but at least she would be safe...safe with our child.*

"What are your thoughts, Arythan?"

He smiled miserably and shook his head.

"Othenis, I'm going to head back," Nistel said. "I will check my book and see if there is a remedy I have overlooked." The wizard took his leave, and the Ice Fly leader sat adjacent to Arythan.

"We cannot despair," Othenis said. "Your brother was ever the optimist."

"'E wasn't blind."

"No, but he was sick, wasn't he? In the time you traveled with him, I'm sure you were aware of his suffering."

Arythan did not reply. He did not like to recall what Hawkwing had endured through the Quake, though he had experienced many of the symptoms himself. He had no doubt that if the Larini had not stripped him of his Shadow, he would never have made it to Cerborath.

"I knew your brother more by reputation," Othenis admitted. "He was well-respected in the eyes of his peers, and he was one of the few given instruction by the Three. So much had crumbled when the Gray Watchers dissolved. The Three disappeared, and the knowledge they guarded was lost. It is of no wonder to me why the Seroko pursued Hawkwing. He was their last hope at finding the Archives."

"So why'd they kill 'im?" Arythan demanded. "The dead don't talk."

"Well...I can only speculate," Othenis said. "The Marksman took a gamble. You were in Hawkwing's company. Whether or not they knew you were his brother—"

"They didn't."

"They figured you were important to him. And Hawkwing knew he was dying."

Arythan felt for a blanket, and Othenis helped cover him. "So they thought 'e told me all the Watcher secrets," the mage summarized.

"Possibly."

"My brother never told me anything. 'E tried to keep me safe that way."

"Hawkwing was subtle in all that he did," Othenis said. "Think hard, Arythan. Did he ever mention anything about a Key or the Archives?"

"'E never said anything about a bloody key," Arythan said, his temper rising. "'Is secrets died with 'im."

"When Hawkwing died, did he say anything to you? Any final words or message?" Othenis pressed.

"What do y' want to know?" Arythan seethed. "If 'e 'anded me a magic key to keep secret from the world? Sure, 'is last words were: long live the Watchers." He remembered the agony in his brother's face as he lay dying. In his mind, he could still see the light fading from Hawkwing's eyes. Arythan wiped the tears away from his own. "'E didn't say anything. 'E looked up at me, an' then 'e died. That's it. The end." He rubbed his brow in grief. "Y' sound just like them," he said bitterly.

"Arythan, I'm sorry. I should not have pressed you. Hawkwing was so loyal, so committed to the cause…I merely thought he would have kept the legacy alive through you."

"I don't carry 'is legacy," Arythan said. "I've tarnished it."

"The reason you are here now is because you were trying to do the right thing," Othenis said. He placed a hand on the mage's shoulder, and Arythan flinched at the sudden touch.

"I've never done the right thing. An' now I 'ave to choose whether or not my wife will be a traitor to the king. 'S not bloody fair—not to 'er, not to our kid."

Othenis was silent a moment. "I think that, perhaps, your brother did face a similar dilemma. He knew he would be pursued by the Seroko, yet he chose to keep you at his side, knowing the danger you were in. It is the price we pay for having loved ones. I have no children, no wife. I devoted my life to the Watchers and now to the Ice Flies. I believe in what I do, but every now and then, I wonder what I have missed. I wonder what it would be like to be held by someone I love, to hear a child call me 'father.' You can still have your family. I promise I will do all that I can to see all of you safe."

Arythan closed his eyes and tried to imagine what it meant to be "safe." Would it be some little cottage or farm? Would it be a shop in a distant city? There was only one place he had ever felt safe, and it had been a strange site from which he had ventured with his brother. Without knowing why, he recalled it aloud.

"There was a place in the mountains," he said quietly. "A gateway, as Em'ri described it… We 'ad passed through another world—a world o' Shadow—trying to escape… We came out o' the dark, out of a white tower. 'E 'ad a name for it, but I can't remember now. Thought 'twas odd that it be there. 'E never said 'oo built it or why. I just remember feeling connected to it."

"What did you do in this place?" Othenis asked.

Arythan's brow furrowed as he tried to remember. "Nothing. We didn't linger."

Othenis was about to question him further when the sound of footsteps made both their heads turn. "Nistel, what's the matter?"

"We found a woman, Othenis. She was heading toward the Ice Plains. We recognized her as the healer, Diana Sherralin."

"No doubt she was looking for Arythan," Othenis said.

Nistel glanced behind him. "We intercepted her. We thought she might be able to help him."

Othenis rubbed his beard, uneasy. "This is a big risk. Have you questioned her?"

Nistel nodded. "She seems genuinely concerned for the medoriate. She agreed to the oath. Do you want to see her?"

Othenis looked at the mage. "How well do you know her, Arythan?"

"I trust 'er," he said.

Othenis turned back to Nistel and nodded, and the healer was brought inside the cave.

Diana said nothing until she was at Arythan's side. "Jedinom's Grace, what have you done, Medoriate? What have you gotten yourself into?" she whispered to him.

"Be more specific," he said.

"These people—who are they? What have they done to you? Your eyes...."

"They're friends," Arythan said. "An' they aren't responsible."

"No questions, please, Lady Sherralin," Othenis said. "You are here to help Medoriate Crow, if you are able."

"Don't be afraid," Arythan told her.

"Afraid?" Diana asked. "I'm not afraid. I'm appalled. How long has he been this way?" she demanded.

"Blind, y' mean?" the mage asked, humorless.

"How long?" Diana repeated.

"About a week now," Othenis said.

"What has been done for him?"

Nistel stepped forward. "I've applied various salves for the blisters. I haven't had any luck with his vision. I hoped the blindfold would keep it dark enough for—"

"You fool," Diana muttered. "I need my bag."

"Your pardon?" Nistel asked, offended.

"Give her the bag, please," Othenis said.

Grumbling, the wizard handed her the item, and Diana began to sift through it.

"You know what it is that afflicts him," Othenis inferred.

"Dragon's Eye," she replied. "It is a rare fungus that grows amongst damp ledges. How by the Golden Sword did you encounter it, Arythan?"

"'Twas in a book."

"A book."

"'S what I said."

Diana shook her head. "In periods of dry weather, the fungus goes dormant. It waits for the next rain—for moisture—so that it can send out its spores to reproduce."

"You are saying it sensed the moisture in his eyes," Nistel said, skeptical.

"He would not be blind if it hadn't," she replied. "By keeping it dark, you have helped the spores to germinate and multiply. What he needs is light. If we can kill the spores, we might be able to save his vision…if we're not too late."

"What do you intend to do?" Othenis asked.

"I need extract from blueroot to drop into his eyes. The remedy will depend on whether or not his eyes will respond by becoming sensitive to light." Diana glanced at Othenis. "You will want to stoke the fire." She turned to Arythan. "This will not be pleasant."

"So I figured. Just don't melt m' eyes."

"That would be counterproductive. But even if I did, you would be no worse off than you are now." She found the bottle she wanted and removed the lid. "Tilt your head back, and keep your eyes open as wide as you can." When he did as she requested, she took a thin glass rod, dipped it into the fluid, and then held it over his left eye. No sooner had the drop made contact, he clenched his teeth and swore.

"Yes, it burns. That's what we want," Diana assured him. She repeated the process with his right eye, and he slammed his fist into the ground. "We will wait just a minute, and then we will direct him toward the fire." She gave a nod. "Hold his head so that he's forced to look at it."

Arythan cried aloud.

"Don't let him look away," Diana gritted, struggling to hold the mage in place.

"Enough!" Arythan begged. "Stop!"

"No," Diana said.

"Stop! Stop!" he pleaded. *"Sieqa! They burn!"*

"Another minute," Diana said, and when it had passed, they released him.

Arythan pulled away and covered his eyes with his hands, shaking and breathing hard.

"Let me see," she said in a voice that was surprisingly gentle. She coaxed his hands away, and Nistel gasped.

"His eyes are bleeding," the wizard said.

"Quiet," Diana snapped. "They are not bleeding. The red spores are running out with his tears."

"Tell me y' won't do that again," Arythan said, his voice quavering.

"Can you see?" she asked.

He sighed in despair.

"I think we can save your sight. Time to be as tough as you try to act."

The wizard chuckled.

"*Nigqor-slet,* Nistel."

"How long will it take?" Othenis asked.

"I would repeat the process twice each day, for three days," Diana said, and Arythan groaned. She handed Othenis the bottle. "I trust you will see it done."

The Ice Fly leader nodded. "And I trust you will keep the vow of silence you have given. To breach it would be to place the medoriate's life in danger."

"He does that well enough without me," Diana said. "And I'm sure he will thank me one day."

"Thank y'," Arythan said weakly.

"Nistel will escort you back to where you were found," Othenis told her.

"Dianar," Arythan said. "'Ave y' seen Tori?"

The healer froze at the cave's entrance. "Yes."

"She went? To Summerfall?"

"Yes, and she was very concerned for you. She is the reason I'm here."

"Was she…er, did she look—"

"Pregnant? Yes."

"Pretty," he finished flatly.

"I suggest you go and see her for yourself once you have recovered," Diana said.

Arythan nodded. If and when he regained his vision, he intended to stare at his wife until her image was burned into his mind.

9

RETURN OF THE KING

"You brought me a gift?"

For a moment, Arythan thought the healer would strike him. She was incredulous, to be certain, but was she touched? Insulted? He honestly did not know. "Open it?" he suggested.

Diana looked at him and began to untie the string from the linen-wrapped box. "This was hardly necessary, Arythan," she said, as if reprimanding a child. "I was merely doing my job."

"Y' saved m' eyes," he said in a low voice. "I would still be blind if y'adn't come." He watched her gently pull away the material to reveal an ornate wooden box covered in carved roses.

Her expression was pinched. "It's very…nice."

"Y're not done yet," he said with a sigh. Now he wondered if he had made a mistake by giving her anything at all.

She opened the box and lifted one of the many small vials inside, holding it up to the light from the window. "Buttermint?" she asked, reading the label. She lifted another. "Sweetberry Oil. Honey Sugar." Diana put the vials back. "These flavorings must have cost a fortune."

Arythan shrugged. "Now y' can give people medicine that tastes good—without getting them drunk or loopy."

"You are so very naïve…and sweet," she added grudgingly.

"Thanks."

"But I cannot accept this." She placed the box back in the linen. "I do not take gifts from my patients."

"Why not?" he asked, trying not to sound as hurt as he felt.

Diana's tone softened. "It complicates the relationship between healer and patient."

"'S not like I asked y' to marry me," he mumbled, ignoring her as she held the box out to him. He moved to look outside the window at the overcast sky. "If y' don't like it, y' can give it away. I just wanted to say thank y'."

Diana set the box down and stood beside him. "Why don't you tell me why you are really here?"

He turned to look at her, expressionless.

"You want to make certain I will keep my silence. Whoever those men were, whatever you were doing in the cave…I was not supposed to be there." Diana shook her head. "You have made decisions that I fear have you buried deeply in trouble. I am not your mother. I am not your king." She sighed. "I'm not your wife, either. For what it's worth, I am concerned for you, but I won't preach what I suspect you already know." She turned away. "Do not worry. I'll hold my tongue. I've seen enough to know when silence is my best defense."

"Y'ave a visitor," Arythan said flatly, his eyes upon the approaching figure on horseback.

"Prince Banen?" she mused. "I think he is here for you."

Arythan folded his arms as Diana met the prince at the door. "Good morning, Your Highness. How might I serve you?" she asked.

Banen's eyes were already on the mage. His scowl said all

Arythan needed to know. "I have business with your visitor," he said shortly.

"I will leave the two of you in privacy," Diana said, giving Arythan a wary glance before she disappeared into the back room.

"You have a lot to answer for," Banen said, stalking up to him.

"Do I?"

"The Merchants' Guild," Banen spat. "Why are they still in the Ice Plains?"

"Ask y'r brother."

"I am asking *you*," Banen said, his voice rising. "And I want to know where you were the night of Summerfall. You certainly weren't sick in bed."

"'Ow would y'—"

"I went to find you," the prince interrupted. "You weren't there."

Arythan said nothing.

"Your silence further incriminates you. What is this game you play?" Banen demanded.

"There is no game," Arythan said darkly. "I was sick, regardless of what y' believe. An' I don't 'ave to answer to y'."

"Then you might consider answering to your wife, who came to Summerfall by herself, carrying your child for all to see." Banen inched closer. "Where was her faithful husband? Not hard at work in the Ice Plains. He was hiding, guarding his secrets, conspiring against—"

"Arythan, I mixed up more of your medication," Diana said, emerging from the back room, a bowl in her hands. "If you lapse in your doses, you will not be able to stomach water, let alone anything else you consume."

Banen backed away from him.

"Your Highness, it was fortunate Medoriate Crow did not attend the festival. When I found him, he was the color of ash, his head hanging over a bucket of his own vomit. Fortunately, I found a remedy." She held up the bowl and set it on the counter. "Pray that you do not find yourself in such a state, lest I must tend to you as well."

The prince huffed in disgust and moved toward the door.

"Is there nothing you need, Your Highness?" Diana asked.

"No," Banen muttered, giving Arythan a lasting, venomous stare before he shut the door behind him.

"Well," Diana said, "I think that should speak well enough for my integrity."

"Y' didn't 'ave to do that," Arythan said.

"Don't worry; I won't be able to help you through whatever complicated web you've woven." She held up the box of flavorings for him to take.

Instead, he put on his coat. "Y' think this was a test. A bribe." He did not look at her. "Sorry if it looked that way. Because o' y', I can see again." He gave her a nod and opened the door. "Thank y'."

Even after he had gone, Diana continued to stare at the door. Eventually her watering eyes turned to the box in her hand, and she clutched it tightly to her chest.

~

"MILADY, YOU HAVE A VISITOR."

Victoria paused from her needlework. "I am not inclined to take visitors right now," she said.

"Pardon, milady, but he says he is from the castle. He introduced himself as 'Thorn.'"

Banen? Why would he come here—unless he has word of Arythan... Victoria set down her work and stood. "Allow me a moment, and I will come to meet him." When the attendant had gone, she moved before the mirror to adjust her hair. In her time at the manor, she had forsaken her wig. She had not bothered to paint her face, either. The more she thought about it, the more she realized she had come to neglect her appearance, but in a strange way, she did not care. Who would she aim to impress, tucked away in the country? She smoothed at the wrinkles in her dress, taking note of her fuller figure and knowing she still had months before the baby would be born.

Her face was rounder, her arms and waist were thicker—not to mention the slight swelling of her belly. Her current dress was comfortable, but it was showing signs of stress along the seams. Soon she would need the skills of the tailor…again. Banen had already seen her at the festival, so she had no reason to pretty herself for him. She smiled at the mirror and swallowed her anxiety over Arythan. *Please be good news,* she thought, and left the room.

There was someone sitting in the parlor, but it was not Banen. She stared at the man while he was yet unaware of her presence. He was well-dressed in dark attire that fit his lean frame. His warm-complexioned face was clean-shaven and strikingly handsome—even with the dark tattoo over his eye. Short-cropped, dark blond hair was brushed back from his face, accentuating his features, his large, intense blue eyes….

"Arythan?"

He turned to her with a smile that made her dizzy. Before he could stand, she was rushing toward him. Victoria reveled that he was truly there, his body solid beneath her fingers, his scent—which she believed to be the scent of the wind—alive in her senses as she breathed. Her lips found his, and she could feel the magic tingling even as she pulled away. His eyes snared her, and she could not turn away—not that she wanted to. Her fingers traced his smooth jaw and tousled his hair. "By Jedinom, you're a little boy," she exclaimed, stunned by the change.

"No, I'm not," he protested.

"What is this?" she asked, ignoring him.

"Same as this," he murmured, touching her belly. "A new beginning."

Victoria blushed. "Oh, I am a terrible mess. If I had known it was you, I would have—"

He pressed a finger to her lips. "Y're beautiful. I could stare at y' forever."

"By Lorth, I would hope not," she muttered, but she found his eyes had not stopped studying her. "What happened to you? You are acting strangely."

His smile diminished—just a little. "I've missed y', 's all. I've been sick, y' know."

"Yes," Victoria said, lifting her chin, and pulling away from him. "And I should tell you what I endured without you. Those women and what they said, how they looked at me."

A shadow crossed his face. "What did they say?"

"They called you a savage, and they said our child was a monster."

"Do y' want me to destroy them?"

Victoria waved a hand. "They would not be worth the effort."

"I'm sorry I wasn't there."

She could hear in his voice that he meant it. "I managed, Arythan. But I did realize something."

He looked at her, questioning.

"You were the only reason I ever had fun at such gatherings."

She saw his cheeks redden.

"I 'aven't been to that many."

"Even so," Victoria insisted. She sat down on the couch next to him and took his hand. "I was so worried, and your letter explained nothing. Who wrote it for you?"

"A mate," Arythan said. "'Twas good y' didn't come. I was in a bad way."

Victoria bit her lip and fought back tears. "Next time, I don't care what you say. I will be there at your side." She squeezed his hand until he made a face. "Don't ever think you can keep me from you, Medoriate."

"Alright, alright," he said, and she eased her grip. "Y' should know 'tis y'r fault I'm better."

"My fault?"

"Y' sent for Dianar."

"I did," Victoria said, "but I wasn't sure if she would go. Were you really in so bad a state?"

He did not answer, confirming her suspicions.

"Oh, I want to hit you and kiss you at the same time," she seethed.

"Sorry. I'd prefer the kiss, though."

"Except that you've regressed back to boyhood."

"Y' don't like it."

"I *do* like it, but I have to adjust to it. I will miss the prickly beard."

"I won't," he admitted. "Took me three years to get rid o' the bloody itchy thing."

"Hm." She rested her head on his shoulder. "How long are you here this time?"

"We 'ave the 'ole day," he said.

"Amazing," she returned, disappointed.

"Garriker is coming back. Michael wants me at the castle."

"To tell him what a dedicated medoriate you are."

Arythan frowned. "I don't look forward to it."

"You should know that the magic show Michael had at Summerfall was boring compared to what you can do."

"Michael did magic?"

Victoria swatted him. "The Merchants' Guild wizards, actually. I thought the Guild was gone."

Arythan sighed. "Le's not talk about it, luv. I'm 'ere for y'."

"And for Reiqo." She stood and proudly flaunted her figure. "You see that I, too, am working hard to feed our child."

He laughed—actually laughed. The sound inspired a true smile from her as well. "You will join me for the midday meal, Medoriate Crow."

"I am 'ungry."

"I am *always* hungry," Victoria boasted, patting her belly. She gave a cry as he swept her up and carried her into the dining room.

THE DARK WIZARD of the North wished for the power to master time. Then he would hide in yesterday, where his wife's arms would shield him from the anxiety of the future. But the future could not be stalled, and the moment Arythan had dreaded had arrived. King Garriker II had returned from Desnera, and he awaited an audience with both his son and his royal medoriate.

Why me? Arythan wondered. *Why am I being dragged into this?* Of course, he knew why. He had only to look over at the man walking beside him. Prince Michael carried his head high, his shoulders squared. Michael was ready for this; Arythan was not. The mage could not help but feel he stood balanced upon a taut rope, the king at one end, the prince at the other. No matter how they pulled, his fall was inevitable.

Their footfalls echoed down the corridor, though neither of them spoke. The guards opened the large, double doors to the Great Hall, revealing the king at the opposite end, waiting expectantly upon his throne. Simultaneously they bowed, and the king waved them in. The doors shut behind them.

"Good evening, Father," Michael greeted. "I trust your journey was a pleasant one."

Garriker merely stared at his son, no expression at all upon his face.

"You see that all is in order," Michael continued, undaunted. "I have no news of consequence to report."

"Banen tells me the Merchants' Guild is still present in the Ice Plains."

Michael straightened. "It is."

"Then you have blatantly disobeyed my command to have them removed," Garriker said, raising his voice so that it filled the empty hall.

"Their presence has been reduced," Michael said. "Medoriate Crow is responsible for the majority of the production of—"

"I ordered them out!" Garriker barked.

Michael's face colored. "It was a poor decision on your behalf."

The king's eyes widened, and his own face turned a shade of red-violet. "Michael—"

"Listen to me, Father. You granted me the authority to oversee this land while you tend to business in Desnera. I exercised that authority as I saw best. Our kingdom depends upon the Enhancement. We still rely upon the Guild for its production. Medoriate Crow cannot shoulder this labor alone."

Garriker's heated stare shifted to Arythan. "I cannot help but feel betrayed by you, Medoriate. As I recall, we had discussed the nature of your work. You assured me you could manage it. And you assured me to whom your loyalties are pledged."

Arythan's gaze fell to the floor, and he wished he could sink beneath it.

"I committed him to this project," Michael defended. "I acted on your behalf. Medoriate Crow is merely following the instructions I gave him."

"In my eyes you are both guilty. The medoriate never informed me of this situation, and you, Michael, overturned my decision. I question your ability to rule in my stead. You disappoint me."

The prince, who had been standing rigid, fists clenched at his sides, broke. He took a step forward. "I disappoint you? Have you seen the faces of your people? There is doubt where none had been before. They wonder why their king has abandoned them to be a second voice in the Desneran monarchy. They cannot fathom what it is that Desnera stands to offer. They do not care about any alliance. Ours are a proud people, and they believe in independence. They would sooner stand upon their own feet than bow to that queen.

"I have sought to appease them. Our one golden investment lies buried beneath the frozen ground, and you want to abandon this untapped resource because it will better our appearance in the eyes of the Northern Kingdoms. To Lorth with Desnera!" Michael cried. "To Lorth with those who question our morals! Our people come first, Father."

"Is that all you believe this is about?" the king challenged. "A carefully crafted image? A model of virtue? When have I ever wasted my time in such a way? You question my motives. You should mind where you step. I am yet king, not you. The Guild challenges my authority. I will not tolerate such insolence in my kingdom."

"There is no harm in their presence," Michael protested.

"You are a blind fool, Michael. How can I have faith in you when you fail to see our dependence upon that organization?" Garriker rubbed his brow. "Perhaps I am wrong to believe you can rule Cerborath."

"Then who else?" the prince demanded. "Your bastard son? Banen has no desire to lead, and no one will follow him. *I* hold the legacy. I have a son. I have honor in our name. It is you who threatens me with this unborn rival—the one who will grow to loom over my head once you and Sabrina Jerian are gone and buried. *I* will be the one to contend with Cerborath's future beneath Desnera's watchful eye. It is insulting to think you believe you have made a decision for the betterment of our people."

"My decision was made to secure peace and a valuable alliance," Garriker said, his temper rising again.

"You have a perverted notion of peace, Father, when you

concoct an elaborate plot to murder the queen. Do not think the rumors have not reached us. Lucinda Jerian, the Revered of Jedinom's Warriors, Desnera's royal medoriate—all conveniently perished in one deadly blaze. Meanwhile your elite run rampant, and your medoriate is rumored responsible."

At this, Arythan paled.

"Tell me how we look in the eyes of our people," Michael continued. "Tell me what upstanding image we hold in Desnera."

"In times of change, there is sacrifice," Garriker said. "I place my wagers carefully, and I make my investments where they count. It is how this kingdom has survived. Do you believe it matters to me what some Desneran peasant thinks of the way I wear my crown?

"You may stand to inherit this kingdom, Michael, but you are not ready. Not yet. You must prove to me you are capable—not by following your own ambitions, but by following my directives. This will be your second chance. Your coronation will be at the Festival of Kings. I want the Merchants' Guild gone by the time I return. If they are not, I will withhold the crown until my orders are obeyed."

"Consider what you ask, Father," Michael said. "You cannot believe this is the best decision."

"Do not question me!" Garriker shouted. He recomposed himself and lowered his voice. "When I return to Desnera, I will take Medoriate Crow with me."

Michael threw his arms before him. "Production of the Enhancement will cease completely," he said, incredulous.

"We have survived without it. This will be a lesson in dependency."

"A lesson to who? To me or to your people? Are you so proud?"

"Enough, Michael! You have tried my patience enough. You are dismissed." Garriker stood and turned his back to them.

Michael was stunned to silence, though Arythan was all too eager to leave the hall.

"Medoriate Crow," Garriker said from over his shoulder. "We leave in three nights. I expect you to be ready."

"Yes, sir," Arythan replied quietly.

He and Michael left the hall the way they had come: in silence. Arythan did not know if the prince would have some parting remark for him, but it was not surprising when Michael veered from him without a glance. Where the prince was outraged, Arythan was disheartened. He would be farther from Victoria, and if anything should happen to her, he would be beyond her reach. Perhaps this was Garriker's way of punishing him for insubordination, though Arythan hardly felt there had been any choice in the matter.

He considered, too, that he would be venturing into a kingdom that blamed him for their queen's death. How had these rumors escaped him before? Arythan wondered just who held more reason in this battle: the king or his ascending son?

He needed to tell Othenis of his pending departure and the king's latest decree. Would the Seroko willingly leave the Ice Plains? Their withdrawal was unlikely so long as they still stood to gain from the Enhancement. But was Michael in control, or was the Seroko's hold deeper than anyone realized? He had been there when Michael signed the contract. He expected the true battle was yet to come.

There would be no manipulating the Enhancement—no opportunities to learn how to destroy it. Instead he would be at Garriker's side, looking like a murderer and a scoundrel before an unhappy people. *Is he mad?* Arythan started to wonder. *Or is the king so desperate to prove a point to his son?* He altered his course for the stable, where Narga awaited him.

~

THE DOOR OPENED to reveal a man and a woman waiting outside. The man was clearly a foreigner, dark in complexion, though he was garbed in northern attire. The woman, too, was from elsewhere, for her hair was blonde, perhaps with a touch of silver. "May I help you?" the steward asked.

"We hope that you can," the middle-aged woman said, stepping forward with a smile. "We are searching for a foreign gentleman—one who had traveled with the Crimson Dragon. We were told he had taken lodging here."

The steward studied them. "You would be referring to Lord Erik Sparrow."

The pair looked at one another. "Might we speak with him?"

"I am afraid he and the lady of the house left nearly a year ago. I do not expect they will return."

"That is most unfortunate," the dark man muttered.

The steward regarded them questioningly.

"We wanted to ask him a few questions," the woman said, disappointed.

"I am sorry. Good day to you." And the door closed.

"Do you suspect they are lying?" the dark man asked as they walked away.

"What cause would they have to lie to us?"

"What cause would they have to speak the truth?" he countered.

They both turned at the sound of approaching footfalls. A girl was running toward them, and they stopped to wait for her.

"You're looking for Mr. Sparrow," she panted. "You must be here to help him."

"Do you know where he has gone?" the dark man asked.

"Not for certain, but her ladyship said she would go with him to the mountains."

"What mountains?" he demanded.

"The Nightwind, sir. He had taken ill, and he hoped to find a cure…."

"No one goes to the Nightwind Mountains."

"Mr. Sparrow did," the girl insisted.

"What is your name, dear?" the blonde woman asked gently.

"Sara, milady."

"What was the nature of Mr. Sparrow's illness, Sara?" she asked.

"It was terrible," Sara said, upset. "He lost his magic. His Light."

The man straightened. "His Light," he repeated.

Sara nodded.

"If you do not mind," the woman said, "we would like a moment of your time...."

10

DIRTY HANDS

Three men lounged in the small room at the gatehouse. The lone slit of a window was hardly enough to expel the smoke accumulating from two lit jacks and a pipe, though it did seem to allow the brisk autumn air to permeate the choked space. Two of the men were clad as Cerborathian guards; they sat facing each other at a table, cards in-hand. The third stood shivering at the window, hiding beneath a hat and scarf.

"Cold bloke stands by the window," Dagger said, glancing at the mage. "Dumb-arse."

"I doubt it is any warmer where we sit," Hunter said in Arythan's defense.

"Smoke burns m'eyes," Arythan grumbled.

"'Smoke burns m'eyes,'" Dagger taunted in a high voice, and the mage glared at him.

Hunter removed his pipe. "Do not stir a fight," he warned.

"Why not?" Dagger asked. "We've been sitting around on our arses for days. I can't take it no more. I need bloodshed." He pounded his fist into his hand.

"I'll 'elp y'," Arythan offered.

"No," Hunter repeated. "We are to behave civilly. Her Majesty may be the only wall of protection we have against those who know who we are."

"'S insulting," Dagger spat. "Wearing the garrison girls' dresses." He crushed his jack into a corner of the surcoat, soiling the color. "We're s'posed to be feared. An' all we're doin' is following Garri around like dogs."

"That is our job," Hunter said. "We are his protection, in case you have forgotten."

"Frosty ain't 'iding."

"Crow can hardly hide who he is," Hunter said. "And for the rumors, his appearance has not won him any favor."

Arythan lifted his hat to reveal a scowl. "I never killed anyone, let alone their bloody queen." He took a hit from his jack. "I'm not even sure why I'm 'ere, 'cept to punish the prince for keeping the Merchants' Guild."

Dagger grinned. "Aw, y're jus' sore 'cuz y're missing y'r lil' rabbit." He pointed a knife at the mage knowingly. "An' as I 'ear it, y' got a reason to be all tight and itchy away from 'er."

Hunter turned to Arythan, curious.

"'E won't say nuthin'," Dagger said. "So I'll tell y'. 'E knocked up the lil' rabbit. 'E's gonna be a daddy."

Hunter's eyes widened, and Arythan's narrowed. "Is this true?" the giant asked.

"Me rumours are always true," Dagger said proudly.

"Life with the syndicate is not conducive to a family," Hunter said.

"Sorry. Forgot to ask permission," Arythan responded and turned back to the window.

"Regardless, I do extend my congratulations to you and Lady Ambrin."

"Lady Crow," Dagger corrected. "'E got tied to 'er, too."

"Anything else y' want to add?" Arythan asked.

"Not yet. Not 'til I 'ear more."

The door opened and interrupted the conversation. Tigress strode inside and took a seat at the table.

"Well, Kitten?" Dagger asked. "Why're y' grinnin'?"

"Because we have a mission," she said. She gave a nod toward Arythan, inviting him over. "There is an important meeting tomorrow."

None of the B.E.S.T. seemed surprised, and in fact, Dagger groaned, and Hunter rubbed his brow. Tigress's smile broadened. "People of power and authority are invited to attend—to ask questions of the newly wed regents and their proposed future for Desnera and Cerborath."

"Y're sick, Kitten. Stop smiling. These meetings are torture. I'd give my left—"

"Shut it." Tigress's expression grew serious. "His Majesty knows his enemies. The Warriors of the Sword have been poking around since the Revered's death. They even scoured the room for evidence after the fire. The queen had to allow it to alleviate any suspicion."

"It would seem that gesture did not work," Hunter said.

Tigress stared at him. "It would seem the fanatics found what they were looking for." Her eyes moved to each of them in turn. "Thorn's ring."

"Aw, shit," Dagger said.

"The evidence that we were involved cannot be presented at tomorrow's meeting. Too many people will be witness."

"Thus we must retrieve the ring," Hunter finished.

"They are staying at the Temple of the Golden Sword in the city," Tigress said.

Dagger swore again. "Y' won't catch me in the temple."

"Because you're not going," Tigress said.

The brute looked relieved.

"This mission is for Hunter and Crow. Hunter knows about the workings of the temple." She gave the giant a nod. "You will fill our heretic mage in on temple etiquette."

"I'm not the best choice," Arythan said, and his frown threatened to drag him to the floor.

"You're just the man for the job," Tigress said with a wry smile. "I'm counting on you to find the ring."

"Because 'e's a good lil' thief," Dagger said with a smirk.

"Because he lost it in the first place," came the flat response.

Arythan folded his arms.

"'Struth, Frosty, y' did," the brute admitted. He stood and stretched. "C'arn, Kitten, time for a beer. These blokes got it 'andled."

"THE PREVALENT TALE by far is that the Revered initiated the conflict that resulted in the fatal blaze," the giant said in a voice surprisingly quiet for his size.

Arythan knew Hunter was studying him as they walked in the fading light. His focus, instead, remained upon the austere structure before them: the Temple of the Golden Sword. It was not so much the dark and hard-edged building that gripped his thoughts but his uneasy relationship with the religious fanatics inside. Warriors of the Sword had murdered the Crimson Dragon, tortured Cyrul Frostmeyer into joining them, and would have taken Arythan's life had his Shadow not briefly returned. Jedinom was but an image that propelled the fervor of Humans' fear of magic. And now *he*—Garriker's Dark Wizard and rumored assassin—would have to raid the hornets' nest to protect the king's integrity.

"Hmph," Arythan responded. He was the easy target for blame, and there were a multitude of theories as to how Garriker's medoriate had killed Queen Lucinda Jerian, her royal medoriate, and the Revered and his warriors in one massive and sorcerous inferno. *He* was the prevalent tale.

Hunter continued. "Her Majesty has lent her own guards to protect the temple from any acts of vandalism by the people. She wanted to demonstrate that the Crown and the House of Jedinom have not soured their terms, that the unfortunate tragedy was the outcome of individuals acting in self-interest."

Isn't that the truth? I thought that was what politics were all about. Greed and lies. Arythan did not see much difference between politics and religion, except that in religion, the true power was wielded behind the guise of an imaginary deity. He rubbed at his eyes and caught himself, not wanting to smear away the dirt he had used to cover his tattoo. A beggar's guise was the most convenient, and Hunter had not objected to his choice. The giant, however, did not don similar rags. He was a social status above Arythan: a commoner who would have been plain enough if not for his marked size.

Arythan stopped and folded his arms. "So what're y' staring at?"

Hunter had stopped as well, though he did not speak immediately. When he did, his voice was low and weighted with sentiments of apology. "I should explain to you what we are about to do."

"Thought 'twas pretty clear," Arythan said warily.

"Our mission, yes. But in order to complete this mission, you must partake in a Cleansing."

Arythan wanted to reply that he had taken a bath that day, but he sensed this was a moment of gravity. He remained where he was, waiting for the explanation.

Hunter closed the distance between them. "A Cleansing is a ritual of purification. You must clean your mind, heart, and spirit so that Jedinom can speak to you."

"Never mind the speaking. What do I 'ave to do?" Already his thoughts were darkening.

"It is the only way a beggar can partake in Jedinom's grace—the only way you would be allowed in the temple," Hunter said. He attempted a serious smile that looked more like a wince. "I believe the ritual will work to our advantage. When we enter the temple, you will be prepared to meet a Keeper. The Keeper wears a blindfold, because he is impartial to your confessions."

Arythan blinked. "Confessions? As in clearing m' conscience?"

Hunter rubbed the back of his neck. "It is at your discretion what you choose to tell him. He will impart advice to you, and then he will show you a better path to your future."

Ha! Arythan tried not to smirk.

"You should attempt to cover your accent," Hunter said.

"No worries," Arythan said dismissively. "What then?"

"There is a period of inner reflection in the gardens. That will be the moment you will go to find the ring."

"And then we leave," Arythan said.

"Yes." Hunter lifted his broad chin. "Even as a heathen, you may find that possessing faith in a supreme power is liberating as well as cleansing."

Arythan stared back defiantly. "Really eats at y' that I don't believe in 'im."

"I believe you are misguided but not beyond Jedinom's salvation," Hunter answered.

"Sun never rises on black earth, mate."

The giant did not verbally respond, but he appeared to be thinking on the mage's words. They walked the rest of the way in silence, and Arythan tensed when he realized just how large the temple was. It did not vault upward like the castle; it sprawled like the legs of a smashed spider. He wondered what all that space was for.

The pair of guards stationed outside the temple doors barely glanced at them as they passed. Beyond the doors was a round atrium with a low ceiling obscured by the smoke of incense. A fire burned in the heart of the chamber, surrounded by colors of wine red and gold. Above the fire, on a stone pedestal, stood a statue of an enormous man, a golden sword in the hand at his side, a distant and righteous expression upon its immobile face. There were twenty-some people sitting around the fire, gazing into the flames or up at their god with wide eyes.

Arythan stirred uncomfortably and pulled his hood a little lower. He caught Hunter's nod to join the people on the floor, and so he sat with a generous distance between himself and his neighbors. Rather than gawk at the statue, his eyes searched the room, locating various dark passages through the haze.

"You should remember that this is a sacred place for those with faith in the Great Warrior."

Arythan jerked his attention toward Hunter, surprised by the statement. The giant's regard was not filled so much with distrust as with caveat. *Really? What do you think I'm inclined to do? Crumble their statue? Fizzle their fire?* The mage refocused upon the statue and exhaled a long breath. *Last I checked, we were both working for a scoundrel king, wearing the same black mask.*

Three men in white robes appeared, each holding a gilded bucket. There was no introduction, no audible word spoken, not even a friendly bow of greeting. The three Keepers circled their audience slowly, dipping their ladles into their buckets and flinging water upon the on-lookers.

"Cleansing." Right. Arythan frowned as a large splash hit the back of his hood, soaking through the material. Everyone around him—Hunter included—had bowed their heads reverently upon receiving the holy shower. He did the same, wondering just how wet he had to be before the Keepers were satisfied. But then he recalled Hunter's words and wondered if this was only the preparation before the ritual. He thought it would be a benevolent gesture if the next phase would be a sacred drying of those dampened. Hunter had promised, however, that there would be a "con-

fession" of sorts, and Arythan could not begin to imagine what he would impart to a holy man behind a blindfold.

The Keepers ceased their flinging and stepped away from the circle. One of them spoke, but for the haze and his lowered head and hood, Arythan could not distinguish which. "When you are ready to be guided by the Great Warrior, you may seek the company of the Keepers of Truth." The robed men gestured toward the dark passages behind them.

All right, then. Arythan took a breath and stood. He was the only one who did.

A slight shake of the head from Hunter told him he had done wrong. Heat rushed to his face as he sat back down.

"You should take more time to reflect upon your impurities," Hunter said.

"Sorry," Arythan snapped. *Guess you have more of them than I do. This is stupid, but I bet you're enjoying it.* He closed his eyes and tried to push away his anger. *The only reason these "Keepers" even have a job is because you believe what they tell you to believe. Big bloke with a golden sword—which would be too heavy to wield anyway—magically appears and battles a winged monster. He happens to win, saving only Human-kind, and disappears from all of Secramore. But somehow he's still here, and wants his due respect. And somehow that means I need to clear my conscience. I want no part of this "necessary deception."*

Necessary deception. Arythan had heard that phrase before, and he could scarcely believe it was resurfacing now. It had been something his father had said—a lesson that had followed him through life, though not quite in the way Qaidao Altyrix had intended.

Quolonero Altyrix had just reached his eleventh year of life, and his father had even hunted the dangerous horned cat for the commemorative feast. By tradition, other members of the tribe—

supposedly distant relatives—were invited for his "farewell to childhood." The boy had never seen them before and would not likely see them again—not until his coming of age the following year. Even at eleven years, he knew this was not a celebration of life so much as a last fling before his inevitable death by the hands of his opponent in the arena.

As it was, the priest-king's son need not have been present. He slipped amongst the guests like a moth, unheeded and silent. They knew he would be of little consequence to the future; they knew his father's legacy was at an end. Qaidao's only son was a frail, sickly boy cursed by family misfortune. Yet so long as Lord Altyrix held his title, the priest-king was best humored by his tribal subjects. What the guests did not admit was that they feared the skull-masked warrior who cut out hearts in the time it took to draw a breath.

During the thick of the feasting and ingratiating, the boy did what he did best: escape. He retreated to his room to stare out at the stars and wonder about his mysterious brother who lived somewhere in Secramore. His imagination did not drift far before his father found him. Expecting a beating for his antisocial behavior, the boy stood and waited tensely for Qaidao to present the switch.

Instead, the boy was presented with a wrapped bundle. *A gift?* Such tokens were as rare as smiles from his father. He looked at it a long while, almost afraid to pull away the material.

"Open it," came the command, and so he had to comply.

Scarlet plumes and a zigzag of black paint adorned the bone mask inside. It was a ritual mask. A death mask. Smaller than his father's, it was perfect for his young face… Quolonero gaped at it.

Mistaking his son's reaction for awe, the priest-king of Gento took the mask and held it before him reverently. *"You will soon learn what it means to take up my mantle. The people will look to you as a god. You will be the hand of Oqrantos, the eyes of the future, the voice of justice."*

The boy turned his eyes to his father.

Qaidao knelt before him, still towering. *"There are truths you must understand. Faith is for the ignorant, but there is power in faith. You must wield this power carefully, and you must behave as though you believe."*

The boy considered his father's words, realizing for the first time that Qaidao Altyrix had no faith at all. His eyes widened. *"Oqrantos—"*

"There is no 'Oqrantos.' There is only a tale to explain what cannot be explained."

Quolonero's fingers were just shy of grazing the mask. *"This is a lie. You told me never to lie."*

"It is not a lie," Qaidao said simply. *"It is a necessary deception. The people will believe in their god, and for them it is a truth. You must use their faith as they expect it of you. That is the role of a priest-king."* He held the mask over his son's face. *"You will wear this when you join my side at the altar, when you have earned your name."*

"Father," the boy said, *"What if I do not earn my name?"*

Qaidao's face hardened, and he took the mask away. *"Then this will belong to another."* He stood and rewrapped the object. He paused at the door but did not look at the boy. *"You may remain here. Sazoq will see to your needs."*

Quolonero felt as though he had looked upon the face of his future, held it in his hands. It had been ugly, frightening. But perhaps he would not have to worry about a future he would never see.

All right, Keeper of Truth. Time for my confession. Arythan's unease had abated with the memory. He stood, not caring if Hunter was watching or not. One of the white-robed attendants trailed him to the dark passage and gestured for him to enter.

"The door is open for you. Ring the bell when you enter."

Arythan followed the torch-lit passage to its end, where it opened into a small, bare room lit with many candles. He saw a table with two chairs opposite each other. One chair was occupied by a Keeper in a red robe. He was an older man—balding, with a scruffy chin, his hands folded upon the table. And as Hunter had said, the Keeper's eyes were concealed behind a white blindfold.

As the mage passed through the door, he noticed the string and small bell suspended above him in the frame. The thought occurred to him that he could slip past this man without a sound and leave through the door at the back of the room. He could bypass the whole confession entirely and waste less time.

"Is there someone there?" the Keeper asked, his head inclined toward the doorway in which Arythan lingered. "Please ring the bell if you are there."

Arythan hesitated, but he did not know why. It was also a mystery why his hand moved toward the string, why seconds later, the tinkle of the bell alerted his presence to one who could be considered his enemy.

"Ah, you are there," the man said, beckoning him closer. "This must be your first Cleansing. I assure you that there is no reason to be afraid. I am Jedinom's ears and voice. He alone will know what you confess, and he will give you guidance. Please, sit."

Arythan sat, watching the man carefully to make certain he truly was blind. Beside them on the table was a bowl of what looked like fine white sand. The Keeper unfolded his hands and presented them, palms up. Arythan drew back as if he had been slapped.

"Please give me your hand, friend. I will search your future as you tell me the burdens of your heart."

The mage stifled a sigh and did as asked. The Keeper dipped his hand into the sand and sprinkled some of it upon Arythan's palm. Then he began to smear the substance to coat every finger and crease. "You are so very quiet, my friend," the Keeper said. "What is it that troubles you?"

Arythan cleared his throat. "I have a confession," he said in a clear voice bereft of any accent. A spark of mischief was threatening to assert itself.

"Go ahead, friend."

"I confess that I do not believe in Jedinom." He had told himself not to say it, but then he had said it anyway. For one wishing to avoid trouble, he seemed equally compelled toward it. He waited for an expression of shock, an offended cry, or disappointed shake of the head. Instead, the Keeper laughed.

"Your honesty is refreshing. You must be here because someone has brought you here… Unless you are merely curious."

"I'm just a beggar," Arythan said. "My friend brought me because he thinks I can be saved."

"Beggar or not, you are a person, gifted with life. Your friend's intentions are noble, but I cannot save you." The Keeper continued to rub the sand in Arythan's palm, but its consistency had started to change to a gel. "And from what would I save you? We make our choices, knowing whether they are right or wrong. We are responsible for our own paths."

"That's what I say," Arythan mumbled, almost slipping back into his dialect. "But then why am I here?"

"Sometimes our vision grows cloudy," the Keeper said. "We need a hand to guide us through the fog we have created."

"No offense, but I don't believe an imaginary god is going to help me."

The Keeper stopped rubbing his hand, the gel now a viscous liquid. There was a moment of silence before he spoke. "Be it Jedinom or some other name, the idea of a greater being is for you to shape. In what do you believe, my friend?"

"I believe in myself," Arythan answered.

"And that is good, but there is more than you or me. This world in which we live, the foundation of right or wrong and all we believe... Tell me, have you ever considered your purpose?"

"What makes you think I have one?" the mage challenged.

The Keeper smiled. "We all have one, whether we know it or not. We influence the world around us, and in doing so, we contribute an immortal piece of ourselves. Good or bad, it cannot be undone. It is the truth of life. Without purpose, we would be empty, meaningless."

Arythan stared vacantly at his slimy hand. Before the Larini had stolen his choice from him, he *had* wondered about the value of his life. He had spent his childhood training to defend himself when no one else believed he would survive his coming of age. He had lived on the streets as a vagrant, moved unseen as a thief and a monster. His life had existed only in the present, for that was all he had.

His brother had started to show him that there was a future, and then his brother died. Only now, as Arythan Crow, had he rekindled a vision of what could be—what *would* be. He had a wife, and soon there would be a child. Victoria and Reiqo needed him.

"Have you lost someone close to you?"

The question jarred him from his thoughts, and he blinked. "Yes," he said quietly.

"What do you believe happened when this person died?"

"What? I— Nothing. Nothing happened," Arythan said, irritated.

"You do not believe that some part of this person still exists?"

"Just a memory, that's all."

The Keeper shook his head. "Perhaps. Perhaps not. The question I pose to you, my friend, is this: Is there only an ending? And if there is, then what is our goal in living?"

Arythan smirked. "I thought you were supposed to be the one to guide me, not ask me questions."

"Questions are merely the gateway to discovery, but you will find that advice is free; experience has its price." The Keeper lifted Arythan's hand. "You feel the change. Your emotions are the cause of this." He pressed his fingers into the liquid now dripping down the mage's fingers. "You are wrought with conflict, and the tension I sense…" His brow furrowed.

"We all have problems," Arythan said.

"Of course, but…" The Keeper frowned and gripped Arythan's hand with both of his, as if trying to sense more. "It is strange. I've not felt this before. It is more than tension, more than stress…."

Just then the little bell rang, and Arythan glanced back to find a new victim waiting in the doorway. He tried to pull his hand free, but the Keeper seemed reluctant to release it.

"Some kind of unseen force…" he murmured. "Very cold and—"

"You have another visitor," Arythan said without emotion, snatching his hand back. He stood. "Thanks for the questions."

"Er, yes," the Keeper said, still bewildered. "You…you can head through the door behind me, to the garden to reflect…."

Arythan was already pulling at the handle, eager to be on his way. The encounter left him confused and uncertain—two states with which he was less than comfortable. He knew deception when he heard it, and he could play his cards well as he could deal, but the Keeper had no motive to mislead him. There had been nothing for the man to gain. So was the experience merely nonsense, or could there actually be some truth to all of it? The fact that he may have sensed Arythan's lingering Shadow only unsettled the mage further.

There would be time for reflection later. As he entered the garden, he was surprised by the roof and walls that encompassed the space. The air was warmer, the light as bright as the outdoor sky. A stone path meandered before him and around stands of small orchard trees and herbs. He walked slowly forward, staring at this indoor oasis and wondering what sort of magic maintained it. There was a small pool with fish—in which he washed his soiled hand—stone benches tucked away in quiet niches, and he even glimpsed a bird flit overhead. In a distant way it reminded him of his island home.

There was another doorway tended by a Keeper, who smiled at Arythan, and gestured for him to pass through. "Follow the Hall of Roses to find your way back to the atrium."

The title could not have been more obvious. Roses had been carved from the stone in the walls, some of them painted in vibrant scarlet and crimson. The passage turned, and just when he believed he would have no choice but to return to Hunter, he found a solitary door that proved his only alternative to the atrium. It led him to another hall bereft of roses but haunted by voices. The noises were familiar—the clatter of cups and utensils, the chatter that accompanies a leisurely meal. Arythan peered into the adjacent dining hall to see red, white, and yellow-robed attendants alike, feasting merrily upon the bounty spread before them. They were distracted enough that he did not fear being spotted as he slid past the entrance and continued his route. A door at the end of the hall opened into a broad dormitory, filled mostly with cots.

It can't be this easy, Arythan thought, studying each bed as he passed. He knew the Revered had traveled to reach the castle, and so his emissaries would likely have travel bags and provisions they had brought with them. Most of the cots were neatly tended and indistinguishable from each other. He had nearly walked the span of the dorm when he found what he had been looking for. Underneath three neighboring cots were stashed plump shoulder bags.

The mage crouched low beside the first cot and began to sift through the contents of the bag. Cloak, knife, charcloth, coin purse… He proceeded to the second bag and was rewarded with a small wooden box with a latch. *It really can't be this easy,* he marveled. Even before he opened the box, he knew his search was over. Nestled in the velvet interior was Banen's ring.

Arythan pocketed the box and replaced the bag just as he had found it. He half expected a Keeper to appear and demand what he was doing—like a baited trap that had been sprung. But no one entered the dorm, and Arythan left the space, strolled past the dining hall a second time, and returned to the Hall of Roses without any encounters.

Hunter was not in the atrium, but he was waiting outside, a short distance from the temple entrance. His hulking form lingered ominously in the shadows of late twilight, and Arythan wondered if he believed he was being subtle.

"Well?" the giant asked.

"I 'ave it," Arythan said.

"Were you seen?"

"I was cleansed," he replied with no small inflection of sarcasm.

"Yes, but—"

"I 'ave the bloody ring, mate." Arythan continued past his teammate without a glance. "No worries."

"Good," Hunter murmured, following behind him. "His Majesty will be relieved."

I'm bloody relieved.

11

BROUGHT TO LIGHT

If it had been possible to start a game of cards in the midst of King Garriker's "very important meeting," Arythan would have had an easier time trying to keep his eyes open. He and his B.E.S.T. teammates occupied the corner of the room, adjacent to where Queen Sabrina Jerian sat with her husband upon their thrones in the Great Hall of the Desneran keep. The others in the syndicate were as lively as the mage, but Tigress and Hunter had better experience masking their boredom. Dagger did not so much as attempt to pay attention to the interactions between the regents and their audience.

Arythan could not help but notice that none of those waiting in line to see the regents were peasants or even middle-class merchants. They were lords and ladies with concerns about status, titles, and questions of property. After a few hours of the same questions by various parties of the aristocracy, even the king and queen seemed to grow weary, and their answers shortened with their patience.

Just before the break for the midday meal, a party of three conspicuously robed men marched with the herald down the center aisle of the hall. Dagger grunted, and Arythan tensed, though everyone else maintained flawless composure. The trio bowed, and the herald announced them.

"Of the House of Jedinom, I present to Your Majesties, Master Warriors Trylan Erun and Hethris Blackbow, and Master Keeper Seldwin Mistel."

"Welcome, Masters of the House," Sabrina said with a nod. "I trust you have been well-received in our city."

"As well as one might expect, Your Majesty," the leader of the group said. "Already you know the purpose of our presence here."

"How fares your investigation, Master Erun?" the queen asked politely.

"We have learned much from the evidence we have discovered," Trylan Erun said. His eyes and the eyes of his comrades locked upon Arythan. "We wish to present this evidence to you, to allow Your Majesty an opportunity to support justice rather than ignore it."

Arythan felt his confidence shudder as he stared back at the Masters of the House. He knew without averting his gaze that Tigress was regarding him questioningly. Yet she had seen the ring for herself. She had been there when he had presented it to Garriker. All loose ends had been tied...or so he thought.

"Please explain yourself, Master Erun," the queen said. "You know that I uphold justice in this kingdom, and I have given my support to the temple and those who represent the Great Warrior."

"*You* have, Your Majesty, but our concerns are rooted in the alliances Desnera has so recently formed."

Garriker rose to address the blatant implication. "Speak plainly, gentlemen, and do not forget that I, too, am an authority in this kingdom. What is your claim here?"

Hethris Blackbow stepped forward with a nod from Erun. "Medoriate Crow was involved in, if not directly responsible for, the deaths of the Revered, Her Majesty Lucinda Jerian, and her royal medoriate, and that he may or may not have been acting under the guidance of a Cerborathian authority."

Garriker bristled in the tense silence that followed. "That is a dangerous insinuation."

"Our evidence supports our claim," Blackbow said, his head high.

"Let us hear it, then," the queen commanded, her voice still even.

Garriker sat down, his eyes locked upon his audience. Arythan's eyes were upon them as well, but he was not strengthened by self-righteous anger. He may not have killed the occupants of the room that night, but he had no means of proving otherwise.

"Medoriate Grim had sent an urgent request for the Revered's presence at the castle," Erun said.

"How do you know this?" Garriker demanded.

"There were those who saw the letter," Erun insisted. "We would produce it now if the Revered had not taken it with him on his journey."

"So we are to trust your word," the king said, skeptical.

"Regardless, Your Majesty, the Revered left our temple immediately," Erun said. "He took with him Jedinom's Light." The warrior produced a small leather pouch from his side. "Our investigation awarded us with the shattered remains of the vial." He spilled the contents of the bag into his palm, holding the shards for the regents to see.

Arythan felt the warmth leave his face, and he gripped the arms of his chair.

"What is the significance of this?" Garriker asked, not hiding his impatience.

"Jedinom's Light is from the Great Forest, a magic elixir that has only one purpose: exposing Ocranthos's taint," Blackbow said. "Medoriate Grim had exposed Medoriate Crow as a heathen, and perhaps as more than that: a follower of the Dark One. Medoriate

Crow certainly had motive to dispatch those who knew of his dark dealings. If the Revered exposed him with Jedinom's Light, then Medoriate Crow could have acted out of desperation to eliminate all witnesses."

"What you present sounds more akin to speculation than fact," Garriker said, dismissive. "You present shards of glass when you have no evidence Medoriate Crow was even present!"

"There are no other questionable medori here," Erun said. "And as I understand it, Medoriate Crow himself proclaimed he does not believe in the Great Warrior."

"That does not make him a murderer," the queen reasoned.

"Forgive my interjection, but Medoriate Crow was in Medoriate Grim's care," came a new voice from the opposite corner of the room. Desnera's "Worst," until now, had held a silent presence. The one who had spoken was the scarf-concealed man known as Keeper.

Garriker was about to speak when his wife placed a hand upon his arm. "What do you know of this?" she asked.

Keeper bowed his head. "At the time we were under Medoriate Grim's authority. He ordered us not to speak of the incident, but seeing as he was unjustly murdered, I cannot help but contribute what I know."

The queen nodded for him to continue.

"Medoriate Crow was subdued by Spight." Keeper gestured to his teammate. "His subsequent injury necessitated Medoriate Grim's skill in magic. We knew Medoriate Crow was in his care, but that was all we knew."

"Why was this not brought to my attention earlier?" the queen demanded.

"Forgive us, You Majesty, but as I said, Medoriate Grim—"

"Was not your overseer," the queen said. "My sister was your liege."

Keeper's head dipped lower, as did his teammates'.

"Your Majesty," Erun said, "this solidifies Medoriate Crow's involvement and proves his presence that night."

"But it does not prove he is responsible for murder," Garriker asserted, though the force behind his words was gone.

"Perhaps Medoriate Crow would speak for himself," the queen said.

The conversation seemed to pass around him, words flying through the air without sinking in. As it happened, Arythan had taken to staring emptily at the doors leading out of the hall. The tale was convoluted enough that should he speak the truth about that night, he would inevitably point a tarnished finger at Garriker and the B.E.S.T.. If he upheld the lie, what consequence did it mean for him, and then for his family? There was no one to defend him, and all eyes were upon him as he realized he must speak. Struggling to find his voice, he took a deep breath and swallowed. "I was tortured by Grim, but I didn't kill anyone." His words sounded weak—in volume as well as in content.

"Why would Medoriate Grim torture you?" the queen asked gently.

"We know the answer and have already asserted it, Your Majesty," Erun said, his patience waning like the king's. "He sought to uncover the truth about Medoriate Crow's loyalties."

"Or tarnish a newly-forged alliance," Garriker accused. "Cerborath, it seems, is favored by an ill light."

"Perhaps not unjustly," Blackbow added.

"You step too far," Garriker warned.

"Hardly, Your Majesty. We merely want justice." Erun held out his hands. "Our leader perished in highly questionable circumstances. While we know the truth, we understand your need to hide behind a lack of solid evidence. We are not here for vengeance, and because Her Majesty has been supportive to our cause, we offer a proposal."

"You have forgotten who it is that rules this land," Garriker said.

"We will hear your proposal," the queen amended, eyeing her husband, "and we will reconvene to discuss how best to approach this situation."

"Very well," Erun said. "Our proposal is this: the king of Desnera relinquishes his royal medoriate and his specialized force that they be exiled from the kingdom. For our part, we will continue favorable relations with the people and the regents of this land." He leveled his gaze. "Given our esteem among the people, our support would be of no small value to you in this time of transition.

"The alternative would be for Medoriate Crow to submit to our Order and profess himself a Warrior of the Sword. I would think this a small concession given the people's opinion that their new king harbors a servant of the Dark One. It would be a way to strengthen trust between His Majesty and those yet reluctant to accept his rule."

"We appreciate your consideration," the queen said, standing. "In turn we will consider your proposals." She nodded for the herald to escort the Masters of the House from the hall. "I will send for you with our answer presently."

The Masters bowed and left the hall. Garriker's sigh was the only audible sound, but no one was certain if it was a sigh of frustration or of resignation. He pinched the bridge of his nose and closed his eyes. "How is it we are given this ultimatum? Our authority should not be questioned," he said, his voice low.

"They are as much an authority," the queen said, "but their kingdom is greater—the hearts and minds of the people. Like it or not, the House can be a valuable ally or a formidable enemy. We must make our decision carefully. How much are we willing to sacrifice?" She touched his shoulder, and the king opened his eyes.

Without looking at anyone, Garriker addressed the remaining

witnesses in the room. He did not raise his voice, but his words were clear and strong. "I want everyone but Medoriate Crow to leave the hall."

After a moment, the Desneran elite and the Cerborathian syndicate stirred and soundlessly followed the king's instruction. Only Arythan and his grim countenance remained.

"Medoriate Crow," Garriker said, "please join us."

Arythan came to stand before the regents, resenting the sympathy in their eyes, resenting their words before they were uttered, resenting the entire bleak situation. "Sir, y' know I didn't kill anyone," he said, dispensing with formalities.

Garriker gave him a grim smile. "I know, Medoriate. And you know that it does not matter."

Arythan turned away. He knew what was to follow.

"This is a difficult predicament for us both. Much was sacrificed to achieve this union between Cerborath and Desnera. It is very important to me that those sacrifices not be in vain."

So you want me to sacrifice my freedom and my family. Is that it? Now the heat had returned to Arythan's face—overwhelmingly so.

"What I ask of you is no small request, but it is my preference to your exile." The mage did not have to look at the king to know that Garriker was assessing his reaction in the following silence. "By joining the Warriors of the Sword, you will still be my royal medoriate."

"Just as Medoriate Grim remained in the service of my sister," the queen added.

"They murdered m' mates," Arythan said in a low, bitter voice.

It took the king a moment before his eyes lit in recollection of the Crimson Dragon's demise. "The dead have no need of our worries, regrets, or desire for vengeance. You must consider your future, your family."

You bastard. The mage clenched his fists. Of course Garriker knew about Victoria and their child. He simply did not care, which was why Arythan had been torn away from Cerborath to remain the king's worthless puppet in Desnera.

"Your wife and child could reside in Desnera with you," the queen said, as if reading his thoughts.

Leverage to keep me complacent in your grip. "Cerborath is their 'ome." His words were quiet but rigid.

Garriker's already shortened patience shortened a bit more, and he drew himself upright in his chair. "Might I remind you that you had taken an oath to serve me? Are you willing to face the consequences of treason?"

The queen put her hand on her husband's arm again, trying to stave his temper.

"My oath was to y', sir, not the Warriors of the Sword." He folded his arms. "An' 'struth I don' believe in their god."

"So you are telling me, your king," Garriker said slowly, "that you will not do as I bid." It was not a question but a confirmation. He drew his arm away from the queen's grasp and stood.

"I will not join the Warriors of the Sword," Arythan said, standing his ground.

"The alternative is exile," the queen said. Desperation rose in her voice. "You will earn the Warriors of the Sword as your enemy. There will be no protection for you or your family should they pursue you."

"They were always my enemy." Arythan waited for Garriker to erupt, but the king merely regarded him with a hardened stare.

"Are you ready to earn another?"

Arythan blinked. Even the queen seemed surprised by the threat, staring at her husband with wide eyes.

"You have made your choice, Medoriate Crow," Garriker said, unyielding. "You should hope you do not come to regret it." He waved his hand in dismissal. "Gather your belongings and leave."

Stunned, the mage did not move immediately. Was this really happening? Was he being exiled for a murder he never committed?

Exiled trying to save the king's son? Exiled for becoming the "Dark Wizard" Garriker had created him to be? With feet that did not seem his own, Arythan slowly turned and walked out of the hall. His anger had fled, replaced by uncertainty for the future.

As he passed beyond the grand double doors, he found the B.E.S.T. and the Worst were waiting in the atrium beyond.

"Ah, if looks do tell..." Keeper mocked.

"Shut y'r 'ole," Dagger growled, then turned with a furrowed brow toward the mage who had not stopped walking. "Oi, Frostbite—what 'appened?" He started after Arythan, but Tigress grabbed his arm.

"Later," she said, watching as the former royal medoriate disappeared from sight.

LEAVING Desnera was not as easy as Arythan had expected. It was not that he bore any great weight other than the burden of his heart; it was the fact that there were people in his way. They had heard about his exile—whether through the House of Jedinom or the Worst—and they had flooded the streets to give him a fond farewell. The people cheered, shouted insults, threw rocks at him —all because they believed the Dark Wizard had killed their queen.

"Good riddance, bloodrot filth!"

"Drown in the mires of Lorth, you murderer!" A large stone glanced off Arythan's shoulder. It was not the first, and it was not the last. The crowd grew bolder when he failed to react, though Narga was in a fury, biting and rearing at any who came too close. If not for her, they would have torn him from the saddle. It seemed, however, the new plan was to stone him where he sat, or at least wait for him to fall.

Arythan remained expressionless, seemingly calm, though the

truth was that his anger, frustration, fear, and disappointment roiled in a mass in the pit of his stomach. Yet amidst the maelstrom of his hidden emotions, there was the Void—that empty, black hole of nothingness that waited to take him. He fought that silent internal battle now, while his body took the brunt of the crowd's fury.

Another sharp projectile struck his temple, and his enemies nearly had their wish. He gripped Narga's mane and righted himself, though a warm trickle crossed from his brow into the corner of his eye. He wiped it away and stared blankly at the dark red fluid on his glove. The pain was distant, almost not his own, though somehow he was aware of every blow. And there were glimpses of the crowd—angry faces, spittle in the air, mouths open and assailing. All of this hatred was for him, and he did not know a single person around him. Another large rock came for his face—narrowly missing its mark.

Then he heard a roar and the sound of hoof beats. Many hoof beats. From behind him. He did not turn to see who was approaching; a moment later the force of black steeds and riders parted around him and compelled the crowd to retreat. Dagger's unintelligible bellowing was like thunder, the glint of metal weaponry in the syndicate's hands like lightning.

"Back off!" Tigress shouted, and the crowd obeyed—for a moment. The people's fear was quickly being consumed by fury.

"Couldn't wait for us, eh?" Dagger asked the mage, and in the moment it took for him to finish the question, an arrow skimmed his shoulder. The brute twisted in the saddle and lost his balance. No sooner than he was on the ground, the crowd began to close in. His own horse posed just as much a danger, its massive hooves dancing precariously around his body. Tigress made a gesture for the rest of her crew to move in protectively, but in time the crowd would overwhelm them and tear them all to pieces.

The sight of his frantic teammates drowning in a sea of angry

Desnerans roused Arythan from his numbness. He heard Dagger's pained shout, saw rocks fly, became aware of Hunter's bloodied face. At least a dozen hands grappled for Tigress's legs. There were hands on him as well, pulling and clawing, and Narga's snorts turned to screams. Arythan released the reins and allowed himself to be dragged from the saddle.

The pain enlivened him, drawing blackened fury from his heart and through his veins like ink that had spilled across a blank piece of paper. He was trapped—surrounded by feet and faces and hands—all of them spurred by hatred. His hatred, however, stained darker. Hatred for those who wronged him by their ignorance. Hatred for those who would harm his friends. Hatred for those who had betrayed him and abandoned him—leaving his wife and unborn child defenseless.

Without warning, a torrent of blue flame blazed upward from his body. He could not smell the odor of burned hair and flesh, but he could hear the screams of those who had been too close, and he did not care. His intention was to defend, not to kill, but if the Humans got in his way, he accepted no responsibility for their stupidity. They were, after all, trying to kill *him.*

Arythan got to his knees, challenging the terror-stricken crowd to defy him. His flames rose from his back like dragon wings unfurled, and he got to his feet and waited. Those who had not fled remained frozen. He turned slowly, staring back at each face before him. *Don't meddle with me.*

Behind him Tigress had dismounted and helped Dagger back to his horse. Arythan snapped his fire wings, and the people recoiled. By then his teammates had all returned to their saddles. He began walking in the direction he had been headed originally, and the angry sea parted, giving wide berth to the company in black. There was not a sound as they passed. One old man was bold enough to throw a stone, but Arythan had seen him, and the projectile burst into dust in mid-air. There were no more acts of malice, and when they passed beyond the city gate, the flames died. Arythan did not care enough to wipe the sweat from his brow. He clicked to Narga, who trailed the group, and managed to pull himself atop her back.

For a long while they rode in silence, and it was not until they had left Desnera's boundary far behind them that any one of them spoke. They had retreated from the road to tend to any withstanding injuries, and Arythan sat alone, staring absently into the trees.

Tigress came up behind him and handed him a wet rag. "This wasn't your doing."

He merely glanced at her, then looked down at the rag.

She crouched beside him. "We knew change was coming. The sun never rises on black earth." She took back the rag and started to dab at the bloodied wound on his brow. He did not resist her, nor did he acknowledge her words.

"We have only been exiled from Desnera," she continued in a voice almost gentle. "We will ride back to Cerborath and seek allegiance under Prince Michael. Given his status with his father, I find little reason to believe he will not have us in his service."

"'M already in 'is service," Arythan muttered. "'Twas the problem. Still a problem. Is it treason? Will Garriker send someone after us?"

Tigress finished cleaning his wound without an answer. At last, she said, "Garriker had always been a fair man. We have done nothing wrong. I doubt he would waste his time."

Arythan replaced his hat and stood. "The sun never rises on black earth, Cap'n. Things 'ave changed." And he went to see to Narga, knowing the eyes of his leader followed him.

12

THE OLD MAN

The sun had bleached the color from the sky in what was already a blistering afternoon. There were but few sparing moments of a breeze, but mostly the air was still. The birds had ceased their calls, and even the insects were silent.

Erik wiped his brow with his handkerchief, though beads of sweat still ran down from beneath his hat—hot and sticky like tree sap. His eyes burned, his arms were burned, and he felt there was not much else left to bake, given his state.

"You all right, Mr. Sparrow?" one of the young men asked.

Erik looked up at him and gave a slight smile. "Is my hat afire?"

"No, sir, but I wouldn't be surprised if it caught right now," the youth said. He extended a hand. "We're all taking a break from weeding. Come and have a drink with us."

Erik accepted his assistance, standing somewhat shakily. The youth fetched his cane and handed it to him.

"I have to say, sir, we weren't sure how you'd hold up. It's strange that the mayor gave you this job." He walked alongside him, heading toward the well. "Seems like rough work for you."

"Work is what I need," Erik said in a parched voice. "But if you mean to imply the strain is too demanding for one of my years, then I would have to argue the point."

The youth scratched his head, embarrassed. "I'd not have said it so, Mr. Sparrow."

"Of course not." They reached the well, and Erik cleared his throat before accepting a cup of water. Most of the other laborers were young men, though there were a few women as well.

"Not even a breeze," one of them lamented, dabbing her neck. The others seemed too tired to talk, or perhaps it was that the water evaporated in their throats the instant they consumed it. They noticed a figure heading towards them, and everyone straightened for Halgon Thayliss. They greeted him, and he tipped his hat toward them. He was nearly as damp from sweat as the laborers.

"The lot of you is more wilted than the crops," he said. "This is an uncommon heat we have." The mayor's eyes fell upon Erik, and his lips curled into something more genuine. "How fares Mr. Sparrow?"

"Like iron in the smith's forge," Erik said. "Quite hot but withstanding."

It was not an answer anyone would expect, and Halgon's face betrayed his surprise, followed by contemplation. He turned to regard the others. "All of you work very hard, I know. But this weather is not fit for man or beast...or Mr. Sparrow."

A few of the workers chuckled, though Erik's blank expression remained unchanged. Halgon straightened and cleared his throat. "Take an early leave. Go home and rest. No sense in watering these crops with your sweat."

There was a collective sigh of relief and many words of thanks as the group dispersed and went to collect their weed baskets. Halgon caught Erik by the arm. "How is Lady Catherine? I see the two of you have much improved your home."

Erik nodded. "It is much more habitable, and Catherine is pleased."

"I am glad to hear it," Halgon said, and patted him on the back. "One must keep the woman happy."

Erik looked at him curiously, but the mayor did not elaborate.

"Do not let me keep you." Halgon gestured to the field. "You can surprise her with a visit."

"She will appreciate a surprise," Erik agreed. "Thank you." He worked his way back to where he had been, his energy revived by the idea. The basket was waiting for him, full of drooping plants.

"I do not understand the concept of a 'weed,'" he murmured to himself. "A plant unwanted, yes, but a plant unworthy? I admire its tenacity." He gazed thoughtfully at the field and flowering "weeds" threaded amongst the crops. "If they are unwanted here, they may be welcomed elsewhere." And he began picking blooms of various colors, thinking of the roses Orilian's betrothed had presented to her.

One stalk in particular bore a golden-petaled flower with a scarlet center, and as he bent to pick it, a drop of sweat rolled into the crook of his eye. He rubbed it to stop the burning, and just as he looked up, he saw that he was not alone. The other laborers had already gone, and though his vision was hardly clear, he could tell this person bore no hat. No one went anywhere without a hat—not unless you were a visitor.

Erik straightened and cleared his throat. "May I help you?"

The figure did not move or make a sound.

Puzzled, he began to walk closer so that he could repeat the question. As the person sharpened with his proximity, he could see it was an older man—older than him, perhaps, with a long, gray beard, and hard, dark eyes. He had never seen this man before—at least, not that he knew. "May I—" Erik was silenced by the man's eerie stare. Neither of them moved, but he finally summoned the words to ask, "Who are you?" They escaped him in a whisper only, but he doubted he would have been given a response.

Erik wiped another drop of sweat from his eyes, and when he looked again, the man was gone. Unsure what to think, he merely stood there, half wondering if the man would reappear.

"My friend, are you all right?" Halgon Thayliss came up from behind him.

"I thought I saw someone," Erik murmured, his eyes still affixed to where the stranger had been.

"I think the heat has gotten to you," the mayor said. "I can escort you home."

At last Erik turned away, his eyes falling to the basket still gripped in his sticky hand. "No, thank you, I'm fine."

"Are you certain?" Halgon looked at him dubiously.

"I am." Erik met his gaze. "Thank you."

"Very well. Be careful. And please give Catherine my regards."

Erik nodded and went on his way, stopping only to pick the flower that had caught his attention before. He poked his head inside the tailor's shop, and Catherine stopped her work to greet him with a warm smile. "What are you doing here?" she asked. Then her eyes swept over him, and concern replaced her smile. "You are very warm and not a little burned."

"Thayliss sent us home because of the heat," Erik said. He grabbed the bouquet from his basket, but all of the flowers had wilted and withered. His shoulders drooped. "They had been beautiful," he mourned.

"The gesture is still beautiful," Catherine said, taking the basket from him and reaching to kiss his cheek. "Thank you."

"You would not know if I were blushing," he said shyly.

"The sun loves fair skin," Catherine agreed. She pulled at his hat. "I must finish my work, but I will be home soon, and then we can go."

Erik's brow furrowed. "Go?"

She looked at him, just as perplexed. "Tale Telling Night. We spoke of it this morning."

"I...must have forgotten," he admitted.

"You never forget Tale Telling Night. You look forward to it every week." Deepening concern had also deepened her frown.

"Perhaps it's the heat, then," Erik said hastily. "I will head home for a bath. I will be ready for tonight."

Catherine squeezed his hand but said nothing as he left the shop. She turned to resume her work but stopped in her tracks. He had forgotten his basket.

"ARE you certain you feel well enough to go? You have barely touched your dinner."

Erik looked up at her from where he sat at the table. "I'm sorry," he said. "I was lost in thought." He ate a piece of toasted fruit in good faith.

Catherine was not convinced. "The bath did not help as you thought it would," she said. Since he had started working in the fields, he had dropped any excess weight from his minstrel days. To her it made him look worn, and the darkening of his skin only aged him more. When she thought about him laboring in the sun, it angered her that Halgon Thayliss had given him such a job. But for her to discourage Erik would be wrong, and the truth was that he did contribute to their way of living. She wondered if she might secretly ask the mayor to reassign him.

"You worry needlessly. And," he said, spearing another piece of fruit, "I have already devised a tale to tell."

"Have you?" Catherine forced a smile. If he was in a fair mood, she would not spoil it with her concern.

Erik nodded but was pointedly silent.

"Very well, Mr. Sparrow, keep your story to yourself until the time is right," Catherine said. "I will just have to be patient." She watched him look away with a pensive expression, and he did not regard her when he posed his next question.

"Have you heard of any newcomers in town?"

"There are newcomers every day at the port," she said.

"Yes, but they have no cause to venture into the field."

Catherine tried to read him—unsuccessfully. "Did you meet someone today?"

"Not officially. Mine is a query of curiosity and not of purpose." He sipped his drink and caught her gaze. "I thought someone of consequence might have come to town." He shrugged. "You hear more than I do."

Catherine shook her head. "I haven't heard of anyone notable in Brandeise. If I learn differently, I will tell you."

"Thank you," Erik said quietly. "The mayor sends his regards."

"You say that as if it is a misfortune," she teased. She stood and began to clear the table.

"I'm not so fond of him."

Catherine paused. "Why not?"

"While I am grateful for the work I have been given," Erik said, "there is something hidden behind his actions. I can't explain."

She glanced his way to find he was watching her again. Her face warmed, but she was not sure why. "We should leave soon. The others tend to arrive early."

THERE WERE three other couples who had taken an interest in Tale Telling Night, and all but one of them were younger than Catherine and Erik. San Becker was the oldest of them all, a bachelor with a talent for telling enthralling tales. Each night they met, one member of the group was assigned to concocting a new tale. Often there was a theme dictated by the others, but sometimes the topic was left open, and such was the case on this night.

They gathered beneath a rocky overhang, a shallow shelter in the stone that had been carved by wind and water. Old San was the designated fire lord, and his talents extended to the construction of a healthy blaze. The fire was already crackling when Catherine and Erik arrived, and the youngest couple was the only one not present, but it was accepted that they always turned up late.

"I expect greatness from you tonight, Mr. Sparrow," San said to him with a firm hand clasp.

"I will try not to disappoint you," Erik returned.

When the initial greeting and chatter quieted, and even the tardy couple was seated, Erik took his place upon the broad rock before the group. He was not hasty to start, glancing at the darkening sky over the ocean and taking note of the clouds drifting in above the distant horizon. A breeze swept past them and teased the fire, and Erik leaned forward, his elbows upon his knees. "Listen," he invited.

There were a few seconds of silence where his audience strained to hear past the wind.

"Did you hear the sound of the advancing night?" he asked. "The sigh of the sun as it takes its light beyond the horizon?" He took a breath and assessed his audience, smiling at Catherine. "I am told these sounds are melodies that belong to the spirits. We are deaf to them without the gift of the divine. But if you could imagine what such melodies would be, if you could perceive just one note, what would you expect?

"I am told," Erik began again, "that every being has a color—a halo of light that surrounds it. The color of life itself and the energy that feeds it." He held out his empty hands. "But not for our eyes. We are blind."

"Even the wind can graze our flesh, but what of the unseen spirits that slip beside us, prod at our backs? What of the scent of the clouds and the breath of a butterfly? We are locked in a world so tangible that to dream of anything more would be nearly impossible."

Erik brushed the hair back from his face. "There was one man who knew what the spirits knew. He was not born with such keen perception, but the gift was granted him on the Twilight Hour, the breath between night and day, when for a moment, spirits and Humans walk together.

"What he thought was a bird had been trapped in one of his hunter's nets, and a bird can hardly suffice for one's dinner. A stirring of kindness had him free the creature, and when he had done so, it changed before him so that he could see its true form. No longer a bird, but a woman. But not a Human woman. Hers was an ethereal beauty, as though she had been born from sunlight and shaped by the wind.

"When he—"

"Wait now, Mr. Sparrow," one of the young men asked. "What did she *look* like? I mean, her hair, her eyes..." His wife elbowed him, and he blushed.

Erik looked at him thoughtfully. "It is not for me to describe beauty. To each, it's different."

"The proper response, Ben, would be to say she looked like your wife," Old San said with a grin.

Ben's blush deepened. "Well, sure."

Erik waited for quiet before he continued. "The man was quite taken by her, though he knew that when the hour was up, he would not see her again. She promised to grant him one favor on account of her liberation, provided she could not grant him immortality. He asked for the next greatest wish.

"He wanted to see the spirit world, to hear the songs, to know the scent, and feel the Unseen. He wanted to see *her*, to gaze upon her the rest of his days. She told him there was but one way to grant his wish. She would bestow upon him her light, the light of the divine. But within him, the light would burn, and it would burn quickly, and with it his life would flee. She bid him to ask a different favor of her, that he would not spend his years so."

Erik lifted his chin. "Would you think the price too great?"

"Give my life to see a world I couldn't reach?" one of the women asked. "No. I wouldn't do it."

"But to see beauty to its fullest and die happy?" another husband said. "Might be worth it."

"Depends on whether or not he had a family," Ben's wife said. "It would be selfish to abandon his family, but if he had none, then he would be free to make that choice."

Ben looked at Erik. "Did he have a family?"

"That is not part of the tale," Erik said. "Think on it what you will, and I will tell it as I must."

"Beauty does not grant happiness," Old San said. "In fact, I would believe it opened a door to longing. This would not be a tale if the man did not hold true to his desire."

Erik looked at Catherine, surprised to find her expression melancholy. "Catherine. What do you believe he chose?"

She drew a breath. "As San said, this would not be a tale had he not chosen the light."

"But what would you choose?" he asked, curious.

"There is beauty even without special sight," Catherine said softly. "But for so special a spirit, for one with true beauty inside, I would give my life to remain with it."

Whether surprised or contemplative or both, Erik betrayed nothing through his expression as he gazed at her. His lips parted as if he would speak, but then his focus moved beyond her, and his eyes widened.

Catherine turned around, perplexed. "Erik, what is it?" When she turned back, he was on his feet, his eyes still riveted to the landscape.

"Is there something you want?" he asked, projecting his voice.

"Is this part of the story?" Ben asked his wife. "The Unseen, perhaps?"

Everyone turned around to face the ocean.

"What is it you want?" Erik repeated, frustration creeping into his voice.

"Who is there?" Catherine asked him, trying not to sound as unnerved as she was.

He looked at her incredulous. "You don't see him?"

"Quite enough, Mr. Sparrow, thank you," Ben's wife said politely. "If this is the ending to your tale, I admit I'm a little confused."

"This is not my tale," Erik said. "He is there. He was in the field before." His brow furrowed. "By the shore—the rocks. Can't you —" It was plain no one else did see the man with the long, gray beard. And the man made no move to make himself noticed. Erik rubbed his brow, confounded.

Catherine was at his side, her hand protectively on his arm. "You were right, earlier. You have suffered from too much heat. I should not have allowed you to come in such a state."

He merely gaped at her.

"For anyone to be out in this heat..." Ben said, supporting Catherine's diagnosis. "You should get some rest, Mr. Sparrow."

"I can finish your tale," Old San said, patting Erik on the shoulder. "Don't worry, young man."

"I feel fine," Erik muttered. He looked at the shore, but the man was gone. "I'm not ill. I'm not."

"You may not feel ill, but rest has never caused any harm," Ben's wife said.

"Which is why we are headed home," Catherine agreed, already pulling the reluctant old man away. "Good night to all of you. We will see you next week."

"Speedy recovery, Mr. Sparrow," San said, and they departed.

Erik said nothing on the walk back home, his face drawn and

tense. Try as Catherine might, she could not calm him. Once inside, he sat down heavily, his head in his hand. "I'm sorry, but I know I saw him."

"Maybe you could describe him for me," Catherine encouraged.

"He was old, with a long—" He gestured to his chin.

"Beard," she supplied, and he nodded.

"A long, gray beard. And dark eyes. Eyes that just stared at me, as though I had done some unspeakable wrong." Erik looked at her with desperate eyes. "You didn't see him, though. You don't believe me."

"I did not see him," she confirmed, "but that does not mean I don't believe you. I think, however, it is best we not over-think what happened tonight." She squeezed his shoulder. "Please. Come to bed. Rest. We will have clearer minds tomorrow."

Erik sighed and nodded and allowed Catherine to escort him to the bedroom.

13

THE DEEPEST CUTS

"I confess, I am utterly shocked. Flabbergasted. Awestruck."

"I understood the first one," Arythan muttered to Prince Michael. He ignored the weapon the prince was presenting to him.

"The fact that my father has exiled both his elite and his medoriate illustrates how eager he is to abandon his people." Michael shook his head. "To think he was once proud of what his ancestors had built here. Now he scoffs at it. I will maintain what he has forsaken." He gestured with the foil. "Come, Crow! It has been some time since we have dueled."

"I'm sorry," Arythan said, turning away as if to leave the training arena. "I really just want to see m' wife."

"And you will. After a quick bout." He pressed the hilt into Arythan's hand. "What will you tell Victoria?"

"What she needs to know. I'm out o' work." Arythan gave a heavy sigh.

"I beg to differ." Michael took his stance, forcing the mage to do the same. "You and your syndicate work for me now. Nothing has changed." He made a lunge, which Arythan evaded. "In fact, I would argue the situation has improved. We are free to mine the Ice, and your family has my protection."

Arythan looked at Michael warily.

"If I were you, I would not tell Victoria anything."

Arythan parried his blow. "What?"

"Consider the stress you both have endured. You are about to be a father. Why lay any weight upon her shoulders when your fortune has scarcely changed. Your work is the same, and I will demonstrate loyalty where my father has failed." They entered a lively bout until Arythan tapped his arm. "One day, I will best you," Michael vowed.

At that moment, Banen stormed into the arena. "What have you done, bloodrot?" he demanded, ready to spark a fire.

"What is this intrusion, brother?" Michael asked.

"The B.E.S.T. are in exile, in case you haven't heard," Banen snapped, approaching his brother. "And *he* is responsible."

"I rather thought our dear father is responsible," Michael said. "Though I am certain you are not included in that verdict. So sheathe your sword, brother, and relax. I am in charge here."

Banen snatched Michael's sword before the elder prince knew what was happening. He thrust the weapon at Arythan, who narrowly avoided being speared. "You seek to take everything from me," he seethed.

Arythan said nothing, moving into defensive posture again. He had a feeling Banen had every intention of permanent revenge. The bout was quick and it was furious, and Michael's angry shouts went unheeded as the younger prince came at the mage again and again.

There was fervor in Banen's eyes, a rigid expression that only intensified each time Arythan evaded him. His desperation made him more dangerous, and rather than tire, he fed off his bottled emotions—which must have been many.

But Arythan had more than a few of his own frustrations.

It was difficult to say who made the first hit, but ultimately both adversaries were responsible for a number of dark stains upon the ground. There was also growing doubt as to whether either of them would emerge as a victor, or if unbridled rage would see them both finished. The would-be king of Cerborath was unwilling to let that happen. His voice rose above the labored breathing and the sound of scathing metal, penetrating the tense atmosphere like thunder.

"Enough!"

Like boys chastised by their father, they stopped, and Michael stormed down upon them and took their weapons. "At a time when your integrity has been called to question, you are at each other's throats." He stared at them. "This is a time when support is paramount, lest we all fall."

"You are not king yet," Banen asserted, though it was plain that he knew his mistake the moment the words left him.

"Our father has abandoned us for a Desneran whore," Michael said harshly. "I will preserve this kingdom, and you will either help me, or you can find yourself a home in Jerian's castle. Which do you prefer?"

Banen turned away.

"We are allies, not enemies," Michael continued. "There are to be no further childish skirmishes. Extend your hands in truce."

Arythan held out his hand, and Banen stared at it. Finally, he took it and pulled Arythan close. "Remember that I know who you are," he whispered venomously.

"And I know what y're not," Arythan returned. They pulled away, though their eyes remained locked.

"Good," Michael said. "Banen, clean yourself up. I have business to finish with Crow."

With a fine scowl for the both of them, Banen left, and Michael turned to Arythan. "It is amazing how a little fear can reinstate order."

"I always thought 'twas respect," Arythan said.

"Ah, and that as well. There is more than one way to earn respect. Regardless, when I am king, I will be heeded—by everyone."

Arythan looked up at him, knowing a threat when he heard one.

"But as I had been saying, our situation is secure. We will continue with the Ice. My father will not detect a skeleton crew. His eyes are obviously on loftier ambitions."

The mage restrained a sigh. "Y' want me at the Ice Plains tomorrow?"

"After you have seen your wife." Michael looked him over. "You should also tend to your wounds, lest you stain the castle halls with the fruit of your anger. It is all I can do to tolerate one rebellious brother. I trust you will serve me loyally, as you have thus far."

Arythan paused in the inspection of his injuries, most of them minor cuts and scratches. What, exactly, was that supposed to mean?

"Our business associates at the Plains have taken quite an interest in you." The prince paused. "They wish to know how we found such a talented medoriate."

Arythan waited, his stomach twisting, though he tried to keep his expression blank.

"I did not say much, for I can be mysterious too. Should they try to recruit you, they will have to contend with me. Still, I wonder why, when they have wizards at their disposal, they should set their curiosity on you."

"Tha's easy," the mage murmured. "Wizards are stupid."

Michael smiled but did not laugh. "I will need you to give me a full report of all activity when I send for you," he said, serious.

"Yes, sir," Arythan responded, feeling as though he was addressing the king. He supposed that was what Michael was to him now. He left the arena and went to change his bloodied clothes. He wanted to focus his thoughts upon Victoria, how good it would be to hold her, see her face. But the truth was that after a conversation that was supposed to reassure him, he had never felt so uneasy.

Banen knew him. And most likely the Seroko had discovered who he was as well. His trip to the Ice Plains would be telling to say the least.

THE PASSAGE of a couple months in Cerborath could bring about a season of change—literally. When last Arythan had visited Victoria at the manor, the leaves had started to color, and the last of the warm days were fleeting. Now it was cold, windy, and the branches were dark and bare. Winter would be upon them soon enough.

When he first saw his wife, Arythan realized that the season was not the only change that had taken place. Victoria was as round as the apples at harvest time, and she was soft and plump and beaming with joy at the sight of him. Her thick arms snared him and threatened to confine him forever, except that he gasped in shock when he felt her belly twitch.

"Was that—"

"It was," Victoria said proudly. "He knows who you are." Then tears sprang from her smile. "I didn't know when you would return...if you would return."

"Y' knew I'd come back," Arythan said softly.

"No." She shook her head. "I didn't. I thought maybe His Majesty would keep you there."

"Actually," Arythan said, "there's been a change o' plans." He watched doubt cloud over her face, her smile vanish. *You should always smile,* he thought, and he considered what Michael had said. He could tell her that the king had exiled him and the syndicate from Desnera. He could give her good cause to worry for their family. And she would worry—but even so, there would be nothing to do about their situation. In truth, their future rested almost solely in his finding a way to destroy the Enhancement and escape with the Ice Flies. But she did not know about them, and if he told her, she would worry about treason, and the baby, and where they would go, and how—

"I'm needed back at the Ice Plains," Arythan said, and it was not a lie. "Michael wants me working on the En'ancement. I'll be closer to y'."

Her smile returned. "Yes, that is good," she said, obviously relieved. "It won't be long now, you know. I am fit to burst."

"I 'ope to be 'ere when y' do," he said.

Victoria cupped his hands in hers. "I want to walk with you."

Arythan glanced out the window. "'S not pretty out there."

"They never let me out of here," she whispered. "They want me to sit around and sleep and eat and talk. I feel like a hog being fattened for the slaughter."

That coaxed a true smile from him. "If my lady wants to walk, my lady will have her walk."

Her eyes grew round, and her pert lips parted. "You spoke without your accent!"

"No, I spoke with *your* accent," he said.

"You must stop. I love how you speak. Don't change it." She pulled him to the coat rack, using him as a shield while she snared her cloak. Arythan took it from her and carefully covered her. She thrust on her gloves, and drew her hood, and together they slipped outside into the brisk autumn air.

"Am I going to be in trouble for 'elping a prisoner escape?" Arythan asked.

Victoria had closed her eyes, relishing the wind in her hair. "Maybe."

"Ol' Lyndi driving y' crackers, luv?"

Victoria opened her eyes and sighed. "Oh, she is very sweet. She is more of a mother than my mother was." She stopped to watch a crow in the tree above them. "I admit I'm not accustomed to so much attention."

"Y' want me to tell 'er to back off?"

"No," Victoria laughed. "I think it makes her feel good to care for someone. I think she is very lonely."

Arythan allowed her to take the lead, and she waddled slowly toward the pond. The water sat low, and the reeds and cattails were now broken and faded. The ducks had fled to warmer grounds, leaving only the echoes of life that had been there that summer.

"When 'e's born, do y' still want to live at the castle?" Arythan asked.

"You mean that we would have a place like Lyndi's?" she asked.

"Whatever y' want, luv." They stood a distance from the shore, and he pulled her close to keep her warm, though he suspected he was colder than she was.

"That's what is so strange, Arythan. I'm not sure I know what I want right now. So much has changed—with me, anyway. I've had only time to think here, and all my thinking has only led me to question." Subconsciously her hand moved to her belly. "I always wanted to live like royalty—ever since I was a little girl. I wanted to live in a castle, wear beautiful gowns, have a wealthy, handsome husband...."

"So y've said," Arythan said dryly.

She poked him. "I have a handsome husband. But do I need those other things? What would Reiqo need? Is the castle the best place for him to grow up, with all those wicked ladies, and the rumors...? Would it be better to be somewhere quiet where he could run and play without a care? I could trade my fancy dresses for an apron, and I would not mind so long as he is happy."

I can make that happen, Arythan thought. *I can make certain we are all happy, living a quiet life somewhere other than Cerborath. I just needed to hear it from you.*

"You are awfully quiet, Medoriate," Victoria said, tilting her head back to look up at him. "You look tired. And I miss this." She rubbed his smooth chin.

We all go through changes. "'Ow will I know when to be 'ere?" he asked, voicing the other concern on his mind.

"Well, as Lyndi tells me, there will be signs."

"Signs?"

"Like labor. The baby doesn't just pop out," she said, gesticulating with her hands. "It could be hours of labor before he is actually born."

"So is 'labor' like 'work', then?" Arythan asked, confused.

"Work for me," Victoria said. "Apparently I have to push him out. And it will hurt." She turned around to face him. "I will be crying and screaming, and I am sure I will say some foul things." She smiled sweetly. "But I would love it if you were here."

Arythan scratched his head. "So y'll send for me if I'm not 'ere?"

"Yes, Medoriate."

"Bonzer," he said with a nod.

"You are so naïve."

"Thanks."

Victoria looked back at the manor. "I don't suppose you could carry me back in your arms."

He certainly would try, but before he could position himself, she laughed and swatted him away. "I was only teasing. Do not be ridiculous. You may be strong, but you will hurt yourself."

Arythan reddened.

Victoria tugged at his hand. "Come, Medoriate, I am certain dinner is nigh. Lyndi will be looking for me."

~

THE FOLLOWING DAY, Arythan was eating his dinner alone, in the darkened hall of the Ice Plains. His mind kept drifting back to Victoria, her face rosy over the wine, her laughter bright and heart-felt. The candlelight gleamed upon her, and they had been in good company at Lyndi's manor. He had hated to leave, and what had made it especially hard was knowing he had to return here, to the desolate, lonely world where he worked alongside his enemies.

He forced down a lump of cold mashed potatoes, knowing he would need his strength later for his personal experiment with the Ice. He had not bothered to light a fire in the hearth, figuring it was just as well he ate in the dark and the silence. Instead, he had bundled a coat and a cloak around himself, not caring how ridiculous the arrangement was.

No one had been there to greet him upon his return, and he took small comfort in that one virtue. Brann Alwin and the Seroko had turned in for the day, or so it seemed. A glimmer of light at the end of the hall caught his attention. While his night vision was now poor, the dim glow of the candle flame illuminated enough of the figure's features for him to tell it was a woman. There was, of course, only one woman left in the Ice Plains.

Losing his appetite completely, Arythan shoved the plate away and waited for her to approach. The flame accentuated the lines upon Sulinda Patrice's face, and he found there was really nothing flattering about her at all. Of course, his vision was tainted by the knowledge of what she was.

"Good evening, Medoriate," she greeted, sitting across from him. "It was not my intention to interrupt your dinner."

Yes, it was. He gave a slight nod, not bothering to remove his hat.

Sulinda peered beneath it as best she could. "It is amazing. I would never have thought… Of course, you have shaved, cut your hair… I can see it now."

He continued to stare at her.

"I cannot speak for you, but I am under no guises," she said, setting the candle down between them. "That our paths have crossed again can scarcely be coincidence, don't you think, Hawkshadow?"

"What do y' want?"

Sulinda smiled. "That is a question for us all, and I think we can reach an arrangement that will make everyone happy."

"Unlikely." *There is nothing you can say that I want to hear.*

She was undaunted by his attitude. "We did a little research."

Arythan clenched and released his fists, trying to quell his rising anger. Of course she did not know her crime. She did not know what her people took from him. To her, he was just a thief, just a boy. In a determinedly calm voice he said, "Didn't know Safir-Tamik was part o' y'r criminal organization, and I didn't know 'oo y' were. I never would've signed on for the Secrailoss voyage."

Sulinda placed her hands, open, upon the table. "I am not sure I understand."

Of course you don't. "The Seroko," he said, darkness creeping into his voice. He toyed with the flame of the candle, turning it blue.

"Whatever past you have shared with Lord Tamik, I know it has you bitter. You see that I have come without him, as a gesture of peace." Her eyes moved from the candle back to him. "He has only recently proven himself worthy of our cause. Had you not been on that voyage, you never would have provided us with the map to mine the Enhancement. And you would not have freed the Stone of Prophecy with whom you gallivanted though Northern—"

"*Erik* didn't belong to anyone, and 'e's not 'ere. And I would never *willingly* 'elp y', map or no."

"Yet we owe much of our success to you," she said.

Nigqor-slet. I hate this. I hate that I've done anything to contribute to your cause. I hate that I have to work with you now, and I can't do a damn thing about it...yet.

She lifted her chin. "We no longer need the Stone. The Ice, however, is where our business here has collided with yours."

"What do y' want?" he repeated more forcefully.

"My suspicion," Sulinda continued calmly, as though she did not hear him, "is that you are a spy. You have changed your name and your appearance and ingratiated yourself into this kingdom. For what cause? Who do you work for, Hawkshadow? Is it Garriker, or is it someone else? Perhaps the ones who are intent on hindering our progress here?"

What business is it of yours? His irritation reached its limit, and the flame soared high in a thin pillar. "I won't ask again," he gritted. "What do y' want?"

Sulinda drew back, her voice tenuous. "We might be able to offer you a proposal, if you are willing to hear me."

Arythan drew a jack and lit it. "Does Garriker know why y're really 'ere?"

Now it was her turn to stare.

"I'd think 'e'd be more supportive if 'e knew. Immortality would fetch a good price, no?" His dark smile prompted her frown.

"What is your gain?" she asked, leaning forward.

Arythan sent a stream of smoke into her face. "I don't 'ave one."

She withdrew, coughing.

He could not hide his loathing. "In case y'aven't guessed, I 'ate the lot o' y'. I'd love to do away with y', but *I'm* not a murderer."

"Murder? I don't—"

Arythan slammed his fist on the table, rattling the plate, and causing the flame to waver. The woman jumped. "No, y' don't. The

Seroko destroy everything they touch, an' they don't bloody care. Y' search for immortality, and y' kill the blokes 'oo stand in y'r way." He crushed the jack in his trembling hand.

"I don't—"

"'Awkwing," he said, his voice nearly breaking. His eyes cut into hers, digging for a sign of recognition. He was not left expectant. Her lips parted, but she was speechless.

"Y' murdered 'im because 'e wouldn't tell y' where the Archives were. Am I right?" he seethed.

"H-how do you know about Hawkwing?" Sulinda asked in a whisper.

"I was there," he hissed. "I watched 'im die." It was all Arythan could do not to set the hall ablaze.

"That was an accident. The Marksman was supposed to take him alive." She paused in the midst of a hasty excuse and straightened. "I don't see how this relates to you."

"An accident?" he mused, barely audible. He snorted. "An *accident?" I could arrange an accident right now. I could kill you with a thought, but better I run you through—just as you did my brother. You clearly had a role in his pursuit. You chased a sick man through the mountains, only to take his final days from him by the blade of a sword. You bitch.*

Sulinda was eyeing him warily, as if deciding to leave this madman to his solitude.

"I thought y' knew 'oo I was," Arythan said. "I thought y' bastards did y'r research." He snared her hand in a quarter of a second, catching her by surprise. Somewhere in the back of his mind, he heard Othenis's warning. So long as the Seroko did not know his identity… The rest of the message was lost when he shoved it away with his anger. *Let them know.*

He squeezed her hand so that she yelped, then pulled her across the table so that her nose was nearly touching his. He stared at her, unblinking, until his eyes burned and watered. "I am the Demon, the one 'oo was with 'im. *'Is brother.*" He made sure his words struck her, made sure they buried themselves in her ears. Then he shoved her away with as much force as he could muster.

Sulinda flew back, toppling over the bench and to the floor.

Arythan leapt over the table and stood over her.

"H-he had no brother," she whimpered, backing away from him. "We would have known."

"He was m' brother," Arythan said, nearly shouting. "And y' killed 'im. *By accident.*" The flame ignited the table behind him.

"Is this...is this your revenge?" Sulinda cried, terror upon her face. "Will you kill me?"

I want to. I want to sear your heart as it beats inside of you, burn you from the inside out. Watch the smoke pour from your nose and mouth, see your eyes burst. The look upon his face must have betrayed his thoughts, for she began to scream. *"Quiet!"* he shouted.

Amazingly, she obeyed.

"I'm not a murderer," he said, his voice nearly inaudible. "I'm not like y'." Arythan spat on her. *Walk away before you change your mind,* he told himself. *She knows now. They'll all know. Not that it matters.* He stormed out of the hall. *My brother is still dead.*

"WELL? WHAT DID YOU LEARN?" The Jornoan was not oblivious to the fact his counterpart had returned visibly shaken and pale.

"He is who we believe he is," Sulinda Patrice said quietly.

Safir-Tamik watched her from his desk, his chin on his hands. "Why is he here?"

She did not look at him as she smoothed her hair and tried to compose herself. "He did not say."

"You mean to say you did not find out."

"I tried. For all appearances, he works for Garriker. Did you really believe he would tell me anything?" She glanced his way but continued to fuss with her hair.

Safir-Tamik said nothing.

"Even if he is a spy, we must continue to work with him. It's not as though we can do away with him." Sulinda sat down in her own chair and rubbed her brow.

"We will do what we must. He is nothing in the grand scheme of our plan." His dark eyes watched her every move. "You failed in your one task."

"I did not fail!" she snapped. "And we cannot touch him. He may well have value—value beyond what you can conceive."

"I find that hard to believe."

"You have not served our cause long enough," Sulinda said, irritated. "What I did learn from him was that we killed his brother, a notable Gray Watcher named Hawkwing." She shook her head. "It was an accident. The Marksman was over-zealous in his mission."

"What does this have to do with anything?" Safir-Tamik asked, his patience waning.

"Hawkwing was the last Gray Watcher known to possess the Key to the Archives. If we had access to the Archives, we would have all the knowledge we could dream of at our fingertips. We would rule Secramore."

"You suspect Hawkshadow now possesses the Key," he said, thoughtful.

"It is possible." She sighed. "So we need to watch him carefully. Take note of all he does."

"I hardly see how that will be fruitful in learning about the Key." He drummed his fingers on the desk. "We can extract the information from him."

Sulinda narrowed her eyes at him. "And have the Crown suspicious of our intentions? No. We will wait and see if he has other allegiances. There will be plenty of time to act."

"Do not misjudge him," Safir-Tamik said, rising. "Now that he is aware of what we know, he will not be careless or idle. And to forget about the prince would be a grave error. I will be certain you are held responsible for any failure to act."

Sulinda looked at him in indignation, but the Jornoan had turned his back to her, his mind already working in other directions.

14

TIMING

For the hundredth time Arythan glanced at the owl feather he had hung from a string at the mouth of the cave. *Where are you?* He sighed and leaned back against the rocky wall. Dawn would come before long, and he would have to return to the hall. Now that the Seroko would be watching him, he would not be able to escape to his hideaway as often as he would like. Nor would he be able to communicate with Othenis as freely as before. Nor would he be able to experiment on the Enhancement without drawing attention.

I can thank my anger for that. Not that I regret what I said. Not that anything has changed. He removed a crystal of Black Ice from a bag and stared at it in the pale blue firelight. *Only I can decide when change will come. Othenis is waiting. Victoria and Reiqo depend on it. It will end the Seroko's little endeavor of immortality. If I can just destroy it.*

The feather fluttered in a passing breeze. *Where are you? I may not have another chance to explain.* It was not like the leader of the Ice Flies to miss a calling, but Arythan knew he had been away for awhile, wasting time in Desnera. *I wonder if he knows about my exile.*

Time was his adversary, and here he was sitting idle. Waiting. *I can't afford to wait.*

Arythan stood, Ice in-hand, and moved outside the cave. He walked a distance to where he had generated the storm and danced with the wind. He had learned more in that moment than he had in the years he had spent with the wizards in Mystland. Since then, he had felt a different sort of harmony with his magic and with the elements.

He set the crystal upon a rock, and it looked like a hole in the landscape. It was not an element. It was a combination of life and death, Light and Shadow, merged into one object. Arythan rubbed his chin. It was Brann Alwin, of all people, who had intrigued him by what he had said. *I'm not a wizard. I cannot create anything new.*

"'The elements cannot be combined. They oppose each other,'" Arythan murmured. "I 'ave to work with them as they are." He smiled and shook his head. "Just like a wizard to be wrong."

Fire needed air to burn. The earth was full of moisture. Storms were a combination of water, air, pressure, and charges—the ultimate orchestration of elements. The elements were dependent, not opposing. They could be worked in combination, but could he combine them to create something new? He had learned how to dance, but these were new steps entirely.

Arythan sat down and closed his eyes, the image of the crystal solid in his mind. Surrounding him was rock, frozen water, and cold. Rock and water—one was stubborn, rigid, and crumbly, and the other was slippery, fluid, and undefined. Neither element was his favorite, but he had come to know their nature, and he understood the energy surrounding each. Could he make them dance with one another? Even for just a moment?

As he tapped into the resources around him, it became clear that he would not be able to produce "water rocks" by physically combining the elements. In fact, the whole idea was stupid and likely impossible. What he needed was purely the *energy* of earth and water—a fusion of potential force directed at the Ice on the rock. The difficulty was coaxing that energy around him and forcing it to mingle. They were like oil and water; what they needed was a binder—a medium that would hold them together.

His entire body trembled with effort, and a growing pain burned in his chest. He could feel the energy swirling and racing around him, but he was not sure if it was dancing or churning. The pain spread from his chest to his shoulders, feeling much like the tearing of a muscle—only deeper. He ground his teeth and exerted more effort toward the crystal. The vibration in the air began to change. Something was happening. The energy spiked with vigor, and with a sudden burst it—

"'S OUR FINAL SENTENCE. Y' both bloody know it." The brute picked his teeth from atop his horse as the trio plodded along. "We're sent to a bloody mud pit to watch Frostbite dig up rocks. Tha's what we're good for, mates. Nuthin'."

Hunter and Tigress did not glance back at him, so Dagger continued.

"And after all we did for 'Is Mighty 'Ighness, Ol' Garri shows is gratitude just fine." He spat out whatever he had dislodged from his tooth. "Still waitin' for that bloody arrow to 'it its mark. 'S gonna 'appen. Maybe not today, but 'twill. Mikey 'as no need for us, so if daddy 'unts us down, 'oo's to know, eh?"

Still no response.

"Y' wanna know what I think? I think we're worth mor'n that. I think we oughta go rogue. Leave this bloody ghostyard an' 'it the Ring. We can even do it 'onest. Like the ol' days, Kitten. Then we keep our skins, an' we're outta sight o' the bloody Garrikers."

At last Hunter turned to scowl at him. "You speak of treason."

"'Tain't treason, y' nit. Garri let us go."

"You would abandon Thorn?" Tigress asked. "He is as much a part of our group. He bears the mark."

Dagger shrugged. "So does Frosty. But both o' them're committed, luv. Mikey's got Banen onna leash as 'is pers'nal protector. Frostbite's 'ere playin' in the dirt. We gotta think of ourselves."

"You do that exceedingly well," Hunter said. "If we were without value, His Highness the Prince would have dismissed us. As it is, we have been charged with this duty to protect the royal investment."

"From 'oo?" Dagger bellowed, incredulous. "From a few Guild wizards? From some pesky flies? 'Oo bloody cares?"

"For all that it seems," Tigress began, "there may be more to this assignment than we have been told. Crow will have the answers for us. 'Til then, I want no further discussion of 'going rogue.' We don't need more enemies, and I'd like to read the hand we've been dealt. Got it?"

Before an answer or a protest could be issued, the earth trembled, and the horses spooked. What sounded like thunder echoed in the nearby peaks, but the clouds that night were scattered and thin.

"What in bloody Lorth was that?" Dagger cried, jerking the reins to control his horse.

They stared into the distance as if waiting for more to happen. "Avalanche," Tigress said, spurring her mount forward. They continued through the pass and into the Ice Plains under the pall of silence. Even though it was night and the few occupants of the Plains were undoubtedly asleep, there was a stillness and a vacancy that permeated the atmosphere. Buckets and shovels lay abandoned, half-submerged in mud. The stable, wizards' dorm, cook's house, and other buildings were dark and showing signs of neglect.

"As I said," Dagger muttered, "ghostyard."

Tigress had them shelter their horses at the stable and continue on foot. They entered the wizards' dormitory without the aid of candlelight, their footsteps echoing down the hall as they searched the cells for the mage.

"I don't think 'e's 'ere," Dagger said. "We almost checked 'em all."

"Where else would he be?" Hunter asked.

"Wherever he wants," Tigress answered.

"That's 'elp, Kitten."

"Excuse me."

The new voice was cold and impatient. It belonged to a broad-shouldered man in a robe. He bore a candle in his free hand; his other arm was folded across his chest. "Most would think twice before intruding upon a medori dorm."

"We are here on the order of Prince Michael," Tigress said. "We are seeking our companion, Arythan Crow."

The wizard moved closer, inspecting each of them. They were garbed in their black uniforms except for their masks, and Brann Alwin gave a nod of recognition, though his face remained hard. "A visit from the syndicate. An interesting hour to arrive."

"We travel when travel is most convenient," Hunter said.

"For you. For me, this is an inconvenience. I work here, and I value my rest."

"We've been stationed here with Medoriate Crow," Tigress said in a monotone, though the corner of her mouth twitched upward when she saw the wizard frown.

"Is he not in his cell?" Alwin asked, suspicious.

"It would seem he—" Hunter did not finish his thought, for a familiar wiry figure slipped in the door like a shadow.

"What?" Arythan asked, stopping a distance away.

"Apparently you have visitors," Alwin said.

"I see them."

"Were you expecting them?"

"Does it matter? They're 'ere."

"Then I will leave you to contend with them," the wizard said. He gave them all a final glower before disappearing into the dark with his candle.

"Where were y'?" Dagger demanded and none too quietly.

"Outside," Arythan said, and slipped back through the door.

The trio looked at one another before following him. He led them to the dining hall where he sat at a charred table, his hat low upon his brow.

"Where's the beer?" Dagger asked, and Tigress punched him.

The hearth lit itself once they were all seated. Only then could they see the dirt upon the mage, his torn clothes, the small cuts upon his face. He took his hat off and ran a hand through his hair, further disheveling himself.

"I assume you will explain all this," Tigress said, though her tone was lightened by her curiosity.

"Yeah, well..." Arythan shook his head and gave a short laugh. "Welcome to m' personal nightmare. If y're 'ere to stay, I'm sorry."

"'E's been at the ale," Dagger said, his eyes narrowed.

"No," Arythan said, his face buried in his hands. "I've been in the mountains."

"You caused the avalanche," Tigress said.

"Prob'ly."

"You do not remember?" Hunter asked.

"I blacked out." Arythan lifted his head. "Why *are* y' ere?"

"Mikey sent us to waste our—"

"To watch over the Plains," Tigress interrupted.

"Really?" The mage gave another short laugh that terminated in a sigh.

"What is the truth, Crow?" she said, her eyes even with his.

"The truth, Cap'n, is that our 'business associate' can't be trusted."

"You mean the Merchants' Guild." She folded her arms. "I was never under the impression we *did* trust them."

"Michael secretly signed a contract with them," Arythan said in a low voice. "The king doesn't know, but 'tis the reason I'm still 'ere with them. 'S all a grand secret."

"Which means we're all likely to be strung up if Garri finds out," Dagger said, and Tigress shushed him.

"'S not what it seems," Arythan continued. "The Guild is a guise. These blokes, they're the Seroko."

Hunter's expression remained blank, but Dagger and Tigress exchanged a look. "Are you certain?" she asked.

"I was there when the contract was signed. 'Twas Michael 'oo told me."

Tigress frowned. "So the prince knows who he's dealing with."

"'E knows their name," Arythan said, "but I don't think 'e knows their nature."

"I do not understand," Hunter said. "What is this 'Seroko'?"

"A very powerful and clandestine criminal organization," Tigress told him. "If you walk down a street lined with twenty shops, the Merchants' Guild will have ten marked with their symbol. Of those ten, five may have a direct connection to the Seroko and not even know it."

"Kitten n' me tussled with 'em when we ended one o' their street rats," Dagger said, and took a hit from the jack. "We were 'ired to take care o' things, and once we did, we sawr blokes following us. More an' more, 'til we was surrounded. They kicked the shit outta us an' took us to some shadow-faced bloke in a dark room. 'E asked 'oo we worked for, an' since we liked livin', we told 'im. 'E took our money an' let us go. Not a day later, the bloke 'oo 'ired us was found with 'is guts torn out."

"I saw an entire town fold beneath their weight," Tigress said. "The merchant families refused to pay their dues, and the town was blockaded. All supply wagons were intercepted, robbed, and sent back. If anyone tried to leave, they disappeared. When the town was on the brink of starvation, the Seroko set fire to their fields. There was nothing left."

In the grave silence that followed her tale, Arythan spoke in a low voice. "They killed m' brother."

"Why?" Dagger asked.

"'E knew about a secret place," Arythan said, quieter still. "An' when they took me as bait, 'e gave 'is life for mine."

Hunter stared at them all in disbelief. "How can such a faction not be brought to justice?"

"Didn't y' listen?" Dagger asked, smashing out his jack on the table. "They're everywhere. Like bloody ants. Y' squash one, they swarm all over y'. Better y' don't ask, 'cuz then y' don't know."

"I can't turn a blind eye," Arythan said. "I won't."

"Well," the brute said, "when y' decide to get y'r revenge, tell me. I'll make sure I'm long gone."

"A true coward," Hunter scoffed.

"A wise bloke." Dagger pointed to his head. "An' one 'oo's still alive."

"You look out for yourself," the giant said to him, "but Crow has a family. He should not waste his life with thoughts of revenge."

Arythan clenched his fist. "They know me, but they don' know about Tori. They can't find out."

"They know you?" Tigress asked.

"I didn't know it, but I did a job for them," he said, shame weighing upon his words. "As a thief."

"After they killed y'r brother?" Dagger asked, astounded.

"I didn't know," Arythan said, his eyes blazing.

"Enough," Tigress said. She closed her eyes and folded her hands. "The prince has good cause behind us being here."

"Why?" Dagger asked, another jack in-hand. "Because they're likely to kill a Crow?"

The captain opened her eyes. "Because they are capable of far worse than murder."

~

ARYTHAN DID NOT SLEEP that night. He had too much to consider. Instead he sat at his desk, distantly focused upon the white-encrusted crystal in front of him. Whatever magic he had used to change the Ice had met with moderate success. That was to say, *something* happened. The white residue was just that—a surface phenomenon. But it had been part of the crystal, of that he was certain. He had initiated a change—even if it was only visible on the exterior of the Enhancement. He spent much of the night scraping the residue into a bowl and testing its properties. His conclusion was that the substance was equivalent to ash. It was inert, and he felt nothing from it in the way of magical energy.

I am still missing the binder—that extra element that would make this work completely. I would bet my life that my Shadow would have been the answer, but I will never know. He ran a hand through his hair. *No, I can't lament what I no longer possess. But if that would work...* Arythan closed his eyes. *All I need to save my family, and I no longer have it.*

He rubbed the powder between his thumb and forefinger. "If I want it badly enough, I can do it. I just 'ave to work 'arder. If I go at it longer, I can work past the surface." The more he considered it, the more it seemed like a failure in his determination that he did not succeed the first time.

I'll have to tell Othenis I've found our solution. Somehow I'll have to reach him. Meanwhile, I should work at this more. And he knew just how he would practice—right under the noses of his teammates. They knew nothing of magic to suspect his intentions, and they would likely keep Brann Alwin at a distance. The situation was perfect.

"Crow."

He turned at the sound of Tigress's voice, instinctively covering the crystal with a rag. She regarded him suspiciously. "You have not slept, have you?"

"What?"

"You have been up all night."

"Sun up already?"

The captain folded her arms.

"Am I late?"

"Crow." She sighed. "We've been here before, but I thought we'd start a routine round. I need you to update us on the status of the facilities."

"I'd be delighted." He set his hat atop his head and stood.

"Afterwards, you might consider some sleep. I am starting to doubt your sanity."

Arythan nodded. "Fair enough."

Tigress motioned for him to follow. "The others are awake. They're not in the best of moods."

"What mood are they in?"

She did not respond as she led the way outside to where Hunter and Dagger waited by a wagon. They did not say a word; they did not even look in their direction. "Look alive," Tigress said and swatted Dagger on the back. "We're here, and you better get used to it."

The brute grumbled something under his breath and narrowed his eyes at Arythan.

It was a relatively silent walk around the premises: to the dining hall, then the stables. He showed them where the laborers stayed, and then, with some hesitation, led them towards the medic's ward. He stopped at a distance. "Tha's where they stay. The Seroko," he said in a low voice.

"Ain't that part o' the inspection?" Dagger asked, already walking in the direction of the building.

"He is aching for mischief," Hunter said.

Tigress headed after Dagger, not to stop him but to join him.

Hunter shrugged and followed, and Arythan trailed behind them. He could not imagine what they hoped to accomplish other than peering through the windows. He was not particularly in the mood to encounter his enemies—not after his last meeting.

As they came nearer, however, Arythan's attention was drawn to the darkness inside, the broken glass, the busted door. Tigress looked back at him as if to confirm that the ward had not always been in such disrepair. He frowned and shook his head.

She made a gesture to follow her, and she cautiously, soundlessly, slipped through the gap in the doorway. The space was dark, but there was enough light to distinguish a figure splayed ventrally upon the floor. Tigress bent down and brushed the victim's hair aside to see if she could detect any life. Dagger and Hunter went ahead to check the adjoining room.

Arythan stared as the scene unfolded, his thoughts spinning. He crouched beside Tigress. "Sulinda Patrice," he murmured. "One o' the two Seroko stationed 'ere."

"She's dead," Tigress said flatly. She rolled the body onto its back. "Just starting to get stiff." Their eyes roved over the corpse. "No blood. No visible wounds."

Yes, but look at her face... Sulinda's eyes were wide—nearly bulging, her mouth twisted and agape—an expression of shock or horror if Arythan ever saw one.

"Magic?" Tigress asked.

"Depends on 'oo killed 'er," he said. He wished he could say he felt remorse, but he did not. Even to feel a sense of justice might have been appropriate, but Arythan felt nothing at all. *Where is her partner?*

"Oi, we found anotha," Dagger said as he and Hunter dragged a man into the room.

Arythan narrowed his eyes at Safir-Tamik, who seemed barely conscious. The Jornoan bore a nasty wound upon his temple, and

Arythan was almost jealous he was not the one who had walloped him.

His teammates set the Jornoan near Sulinda Patrice. Safir-Tamik did not stir.

"He could be a witness," Hunter said.

"Or the murderer." All eyes turned to Arythan. "She was 'is partner."

"So he is with the Seroko," Tigress said, now focused on the man. "Why would he kill one of his own?"

Arythan scowled. "Because 'e's a nice bloke." *Or because he was unhappy with how his lady handled the situation with me. Or maybe he was just having a bad day. I'm sure he has his reasons.*

"We should not create our own conclusions before he has a chance to speak," Hunter said.

"Why not?" Dagger asked. He had started anxiously pacing the room. "We 'ave nuthin' to do with these blokes. If they wanna kill each other, fine. 'S no thorn in our side. I don't like that we're 'ere with 'em now. What if 'e decides to blame us? 'Oo's to say otherwise? The Seroko—tha's their style." He stopped and stared at his teammates. "We got no protection now. We'd 'ang for sure."

"Enough, Dagger." Tigress stood. "If anyone saw us come here and then witnessed us leave, we would only incriminate ourselves further. We need to hear what this man would say."

"An' if 'tisn't the right thing, we kill 'im," the brute added.

Tigress frowned.

I'm with him, Arythan thought. *And I doubt I would feel any remorse.*

Safir-Tamik groaned, and his eyelids fluttered.

"'Ere we go," Arythan muttered, and all of them waited.

The Jornoan's dark eyes moved around the room, from the syndicate, to Sulinda's body, and finally to Arythan. They remained upon the mage for some time before turning back to the corpse. "You are Garriker's men," he said weakly.

Tigress ignored the statement. "What happened here?"

"It's obvious," Safir-Tamik said. "The Ice Flies murdered my companion."

"I thought the Ice Flies were gone," Tigress said.

"Then you fell for their trap," the Jornoan returned. He gingerly touched the wound upon his head.

"Y' seem really broken up about this," Dagger blurted, and Tigress flashed him a dark look.

"What do you expect of me? Tears? Sobbing?" Safir-Tamik snapped. "This is a matter of business. I am fortunate to escape with my own life." He winced and eased his head against the wall.

"I liked 'im better without 'is wits," Dagger grumbled.

Safir-Tamik scowled at him. "You have arrived too late to be of any use."

"We serve the Crown," Tigress said, "not the Guild. Your protection was never our responsibility."

"Interesting." The Jornoan had returned his focus to Arythan, who remained a blank slate. "I understood that you were to defend this territory and the king's investment. Yet you allowed these marauders to infiltrate this site and jeopardize the lasting agreement between the Crown and the Merchants' Guild."

"Then your understanding is wrong," Tigress said.

"Is it?" His dark eyes flashed to her. "I can write a letter to my overseers to inform them of this situation. They will demand an investigation, and I am certain the prince will be discomforted by the attention."

Tigress lifted her chin.

"Or," the Jornoan said easily, "You can do your job and investigate on the Crown's behalf."

"What good will it be for us to investigate when you witnessed the crime?" she asked. "You know who is responsible."

"And should you not try to apprehend them?" Safir-Tamik bore into her. "Or will you do nothing for your liege?"

"Perhaps that is a question best answered by him," Tigress challenged.

"If you think that is what is best," he said snidely, knowing they were cornered.

Tigress turned to Hunter. "Ride back to Crag's Crown. Inform the prince of what has happened and await his instructions." She motioned for Dagger and Arythan to follow her outside.

"You are leaving?" Safir-Tamik called after her.

"We have to investigate this matter," she returned with a flavor of sarcasm.

"What of this corpse?"

"Last I saw, there were shovels in the mud pits." Then they left the Jornoan behind.

Arythan could tell Tigress was furious. Even when Safir-Tamik was almost certainly the culprit, he had a way of gaining the advantage over his enemies. Already Arythan knew their search would turn up empty, just as it had before. The only question was how Michael would treat the situation. Murder in his territory would leave him indebted to the Seroko. How could he smooth out this wrinkle, if he could smooth it at all? What would the Seroko ask as compensation?

"You were right, Crow," Tigress said in a low voice. "He is a murdering bastard."

Not my words exactly, but nicely phrased. Now what?

They headed for the stable. "We have to tread more carefully than ever," she said. "Let's hope Prince Michael has the conviction his father once had, or Cerborath will crumble beneath our feet."

Arythan was both surprised and relieved by her statement. Surprised that she should voice her fear so openly, relieved that at least one other person recognized just how powerful an enemy Michael had allied himself with.

15

OUT COMES THE TRUTH

T*here was something else...* His hat was atop his head, his basket was in his hand… *I know there was something else.*

"You look as though you're troubled," a man said, coming up beside him.

Erik barely glanced at him, trying to focus his thoughts. "I just need a moment," he murmured, looking at his empty basket.

"Are you looking for this?"

Erik turned to him, his eyes lighting upon the knife in the man's hand. "Ah, that is just the thing!" He took it gratefully. "My name is Erik Sparrow." He held out his hand.

The man's face clouded in confusion. "It's me, Sparrow. Firik."

"Firik," Erik echoed, uncertain.

"You're trying to play a joke on me," Firik said, a slow smile settling upon his face. "That sense of humor you have…" He shook his head and patted Erik's shoulder. "Better get started before the heat settles in."

Erik watched him walk away. *Firik. I must work with him. Or work for him? One or the other.* He brushed the thought away and headed for the fireberry shrubs. With a quick bite of the knife, he severed the ripened fruit from the woody stems and tossed them into his basket. He kept his eyes on the berries and deliberately began to hum a tune Catherine had taught him. The words came only in bits and pieces in his head, but at least the melody was memorable.

A fly bit his arm, and he swatted it, watching the blood well from where it broke the skin. *Do not look up,* he told himself, and then he went back to work. "Spring is born from Winter's sorrow," he murmured as the lyrics pattered down upon him like scattered raindrops from an overcast sky.

"Blossoms amidst the snow…" A bird flitted above him, and he made the mistake of watching it. *No, no—now you've seen them. You fool. Now they will never leave.* His gaze fell upon his audience, a strange conglomeration of a dozen or so people who often appeared to stand and watch him soundlessly. *Not that they ever truly leave. The old man brings new friends when he sees fit.*

Erik returned to the berries. "Amidst the snow," he repeated. *I may have already said that line.* "When in time they turn to the sun, they…they…" He rubbed his brow. "What is it you want?" he whispered. "Just tell me why you haunt me. Do I know you? How do you know me? What do you want of me?" he pleaded.

The specters remained fixated upon him.

"I don't understand," he cried, clenching his hands and accidentally drawing blood with the blade of his knife. "Do you seek to drive me mad?"

It was so very hard to ignore them. Not when he saw them every day. They watched him when he ate, they watched him as he drifted to sleep, they watched him at work and at home. They were always watching. Always. And try as Erik might to hide the fact that he saw them, he knew that Catherine watched him as well. She watched him with deepening concern and brooding silence. What she must think, he could only imagine.

Calm yourself. You must calm yourself. He drew a deep breath and slowly exhaled. He set the knife in the basket and faced his intruders, determined to voice his theory. "You are here because I knew you somehow. When I was a minstrel, perhaps even as a youth. There must be some unresolved matters between us, that you should appear to me. I beg you make them known. We want the same: we want peace."

Erik waited for a response, but as the silence persisted, he sighed and began to wrap his bleeding hand in the bandana from his neck. There was a stir in the air, and despite his growing deafness, he still heard it as though it had been spoken into his ear.

"Remember!"

With the word came a chill that pricked the flesh of his arms and triggered a shudder. His mouth fell open, a chasm with nothing beyond. He looked up, and they were all gone. All but one: the old man. As Erik stood, stunned, the old man advanced without taking a step. The misty figure steadily dissolved in its slow approach, but the instant it was upon him, it passed through him, permeating him like water beneath his skin.

Erik gasped, the cold filling his nostrils and lungs. The field had vanished, and in its stead was a blustery world of snow and rugged earth. A cloaked form was crouched above him on a precipice, like a mountain cat waiting to leap upon its prey. He tried to see the face beneath the hood, but the eyes that stared back at him were not Human. They burned like violet embers—from wide, foxlike eyes.

The non-Human stood, and a pair of white, leathery wings unfurled in the whirling snow. The wind threw back its hood to reveal a white-skinned, white-haired creature with all the appearances of a young man save for a set of long and tapered ears and a smile comprised of sharp teeth.

Terrified, Erik turned and started to run. The creature's silhouette loomed above him in the sky as it soared on those dragonlike wings. Erik stumbled and gasped for air. His legs refused to carry him, and the creature descended like a vulture.

But it did not descend upon him. With its sharp claws it tore into a body near him, and blood stained all that had been white. Erik realized there was not one body but many—faceless men that had already fallen victim to this monster's dark intentions. Frozen in horror, he watched it rip the body apart.

It lifted its head to glare at him, and then it spoke, but he could not understand it. He knew, somehow, that it was a warning. Then the creature turned upon him.

Erik cried aloud, kicking and pushing with all his strength as he was pinned to the ground. His attacker was stronger.

"Stop, Mr. Sparrow! Stop!" it cried, but it no longer looked like a white-skinned monster. It was a man smeared in blood.

Erik stopped struggling, but he could not catch his breath. His vision dimmed, his ears were ringing, and his limbs tingled.

"What by Lorth has taken you?" the man cried. They were surrounded by half a dozen others, and they were in the field once more.

"It was a monster," Erik wheezed. "It had fangs and glowing eyes…."

The on-lookers turned to one another in disbelief.

"It would have torn me apart," he said, then gaped at the blood on the man restraining him.

"He's mad. He's gone mad," someone said.

"There's no monster, Mr. Sparrow," said another. "Firik saw you fall, and then you started to thrash around. He was sure you'd hurt yourself."

Erik's eyes had not left the man above him. "Do I… Do I know you?"

"I'm Firik," the other returned, disconcerted. "You work for me." He looked over his shoulder at the men. "Someone fetch Orilian. We need to get him inside."

"I don't understand," Erik said, but the ringing in his ears had intensified, and he heard none of the explanation offered him. His limbs had gone numb, and spots had clouded his sight. He closed his eyes so that it would all go away; instead it was his consciousness that left him.

~

WHILE IN THE blanket of his darkness, Erik dreamed of light. He reached toward a bright and shining beacon—a source of illumination that warmed him with vivacious energy. Strength flowed into him, revitalized his body and clarified his thoughts. Was this what youth felt like? He did not know; he could not remember. Regardless, the way he felt now was euphoric, and it sent him reeling.

But the light began to fade, and with it went all the life that flowed through him. A shadow settled over him, and he felt drawn and weak. His spirit withered, and years weighed upon him before the eyes of Death. It was so very cold, and as the shadow deepened, so did his longing for the light. But the light was gone.

It was Erik's own shivering that woke him. He was in a bed, covered with a knitted blanket that should have warmed him. It could not, however, reach the coldness inside him—the creeping decay that would one day claim him.

The pretty young healer, Orilian, was wringing out a cloth over a bowl. As soon as she noticed he was awake, she hurried to his side. "Mr. Sparrow, how are you feeling?"

"I don't know," he said weakly. "Foolish, I suppose." Just beyond her, the old man stood in the corner, watching him.

"The men said you were seeing monsters," she said, and placed the cool, damp cloth upon his brow.

Erik managed a fragile smile. "Too much sun, perhaps."

Orilian gazed at him a long time. "Mr. Sparrow," she said, "you cannot continue like this."

"I don't understand," he said, picking at the blanket.

"I think that you do," she said sadly. "Perhaps too well. Firik Lasting has decided not to allow you back in the fields."

"Who is he to say how able I am?" Erik asked, hurt.

"He is your employer," Orilian said. "And he is afraid something will happen to you. The others you work with were very upset. They harbor no ill will toward you, but they had never seen anyone in such a state."

Movement outside the door caught his attention, and Erik glimpsed Catherine standing with Halgon Thayliss in the adjoining room. Her face was careworn, her features burdened by sorrow. She looked vulnerable, lonely. An arm moved protectively around her shoulders. Halgon's arm. She did not ease away from him, nor did she fold into his shelter.

She is so very strong, but she cannot endure this alone. I have only caused her grief in my weakness. He watched as Halgon's hand soothed her, gently rubbing up and down her shoulder. Erik turned away, unable to witness any more. This was a new feeling—one that tore at his heart in a way that made him physically ill.

"Ms. Lorrel is here for you," Orilian said, having followed his gaze.

"Too late," Erik murmured.

"Mr. Sparrow?"

He looked at her with glassy eyes. "I am too late for her," he said.

The healer held his hand, a knowing look upon her face. "She loves you, Mr. Sparrow. You know she does."

Erik did not reply. In another moment, Catherine appeared at the door, and Orilian gave her farewell. He could not look at her—not when he had failed her, not when he was the cause of her grief. All he could feel was shame. "I'm sorry."

Catherine did not reply. She sat on the bed beside him and smoothed the hair from his brow. The silence was oppressive. He wished she would say something—anything. The fact that she could not find words tore at him even more.

"I would like to walk along the shore with you," he said, finally accepting her gaze. "We could watch the sun set."

Her reaction was terrible. Her eyes sprang with tears, and she shook her head. "I would watch every sunset with you until the end of my days if that would help us."

"What is it you wish of me?" he asked, desperate.

"Nothing, Erik," she said, taking a breath. "This is not your fault. I wish you were well, but you are not."

"I…I know how this must upset you…" he said slowly.

"But does it not upset you? The ghosts? The visions? I know you see them. I see you staring—"

"Yes! They are there. They are always there," Erik cried. "And every day I try to ignore them. But every day I feel I know myself less and less. The things that I kept here—" he tapped his head, "—they fade. I fear that everything will one day fade, and there will be naught left of me." He tore at his hair, agonized. "And I fear you will be left alone with this empty shell."

Catherine clutched at his hands as though her grip would keep him from slipping from her. "I don't want to lose you," she wept. "I did all I could to keep you, and I thought it would be all right. I was wrong. All of it was wrong. I am so sorry."

Erik only heard part of what she had said, and it made little sense to him. He knew only that she had acknowledged this ending to be real. She shared his fears, but it made him feel no less alone. He freed a hand and brushed it across his own eyes, surprised that they, like hers, were damp. *So this is madness,* he thought. *Like a slow, rising wave that carries with it all reason, all knowledge. It will swallow me and all that I am into oblivion.*

Catherine attempted to clear her throat and dry her eyes. "Erik. Halgon has offered that we stay in his home, so that we could better see to you. You won't need to go back to the fields."

He nodded numbly.

"It was a difficult decision," she said. "But when I'm away, I do not want you to be alone."

I am *alone in this.* "I understand," he said quietly. "It is generous of him, to offer his home and his support."

"He means well, but so do I," she said, embracing him. "I will be with you. I promise."

As they held one another, Erik saw the old man in the corner watching them. *"Remember,"* he heard the specter say, and then it faded away.

"IT'S LATE," Diana Sherralin said to whoever was knocking at her door.

"'S me, Dianar."

"Arythan Crow," she muttered. "It's still late," she told him, though she opened the door. She blinked. "You *are* Arythan, aren't you?" He looked so much younger without the beard.

"Last I checked," he said. "Sorry about the hour." Arythan looked past her. "Can I come in?"

"Yes, of course," Diana said hastily and moved aside. She shut the door behind him and watched as he removed his hat, further intrigued by the short and tousled head of blond hair beneath it. "You, ah, look different."

"Hm?" He lifted his head from the paper that had spontaneously appeared in his hands.

Diana folded her arms. "I said you seem distracted."

"Always." The letter disappeared into his coat before he removed the clothing from his shoulders, hanging it on the back of a chair.

"What brings you here at this unusual hour?" She gestured for him to sit down. "Are you ill?"

Arythan hesitated before following her suggestion. He ran a hand through his hair, further messing it. "Y' may've 'eard, but m' wife is pregnant."

"Yes," Diana said. "Old news. Though I suspect she is ready to deliver soon."

Arythan pointed a finger at her and nodded.

"I wouldn't dare say you are nervous," Diana said, amused by his uncharacteristic behavior. "And I wouldn't dare say you have a favor to ask of me." She leaned against her counter and waited.

"I can trust y'," he said, and Diana smirked.

"That, Medoriate, is not how to begin."

"'S'truth, though," he said, his feet tapping upon the floor as he leaned forward in the chair. "With the king gone, I was 'oping y'ad the time to take a lil' trip to a country manor. Like a retreat o' sorts."

Diana turned to produce two cups and a ewer. "A retreat. And I would find the role of a midwife relaxing, right?"

"I will pay y' whatever y' want. I just want to make sure someone is there—in case I'm late."

"Oh." She handed him a cup. "I thought it might be because you know nothing of childbirth."

"An' that too." He peered into the cup. "What is this?"

Diana sipped from her cup. "My special mint tea. It will calm you."

"'Oo wants to be calm?"

"At this hour, I want *you* to be calm." She gestured for him to drink, and he did. "So if I pack and take the journey, leaving my shop behind, what do I gain from this venture—other than seeing your child greet the world, of course?"

Arythan licked his lips. "I said I'd pay y'. Unless y' want something else."

"Yes. Something else." Diana took another drink. "But will you honor my request?"

"I will," he vowed warily. "What do y' want?"

Diana pulled over a chair and sat across from him. "I know about your exile."

Arythan started to speak, but she held up a hand.

"I know you're not a murderer, though you took the blame for the incident. I know the other thugs are in exile with you, in the Ice Plains. I also know that you are at Prince Michael's mercy." She paused to allow him to speak.

"Y' know a lot," he said, impressed. "But I thought y' didn't buy into rumours."

"Well these would be statements of fact, would they not?" Diana asked. She set her cup down. "Since last we spoke, I have had much to think about."

Arythan frowned. "Y' were supposed to forget about what y' sawr."

"I can't forget it any more than you can relax about your pending child." She leaned toward him, and he drew back. "What is going on, Arythan? Are you a spy? Be honest with me."

He merely stared at her.

"I'm not trying to incriminate you."

"Don' know what that means."

"I'm not going to tell anyone. This is for me, because I want to know what sort of trouble you're in."

Arythan shrugged. "'Oo said I'm in trouble?"

Now it was Diana's turn to frown. "You want to be evasive? Fine. I'm in no great hurry to leave my cozy shop behind."

His expression softened. "Alright." He sighed. "Alright. For all the good it'll do y'. I wanted to spare y' the danger in this."

"Spare me the sparing," Diana said. "I know what I'm asking of you."

"But I don' know why," Arythan countered. "An' I'm guessing y' wont' tell me."

Diana merely waited for him to continue.

Arythan took a longer drink. "I'm 'elping the Ice Flies."

She nodded, hardly surprised.

"The Seroko—the Merchants' Guild—killed m' brother, an' so I'm 'elping the Ice Flies find a way to destroy the En'ancement."

"Even if it means betraying your friend, the prince?"

"'S nothing against Michael," Arythan said.

"Do you believe he will see it that way?"

The mage's expression did not change. "'E doesn't need to know."

Diana narrowed her eyes. "He doesn't need to know that you're working against him? If you destroy the Ice—which, by the way, I thought was impossible to destroy—you are being counterproductive to Cerborath's economic success."

"There's a bigger story 'ere," Arythan insisted. He downed the rest of his drink. "The Seroko 'ave another motive. They're using the Ice as a path to immortality."

Diana froze before she started to laugh. "You cannot be serious. Immortality? That is not even possible!"

His face darkened. "Until y' think about what the En'ancement is."

Her smile faded a little. "What is it?"

"The remains o' dead immortals."

"That makes even less sense," she said, her hands open. "If you are immortal, you can't die."

Arythan rubbed his forehead. "According to the immortal *I* knew, yeah, they *can* die. But if y' don' kill them, they can live a bloody long time. Apparently they all killed each other at some point, an' the Ice Plains were their battlefield. Magic corpses turned to crystal, and now we let blokes drink them in their wine."

She stared at him.

The mage leaned back, his hands behind his head. "Great story, eh? Michael doesn't know about this, an' 'tis better that way if I'm going to destroy it. 'E'll find another way to make Cerborath rich."

He yawned. "I did find a way to destroy it. 'S not easy, but I know I can do it."

"And once you do, you will label yourself an enemy of the Crown. What about Victoria? What about the child?" She bore into him. "Have you even thought this through? Or is revenge the only consideration you've had?"

"I thought it through," he snapped. "Othenis and the Flies are going to 'elp us leave once I destroy it. We'll be under their protection, living far away. 'S too dangerous for us to be 'ere."

"I'm surprised Victoria approves of this," Diana said, and then she caught his expression. "You haven't told her."

"Yet. She 'as a lot on 'er mind."

The healer let out a long breath. "So what's stopping you, Arythan? Why not enact your plan, destroy the Enhancement, and run away with your family?"

"'S all timing," he said, irritated. "An' I 'avent' been able to meet with Othenis yet. 'E doesn't know I'm ready." Arythan pulled out a jack and moved it between his fingers. "But 'e'll know soon," he said more to himself. "'E'll find the book, and 'e'll know."

"Book?"

"The Seroko 'ad a book to tell them where the Ice is underground. A map o' sorts. I stole it for them a long time ago, and now I stole it back."

"Would this be the same book that blinded you?" she asked, suspicious.

"The same. But Othenis knows about it. 'Tis safe in the cave, an' I didn't open it this time."

"Obviously, but if you stole it, and someone saw you…."

"No one sawr me," he said, exasperated. "Safir-Tamik was prob'ly burying 'is partner when I took it."

"What?"

"The Seroko murder each other, 'parently. I know 'e did it, but 'e's blaming the Flies."

Diana took a moment to process this disclosure. "Does Michael know?"

"The syndicate did a search," Arythan said, "just for show. There was nothing to find."

"Why would—all right—never mind. The more I ask, the more complicated this tale becomes. How is your head on straight? How many strings are tied to your fingers? All you need is for someone to pull the other end."

He sighed and looked up at her. "'Twill all be fine once I'm gone." He lit his jack and took a hit, but Diana did not protest. "Tori said she'd like to live away from the castle," he said softly. "I want to give 'er that peace. Our son, too."

"Son?"

Arythan smiled. "She's convinced 'tis a boy." He took another hit. "I lost m' family when my brother died. I never thought I'd 'ave another. I've been running alone for a long time."

Diana regarded him thoughtfully. "Believe it or not, you do have friends." It was her turn to sigh. "I will go to the manor, but I think you should consider telling Victoria about your plans. Regardless of the child, this is no small matter. If escaping the kingdom is what is best for your family's survival, then she will have to trust in you. I just hope you know what you are doing."

She expected him to grow angry or at least make some cocky remark, but he merely nodded. "Maybe you are ready for fatherhood."

"I don't feel ready."

"That's a start." Diana rose, collected his cup, and brought it to the counter. She heard him stir behind her.

"Dianar...."

"You don't have to thank me," she said lightly. "This is part of my work."

"Y' kept it," he said.

She blushed, following his gaze to the box of flavorings he had bought her. "I merely haven't had the chance to find a more suitable home for it." His hint of a smile made her feel even warmer. "Where are you headed?"

"I 'ave to go back to the Plains," he said, his words empty.

"Now? Your poor horse. You may do fine without sleep, but have mercy on the mare. You can stay here tonight and leave in the morning."

Arythan hesitated. "I should get back."

"And you will. In the morning. There's an empty cot right here." She dropped a folded blanket onto it. "It's no trouble. No more trouble than a late night visit."

His head bowed submissively. "Thank y'," he said.

She did not respond, moving about her shop as she tidied her herbs and bottles. When she glanced at him again, he was already asleep, bearing as peaceful an expression as she had ever seen on him. "I hope you find your way," she murmured and finally blew out the candles.

16

MESSAGES

The prince looked up from his dinner. "What do you mean, 'murder'?"

Hunter had already related the tale, but only now did Michael seem to truly register what had happened. "We conducted an investigation, Sire, but we found next to nothing."

"Dagger is a *tracker*," Michael said pointedly. "How did you find nothing?"

Banen smirked, and Michael glared at him.

"It was Lord Tamik's belief that the Ice Flies are responsible," Hunter said, "but we found no evidence of their passage." He had not—by order of the captain—related the suspicion that Safir-Tamik had committed the crime himself.

"We know they are masters of subterfuge," Michael said sarcastically, "but to fail at finding them *twice?* Where is your captain?"

"Back at the Plains, Sire."

"Yes, yes," Michael said, gesturing with his knife. "The Plains. Apparently I need to be there as well, to see that the Merchants' Guild does not point a finger at us for our incompetence in security."

"Sire, we had only arrived when the murder occurred. There had not been a chance to—"

"Enough," Michael snapped. "This is a delicate relation, and excuses will not do." He stabbed a piece of chicken and shoved it in his mouth, chewing furiously. He swallowed and took a gulp of wine to wash it down. "What of Crow? Is he still working? Where was he when this took place?"

Hunter's brow furrowed. "I believe he was in his quarters. I cannot speak for his activities, for I have not seen—"

"His activity with the Enhancement needs to continue," Michael insisted. He scarcely glanced at the members of his family at the table. "Banen and I will join you on your journey back," he said. "We will leave after the meal."

"Michael," Ladonna said softly, "Must you go tonight?"

"Jedinom's Sword, a man has been murdered," Michael said.

"Woman, Sire," Hunter corrected.

The prince waved his hand in indifference. "This is a threat to our operation. I will be there to set it right." He nodded to the giant. "Make certain my carriage is ready. We will meet at the gate."

Hunter bowed and left, and Michael found his brother eyeing him from across the table. "What is it, Banen? Please speak what is on your mind."

The younger prince shook his head. "There is nothing I have to say."

"Good. I would hate to think there is dissention in my ranks." Michael shoveled another mouthful of food. "I will not tolerate opposition."

TIGRESS AND DAGGER were little surprised by Prince Michael's late visit. They had been patrolling outside the medic's ward when they saw the carriage and a rider arrive outside the medori dorm, dark silhouettes against a darker landscape. Immediately they went to meet him and were little surprised by his first words.

"Where's Crow?"

Tigress met his gaze without expression. "He returned to the royal city, Your Highness."

"He did not report to me," Michael said.

"He was set to meet with Diana Sherralin. Prior to that, he aided in our search for the Ice Flies."

Michael bit his lip. "He should have continued the work I gave him. By whose authority did he leave? Yours or his own?"

Tigress did not hesitate. "He told me of his intentions before he left, Your Highness. I saw no reason to detain him."

Michael pointed a finger at her. "I will make this clear. *Your* role and the role of your elite is to protect this land and all that is in it. *His* role is to forward the production of the Enhancement. If Crow seems unclear about his duties here, I trust you will enlighten him."

"Yes, Sire."

"Wonderful. Now show me what you have found."

The B.E.S.T. escorted the two princes to the medic's ward, where Safir-Tamik promptly joined them.

"Your Highness," the Jornoan greeted, "I am pleased that you are here to give your attention to such a dire situation."

"Hunter informed me of the details of this unfortunate circumstance," Michael said. "I am deeply grieved at this tragedy. I am here to contend with what has been done and assure you that there will be no further question about security." He peered around the Jornoan to see the building. "The body...."

"Has been properly tended," Safir-Tamik said. "Your servants failed to find evidence of the perpetrators."

Tigress scowled. "Your Highness, the Ice Flies are known to

have medori forces in their ranks. They may have methods of concealing their trails we can't detect."

"If you claim your tracker is useless," Safir-Tamik said, "then your medoriate must be equally so."

Dagger emitted a growl, and Michael held up a hand. "Medoriate Crow is not here for defensive maneuvers."

"It would seem Medoriate Crow is not here at all," Safir-Tamik said.

Michael frowned. "That is none of your concern."

"I mean to say," Safir-Tamik persisted, "that I seldom see him on the premises."

The prince stared at him. "Mind your wizard, and I will mind mine," he said with finality.

"Very well, Your Highness."

"Might I expect to correspond with your superiors over this matter? I would like to reassure them that progress will continue in good faith. There will be no further incidents."

Safir-Tamik turned his dark stare upon the B.E.S.T. "Of that I have no doubt. I will communicate with my associates and inform you should there be a desire to meet."

Michael nodded, and as the syndicate escorted him from the ward, Tigress voiced herself in a low and careful tone. "We did find one trail, Your Highness, but Medoriate Crow admitted it was his."

Michael stopped. "Crow? What sort of trail? Where? For what purpose?"

Tigress elbowed Dagger. "'E said 'twas to get away from the wizards. 'E 'ates the bloody wizards, 'e says."

"A retreat?" Michael rubbed his chin.

"We should follow his trail," Banen said, speaking for the first time since his arrival.

Michael raised an eyebrow. "You seem eager to roam the mountains on a frigid night."

"I am merely curious," Banen said.

The elder prince nodded. "As am I. Show us the trail, Dagger."

"'S kind o' rough," he warned. "What I seen of it, ennaway."

Michael merely gestured for him to lead on, and so they steadily picked their way along the narrow, obscure trail that ascended into the mountains. As their altitude rose, night quickly advanced, and Tigress lit the lanterns she and Dagger had fetched from the wizards' hall.

"Lil' Frosty's got no fear o' heights," the brute muttered, peering down at the impenetrable shadows over the edge of the trail.

By the time they had reached the shelter where Narga was kept, most of them were out of breath and more than a little shaky. Tigress held the lantern over a bag of oats and a bundled blanket. "The horse climbs this," she said wryly.

"'S not a 'orse," Dagger said. "'S 'is bloody demon nag. Prob'ly 'as wings."

"Captain," Michael said, trying not to sound winded, "let's remain on-task."

Tigress nodded to Dagger, who detected the final leg of Arythan's trail. The thin lip hugging the mountainside was the only possible route the mage could have taken.

The brute cursed. "Let's get it over with."

"Mind your steps, Your Highness," Hunter warned Michael.

"Yes, I see," he replied tightly. Overindulgence in fine feasting had affected his shape as well as his endurance.

The wind and heavy breathing dominated the air until all five explorers had ducked inside the low and narrow opening of the cave. Several curses followed from those who were not as lean as the mage in question--which included the majority of the group.

"Quite an arrangement," Banen said as the lanterns pushed away the darkness, revealing blankets, remnants of victuals, and tracings of Wizard's Sand.

Michael said nothing, picking through the supplies as Tigress held the lantern above him.

"What are you looking for?" Banen asked.

"Just curious," Michael murmured. Folded in one blanket was a hard, rectangular object. He removed a book, motioning Tigress closer with the light. *"Herbs of the Northern Mountains,"* he read aloud, hefting the book in his hands. "Our Crow is quite the reader." Michael slid the book back inside the blanket, and as he did so, he felt another concealed object.

When he withdrew the chunk of Black Ice, he stared at it a bit longer. A peculiar white powder had formed on the outside of the crystals, and he rubbed it between his fingers, wondering what had caused it.

"What is it?" Banen asked.

"What does it look like?" Michael held up the crystal.

"Ice."

"Very good, brother." He tucked the crystal into his pocket and stood. "A retreat after all."

"From one wizard?" Banen asked.

"Crow dislikes wizards," Michael said. "And now that we have invaded his haven, we should leave it as we found it."

"All this way to leave again?" Banen crossed his arms, dissatisfied.

"Then help yourself to his dried fruit," Michael told him. He waved toward the entrance. "I, for one, am done with scaling mountains." He grunted as he crouched low at the entrance. "There will be no need to worry him over our intrusion."

Banen sighed and followed suit as they abandoned the cave.

WINTER STRUCK Cerborath like a hand across the face. It came one evening in the form of a relentless gale, and it brought with it an onslaught of snow. Arythan had been summoned from the Ice Plains by Prince Michael, though the letter never specified the purpose of the meeting. He had been hoping to re-attempt destruction of the Ice that night, but for what seemed like the hundredth time, his plans were postponed. Some sort of interruption always found a way between him and his project, whether it was Dagger's need to gamble, problems with the cooling of the crystals, or Tigress insisting upon a training session. Arythan found it mattered little; he could not reach his cave, and so he did not know if Othenis had found the book or the crystal he had deteriorated. Communication beyond the cave was too risky now that Safir-Tamik watched him with renewed interest.

What Arythan hoped was that Othenis was able to piece his clues together and now held close watch over Victoria at the manor. Arythan would leave with her in a heartbeat—as soon as the Ice Fly leader unleashed him to wreak destruction upon the Plains. But for now he was waiting and none-too-patiently.

Both he and Narga were a chilled and snowy mess when they arrived at Crag's Crown that night. Arythan took extra care to see her blanketed in a warm, clean stall with a few treats in her trough. He doubted he would be compensated so generously for his efforts in expedience during a blizzard. He was still shivering when he entered the Great Hall, only to find it empty.

"His Highness will see you in his study," the servant told him, holding out his arm for Arythan's hat and coat. The mage ignored the gesture, too stiff and cold to part with any of his layers. He did not care that he left a trail of snowmelt prints behind him.

The servant announced him through the door, and it was Banen who opened it from the inside, greeting Arythan with a heartfelt glower. The younger prince said nothing, however, as he stepped aside to allow the mage his entrance.

"Crow!" Michael greeted warmly. "You look a mess."

The elder prince, by contrast, could not look more comfortable. He was in a robe, reclining lazily in his velvet chair, his feet upon the desk before him. Arythan did not have to see the ewer or the glass to know he had been at the wine and likely the Enhancement as well. Michael's rosy face seemed a bit fuller since last Arythan had seen him, and it was clear he was taking his liberties very seriously as a king-to-be.

Arythan removed his hat and gave a short bow. "Y' sent for me, sir?"

"I did." Michael gestured to the blazing hearth. "Warm yourself, please. You resemble a corpse."

The mage needed no encouragement. He hovered near the flames, unable to shake the chill that had settled in his bones.

"The Festival of Kings is coming, my friend," Michael said to him, pouring them both a cup of wine. "Merely a couple months from now, which is no time at all." He smiled. "There is much to prepare." He gestured to Banen. "Hand Crow the letter."

"I am not your servant," Banen grumbled.

"I ask as a favor," Michael said, frowning. "You merely have to take it from me and give it to him."

"It might do you good to get up."

Michael sighed and turned to Arythan. "You see how he tries to darken my good spirits?" He removed his feet from the desk, slowly stood, and stumbled to the mage to deliver the letter. "Read it," he encouraged.

Arythan did not want to read it, but his eyes skimmed over the fine writing, discerning key words and phrases that caused his lips to part in surprise. He looked at Michael.

"Yes, yes, there you have it," he said and took the paper back. "My father will be returning to Cerborath for the festival for 'important matters,'" Michael said, pointing to the exact words. "Cornonation, Crow. This is to be my coronation."

"You behave like Riley," Banen said, referring to Michael's young son.

"Riley behaves like me, brother. And he does so because I am his father," the elder prince said. He turned back to Arythan. "I will need your help in seeing that this transition moves smoothly."

Arythan's brow furrowed, unsure how he could be of any use. As it was, the festival and the coronation were not nearly as stunning as the information shared at the end of the letter. "Y'ave a new brother," he said, unsure if Michael was purposely ignoring the arrival of the king's son.

"So I do. Prince Ryland of Desnera," Michael said with an easy smile. "Little Prince Ryland. I am sure there is much celebrating in the Emerald Hall. I bear no ill will toward him or his parents. He has his day, and I will have mine."

Banen gave a loud sigh. "I hate to be the voice of reason, but how is Crow going to be of any use to you?"

"He is my medoriate," Michael said, retaking his chair and the leisurely position in which Arythan had found him.

"Ah, yes," Banen sneered. "The medoriate Father had exiled for disloyalty and murder."

"Crow is only exiled from Desnera. I am happy to take all that Father throws away," Michael said. "No offense, Crow."

"None taken," Arythan said, "But maybe 'e's right. I wouldn't want the king to see me an' change 'is mind about the ceremony."

Michael pushed the cup to the edge of the desk, in Arythan's direction. "Honestly, what do you think my father expected of you? Your role is here, with the Enhancement, supporting our kingdom. Your wife is here, as are your teammates. How could he not expect you to come to serve me?"

Arythan withheld a wince when his wife was mentioned. Of course Garriker knew exactly where his family was, and it was a fact that made him more than a little uneasy. The king had not had him hunted down yet, but for Arythan to let his guard fall for a moment could result in disaster. "'E may know it, sir, but 'e doesn't 'ave to see me."

"That is ridiculous." Michael gestured for him to drink. "My father is not so emotionally guided. I want you at the ceremony. You have supported me in our accomplishments with the Enhancement. And if you feel so inspired, you might demonstrate a little magic for the occasion."

"It is a serious event," Banen voiced. "Not an occasion for tricks and marvels. Father will never allow it."

Michael shrugged. "Father has done many deeds of which I did not think him capable. A little magic is hardly a disruption to tradition. Regardless, I want Arythan present." He looked at the cup in the mage's hand. "Drink up, my friend."

"Sir…there's Ice in it," Arythan said, watching the sparkling swirls move atop the wine.

"Oh. Oh, I must have…" Michael reached for the cup, and Arythan handed it back to him. "I am sorry, Crow." He poured the mixture into his own cup and refilled Arythan's from the ewer.

"No, thank y'." Arythan could see Michael was well on his way to drunkenness, and he would rather leave Banen to contend with that situation.

"Very well." The future king of Cerborath hiccupped and drank some more. "Perhaps you will be up for a duel later."

"I don' know if that's a good idear, sir."

Michael seemed disappointed. "I miss the duels, the challenge. Eventually we must battle. I have yet to win against you."

Arythan nodded.

There was a knock upon the door, and Banen admitted a messenger.

Michael held out his hand for the letter, but Banen frowned and shoved it at Arythan. The mage blinked and broke the seal. He unfolded the paper, and as he began to read, his hands started to tremble. Whatever warmth he had drawn from the fire left him in a breath.

"By the Sword, you are pale. What is it, Crow?" Michael demanded.

“’S coming,” he breathed.

“What is—oh. Oh.” Michael struggled to push up from his chair. “By all means, go! Go now!”

Arythan needed no encouragement. He bolted from the room and did not stop until he reached the stable.

17

A REBEL IS BORN

Narga had a fine sense for urgency, and the spirited mare was not one to neglect an opportunity to gallop. What hindered the pair most was the growing storm—a storm that seemed to feed off Arythan's anxiety. The wind hurled the snowflakes at them in a blinding wall of fury, and Arythan could scarcely discern the boundaries of the road. The snow melted on contact and froze again in the biting air, layering rider and horse in clumps of ice. Arythan let Narga pace herself, and when she tired, he dismounted and walked beside her. She would push him with her nose when she was ready to run again, and such was how they fought the blizzard, stretch by stretch.

A dim and flickering light caught Arythan's attention from the side of the road. He was amazed that anyone with more sanity than him would be on the road in such a storm. Neither he nor Narga had any intention of slowing, but as they drew nearer, there was a strange sound, and the mare suddenly reared high into the air, her ears flat against her head. Arythan, fighting his exhaustion, had not been ready, and he was thrown clear from the saddle.

He landed on his stomach, the impact against the frozen

ground like a fist in his gut, snatching the air from his lungs. As he lay gasping, he saw the obscured form of a man grappling for the reins of his horse. Arythan tried to focus his magic, to do anything to stop the thief, but the storm pulled at him harder than he could bridle it. It was too much.

In another moment, the man was in the saddle, galloping back the way Arythan had come.

Nigqora.

He stood slowly, realizing the extent of the damage done as pain surfaced on the right side of his body. His coat was torn along his arm, his trousers worn through on the side of his leg, where the frozen ground had abraded the surface of his skin. He could not see the wounds, but the cold air burned wherever the raw flesh was exposed. *Sieqa.*

Arythan took a step forward and found he had twisted his ankle as well. The joint nearly buckled beneath him, and he sighed. *This is no different than Summerfall,* he thought bitterly. *Tori is waiting, and I have to limp my way there only to be too late to see my son born.* He gingerly retrieved his hat from the road. *And my bloody horse has been stolen.*

In an explosion of anger, he erupted in a brief, hot flare of blue flame. The snow around him instantly turned to steam, and he knew he would regret the waste of energy. But that would be later; now he had to limp as quickly as he could to the manor. If he arrived in an hour, he would be amazed. If the child was not born yet, he would praise Jedinom himself.

Not ten minutes later, the heat of his anger gave way to the cold. He pulled up his scarf so that only his watery eyes were exposed, but that did not help his stinging toes and fingers. *Hold on, Tori. Just a little longer.*

Arythan's thoughts drifted to what this event would mean for him. He was about to become a father. What would change? And then a new realization struck him. How would he leave Cerborath with a newborn child? The fact he had not considered this before ate a hole in his heart. If the Seroko should discover his family, or if Garriker opted for vengeance, what would he do? Would Othenis's vigilance be enough to alert him to pending disaster?

How soon before a baby can travel? he wondered, trying not to dwell on a tragic outcome. *Nothing has happened yet. Nothing will happen, either.* He intended to stay at Victoria's side as long as possible—until Michael sent for him. Michael had children of his own. He should understand.

I'm going to be a father. That word—"father"—had always burned beneath his skin. What did he know about fatherhood? Fatherhood was the right to punish, to criticize, to discipline. Fatherhood meant never having to give explanations, never having to speak at all. Fatherhood meant that disappointment was inevitable, that all one's hope and future was placed on the small shoulders of his offspring. Fatherhood was tyranny and hypocrisy, an undefined standard that existed in one's own mind. That was fatherhood.

Not for my child. I won't be like him, Arythan vowed.

What other thoughts cluttered his mind when he finally approached the manor, he could not say. There was a light in one of the lower windows, and there was a rock in his stomach when he knocked upon the door. The servant answered with a look of astonishment. "Medoriate! You—what happened, sir?"

"Someone stole m'orse," Arythan answered, his voice rough. He cleared his throat. "I'm 'ere to see m' wife."

"Come in, come in," the man said, ushering him through the door. "I will fix you a warm beverage, Medoriate, sir."

"Thanks, but I need to see Tori first."

There was a scream from behind the closed door of the adjoining room, and Arythan's eyes widened.

"That is how it has been for a little while, sir," the servant said.

"So it 'asn't—"

"As far as I can tell you, no, sir."

Arythan felt a small sense of relief and headed for the door. The panicked servant barred his path. "No, sir, you mustn't. Only the midwife can be present."

"Why?" Arythan demanded, tossing his ice-glazed hat to the ground. "I promised I'd be 'ere for 'er."

"And you are," the servant said in a whisper, raising both hands to calm him. "But it is best you wait outside."

"Why?" he demanded again, ready to plow through the man.

"It is not proper, sir. She is a lady, and…and… It is not proper!"

"Look, mate, it took two of us to get 'er like this, an' I don' think I'll see anything I 'aven't seen before," he said in a low voice, exercising the last of his patience. His toes and fingers had no feeling, he could see now that his arm and leg were a bloody mess, his ankle was sore from supporting his weight, and he had barely slept in days. This was not the time for an argument.

"Arythan!" Victoria cried from the room. "Is that you?"

"Coming, luv," he said, challenging the servant with his stare. The man looked away and stepped aside, but then Lyndi's large frame appeared in the doorway, her hands on her hips.

"Good to see you, Medoriate," Lyndi said. "Victoria is doing well. You can wait in the parlor until the child is born."

"Lyndi," Arythan said, an edge to his voice. "I'm 'ere to see m' wife."

Victoria gave a cry, and he tried to look past the large woman to see her, but Lyndi was a determined barricade. "Of course, you are, dear, but you must be patient." She moved to close the door on him, but Arythan stopped it with his foot—the foot attached to the twisted ankle. His eyes watered in pain, but he did not make a sound.

Lyndi gawked at his audacity. "Medoriate!"

He leveled his gaze at her. *"I'm 'ere to see m' wife."*

"I tried to tell him," the servant protested.

"I will burn the bloody door down," Arythan vowed.

"Arythan!" Victoria screamed.

"Oh, all right—"

But the mage was already ducking under her thick arm. He stopped in his tracks when he saw Victoria in the birthing chair, her hair plastered to her pale round face by sweat. She was in a simple white gown that was not only dampened by sweat, but by blood.

"Oqrantos mora-miq," he breathed, unable to blink.

"Hello, Arythan," Diana said, humorless. She was on the receiving end of the chair, and she nearly looked as tired as his wife. "You never were one for modesty and tradition."

"I got y'r letter," he blurted.

"I see." Diana glanced him over. "What happened to you?"

"Long story. I would've been 'ere sooner, but—"

"We've been here for hours. You haven't missed anything."

Victoria gave a howl, and Arythan hurried to her side.

"I'm 'ere, luv," he said, letting her grip his hand with all her might.

"Good," Victoria panted. "Sorry if I hurt you."

"Can't feel m' fingers anyway," he murmured. He smoothed the hair from her face and discovered the damp cloth Lyndi had been applying to her forehead. He gently wiped her brow and pressed it to her flushed cheeks.

"You have no idea...how much this hurts," she said, wincing.

"I believe y', luv."

"I wasn't sure you'd come."

He squeezed her hand. "I'm 'ere."

"Arythan..." she said through clenched teeth.

"Yeah, luv?"

"He's coming!"

Somewhere amidst her panting, grunting, and crying, Arythan found a point of uneasy silence in his mind. *He's coming. He's coming. What will* he *be? What if he doesn't look Human? What if—*

And suddenly there was the sound of a tiny being crying at the top of its lungs. Pink and bloody, it was braced in Diana's capable hands. *Mora-miq,* he thought, scarcely able to believe this was his child.

"Can Reiqo also be a girl's name?" Diana asked with a smile.

Arythan and Victoria exchanged a look.

"I was only curious. He is a healthy baby."

Victoria collapsed against the chair, and Arythan held her, watching as Diana took the child away to clean him. "Good work, luv. Y're a tough lady," he whispered in her ear.

"Thank you, Arythan," she breathed. "Thank you for being here."

"I love y'," he said, kissing her brow.

Diana returned with a clean and swaddled baby boy. Reiqo was no longer crying but staring up at his parents with a set of bright, blue-green eyes. "Mage-child," the healer said, handing the baby to its mother. "I hope you are ready for him."

The tiny pink face grew vexed and began a new round of noise. "'E *is* a rebel," Arythan said, and he knew his entire life would never be the same.

MORNING BROUGHT WITH IT A WHINNY, and Arythan ventured outside into the thick drifts of snow to find a black mare bounding in the field near the frozen pond. Upon spotting her rider, Narga trotted to greet him. "'S about time," he said, rubbing her muzzle. The bridle and saddle were still on her, and he led her to the barn for a quick groom and a feed. In that quiet moment, he could almost believe that nothing had changed.

But then he went back into the manor and heard the sound of infant distress. Diana had retreated to the guest room for some much-needed sleep, leaving Victoria and Lyndi in Reiqo's company. "I found m'orse," Arythan said.

Lyndi shushed him and rocked the crying child in her arms.

"He isn't hungry, and I can't get him to stop screaming," Victoria said, pulling her robe back up her shoulder.

"Er..." He almost backed out of the room, but he saw the look of exhaustion upon his wife's face. "I don' think I can 'elp, but I'll try."

Lyndi hesitated before handing him the swaddled infant. "I'll see to breakfast," she announced, and left the room.

"She's still sore at me for being in the room," Arythan said.

"Don't give it a second thought." Victoria yawned and turned over in the bed. "I am glad you were there."

Arythan looked at Reiqo, and Reiqo looked at him. The child's tears had ceased, but it seemed he would potentially start again when the mood struck him. The mage slipped out of the room and closed the door. There were enough rooms in the manor for him to find a secluded place to sit and think. The study contained a desk and a grand chair near the hearth. A couple half-burned logs sat on the firedogs, and they instantly flared blue, catching the baby's attention. "Y' like that?" Arythan asked, making his way to the chair. "Maybe y' can do the same thing...in a few years."

He carefully eased himself down in the chair, watching the reflection of the fire in the child's vibrant eyes. "'S funny," he said quietly, "but these 'ands 'ave done many things. They've been stuck with spikes, wielded all kinds o' weapons, an' even chopped off a bloke's 'and... But they've never 'eld a baby. Not 'til now."

Reiqo's eyes were everywhere—on the flames, on his father, taking in the room around them. It was fascinating for Arythan to watch him. *My son.* "Y' know, y'r father's not the nicest bloke. 'E's made some bad choices, done some rotten things. Y' might be the first good thing to come from m' life. Y' an' y'r mum. There's a chance I can make this right. Turn things for the better. It starts with y'."

Arythan smiled. "Y' got the good blood, kid. Y'ave a family o' demons behind y', but there's not a trace o' them in y'. Y'r uncle was a good mate. I 'ope y'll grow up to be like 'im. If only 'e could see y'. If only 'e could know."

Reiqo had closed his wandering eyes, giving way to sleep. "I will be a good father," Arythan whispered to him. "I'll keep y' safe. Make sure y' don't end up a thief on the streets. Make sure y' don' suffer in any bloody wizard school. They won't let me back into Mystland anyway." He thought about Miria for the first time in a long time. She would be happy to know that he had finally found his way.

The concept of a normal Human life was not beyond his reach anymore. Once he and Victoria and Reiqo left Cerborath, there would only be time. Time to watch his son grow, time to teach him all he knew—or at least the decent things to know. Time, even, to shape himself into a good man his son could admire. If he could be half the respectable person his brother had been, he would have no worries.

"Em'ri was a father," Arythan said. "I'm sure 'is lil' girl loved 'im. I don' 'ave the sickness like they 'ad—not anymore." It was not a thought he ever truly considered. Falquirians were a long-lived race, even with the Quake in their blood. *Will I grow to be an old man?* It was not impossible that he would long outlive Victoria. *I never dreamed I'd survive this long. Is this what it means to consider the future?*

His own eyes began to close as he stared into the fire. Reiqo was his future. He did not need to be anyone's Dark Wizard or hired thief. He was a father.

~

*R*EIQO HASN'T BEEN *in this world a day, and already he and Arythan are missing.* Victoria, still weak and exhausted, had no desire to so much as lift her head. She did, however, turn slightly from her pillow to see the snowy landscape outside. The sun cast its golden light upon the pristine covering, while the shadows stained it blue. She had scarcely been aware of the snowfall—for obvious reasons—though now it struck her that for so much to have fallen, it must have been a fair storm indeed.

And he came anyway, she thought, her lips curving into a smile.

There was a knock upon the door, and Diana came in before Victoria could grant permission. "I thought you would like to know that I found them," she said.

"Where are they?"

"Asleep in the study," the healer said. She picked up the tray she had left in the hall and brought it to the table at the bedside.

Victoria eyed the soup and rolls hungrily, then forced herself to look away. "They are both asleep?"

Diana nodded. "You might enjoy a rare moment of peace."

Victoria pushed herself up just enough to eat. "Thank you," she said when the tray was placed upon her lap. "You have done so much for us...and I know it must be difficult."

Diana looked at her in surprise.

Victoria bit into a buttered roll and slowly exhaled. When she finished the morsel, she explained, "I know how you feel about Arythan, and I know how you feel about me. He asked you to come, to leave behind your shop to watch over me."

"I don't understand you, milady."

Victoria glanced at her. "Of course you do. I do not rank high in your favor—however I have offended you or presented myself the wrong way." She held up a hand when Diana's pale face colored, and the healer looked as though she would protest. "But you care very much for Arythan. You try not to show it, but you do."

The healer grew a shade darker. "I tend only professional relationships with my patients. Arythan, in the past, has been a frequent visitor to my shop."

Victoria sipped her tea. "It does seem like he cannot escape illness or injury, but this is different. You might call it friendship."

"What would *you* call it, milady?"

She did not answer, but her one-sided smile betrayed her thoughts. *Dare I say you might be a little jealous?* Her intention was not to offend the healer, but a little woman-to-woman honesty was not unwelcome. After all, she had spent months with only Lyndi as company, and Lyndi could carry a conversation by herself. It was, in fact, not conversation at all but more like an ongoing lecture from a mother.

"You can sit down," Victoria said, nodding toward the chair by the window.

Diana hesitated and then accepted the offer.

"Arythan trusts you," Victoria said. "I don't believe there are many people he trusts."

"I would say not," Diana agreed.

She is guarded. Very guarded. I wonder why. Victoria took another sip of tea. "When I first met him, I was drawn to him because of his mystery... And his accent, his handsome face..." She waved her hand. "I could tell he was a man of secrets. Piece by piece I have learned about him, but it's like chiseling rock. It takes a long time, and I do not get very far."

Diana studied her. "Men like him are difficult to reach. They often have a painful past buried beneath that rocky exterior. The truth about rock is that it does not change readily."

Victoria lifted her chin. "Wind and rain do wear, though. Even rock can crumble."

"Yes," Diana said, "but then it is broken and no longer what you had first admired."

Victoria gestured to the tea. "Have some, please. I feel silly eating alone."

Diana poured herself a cup.

"Everyone changes," Victoria continued. "Who we become is part of who we are. Arythan is a father now. He can't be mysterious and silent."

"I thought you admired his mystery."

She nodded. "I do. I did. But now I need more from him. I want to know who he is. I think it is only fair, being his wife."

"Is a man defined by his past?" Diana asked. "Is it possible to know him by how he loves you now, as he is? Is it worth digging into him, to unearth the pain he has sought to bury? It could cause him to resent you."

Victoria bit her lip. *Like the time he ran away from me in Desnera. But he was being childish.* "You are so ready to defend him," she said, a little frustrated. "Maybe you know more about him than I do."

"I can't imagine that is true," the healer said, staring at her cup. "And it is not so much that I defend him as I understand…" She had stopped herself.

"You understand him," Victoria finished. "I like to think I do as well. Yet I feel there are secrets he keeps—even now. It's in the way he is anxious despite being tired. The way he falls silent when we talk about the future."

"He was a member of the king's elite; they are not the sort one would label as 'social.' He has obligations to uphold, work to do. Some of it may wear on him, and he does not want you to worry."

"What do you mean *'was'* a member?" Victoria asked.

Diana finally took a long drink from her cup. "Merely that they have been reassigned to the Ice Plains." She glanced at Victoria. "Maybe you should ask him about his intentions."

It is not for a lack of trying. "He is not one to talk about what he does not want to talk about," Victoria said.

"I think he would be honest with you."

Victoria recalled the story Arythan told about his father and the punishment for telling lies. "Honesty is one matter; evasion is another."

"He cares too much about you not to listen." Diana's stare was upon the window, but her thoughts were clearly elsewhere. "He has let you close to him, and men like him seldom have families. The risk is too great. He loves you enough that he has taken that chance, and his every thought revolves around protecting you and your child. Therein is his anxiety and his exhaustion." She fell silent and set the cup back upon the tray.

Victoria did the same, her appetite waning. "I know of the importance of his role as the royal medoriate, but I don't understand these risks and chances of which you speak. Is he in danger? I would think he would tell me if we were in any danger." She searched the healer for any hint of truth.

"I don't know, milady, but if I were you, I would ask him."

Why do I have this sense of growing doubt? I want to trust him, but my instincts are gnawing at my heart. "Perhaps I will."

"I met someone in Mystland," Diana began, in a quiet, uncertain voice that made Victoria freeze. "He was a skilled wizard. Well-respected." Her gaze fell from the window to the floor. "But he had another life—one he wished to leave behind. As we grew closer, I had thoughts of starting a family. At first he was reluctant, but I so wanted a child....

"I became pregnant, and it seemed the more the child grew inside me, he grew more and more distant. I confronted him; I wanted him to face his fears. I wanted to know he would be there beside me, that his family was most important in his life. But it was not true. It was more than he could give. I didn't know it then, but I know it now. I never should have pushed him."

Victoria listened with a twinge of sympathy. "What happened?" she whispered.

"When the baby was born, he was gone. I never knew where he went; he just disappeared. The child—the girl—was stillborn."

Victoria expected tears or a sigh. Instead, Diana straightened, and rose from the chair. The glimpse into the healer's heart had been just that: a glimpse. "For what you cannot change about him, you must accept," Diana said. "Would you like me to leave the tray, or have you finished?"

Victoria looked down at her half-eaten meal. "You can leave it," she said, though she was no longer hungry. *So much for being social. Why do* I *feel guilty? Should I thank her for her advice? Tell her I'm sorry?* When she looked up, Diana was already at thc door.

"When Arythan awakens, I will tell him you wish to see him."

Victoria nodded and found herself alone again.

It was not until later that the family was reunited. The hungry child was nestled in his mother's arms, contentedly nursing as they sat in a blanket by the fire. Arythan sat on the other side of the hearth, an unlit jack weaving between his fingers. His wandering gaze fell upon a set of figurines on the mantle, and he went to investigate them. His suspicions that Victoria was watching him attentively were confirmed when she voiced herself.

"What are you doing?"

"They're lil' birds in clothes," Arythan said, lifting one up. "This one 'as a sword."

Victoria squinted. "It's not a sword. It's a walking stick."

"Not to me."

She made a face. "Do you want to know why I'm right?"

Arythan shrugged.

"It's a children's poem. 'Ten Sparrows.' She began to recite the poem, speaking more to Reiqo than to the mage.

"*Ten sparrows march in time*

Each one different in the line.
One has a flute with melody sweet,
Two has rings upon his feet.
Three has a watch that cannot tick,
Four has a sturdy walking stick."

She gave Arythan a self-satisfied nod at this line.

"Five has a hat with feather in-brim,
Six has a lantern and candle within.
Seven wears a cloak of green,
Eight has spectacles so clean.
Nine reads a book without a title,
And Ten does nothing but sit idle."

"Lazy bastard," Arythan said. "Must be a code o' some sort. Access to a secret guild." He feigned a suspicious look in her direction.

"You are absurd. It is a poem to teach children to count. Everyone knows it."

"Apparently not."

"Everyone who didn't grow up on an island in the middle of nowhere."

"Tha's better." He lit his jack and started to arrange the bird figures in different positions.

"Arythan."

"What?"

"Why are you so anxious? Why can't you sit down and relax?"

"Sit down an' what?" He looked at her blankly.

"Do you always have to be busy?"

Yes. "Not when I'm sleeping."

"Which isn't often, it seems." Victoria sighed. "Back to the first question, and I do expect an answer. Why are you so anxious?"

Now is the time. Tell her. Tell her everything she needs to hear. But as he thought about it, "everything" was a lot. When he had told Diana almost "everything", she had a look of... Was it concern?

Disbelief? A combination of both? Was it fair to load the same burden upon his wife, who had just given birth to their first child?

He knew she was waiting for an answer, and his delay only confirmed that there was truth to his anxiety. *These are* my *fears.* My *burdens. She will only worry over what she cannot control. How could I do that to her? I don't know that I can.*

He picked up the last sparrow—the lazy sparrow—and spoke with the jack between his teeth. "I'm not much of a storyteller."

"Pardon?"

"I 'ave a story. 'Tis a true story, but I'm not so great at telling... not like 'e was." He set Sparrow Ten back on the mantle and removed the jack.

"He?"

"A bloke named 'Awkwing."

Victoria smirked. "His name was 'Hawkwing?' That's a little strange."

"Not if y're Falquirian," Arythan answered seriously. He explained before she could ask. "'S a race that looks 'Uman, but they're magic. They can change into birds."

"Oh! '*Hawk*wing *would* make more sense, then," Victoria reasoned.

"'Twas 'is name, sense or not." Arythan took a hit and slowly exhaled. "'E was a good man 'oo traveled a lot, sawr many places, knew a lot about the world. Too much, actually. 'E knew too much, an' that's what made 'im special. The Merchants' Guild wanted what 'e 'ad." Arythan tapped his head.

"The Merchants'—"

Arythan stopped her interruption by holding up his index finger. "The Guild does a lot o' business, luv, and not all of it is clean."

"Well, what did he know that they wanted so badly?" Victoria asked, watching as Reiqo repositioned himself.

"'E knew the location of a secret library."

At this, she looked up. "A *library*?"

"A secret one. With important information." Arythan took the sparrow with the book and sat it on its head. "'E didn't believe in the Guild's intentions, an' 'e was unwilling to share with them. So they followed 'im everywhere. Chased 'im around Secramore. 'E grew sick an' weary, but 'e was determined to keep 'is secret.

"One day, the Guild caught up to 'im." He stopped and took a breath as the memories returned. "'Awkwing 'ad someone 'oo traveled with 'im, and the Guild took 'im. Kept 'im at knife's edge so that 'Awkwing would be forced to tell them what they wanted to know."

"Did he tell them?" Victoria asked, her eyes wide.

"No." Arythan turned away from the mantle. "'E fought them to save 'is mate. In the struggle, 'is mate was 'urt, and 'Awkwing was run through."

"But why kill him if they needed him?"

Arythan shook his head. "As I 'eard it, 'twas an accident," he said, his voice bitter. "'Awkwing died without a word."

"What about his friend?"

Arythan lifted his shirt to show her a white scar. "'Is sorry arse survived."

She gaped at him.

"'Awkwing was m' brother, and the Merchants' Guild killed 'im. The same bloody blokes I 'ave to work with now." He replaced the jack between his lips.

"Arythan… I didn't know you… I am so sorry." She reached for him, and he came to take her hand. She squeezed it. "For you to face them every day…it must be awful."

He crushed out the jack and knelt beside her to look in her eyes. "'S why I asked what y'd want to do. 'S why I can't be 'ere anymore. We should leave. We should find that quiet place where Reiqo can grow, an' we can be a family. I can make it 'appen, Tori. Soon as 'e's able, we should go."

Victoria blinked. "I-I know you asked me about this, but I did not expect it so soon. There is so much to consider."

"No, there isn't. I 'ave money. We just need to find the right place."

"You're forgetting about your oath to the king. We can't just run away."

He pulled her hand to his lips. "I 'ave a way to make it 'appen. I can't explain it to y', but y'ave to trust me. I want the best for us, an' 'tis not 'ere. Not in Cerborath."

"Reiqo is too young. And winter has only begun," she protested.

"So we wait a spit, but we can't wait too long."

"Why?" she challenged. "Because the Guild is watching you? Aren't you in danger if they see you working for the king? They can take you and force you to talk. They—they could torture you, Arythan." She fussed with the baby, and he began to cry. "Can't you just write them a letter and tell them where the library is? Then they would leave you alone, and everything would be fine."

Arythan could see she was growing more upset—the opposite of what he had hoped to accomplish. "I don' know where 'tis," he murmured. "An' I'd still be working with murderers. So long as I work for Michael, the Guild can't do anything. Once we leave, they'd never find us."

"You sound so certain," Victoria said, doubt in every corner of her expression.

"I am," he said, staring into her eyes. "I need y' to believe in me."

Her frown did not ebb. "I do," she whispered, reaching to touch his face. "I do. I'm just afraid—"

"No. Nothing to fear." He let the baby take hold of his finger and managed a smile. "I promise."

"All right," Victoria said. "I will follow you. *We* will follow you." She leaned toward him, and they kissed.

18

TAKE THE REIGN

For a month and a half, the snow came down. At times it was thin and cutting with the wind, and sometimes it fell sparse and glittering like lost stars drawn to the earth. Mostly, however, it fell heavy and relentless, amassing in large drifts and embankments that may or may not have concealed an object beneath. Yet while the skies remained unforgiving, spirits were high.

Arythan had spent much time with his family before returning to the Ice Plains, and even that venture became short-lived when Prince Michael summoned him to Crag's Crown in anticipation of the king's return. Arythan may have been less than thrilled at the prospect of seeing Garriker again, but Michael more than compensated for his lack of enthusiasm. There was feasting, many lengthy social gatherings, entertainment, drunkenness, and of course, random amorous diversions. Arythan watched it all from a distance, his thoughts upon the future, his wife, and his son.

Reiqo grew in strength and showed more personality with each passing day, and Arythan guarded the hope that they would be able to leave Cerborath sooner rather than later…if winter so permitted. But the season was not all that held him back. He had not been to the cave in a long while, and so there was still no word from Othenis as to whether or not he should attempt to destroy the Plains. It was difficult for Arythan to be patient and wait while the world around him seemed alive with change.

King Michael Garriker II arrived at Crag's Crown a week before the Festival of Kings. Michael was on his best behavior, though he seemed mindful not to mention his pending coronation. He was, however, eager to discuss how lucrative production of the Enhancement had been, how nicely maintained the castle was, or any other demonstrations of his competence at managing a kingdom. The king remained quiet and thoughtful, and Arythan was relieved that Garriker had given him no more than a glance. By contrast, Arythan had noticed changes in the king. Where the prince had gained in girth and in vigor, Garriker seemed lacking in heart and in health. The king of Cerborath had aged since his ascension to the Desneran throne. His shoulders were slumped forward, the color nearly gone from his hair and beard; there were new lines upon his face and heavy circles beneath his eyes. Arythan wondered how Michael did not see this, or if the prince simply did not care to acknowledge it.

The rumor was on the lips of everyone in the castle—the king would make an important announcement at dinner. When the time for the meal finally arrived, it was a feast nearly to rival that of the Festival of Kings itself. Conversation began easily enough, and the lighter topics flowed from Michael's and Ladonna's lips like nectar from honeysuckle. Arythan picked at his food while they spoke of the newest member of the Garriker family, the political intricacies of the modified Desneran monarchy, and, of course, the weather.

Garriker had never struck Arythan as a man of unnecessary words, and certainly he upheld that concept this night at the table. The subtle game was at its peak; he could see it upon the faces of everyone present. Banen ate in brooding silence, occasionally glancing up to frown at Arythan. The children teased each other while Ladonna split her attention between them and the regent. Michael's voice grew louder with the effects of the wine. This had been the hall's music before Garriker had remarried, but now it seemed there was a string out of tune.

Arythan could not help but long for the company of his own family. Even Reiqo's crying was more appealing than the hollow pleasantries of the Garriker family. He was, in truth, rather proud of his son's set of lungs. With a sigh Arythan waved the server away, uninterested in dessert.

"...you see that all is going splendidly," Michael rambled, spilling some of his wine as he gesticulated. "I have worked very hard to see you proud, Father. I have every intention of upholding our legacy. I know I will—"

"Michael." Garriker took a hard look at his son. Then he turned to the younger prince. "Banen." He pushed away from the table and stood. "Come with me."

The brothers looked at one another before following the king beyond sight of the table. Arythan, Ladonna, and the children remained.

"Arythan, when will we see your son?" Ladonna asked, always the polite ambassador.

"I can't say," he admitted, knowing the odds were she would never see Reiqo.

"I had hoped Victoria would bring him to the festival, though I suppose the winter has been less than kindly for travel."

"'Struth."

"Mother says you look younger and more handsome without your beard," Mirabel said.

Ladonna blushed, though Arythan would bet his color was deeper than hers. "An' what do y' say?" he asked the girl.

"I think—"

"Mira says she'd marry you," Riley blurted, and his sister looked as though she would tear him limb from limb.

Ladonna laughed—politely, of course. "Arythan is already married to Lady Ambrin."

"I know," Mirabel snapped. "I meant that if he was not…."

"Y're too pretty for me," Arythan said. "Y' need to find a bloke 'oo's 'andsome." He watched the girl suddenly grow shy and quiet.

"When I'm old enough, I'm going to marry Mother," Riley said.

"Don't be stupid," Mirabel scolded. "You can't marry Mother. She's married to Father."

Ladonna smiled. "That is very sweet, Riley." She turned to Arythan. "You see what you can expect—especially if you have more than one."

"One's bonzer right now," Arythan said.

"Arythan…I was wondering if you—" Ladonna's words snapped and fell at the sound of a door slamming shut. Shortly thereafter, Garriker and Banen reentered the hall.

There was nothing decipherable about the younger prince's face when he took his seat again. Garriker, however, did not sit down. "You will have to excuse me," he said, and that was all. He walked out of the hall, leaving an uncomfortable silence in his wake.

"Something dreadful has happened, hasn't it?" Ladonna whispered to Banen.

"That is a matter of perspective," the prince said lightly.

Ladonna tapped her knife upon the plate. "Arythan." She looked at him, pleading. "You are Michael's closest companion."

He knew what was coming before she uttered it.

"I beg you find him and talk with him." She touched his hand. "I fear he will destroy himself if left alone."

"I don't—"

"He will not listen to me," she said. "But he will value your company." Her fingers wrapped around his. "Please, Arythan."

What if 'e doesn't want company? What if 'e wants to be left alone? Arythan wanted to say, but he held his tongue. Michael had asked him to be present when his father arrived, and what good would he be if he was not there to support his friend? The worst that could happen was that Michael would tell him to leave. Of course, Arythan had not the slightest idea what Garriker could have said to upset the prince as much as he had. Michael was not easily daunted—even by his father.

So the mage nodded and stood, an uneasy feeling growing inside him as he left the hall behind him. Michael was most likely to be in his study, and when Arythan caught the candlelight flickering from beneath the door, he drew a breath and prepared himself to make his presence known.

He lifted his hand to rap on the door but then let it drop. "Sir… Mate… Y'alright?" He felt stupid talking to a door, and there was not a sound to be heard inside. "Just wanted to make sure y'—"

The door opened, and Arythan figured he must have been standing right there, else he would have heard him approach. Michael was unreadable. The prince stood there a moment, then stepped aside. Arythan entered the room, half expecting to see some sort of mess or anything unusual to indicate Michael's distress. But nothing seemed out of place.

The door shut, and Arythan heard Michael behind him. "Sit down, Crow." His voice was strangely quiet.

Arythan sat opposite the desk, and Michael took his seat behind it. When the prince spoke, his tone remained calm, level. "We spend our short, insignificant lives trying to feel as though we matter, as though we could make a lasting difference in this world. We dream, we hope, and we strive to make our mark." His gaze turned from the desk to Arythan. "No, Crow, I am not all right.

"My father has seen to it that I remain insignificant. Not only me, but his entire legacy. 'The blood and bones,' he used to say, upon which this kingdom was built. Our family faced adversity, but we persevered. We stood strong, and we made Cerborath. We *made* it. A true legacy."

Michael lifted his hands to the air. "Gone. All gone because he married the Desneran whore." He leaned across the table, folding his hands. "They are dissolving the kingdom, Crow. Cerborath is to be a mere territory beneath Desnera's thumb. And I—I am to be his underling still. A mere lord with a faded title. He said Cerborath could not stand without assistance, but what have we done all these years? What 'assistance' have we leaned upon? It's an excuse. An excuse to keep his power and take what he wants."

Arythan never knew a kingdom could be dissolved, but then again, there was very little he knew about politics. If there was cause for Michael to be upset, this was it. The future he had waited for did not exist anymore. Arythan could only imagine how the prince must feel; his own future was bright with the promise of escaping Cerborath with his family. If Cerborath was to crumble, all the more reason he should leave and leave quickly.

"How could he deny me? Deny his grandson? How could he shame our ancestors? Has he lost all regard for everyone but himself?" Color was creeping into Michael's voice, and it was a sour shade. "I cannot sit here and watch him destroy this kingdom and destroy this family."

"Maybe y' can talk to 'im. Before the festival," Arythan said, unsure if his words held any value.

"There is no festival," Michael said bitterly. "There is no festival, because there is no king to celebrate. Father intends to make his grand announcement of the dissolution to the nobility, and that will be the end." He slammed both fists upon the table.

Arythan did not know what to say. Michael held no illusions about his father. The situation looked bleak, the decision final. He stared uncomfortably at the floor, wondering why he came. He could pat the prince on the back and say he was sorry, but it would amount to as much as staring in silence.

Michael closed his eyes and rested his head in his hand. "I appreciate your concern, but there is naught to be done. Go back to the Ice Plains, Crow. Continue as you have."

Arythan hesitated before he stood. "As y' wish it."

The prince chuckled. "As I wish it." He shook his head and said nothing more.

Arythan closed the door behind him and headed for his room. He would be glad to leave the castle, but he would rather be sent to the manor than the Plains. If only Reiqo was old enough. He would have loaded the carriage and had his family gone by morning.

ARYTHAN LEFT IN THE MORNING, battling a new onslaught of snow. Against his better judgment, he made a detour to the cave. The path was nearly impassable, but he was determined to know if Othenis had been there. The feather was gone at the entrance of the cave. Whether it had been removed or stolen by the wind, he did not know.

He lit the Wizard's Sand and sifted through the blankets, searching for the items he had hidden. The book was gone, and so was the crystal. *Good,* he thought, relieved. *Then he knows. But why didn't he leave a message? How am I to know what to do? Or am I still waiting?*

There was no telling when he would be able to return to the cave; Othenis would have to find him some way. He looked out the mouth of the cave, watching the fury of the snow whirl and eddy in the rising drafts. *Damn snow.* He extinguished the fire, drew his hood, and went to retrieve Narga.

The B.E.S.T. were starved for news, and Arythan had delivered it. The reaction was just as he expected: mild surprise before confessing they did not care. Then the cards were dealt, and life continued. He realized that uncertain fate was nothing new to them, just as it was not novel to him. Garriker had turned his back on them; their service to him was at an end. Whether Michael was a prince or a king or a noble with some other title, they would obey him so long as he paid them. Cerborath was just a name, and the only loyalty beyond their wages was the camaraderie they had with one another. Black earth.

The days passed without any word from Crag's Crown until only a day remained before the eve of the festival-not-to-be. Arythan was in the company of Brann Alwin, trying to stomach a cold breakfast near the hearth. The mage had awoken queasy, and he wondered if he was not getting sick...again. The thick oatmeal was like rocky mud going down his throat, and it hit his stomach like a bag of sand.

"There was a Silver Moon out last night," Alwin said casually.

"'Twas cloudy," Arythan said dryly. "And 'twas snowing."

"Just because you do not see the moon doesn't mean it's not out." Alwin smiled to himself. "I had brought one of my charts with me. Astronomy was once an interest of mine."

Arythan did not care, and he would not play the wizard's game by asking what a "Silver Moon" was. He had a feeling he was about to find out anyway.

"Being a mage, I thought you might know the history of the term."

Arythan stared.

Alwin was undaunted. "It's old lore from long ago—when mages were a bit more common. Being closer to the elements, they felt the influences of the natural world. The Silver Moon was said to be when the moon drew upon magic, and the mages had little or no control over the elements. It happens once a century, if that."

He looked at Arythan skeptically. "Did you feel differently last night?"

The mage shrugged. He felt like he wanted to vomit. "Dunno," he said with a sigh.

"Come now. You either felt it, or you did not. Satisfy my—"

The door to the hall opened, and a giant of a man covered in snow stood at the threshold. "Crow. You best follow me."

Hunter. Arythan did not like the tone of his voice. Without a glance at Alwin, he rose and went to meet his teammate. Surrounding Hunter's grim face was a beard encrusted with ice and snow. The giant did not bother to dust off his shoulders as he gave a nod toward the outside.

Fortunately for Arythan, he was seldom without his coat—even when inside. He donned his hat and tailed Hunter from the dining hall to the adjacent dorm, where the B.E.S.T. had assumed their quarters. Tigress was by the hearth, tending to someone who was not nearly large enough to be Dagger. As they drew nearer, she addressed them without looking up.

"He said you knew him."

Arythan moved to peer into the unconscious man's face. Red and swollen from the cold and the wind, it was difficult for him to see any familiarity.

"We found him riding through the pass. His horse was in better shape than he was," Hunter said.

Arythan stared harder at the face.

"He didn't say much," Tigress said, "but he did mutter something about Diana Sherralin and an emergency."

The manor. Arythan's stomach clenched. Now he saw it: this was Lyndi's servant.

"Crow?"

"I 'ave to go," he whispered, his feet already taking him back toward the door. If Tigress said anything else, he did not hear it. There was only one word in his mind, and that was, "emergency."

Beyond that, his thoughts raced off a cliff into the unknown. He saddled Narga, and they rode into the storm.

The passage of time, much like the falling snow, was irrelevant. Narga chose her pace, responding to her master's silent sense of urgency. Her endurance was unmatched, but even she began to tire against the drifts. Their greatest asset was his anxiety, which burned in a fury around them. The magical energy kept them warm, but it drew heavily upon Arythan's strength.

Narga's nostrils flared, and she grew skittish. Then Arythan smelled it, poor as his nose was. Fire. Burning. He squinted at the distant tree line, trying to see past the flurries. Where his sense of smell often failed, his eyes had eagle acuity, and they caught the dark trail of smoke rising into the air. He shuddered and spurred Narga as fast as she was able.

Somewhere in that final, brief stretch, Arythan's world changed. There was no sound, no smell, no feeling of cold or snow upon his skin. It became a world of visions—piecemeal visions suspended in one horrific breath in time. Narga disappeared from beneath him, and he was on his own legs, though they seemed detached from the rest of him. Still, they carried him steadily toward what had been the manor.

Like a charred skull, it gaped at him: dark window sockets empty and sightless, its structure half-collapsed and blacker than midnight. The smoke and the snow suffocated the ruin, choked it in much the same way Arythan felt the rigid, constraining pressure upon his heart.

Closer he came, feeling the remaining heat that had destroyed the sanctuary in ravenous flames not so long ago. His eyes were imprisoned by a shape jutting from the wreckage. A blackened hand attached to an arm attached to a body—what remained of the body. Without a reason, he knew it was the old woman. Lyndi. He stared until his vision blurred, and then a living body crossed his sight.

Nistel spoke to him, his face drawn with concern. The Ice Fly seemed to be waiting for a response, and Arythan had none. Nistel pointed down the road, then pointed to Narga and another horse who watched restlessly from afar. Arythan followed him to the horses, and then he was upon the mare again, riding.

They stopped at a cottage. Off the horses again. Inside the dark and smoky room. A fire burned in the hearth, and next to it... Arythan moved toward the blanketed figure. Diana moved in front of him. She spoke, but not so loudly as the tears in her eyes. She took his hand, though it might well have been someone else's hand. Words reached him through the smoke, but they were mere shadows hinting at what cast them.

Sorry... Fire... Three men... Came in time to... Child lost... He brushed past the shadows, brushed past the healer, and he found Victoria in the blanket by the hearth. His heart strained and pulled inside his chest, and his breaths came hard and fast as he looked upon her. Her face—the face that had been his smile and his laughter—was empty. Empty as the smoke. Empty as the skull-manor that had first reached his eyes. And covering that emptiness and the terrible truth of what had happened were linen wrappings. Like the snow, they sought to conceal what lay beneath, but the bandages were stained. Her eyes were shut, her lips silent. He could not reach her.

Beside her was a smaller form, still swaddled. Just still. He could not see Reiqo's face. It, too, was covered—hidden from him. He reached to move the blanket, but his fingers fell short, grazing the material instead. There was nothing to see. His son was dead.

His feet carried him again. From the cottage and into the snow. Narga was waiting; she would take him where he needed to go. It was time to kill his enemy.

19

FINDING THE TRUTH

Dagger sat by the entrance to the stable, watching over the medic's ward as had been Tigress's instruction. He took a swig from the flask on the ground beside him, then puffed on his cigar. Certainly he had been given more interesting tasks, but at least he was out of the snow and the cold—even if all he could smell was horse manure.

He was about to take another swig when a large, black form advanced toward him from the outside. "What the—" He scrambled aside just as the snow-covered mare trotted through the door and to an empty stall. Her bridle and saddle were gone.

Dagger opened the door to the stall while the mare eyed him suspiciously. Then she headed inside and began munching on whatever hay she could scrounge. "Y're Crow's nag, ain't y'?" he muttered, cigar between his teeth. "So where is Frosty?"

He returned to the door and looked outside. There was no one headed his way. "This can't be good." He hastily threw on his coat and hat and went outside to investigate. "Bloody snow," he grumbled, trudging his way through the thick cover. He stumbled upon the bridle and saddle as he headed toward the medic's ward. He looked up in time to catch movement from outside the building—just around the corner.

"Hm." Dagger blew a trail of smoke from his cigar and quietly worked his way along the building wall. Then he lunged around the corner and tackled the figure crouched there. When he saw his teammate, he threw the cigar from him mouth. "What by Lorth are y' bloody doing?"

The brute stared into the face below him. Pale as the snow around him, reddened eyes rimmed in violet rings, the half-frozen mage could barely struggle beneath Dagger's weight.

"Off!" Arythan choked.

"What's wrong with y'? What're y' doing 'ere?" Dagger asked uneasily.

"Justice," Arythan spat.

Then Dagger saw the knife in his hand, which was now pinned to the ground. "Are y' mad? I know the Seroko offed y'r brother, but y' can't just go in and—"

"'E killed m' son," Arythan gritted. "An' Tori."

Dagger's eyes widened. "Y' can't be..." He looked at the mage's face. "Shit."

Arythan's jaw tightened. "Leave me be," he warned.

"No, mate, I can't," the brute said, his voice softening. "This don't make enna sense. We gotta see the cap'n."

Arythan growled and renewed his efforts to free himself.

"Y're afire, Frosty. Y're in no shape to kill anyone right now."

The mage nearly sliced him with the knife, a mad look in his fevered eyes.

"Sorry," Dagger said, and gripped him by the throat. "We'll sort this out, I swear it." When the air-deprived mage finally passed out, Dagger slung him over his shoulder and headed for the dorm.

"Tell us your story."

Lyndi's servant looked at the bear of a woman, then at the broad-shouldered men next to her. Lastly his eyes came to Arythan, who sat in his blankets and stared expressionless at the flames in the hearth. "I'm sorry, Medoriate, Sir," he said. "I am so very sorry about—"

"The story," Tigress interrupted, her voice iron.

He stirred uncomfortably. "I...I went with Lady Sherralin into town. She needed help with some supplies, and the snow kept on falling. So we went, and when we came back, we saw smoke and fire. Lady Sherralin jumped out of the wagon just as we saw three men running away. They looked like they might have been hurt."

"Hurt by the fire they started?" Tigress asked.

The servant shook his head. "No. There was another man there. A wizard. He was chasing them away with his magic. He managed to put out the fire, and he and Lady Sherralin set to finding..." He looked at Arythan and stopped. The mage's head was down, hidden beneath his hands.

"Go on," Tigress ordered.

"I can't," the man said quietly. "That was when Lady Sherralin sent me to fetch Medoriate Crow."

Grim silence fell like a pall upon the room; only the fire continued to talk.

Arythan's voice emerged. "'Twas 'im. Safir-Tamik."

"We have no proof of his involvement," Tigress said. "In fact, he has not left the ward, and no one has come to see him in days. Besides, what motive would he have? If he has something against you, why strike now? The Seroko don't act unless they stand to benefit."

The misery upon the mage's face eased her approach. "We need to deal with this directly. Obtain the evidence we need before we resolve the situation."

Dagger perked at this statement. "We're going 'unting."

Tigress gave a nod. "But Hunter will remain here at our post to cover us."

"Y're coming, Kitten?" the brute asked.

"I cannot unleash you both," she said. She turned to the mage. "Crow."

He was staring at the flames again.

"Crow, are you with me?"

He gave the slightest of nods, and Tigress frowned, watching him carefully.

"Er, milady?" the servant asked, uncertain. "There are two villages near Lyndi's manor—one in either direction. Stagrun and Snowcreek. If the men are injured, they can't have gotten far."

"Which one 'as a medic?" Dagger asked. "An' a bar?"

"Um, Snowcreek is the larger," the man said, his brow furrowed.

"Right, then." Dagger lit his cigar and headed for the door.

Tigress waited for Arythan, who seemed a world away. She stopped him, gripping his arm. "Are you certain you can manage this?" she asked in a low voice, her eyes intent upon him. If she had expected a verbal response, she was to be disappointed. Her only confirmation was a return stare before he pulled away to follow Dagger.

The storm outside had relented, though the snowfall remained steady. They came upon Snowcreek first, stopping at a tavern to rest and pose some tactful questions. Dagger immediately approached the bar while Tigress directed Arythan toward a quiet table in the back of the room. After the initial gawking of the townsfolk, the tavern activities resumed.

"I would be hard-pressed to say these people don't know who we are," Tigress said. Even without their masks, their reputation as the "Brutes in Black" evidently preceded them. A timid-looking barmaid approached them, and Tigress ordered a few drinks, some bread, and a bowl of soup.

Arythan's vacant gaze remained upon the lantern at the center of the table.

"You will eat something," Tigress said, "because I need your wits about you. I know you are not like the rest of us. I know you aren't a killer. We cannot let emotions get in the way, or we won't get what we want." She tried to get him to look at her. "Crow."

Tigress pushed the lantern away. "Arythan."

At last he granted her what she wanted. "I can't 'ave what I want," he said, almost inaudibly.

For a moment she was speechless. Tigress turned away first, changing her approach. "You know that these men were likely hired for this. We will interrogate them, learn what we want to know, and work from there." She could tell he had stopped listening, his eyes back upon the place the lantern had been. They sat in silence until the barmaid returned with their drinks and food, and Tigress pushed the bowl of soup toward him. Arythan did not touch it, nor did he touch anything on the table.

Dagger returned to them, sitting down in his chair heavily. "Yeah, so..." He took the cigar from his lips. "Nobody's seen nuthin' yet." He spied Arythan's soup and pulled it toward him. "But what I think," he said, raising the spoon to his temple, "I think they're still layin' low. We can visit the medic, an' see what 'e knows. Else we wait."

"What about the other town?" Tigress asked, watching him slurp down the soup. "That was for Crow."

Dagger stopped eating and studied the mage. "'E don't want it. An' I think I'll know if they're 'ere after we see the medic." He winked at her. "Got me a real silver tongue, I do."

"And it's constantly yapping," Tigress returned.

"Hm," the brute said, intent on the soup again.

When he had finished, they headed down the road to the medic's home. Tigress knocked upon the door, and Dagger smirked to see someone peeking out at them from the window.

"Tha's a blow a'tween the eyes," he said. "Sure sign this bloke's nervous."

"We make everyone nervous. It's our job," Tigress said flatly.

"*'Twas* our job. Now we just play cards an' watch the snow fly."

Tigress shook her head.

The door opened a crack, and they heard the small, creaky voice from beyond it. "Can I help you?"

"We need to ask you a few questions," Tigress said. "In the name of His Majesty."

The door opened before an old man, his elderly wife not far behind him, peering around a corner.

"Very well." The medic did not step aside to allow them entry.

"Might we come inside?" Tigress asked.

Reluctantly, the old man moved. The trio entered a cluttered space with bottles upon the table, bowls scattered near the hearth, and an untidy cot in the corner.

"Any business lately?" Tigress persisted, walking around the room.

"No, milady. It's been quiet. No one goes out in the storm." The old man watched her, standing rigid by the door.

"It is very important that we know the truth," she said, "because you might think you have something to fear until a bigger threat arrives." She paused and held up a bottle. "There was a crime committed by three men. Three injured men. Have you tended them?"

"Three men?" the old man echoed.

"They still 'ere?" Dagger demanded, his patience gone.

"N-no, sir. I haven't—"

"Y' know 'oo we are. No bullshit." Dagger had him backed against a wall. The medic's wife was whimpering somewhere out of sight.

"There were three men," the old man whispered. "They came,

and they left. They warned me not to say a word. P-please, sir… We don't want any trouble."

Dagger patted him on the shoulder. "No trouble. Jus' tell us which way they went."

"They didn't say," the medic told him, wincing. "But I would guess they would be at the old mill."

Dagger nodded. "Thanks, mate." He patted the medic's head and left.

"Thank you for your time," Tigress added, tailed by the silent mage.

The old mill was an eyesore at the edge of town. Dilapidated and on the verge of collapse, the trio moved in cautiously. There were voices from within, and Dagger looked at his teammates in disbelief. "They're still 'ere," he mouthed. "Idiots."

All three were inside, one groaning, the other two arguing about what to do next. There was only one exit, and so there was only one way for the B.E.S.T. to make their entrance. Tigress nodded to Dagger and gave Arythan the signal to wait. Dagger cocked his ear to the wall as he slid a knife from his coat. Then the two of them stood and strode inside.

The knife had left the brute's hand before any word was spoken, and it lodged itself in the heart of the injured man propped against the wall. "Ladies," Dagger greeted, "we 'ave some questions for y'."

The stunned men looked at their dead companion, then at the advancing duo. "What is this?" one of them demanded. Their appearance was what one might imagine any common thug to have: dirty, scruffy, broad in girth and muscle but not so in intelligence.

"Who are you?" the other demanded. They had moved away from the wall, ready to brawl.

"I said *we* 'ave the questions," Dagger barked, and charged the man on the left. Tigress rushed the one on the right.

The grappling did not last a moment as both men were taken to the ground, stunned with blows, and bound using their own attire. They were dragged and dropped against the wall, next to the body. Dagger retrieved his knife from the corpse's chest and wiped the blood on the shoulder of one of the thugs. "This was too easy," he lamented.

"That's because they are morons," Tigress said with a glower, towering over the men.

"Y-you're with the king," one of them said.

Tigress stomped and ground the heel of her boot into the man's foot. He howled, and she stuffed a rotten piece of wood into his mouth. She turned to his partner. "It's my understanding that you attacked a young woman and her infant."

The man narrowed his eyes and spoke with false bravado. "What's it to you?"

"To me? Nothing." Tigress looked over her shoulder to see Arythan standing in the doorway. "To my comrade, the royal medoriate, they were his wife and child."

The man's mouth fell. "Nothin' was told to me. I didn't know who they were. We did our job. That's it."

"What's the going price for the life of a woman and child?" Tigress asked. "And what sort of coward hires three idiots to do his work?"

The man glanced at the corner of the room and refocused on her. "I don't know."

"Really?" She nodded to Dagger, and the brute locked the silenced man's head in his arms. He forced the thug's head down upon the wood while pushing up on his lower jaw, squeezing so that the man's face turned a purplish-red. The pained protests filled the silent mill.

The speaker glanced nervously in the corner again. "I-I can't say nothin'."

The sharp groans and muffled cries intensified as teeth shattered into the splintering wood.

"Who hired you and why?" Tigress asked, making her way to the corner that held his interest.

The man said nothing.

There was a strange sound—like a jaw popping—followed by intense shrieks.

Tigress pushed some debris aside with her boot. Beneath it was a small leather bag which she retrieved and opened. Inside was a folded piece of paper. She took a moment to read it, then folded it up again. She brought the item over to Dagger and motioned for Arythan to join them.

"Methinks I broke 'is 'ead," the brute said, reveling in the speaker's terrified expression. He shoved the tortured man away and stood. "What is it, luv?"

She had given the letter to Arythan to read. "Apparently," she said in a low voice, "these men were acting on a contract issued by His Majesty. His seal is upon the paper."

"Nuh-uh," Dagger said, astounded. "Ol' Garri? Why?"

Tigress merely stared at him.

Dagger turned to the speaker. "Why?" he growled.

The man's eyes bulged, and he shook his head. "We just did what we were told."

"Don't make enna sense," Dagger said. "'S a trick. Gotta be."

"By whom?" Tigress asked. "The seal is there."

"Revenge," Arythan said.

They turned at the sound of his voice, watching as the letter dropped from his hands. He was visibly shaking...and so, it seemed, was the ground beneath their feet.

"Shit," Dagger muttered. "We gotta end this now, or this bloody place'll bury us." He gripped his knife and headed for the tortured man.

A few loose planks came crashing down from the roof. "Arythan, stay with us," Tigress ordered. She retrieved the fallen paper and slid it into her coat.

Dagger moved on to the speaker, who had watched his companion's throat spill before him. "Y're turn, y' bastard."

"Please," the speaker begged. "Please, I—" The knife cut his words cleanly away.

"We're leaving, Crow," Tigress said, uncertain whether she should snare the mage by the arm. "Come on."

Dagger was already at the door. "Bloody drag 'im if y'ave to," he shouted, and an entire section of the roof collapsed.

Tigress had barely managed to shove Arythan out of the way. "What are you doing?" she cried to him.

"Leave me 'ere," Arythan said.

"Don't be an ass," Tigress said, jerking him upright from the floor. "If Victoria isn't dead, she's going to need you."

Some of the anger left his eyes and his head fell. They made it out just as a wall collapsed.

Dagger watched as the entire structure buckled. "Someone's gonna find the blokes. If Garriker 'ired them, we oughtta—"

Arythan lifted his head, and the whole shamble of the mill flared up in a hot and furious curtain of blue flame.

"Never mind," Dagger said, turning his back to light a fresh cigar. "Now what?"

"We take Arythan back to his wife," Tigress said. She handed Narga's reins to the mage and mounted her own horse.

Dagger looked at Arythan with uncertainty, but he said nothing as he heaved into the saddle and followed them out of Snowcreek.

ARYTHAN HAD TRIED to shut out Dagger's comments as they passed the broken shell of a manor. The world from which he had become detached was slowly reeling him in again. He had not told his teammates that Garriker had been his other suspicion if not Safir-Tamik, and so it was far less a surprise to him to learn the truth. Arythan had chosen not to obey the king's request to join the Warriors of the Sword. Arythan had taken the blame for Lucinda Jerian's murder, and Arythan was still involved in the production of the Enhancement. Arythan had thought—had fervently hoped—that Garriker would simply let him walk away.

Why them? he thought, grief-stricken. *Why them and not me? My son is dead, and Tori....*

"Crow?" Tigress's voice reached him.

Arythan had not realized he had stopped. The cottage was before them, and a sickening sense of dread gnawed at the walls of his stomach. He did not want to go in. He did not want to see it. Not again. *If I don't see it, it might not be real. It might not be true.*

But then Diana appeared. Straight-faced, cool-toned Diana, who had seen sickness to every degree, tended the dying, witnessed death firsthand. Truly his closest friend, who knew his secrets, had delivered his child, and now... Arythan could not face her as she approached, the evidence clear she had spilled tears of her own. She had cried for the loss of his family.

"Arythan," Diana said.

"I can't do it," he whispered, choking. "I can't."

"Victoria is awake," she said softly.

Now he did look at her, and she held out a hand, waiting for him to dismount. She walked with him into the dark cottage, and he was vaguely aware that Dagger and Tigress followed at a distance. "I have every reason to believe she will recover, but she is in a lot of pain," Diana said quietly.

Victoria was where he has last seen her, beside the hearth, her body covered in blankets, her face covered in linen wrappings. She was turned toward the fire and remained so even as they drew nearer. The little bundle was gone.

"Arythan is here," Diana said.

There was no immediate response, but then Victoria took a breath. "I know."

Diana squeezed his hand. "We will leave the two of you to talk." Then she was gone. Everyone was gone, and Arythan and Victoria were alone. He found he could scarcely breathe.

"Where were you?" Victoria asked, her voice quavering. Suddenly her pained eyes were rapt upon him.

Arythan could not speak, hearing the resentment in her words.

"Where were you," she repeated, "when we needed you?"

When he remained silent, she continued, each statement tearing away a piece of him. "Where were you when those men came—when they killed poor Lyndi? When they burned my face and asked me who you were—asked me who you worked for? None of my answers were right. Nothing I said would stop them." Her tears ran, and he could not hold her; he could not move at all.

"They took our baby," she choked. "They took him, and he screamed and cried, and I begged them not to hurt him. But Reiqo cried and cried, and then that monster took him and—" Victoria let out a sob. "He stopped crying, and I knew—I knew!"

Arythan tried to take her hand, his own eyes blurred with tears. "I never meant—"

She hit him with as much force as she could muster. "Don't touch me! Don't even touch me! Our baby's dead because of you. Because I don't know you. I never did. All your secrets—all your lies! You can just keep them, and let them haunt you."

"I wanted to save y'. To take y'away," Arythan wanted to say, but it did not matter. None of it mattered now.

"Go away," Victoria said. "I never want to see you again."

Arythan stood. "I'm sorry," he whispered, and walked outside. Familiar faces surrounded him—they had likely heard it all. But none of their words reached him, because Victoria's were still there—loud and echoing across that abyss that had become his heart. He sat down and did not stir, broken and empty.

~

THE SNOW HAD TURNED a sooty gray as the day withered beneath a dreary and laden sky. A solitary rider returned to Crag's Crown, intent on an exclusive audience. Prince Michael entertained Tigress's request, and the meeting was held in his study, with Banen at his side.

"Jedinom's Grace, Captain, you look like you've been through the mires of Lorth and back," Michael said, offering her a cup of wine.

Tigress declined the drink. "I think you should be aware, Your Highness, that Medoriate Crow has been attacked."

Michael gaped at her. "What do you mean?"

Tigress glanced at Banen, who was trying to hide his attention by polishing his sword. "An attempt was made on his wife and child."

Banen's head jerked up.

"Are they all right?" Michael asked, leaning forward in his chair.

"She was injured, but the child was lost."

"Oh my... Poor Crow must be devastated." He brought his hand to his head. "Is he with you?"

"No, Sire, he is with his wife, near where the manor had been. Diana Sherralin is in their company."

Michael's brow furrowed. "Where the manor had been?"

"It was burned, Sire. The lady of the house did not survive. I'm sorry."

"Who could have done this?" he murmured. "And why?"

Tigress hesitated before withdrawing the paper she had taken from the thug at the old mill. She handed it to Michael and waited for his reaction, which was immediate.

"Golden Sword, this was done by my father," Michael whispered. "The falling out in Desnera must have hit deeper than I thought. But I never would have believed he would target Victoria and the baby..." He looked up to see Banen's face was a palette of emotion. "What are you thinking, brother?"

"I would like to go to her—to Victoria," he said tightly.

Michael rubbed his chin. "Are you certain that is the best course of action—especially with Crow there?"

"I don't care," Banen snapped.

"Of course you do not," Michael said, "but you must think of Victoria. She will be beside herself."

"That is why I'm going," Banen challenged. "She will need more than some bloodrot imbecile to support her."

"Banen," Michael exclaimed, appalled. "Crow has just lost his son."

"Perhaps it was his own fault," the younger prince said, sheathing his sword and moving toward the door.

"I will not stop you from leaving, but I beg you consider your actions carefully."

Banen gave him a final, disdainful look before he left the study.

"Sire." Tigress stepped forward. "How do you wish to proceed? Would you like me to remain here at the castle? I am concerned that—"

Michael stopped her with a shake of his head. "Go back to the Plains, Captain. There is naught we can do. I will see Crow myself, once he has had time to grieve. I imagine Banen will cause a stir, and one unwanted guest will be quite enough."

Tigress stared at him. "Are you certain, Your Highness?"

"Yes," he said, waving her away. "I regret hearing such unfortunate news, but I assume you have already done all that can be donc. You found the hired men who committed this atrocity?"

"Yes, Sire. The situation has been resolved."

"I'd expect no less from you and your men, Captain." Michael took a sip from the cup she had rejected. "I will send for you if there should be a need."

Tigress gave a short bow and left Michael in solitude. Once the door was closed behind her, she shook her head and frowned. There was nothing more to be done.

King Michael Garriker II paced before the desk in his old room in Crag's Crown. It was late—too late for any sane man to still be awake and active. The truth was, however, that he had not slept well since his arrival. Once he had known certainty in his life: seldom had he doubted his decisions, seldom did he act without feeling regret. What was it he felt now? On the verge of a festival to commemorate his ancestors, he was prepared to speak to his loyal friends and family—to inform them that the kingdom of Cerborath would be no more.

No one knew how this decision pained him. No one understood that he had only ever acted in the best interest of his people, and that merging with Desnera was the best way to secure a future for those who depended upon him. The Enhancement had once been his solution to a prosperous economy, but the Merchants' Guild had grown too strong, too greedy. He had known that in breaking his contract with them, his kingdom's prosperity would suffer.

His son Michael was too brash to see the threat the Guild posed to his power. Michael would leap at any opportunity for a prospective fortune; he lacked the foresight to acknowledge danger when it appeared on the horizon. Michael's blatant disobedience had disheartened Garriker more than all else, for he had hoped that Michael would be Cerborath's future. Yet Michael had only succeeded in proving how incapable he was at managing so great a responsibility.

Rather than see his kingdom fall to inevitable ruin, Garriker made the only choice he could. He knew Michael resented him for it, and the prince would not be the only one. And so here he was, struggling to compose a speech that would justify all his decisions and build confidence in his supporters. The task might well be impossible.

Garriker moved over to the desk and drew the candle closer to the paper. He plucked the quill, dipped it in the ink, and scratched out another line from the few he had recorded. By the evening, he would be surrounded by familiar faces, and all he had for them were a few simple sentences. In frustration, he pulled forth a clean sheet and began to write.

"My Son,

I am sorry."

He was surprised by the words that appeared on the page, but for as simple as they were, they were the right words for Michael. He meant them in the most profound sense, and yet he knew the prince would not have the patience or the respect to hear them.

Garriker rubbed his eyes, which were bleary from lack of sleep, but also damp from a rare expression of emotion. "Once I write this, there is no return," he said to himself. "It will all be done."

There was a sound from behind him, and he turned as a dark form emerged from the shadows of the corner by the wall hanging. It advanced upon him so quickly that he did not utter a sound. Hands gripped his throat with incredible strength for such a small stature. And past the hat and the scarf, he saw the tattoo, saw the brilliance of the dark blue eyes that were reddened and brimming with tears.

Garriker was a much bigger man in height and in girth, and he pushed his attacker against the wall with all his force, trying to shake free of him. But the rigid hold on his throat only constricted more, and the king saw the mage's eyes flash. He began to feel sick —sick to his stomach.

He backed away from the wall and smashed the mage into it again, but the sickness intensified. Pain seared through him, and he felt his neck burning beneath Arythan's fingers. His attempt to scream came in a garbled gasp as his neck blistered, and his insides began to cook. The king's body combusted, the smell of burning flesh saturating the room.

When the charred body collapsed, Arythan finally let go and stepped away. His eyes locked upon the corpse, he backed toward the window, his breaths short and raspy. And then he was gone, lost in the darkness of a descending night.

20

THE ONE REMEMBERED

The greasy texture of the markstick had turned her fingers a dull shade of brown, and she tried not to smear it upon the page open before her. Catherine wondered at the effort, because she had already ruined several pages on account of her bottled emotions pouring forth. She used to write in the journal more often, but she had decided that seeing her troubles on paper made them seem all the worse. Or could it be that matters simply *were* worse?

She looked up from the page to watch the sun setting on the horizon. The sky was rosy and golden, a sweet farewell to another day. *How many more days will there be?* she wondered. Absently her gaze moved to the empty sand beside her. She had stopped taking Erik for walks along the shore. He had enjoyed them well enough until the day came when he did not recognize where he was.

He simply fades away. How can you lose someone like this? How can he be there and then be gone? Catherine smoothed her free hand atop the sand, allowing it to slip between her fingers. *I did this to him. I am the real monster. Seranonde aged him, took his immortality, but I stole his spirit and all that remained of who he was.*

She fought hard the tears that wanted to spill yet again, brushing her arm across her face. "And you asked me what I had done to you," she whispered, remembering the moment she had employed the crystal rose—the same rose that was locked in a chest beneath her bed in Jaice's old home. "Now it scarcely seems to matter. And once you had asked me what happens when we die. I could hardly consider it, because I never thought we would fail in helping you. I used to believe in a place like Valestia, a paradise for the spirits after death. Now I find I don't believe in much of anything."

"That is a very sad thing to say, my dear."

Halgon Thayliss's voice prompted her to shut the journal and spin to face him. There was a sad smile upon his face. "I hope I did not startle you," he said.

"A little," Catherine admitted.

"You are alone too much," Halgon said, sitting down beside her. "You should not be alone in this."

"I was alone for much of my early life," Catherine said. "I had grown used to it…until one night, when everything changed." She set the journal down and looked at her stained hands.

Halgon reached over to clean some of the color smeared upon her face. "It is very unfortunate, this degradation of the mind. You do not have to hide your thoughts from me, Catherine. I wish you would express yourself—sorrow and all."

"What room is there for sorrow?" she mused. "And who would willingly hear it?"

"I am waiting," Halgon said, taking her hand.

"You see him like this—a man who seldom sleeps and needs to be reminded to eat. A man who wanders with a vacant look in his eyes, a man who cannot remember where he is or who he is, for that matter. You see him weak and feeble, speaking of nonsensical visions." Catherine shook her head and began to cry at last. "He was the most amazing person I had ever met. His intellect, his wit —unmatched. He had this life and spirit about him that could not be suppressed. When he played his violin, his music breathed like a living being, and it was magic. He could do anything—anything he wanted, and he had set his mind to so many things." She looked at Halgon, desperate. "Where has he gone? I want him back."

He placed an arm around her and held her close to him. "You cannot change what will happen to him. You need to accept it. And you need to think about your own future, because life will not end for you." He withdrew a handkerchief and gave it to her. "What will you do when he is gone, Catherine?"

"I-I don't know," she said, wiping her eyes. "Return north, perhaps. Back to Lorrelwood, my home."

Halgon nodded. "You could return. You could try to reclaim what you had left behind." He lifted her hand and wrapped a white ribbon around it. "Or you could begin a new life here, with me."

Catherine's lips parted, and she stared at him. No thoughts graced her, no words slipped her tongue.

"Lady Catherine, I would be honored if you would marry me."

CATHERINE KNOCKED GENTLY on the door before turning the key to unlock it. It was a necessary precaution lest Erik wander outside the house and lose himself. She hated that he was like a prisoner, but she also wondered if he was past the point of wandering anywhere.

The room was simply furnished, with a bed and a table with a chair. There was a small stack of books on the table and a tray of untouched food next to it. Erik had moved the chair to the window, his eyes transfixed upon the sky outside, his hand extended toward the beam of moonlight that fell upon the floor.

There was an open book upon his lap, his spectacles sitting where the pages were divided.

Catherine took a deep breath. "Good evening, Erik," she said, crossing the room to take his extended hand.

"Good evening," he returned, finally giving her his attention. The book slid from his lap, forgotten, along with the spectacles.

Catherine bent to pick them up and set them on the table. "Have you—have you moved from that spot at all?" she asked.

Erik's brow furrowed. "I cannot say."

"Were you watching the sun before the moon?" she asked.

"Yes." He smiled. "The light was different then."

Catherine tested the cold food upon the tray with the fork. She looked at his gaunt frame and brought some bread to where he sat. "You must eat, Erik. You need food and nourishment."

He began to pick apart the bread and place small pieces into his mouth, chewing slowly. Catherine watched him, waited for the inevitable distraction that would stop him from eating.

"I saw the white monster again," Erik told her, fulfilling her prediction. "He told me I must 'stay out of his head.' What do you think it means?"

"I honestly do not know," Catherine said quietly.

"The others were there when the monster went away. The old man, he watches you now."

She suppressed a shiver. "Eat your bread."

"He is never happy. His eyes see into me; I know they do."

Catherine broke apart the rest of the piece for him.

"He tells me—"

"Erik, I have a question for you," Catherine said. "Do you...do you remember the night of Summerfall, when we first met?"

"Remind me of this," he said, chewing again.

"You were in costume, wearing a mask with a moth. I, too, was in a mask." She searched him, desperate for any sign of recognition.

The clouded blue eyes turned from her to the bread. "Why would you wear a mask?"

"So no one would know who I was. But you knew me, somehow. Not by name, but by something else."

"And you knew me?"

"I did. I knew who you were instantly." She gently lifted his chin so that she could meet his eyes. "You were an immortal. An Ilangien."

"The light was different before," Erik said. "It was gold, and now it is silver."

"Yes," Catherine said, broken, "it is." She kissed his forehead. *Would he understand if I told him? I want to tell him. I want him to know. I owe it to him to try.*

"Erik, you know Halgon—the mayor. This is his home."

"Is it?" He looked at her curiously. "Why are we in his home?"

Catherine turned away from him. "I cannot care for you anymore. I cannot help you. Halgon has asked me to marry him. I am going to accept his proposal." *There. I have said it. There is no better way to say it—not that he will understand.*

"That is good," Erik said. "You should be merry." And he turned his attention back to the moon, his hand rising to touch the light he could not hold.

THE EVENING AIR over the courtyard burned with the passing of Cerborath's most recent king. The pyre blazed in the company of Michael Garriker II's family and closest nobles, the somber atmosphere staining the faces of all present. His eldest son stood before the congregation, the firelight bright upon his face.

"My father would be honored to see all of you here," Michael began, his voice grave. "He returned to Cerborath for my coronation, but the joyous occasion has been marred by tragedy. Those once loyal turned treacherous. Medoriate Arythan Crow, his famed 'Dark Wizard,' has taken his revenge for the exile my father had placed upon him from Desnera." Michael lifted his head, and the light shifted upon his face. "Rest assured that the renegade mage will be apprehended and brought to justice.

"I have sent correspondence to Desnera to inform them of my father's tragic passing. Meanwhile, I intend to uphold my father's legacy. I will serve Cerborath's people as king, and I trust you will support and respect me as you did my father. We will continue on as we have, proud and strong and striving toward that great future that awaits us." He bowed, and the nobility moved in to both congratulate him and express their sympathies. Then they slowly dispersed, the fire died down, and Michael remained. But he was not the only one.

Tigress had lingered at the castle on instinct, and she knew now what would be expected of her. She came to stand before the former prince, now king.

"Captain. Do you know the whereabouts of Medoriate Crow?"

She stared hard at the new king. "No, Sire."

"You know you are not at fault for this," Michael said. "He may be under your supervision, but given the circumstances, there was no telling how he would respond."

Tigress continued to stare.

Michael started walking toward the keep. "I need you to find him. Bring him here alive." He looked over his shoulder. "I trust your men will be able to apprehend a mage."

Her voice was flat. "We will do what is necessary, Sire."

"I know that you will."

Tigress watched him retreat until he disappeared into the keep.

~

Victoria had been moved to Crag's Crown by her own desire and much against the wishes of Diana Sherralin. She kept her physical pain hidden, much like the bandages that covered her face. She could not, however, conceal the deep and bleeding wound of her heart. She would break down in tears, start from her sleep screaming, and would hardly touch her meals. Banen had accompanied her and helped her move into her old room inside the keep, and he coaxed her to eat, calmed her, and dried her tears.

She had only been settled for a day when Michael held his father's funerary ceremony. Of course she had not been able to attend, but Banen had. The scowl had not left his face since the gathering.

"Michael is in his glory," the prince said. He sat in a chair beside Victoria's bed, fidgeting with the cuff of his coat. "He lied to the nobility about his coronation. They had no idea that Father was going to dissolve the kingdom. Michael almost seems a hero, saving the family name. He has achieved all that he wanted."

"As a result of tragedy," Victoria said, propped against her pillow. "I still can't believe your father is dead. And that Arythan is responsible. I never would have thought him capable of such a terrible act." Her voice quieted. "There is a lot I didn't know about him."

"A lot we still do not know," Banen said. "Anyone he has ever been is a lie. He could be a spy, but for whom? What is his purpose here?"

"It would seem he has accomplished it." Victoria shook her head. "How could I have ever trusted him?"

"If he believed my father plotted the attack against you, then Crow's actions were not so deeply rooted."

"Revenge, you mean," she said with a shiver.

Banen stood and started to pace. "My father is not responsible for what happened to you, regardless of any letter stating otherwise. My father would have dealt with Crow directly."

Victoria's voice trembled. "Then who would have done this?"

"The bloodrot has his enemies," Banen said darkly.

"Who? How would you—"

"The answers," he interrupted, "are coming. Crow is being hunted as we speak."

Victoria looked at her hands. "What will happen to him?"

"He will be questioned and executed," Banen said, his eyes flashing. "And we will be better for it. I should like to wield the sword myself, sever his head from his shoulders."

"Banen, please," Victoria whispered.

He approached her. "You cannot claim sympathy. Not after what happened to you, to your son. This is his fault."

The door opened, and Diana stood there, bearing a tray of medicinal herbs.

"Do you not find courtesy in knocking?" Banen snapped.

"My hands were full, Your Highness," Diana said flatly. "I have come to tend to the lady's injuries, but if you would rather I leave...."

Banen made a sound akin to a sigh and waved her in. He turned to Victoria. "Rest assured, there will be justice. I will see to it myself if I must." Then he left the room, and the two women were faced with momentary silence.

Diana brought the bowl of rose water to the bedside table and began to gently dab at the bandages so that she might peel them away. "I know you are angry, hurt," she said in a low voice. "I know how difficult this must be. But you must not forget Reiqo was Arythan's son too. He acted out of passion, because he cares for you."

"Do not defend him," Victoria said, her voice cold. "And do not imply that I have any influence in what he did to the king. If he truly cared, he would have been there. He would not have allowed any harm to come to us. And he never would have kept secrets from me."

Diana gently lifted the bandages. "You're right. One should not guard secrets. But is it fair to judge him by the demands of his other responsibilities? How would he have known of the danger? His intentions may have been to settle elsewhere with you and the baby, once winter was through."

"Clearly he has divulged his secrets to someone," Victoria said, growing angry. "A courtesy he did not extend to me. He did not hear my child cry. He didn't see how we suffered." She moved to brush away a tear, but Diana caught her hand before she could further damage the burn.

"Is it too much to believe that he suffers too?" the healer asked, looking Victoria in the eyes.

"How dare you!" Victoria cried. "How dare you compare this," she tore at the bandages, "to *his* pain!"

Diana held up a hand. "Calm yourself."

"He wasn't there!" Victoria shrilled. She threw the bowl of water to the ground. "Get out! Leave me alone!"

"Your wounds—" Diana protested, but Victoria would not hear her.

"I don't care! Get out! Get out!"

Banen burst back through the door. "What is this?" he demanded. When he saw the fresh wounds on Victoria's face, he hurried to her side.

"Milady is a touch sensitive," Diana said, her words stiff but brittle. "I had not intended—"

"*She* is the spy," Victoria accused. "She listened to every word we spoke. She defends the murderer."

Diana looked sharply at Banen. "Her emotions run high, Your Highness. I—"

"Of course they do," Banen snapped. "You, of all people, should know." He stood protectively in front of Victoria. "I will find another to tend to Lady Ambrin. You are dismissed."

The healer stared at him a moment, assimilating his words. At last, she picked up the tray. "Very well." She stepped over the bowl and headed for the door without a glance behind her.

ARYTHAN AWOKE to hot breath upon his face and the gentle grazing of velvety skin. He was surrounded by shadows and walls, and there was a body beside him. Warm and soft, Narga was nestled in the straw, her head craned toward his. All was quiet save the rustling of other horses in the stable.

He could not immediately recall how he had ended up where he was, and he was afraid to press his memory, for he knew the truth was there, black as any he had ever borne. Was it day? Night? He tried to rise, but his legs refused to bear him. It was an effort to even lift his head. *"Narga,"* he whispered, and the mare's ears pricked toward him. *"Narga, I am finished."*

Arythan could hear her munching her hay. He rubbed his face with his hands, wishing he could rub away all he had done as well. He exhaled in grief, but his tears were done. *"I killed the king, Narga."* It did not matter so much that he had committed regicide; his hatred for Garriker would burn eternally, beyond the fire and smoke that sent the king's spirit to the stars. Garriker had taken everything from him, but it was what Arythan had torn from himself that he mourned most.

He was a killer. A murderer. He had taken a life—deliberately and spitefully, and it was not an action he could ever rescind. His soul was stained, as dark as the souls of his people, who killed and maimed and hated. He was like his father, as his father had wanted him to be. He had allowed the darkness to control him, and the monster had won. It had finally claimed a piece of his mortality.

"He was not the only one," Arythan murmured, no longer talking to the mare. *"I killed my own son. And I killed Victoria."* He could

picture the infant's face, hear him crying. His child—without a future. His child who he had failed to protect—the most precious life he should have defended with his own. In Arythan's mind, the crying turned to screaming, and he pressed his hands against his ears as tightly as he could. But the screaming went on.

"I'm sorry," he breathed. *"I am so sorry."*

"Where were you?" Victoria's face appeared, burned and twisted in pain. "Where were you?" she wailed. He had destroyed her too. He had taken her faith, taken her heart, taken her motherhood, her family, her dreams. All because he had failed to be there. Failed to protect what he loved the most.

Arythan took a breath. He had been given a new life, one with possibilities. One where he had learned the meaning of love. In his hands it had blackened and smoldered, but there was no visible demon to blame. Just the darkness within. Not even Shadow. The darkness of his own destructive mind.

"It's the Shadow in you," his brother once said. Arythan buried his head in his hands. *"Maybe you knew all along, Em'ri. It was never dark magic. It was me. The darkness that is me. The darkness I can never escape."*

He thought back to that night in the Cantalereum, when the Larini had presented him with a choice—a choice they stole from him. But had he been able to choose, how many lives would have been spared his taint? Even before that decision, he had infected so many. His mother, his brother, Miria, Jaice, Eraekryst, the Crimson Dragon—all them right down to his wife and child. It seemed his only purpose had ever been destruction and chaos.

Miserably he looked at Narga. *I could disappear. Ride off and never be seen again. Run away, as I always did.* He closed his eyes. *Only to spread this curse. It needs to end. It must end.* He opened his eyes again. *I can make it end, and I can take one other darkness from the world.*

Nothing but his growing resolution helped Arythan to his feet. He touched Narga's face and weakly made his way to the stall door. He undid the latch, stepped out, and shut the door behind him. Narga rose and stuck her head out the half-door, pawing at the wood as she watched her master walk away. Arythan paused and looked behind him. *"Goodbye, Black One."*

21

KING'S JUSTICE

Tigress brushed the snow from her hood and squinted across the cratered earth. There was no wind to speak of—just thick, heavy flakes falling relentlessly from a sky she could not see. She also could not see the energy amassing in the air like a swarm of locusts, but she felt it as sure as the hair that stood on her arms and the skin that prickled on her neck.

"I can't believe it," Dagger muttered for the millionth time. "Why didn't 'e run? 'E shoulda run."

"You can ask him when we find him," Tigress said. Arythan had made no effort to run or hide. His horse was in the stable, and the earth trembled slightly beneath their feet. Whatever his intentions were, she was uneasy over the inevitable confrontation. He was a man with nothing. So what did he want? She was afraid of the answer.

"Kitten."

She turned back to see the brute had stopped walking. His expression was surprisingly soft.

"Can't we just lettim go, luv? 'E lost 'is kid. 'Is wife don't want 'im. Ol' Garri's dead, an' there ain't no bringing 'im back."

Tigress bit her lip, but before she could speak, Hunter spoke instead.

"It is because he murdered His Majesty that we must deliver justice." The iron voice held no sympathy, as Tigress knew it would not.

"Justice for 'oo? Mikey wanted the throne. Crow did 'im a favour—"

"Enough," Tigress said, hoping to avoid further tension. "This is our order to carry out. We bring him to the king alive."

Dagger half-laughed. "Y' care to tell us 'ow?"

"You will follow my lead," she said, and nodded toward the Plains. It was so very quiet, and all she could hear were their boots compressing the snow. With the ground frozen and covered, it was treacherous enough just traversing the pocked land. They picked their way along the ridged trails, trying not to break an ankle or fall into one of the mined pits. For all she knew, the mage was watching and waiting, ready to spring upon them when they least expected it. Her gloved fingers found the lump of a bag in her pocket, and she immediately withdrew her hand.

The ground shuddered, and all three of them lost their footing.

"Aw, shit," Dagger grumbled, struggling to his feet. "I don't like this one bit."

"Bite it," Tigress snapped. She scanned the setting again, her eyes pained by the brightness of the snow. She swore she saw a fleeting halo of blue light over one of the pits. But in a blink, it had vanished. "This way."

She trudged to the brink of the pit and found she had not been mistaken. Arythan was on his knees at its center, his hands pressed to the earth. His coat had been discarded, as had his hat and scarf. Even through the snow, she could see the strain upon his ashen face, the sweat that darkened his hair and ran down his lean and scruffy face. His eyes were shut, his jaw set. He did not seem to know they were there.

"What is he doing?" Hunter asked, his eyes locked on their target.

"I'm not a wizard," Tigress said. "But I have every intention of asking him."

"Is that wise?"

"Wisdom alone hasn't kept us alive," she said. "I want the both of you to stay here, but be ready. He cannot be in his right mind." Tigress moved to the edge of the crater and addressed the mage. "Crow!" She watched his head fall for a moment, and when he lifted it, his eyes were fixed upon her. It seemed to take him great effort to stand. If he was tired, all the better; their task would be easier to accomplish.

Tigress braced herself and skirted down the slope of the crater so that her back was to the wall. She tried not to recall the melted body of the king. It was hard even for her to consider that this quiet little man had done what he had. And he had probably done it with only a thought. "Crow, it's time to come with us."

He looked at her a long while, his face completely unreadable.

"Did you hear me?"

He glanced at the earth, then back at her. "I need to finish this," he said calmly.

"It *is* finished," Tigress said.

"Please," he said. "Go away."

He really did look awful. His eyes were bloodshot and sunken, his shoulders drooped, his body swayed slightly. She wondered how he was standing. "You know that we can't. You need to face what you've done."

"I know what I've done," Arythan said dismissively. "And I know what I 'ave to do. I'm telling y' to leave." His last words were harder—a definite warning.

She changed her approach. "What is it you're doing?"

He eyed her, irritated. "What I do best. Destroy."

"Destroy what? The Plains?" She looked around her. "Quite a task."

He watched her but said nothing.

"A final act of vengeance against a dead king? Garriker didn't care about the Plains." She began walking toward him. "You're wasting your strength."

"I said go," Arythan returned quietly.

Tigress continued to approach. "Go or what? You'll burn us alive too?"

He shook his head. "Don't."

She was just a few yards away. "I don't think you'll do anyth—"

The force of a runaway horse slammed her against the rock wall of the crater, stealing her breath. She crumpled to the ground, gasping. As much as her body protested from the pain, she was deliberate in holding up a hand for her teammates to wait.

"Makes no diff'rence if I die 'ere or elsewhere," Arythan said.

Tigress managed to get to her knees. "We're…not here…to kill you." But she knew that was his goal: to meet his end.

Arythan drew up his sleeve, revealing the tattoo they all shared. "Black earth, Cap'n!" he said with a grim smile. "Can't y' grant me this?"

"You *killed* the *king*!" she cried. "What choice have you given us?"

"Two choices," he said, raising his head. The wind rushed and whirled around him, lifting his hair. His eyes were wide and luminous—the look of a madman. "Let me finish, or end it now."

Tigress got to her feet. She shook her head in disappointment. "After all I've seen from you, I never figured you a coward." And she knew she had pushed him a little too far as soon as the words left her lips. There was a sound from behind her, and she turned in time to see the wall of rock, ice, and snow had separated from the crater's side and was collapsing down atop her. What felt like fists smashing into her turned into a heavy, crushing and constricting mass. She could see nothing, could scarcely breathe. She gathered every ounce of energy she had and let out a massive growl as she sought to push away her earthy prison. But nothing happened, save the dirt in her mouth and a feeling of utter helplessness. He had buried her alive.

Muffled sounds reached her ears, and there was a shifting of the rocky mass. "'Old on, Kitten," Dagger said, his face appearing as the dirt fell away. While he continued to dig her out, she could see Hunter contending with Arythan. The giant had rushed him, sword in-hand, but then he faltered, gave a cry, and dropped his weapon. Hunter staggered back, clutching his burning hand, and the sword sank into the snow, glowing orange with heat.

The enraged giant came at Arythan again, only to be stopped by the ice that reached up from the earth and snared him. Thick, giant crystals grew with unnatural rapidity, rendering Hunter's legs as useless as stone. Tigress heard him curse, heard him roar with rage.

"We can't take 'im," Dagger told her, taking her arm and pulling her from the rock. She knew she had likely broken a few ribs, and worse than the pain of her undetermined injuries was the feeling of betrayal and the blow to her pride.

She ignored Dagger's questions, her eyes locked on Arythan. She spat the dirt from her mouth and stood as upright as she could. The brute stepped aside as she moved toward the mage. She reached in her pocket, and in one swift motion, hefted the bag at Arythan's head.

He incinerated the bag itself, but the contents inside could not be burned—could not be frozen, melted, or destroyed. The fine, black powder sailed in an explosive cloud past his face, and Tigress watched him freeze, his eyes wide. The blazing color in them fizzled and darkened to black, and those black eyes turned on her.

With a mad cry, Arythan charged her. There was no fire, no rock, no ice, no wind—merely the fury of one who knew his own defeat was at hand. Tigress could not avoid him, and so she braced herself for the impact. What surprised her was the force behind his attack. And the knife that suddenly appeared in his hand. She felt it bury into her flesh, in her side. He struck at her again and again, and all she could see were his black eyes.

Arythan did not relent—not even as Dagger drew his own blade and tried to pry him from Tigress. Wounds cut deeply, blood flowed dark, and spatters blackened the snow. Tigress knew Arythan would not stop until he breathed his last. Dagger had backed away, spitting upon the ground and turning his back to them. Hunter took his place, his massive arms locking and tightening around the mage. She swore she heard a cracking sound, but there was no cry, no groan. Hunter loosened his grip, and Arythan's struggle intensified. The knife had fallen from his hand, and Tigress picked it up, turned the handle toward him, and smashed its butt against the side of his head. Fresh blood poured over his face, and his dark eyes faded but did not close. Arythan ceased fighting.

"Bind him," Tigress ordered between her gasps for air. Though Arythan did not move, his glassy eyes watched her relentlessly. She turned away from him and glared at Dagger. "Nice of you to help. Get his horse."

The brute said nothing but left for the stable. Hunter did a thorough job of maintaining Arythan's immobility with the rope. When Dagger returned with Narga, Tigress had them secure the mage to the mare. "It's time to deliver him to the king," she said, emotionless, but inside the truth she knew ate away at her.

Black Ice was an Enhancement—it heightened the senses of those who consumed it. For any average Human, the sensation was euphoric, revealing a world of dazzling color, light, and motion.

Medori, however, did not consume it, did not breathe it, did not handle it without caution. No one had ever offered an explanation as to why, but Arythan had learned.

To a wizard or a mage, Black Ice was poison. What felt like thousands of stinging hornets crawling through his veins brought to Arythan a new meaning of agony. He twitched and jerked, but the ropes held him fast. His heart raced, and shapeless forms crossed before his blurry, blood-stained vision. The shrill ringing in his ears might well have been the result of the blow to his head, but it vibrated through to his stomach, causing it to cramp and churn incessantly. Without anything to vomit, he could only cough up bile and blood. The magic that once flowed through him had been stopped like a flask; he could access none of it.

It was the longest ride to Crag's Crown Arythan had ever known. Not a word was said from his former teammates; his thoughts alone spoke to him of his failure. He had been unable to destroy the Enhancement. Not merely unable. He *could not* destroy it. Without his Shadow, he was merely stirring smoke. He had not wanted to admit it to himself, not when it seemed that escape with his family was nearly within his reach. It was made painfully clear, however, in his final endeavor that the task was impossible.

The Seroko would prevail. They would continue to mine the Enhancement and eventually discover their pathway to immortality. Cerborath was merely a stepping stone, but Michael did not see that. They would parasitize the kingdom until it had been devoured from the inside out. Michael still believed he was in control, but Michael had been deceived by more than his business associates.

Arythan would have to face him, his one-time friend. Doubtless he would be questioned, have to explain why he killed Cerborath's most recent king—Michael's father. The answers were all there, but they scarcely mattered. There could be only one end for him:

execution. And so despite Arythan's ambitions and best intentions, his life would mean next to nothing once the blade fell.

The company in black left the wilderness for the scattered villages along the road. Somehow the people knew. Somehow they had learned that the murderous Dark Wizard of the North was passing through on his way to face the justice of the Crown. Young and old, faces stood outside their doors to watch him. They did not throw stones, did not shout threats or insults. Their stares were for him, silently condemning the man who stole the life of their great leader.

Then they climbed the mountain to pass through the royal city, where the streets were lined with every resident, come to watch the prisoner be delivered to his fate. Arythan thought he saw Diana, her eyes filled with sorrow, her stern face weighted with grief. He looked away. She was yet another rare friend he had cast aside. Past the city, to the gate, then through the gate and to the keep they continued.

King Michael Garriker III was standing on the steps before the grand doors to the keep, and Banen was at his side. Tigress struggled to dismount, though she refused the help of the guards as she approached the new regent and bowed her head. "Your Majesty, we have brought you Medoriate Crow."

Arythan saw Michael's gaze shift in his direction, though Banen's murderous stare had never faltered. "Good work, Captain. Please bring him inside the hall, before the throne." The king headed inside, and the prince reluctantly followed.

Tigress allowed Hunter to help her remove Arythan from the saddle. There was nothing to be said of her expression, though Arythan could see the underlying pallor and the tension as she suffered her wounds without protest. Hunter's face was brimming with contempt. He dragged the mage unceremoniously to the stairs, then upwards and through the door. Dagger did not join them.

The throne sat before the hearth, and adjacent to it was another chair. Arythan assumed Michael and Banen would preside over him, force him to kneel before them upon the ground. But Michael gestured for Hunter to set him in the chair, and then he asked for everyone to leave.

Michael sat down in the throne, facing Arythan, his chin propped on his hand. "Brother, I would ask for a moment alone with Medoriate Crow."

"I will not leave," Banen said, his arms crossed. "I will not leave you in the presence of this murderer."

Michael waved a hand. "You see he is harmless—a spider with limbs removed. See to Victoria. I am certain she has heard that her husband has arrived."

"A snake has no limbs," Banen spat. "I'll not go."

"You will go," Michael said, his voice rising, "because I have told you to do so."

Banen glared at him.

"Go and see to Victoria, Banen."

The prince did not budge until Michael turned to look at him. Then he marched from the room in a fury.

"Now that we are alone, dear Crow, I must say that you are a mess." Michael rubbed his fleshy chin and studied him.

Arythan said nothing.

"You have been a good friend," Michael said. "It is a shame how desperation can turn a good man into a criminal. But you have seen for yourself the world in which you are immersed. Cerborath —land of scoundrels and hardened men. The aristocracy is no different. In fact, they may be worse." He stood and poured some water from a ewer into a cup. Then he took the handkerchief from his pocket and approached the mage.

"It is difficult for me to see you this way," Michael said, dipping the material into the cup and wiping the blood caked upon Arythan's face. "I suppose it is shame that I feel. After all, I am responsible for how you have turned out." He looked at the white cloth and grimaced at the stains upon it.

"Your father attacked Tori. Killed m' son," Arythan managed.

Michael smiled. "When you came here, you were a boy. You are no longer a boy, but you have learned nothing of this game. And so here we are." He dabbed again at Arythan's wound, but the mage turned his head.

"What are y' saying?" Despite the burning of the poison, Arythan felt his heart grow cold.

"Aren't you listening?" Michael asked. "Here. Wait." He produced a knife and began to cut through the ropes binding the mage.

"All I ever wanted," Michael continued, "was to claim my rightful place as king. When I learned the Crimson Dragon was traveling through, *and* that they had acquired a skilled mage, well... How could I cast aside such an opportunity? If only you had agreed to leave them, they would still be entertaining the fine populous of Secramore."

"The Warriors o' the Sword," Arythan said, his voice barely audible.

Michael nodded. "You had guessed it then, Crow, being the clever boy you are. The Warriors did their job, and you came back. Then I almost lost you to Cyrul, but in a way, he gave rise to my suspicions about your loyalty. Your friend—what was his name? Oh, he would have ruined it all. I did not chase him off, by the way. I had nothing to do with my cousin's amorous spell."

Arythan was speechless.

"Don't look at me so," Michael said, pulling the ropes away. "You were a means to an end. The end, however, has become rather ugly—from your perspective anyway. My father grew weak in his resolve, and he decided to deny me what was rightfully mine. I could not see my fate fall to ruin.

"The deteriorated relationship between you and my father left me the opportunity I needed. I am sorry that Victoria and your son had to play a role in my ascension to the throne, but the blood stains your hands, Crow, not mine. Just as Victoria and your son had been innocent to all this, my father died an innocent man."

"*Why?*" was all Arythan could utter.

"I am not capable of killing my own father. You had the motive. You had the conviction. Unfortunately, there will be repercussions." Michael started to move away, but Arythan snared his arm.

"Would you kill me, too?" the king asked, unconcerned. He shoved the mage's chair back with his foot, and Arythan let go in an attempt to maintain his balance. "I am not a fool. I know you are a spy. You have aided the Ice Flies, working against the Seroko. Unfortunately, it means you are working against me. They know you, my friend. The Seroko know you. They have asked if I would part with you." Michael returned to the throne. "I suspect you have something they want. I should like to know what it is."

"I 'ave nothing," Arythan choked. "Y' took everything."

"Just who are you?" Michael leaned toward him. "Your lovely wife did not seem to know. No one seems to know other than my business associates. And they will not disclose anything not in our contract."

If he had the strength to stand, Arythan would have amended his error. He would have burned Michael alive on the spot. He was, however, completely powerless, and his strength was gone.

"Come, Crow. Talk to me." Michael raised his hands. "What have you to lose? Tell me who you are and what they want from you. I might be lenient in your sentencing."

"I don't bloody know!" Arythan cried, his emotions erupting. *"Nigqor-slet! Nigqor-slet ai Oqrantos!"*

"No need to be nasty," Michael said, blinking at the outburst. "I can see that you need time to consider your position."

Arythan tried to rise, but his arms shook, and he fell to his knees. "If y' don' kill me, I'll bloody murder y'," he seethed.

Michael laughed. "Empty threats. You can't even stand. Oh, my poor friend, I have ruined you. But it seems you still might retain some value." He stood, towering over the mage. "And those items I hold of value get tucked away for safe keeping." He lifted a finger. "I know just the place. You might be interested to know that when the Enhancement was first being tested, we tried it upon prisoners. Common thieves, delinquents, upstarts..." He frowned. "The results before perfection were not so favorable. We had to find a way of hiding our mistakes. I believe you discovered the last one—quite by accident when you were trapped in the old dungeon."

Michael stepped away from the throne, heading down the hall. "Wait just a moment, Crow. I will need a hand in this." He disappeared momentarily, leaving the mage reeling.

All this time, I was his pawn. I let him use me as his fool. Arythan smashed his hand against the chair, but it did not so much as splinter. *Nothing was real. And what was real, he took from me.* He tore a hand through his hair, shaking as he stared at the empty throne. *Michael Garriker, I will kill you.* Even as the thought opened the doorway to the darkness inside him, his eyes were scanning the room for anything he could use as a weapon. The chairs, the hearth, the cup, the ewer...there was nothing....

The rope. Arythan picked up a piece of what had bound him. *Around his neck. I can—*

Michael returned with Hunter and Banen, and Arythan tucked the rope away.

"Your Majesty, he is unbound," Hunter said, alarmed.

"Your observation is of no consequence," Michael said. "Little Crow cannot harm you. I ask that you take him to the old dungeon. I will speak with him later."

Hunter gripped one of Arythan's arms with his good hand, and Banen gripped the other.

"No!" the mage shouted, trying to tear his arms away. "Kill me 'ere! Cowards!"

"We have had enough killing," Michael said, and waved them away.

Arythan was dragged from the hall and to a familiar dark passage. The sight of it nearly stopped his heart. He started to kick and fight, but his limbs were useless.

Banen scowled at him. "It's what you deserve, bloodrot, for killing my father."

"Michael's the one!" Arythan cried, resisting them. "Michael! 'Twas Michael!" His eyes widened when the door opened into blackness. "No—*no! Stop!*"

"Rot in Lorth," Banen growled, and he and Hunter shoved Arythan down the stairs.

The mage scrambled back to the top as the door was closing, frantically stopping it with his hands. Banen trod upon them with his boot, crushing them. He kicked the mage away and shut the door.

Arythan's breathing came hard and fast, his heart pumping furiously in the darkness. He had been here before, locked away and not knowing when or if he would gain his freedom. Imprisonment was his greatest fear, and it had materialized in the form of his future—now his present. Worse than death, he would linger, decay, exist in a whisper unheard while his mind screamed for release. He clutched the rope he had hidden, as though it represented the one link to any logical and clear thought to be had. One way or another, it would be his escape.

22

ESCAPE

It was her wedding night. The fire burned brightly, and Halgon's silhouette waited by the ocean. The air smelled like sweet honeysuckle, and someone was humming her song—the one to which she had forgotten the words. Catherine never thought she would be here—at her own wedding. As time slipped away from her, she had pushed the possibility into the realm of dreams. And she was far too old…or so she had believed. This was a man who wanted her for all that she was, and not for the wealth and title that she had forsaken. Halgon Thayliss was her future—her dream made reality.

She floated up to him, her heart speaking to her in the way it drummed against her chest, and clasped his strong hands. Those hands would never fail her, never let her go. Catherine sighed and looked up into his face.

Her groom was not Halgon Thayliss. It was Eraekryst of Celaedrion. His fair face bloomed into a smile, and his golden hair caught the firelight. His eyes were bright like the moon.

"Erik," she murmured, mystified.

"Lady Catherine," he returned, his voice clear and youthful. He tenderly held her head in his hands. "My lady, do not forget me."

She felt her lips weighted by a frown. "What?"

His smile also faded, and he looked at her in sorrow. "Do not forget me, Catherine. Please, do not let me go."

Even as he spoke, she could feel his hands softening in hers. They seemed to fade from her sight, growing lighter until she could no longer feel them. "Erik?" But the rest of him was vanishing too. "Erik! No!" She could only grasp at the empty air.

A sense of pressure on her shoulder roused her from her sleep. She felt wetness on her face and the sand scratchy underneath her. Yes, now she remembered the beach, a niche in the rock she had declared her hideaway. It was a place of privacy and comfort...and loneliness. But not today. She had company.

Jaice Ginmon, of all people, was crouched beside her, jostling her. Maybe she was still dreaming.

"'Ello, Lady Catherine," Jaice said with a reserved grin. "Or should I say, 'Madame Thayliss.' A lil' surprised at that one."

Catherine blinked. "Mr. Ginmon, I—how is it you are here?"

"By boat, mostly," the adventurer said. "Didn't arrive too long ago, luv. I went to find y', an' the servants at the mayor's 'ome pointed me to the beach. Said y' come 'ere quite a bit."

"I do," Catherine admitted. "But you are supposed to be in Southern Secramore, making your fortune at prospecting." She searched him for any clues of misfortune, but he looked the same as the day he left.

Jaice shrugged. "I 'ad a fair gamble at it. Didn't do poorly, but there's somethin' about keeping me feet in one place I just can't swallow."

"I do believe that," she said, trying to tidy her hair and dress. She tucked the journal in the bag beside her, but Jaice had spied it.

"Y' do some writing, luv?"

Catherine could not help but blush. “I find a journal is a good way to sort my thoughts.” She folded the blanket and tucked it toward the back of the niche, out of the reach of the weather. Jaice handed her the bag, and she placed it over her shoulder. He was not smiling anymore.

“I'm sure ‘tis,” he said softly. They started to walk along the beach. “I sawr ‘im, luv. They let me see ‘im. An' ‘struth, I ‘ad this rotten feelin' while I was gone. Thought about y' a lot, and now I know: I never should've left. ‘Twas a ‘eartless thing to do.”

“Heartless to pursue your dream?” Catherine asked, her eyes on the last sliver of light upon the watery horizon. “Heartless to leave us your cottage?”

“'Twasn't enough,” Jaice protested. “I left without knowing if Erik would wake up. Left without knowing if y'd be alright. What sort o' manners do I ‘ave?”

“There was nothing more you could do for us,” Catherine said. “What has happened would have happened regardless of your presence or absence. What I was told was true: the rose that stole his memories is oblivion.” She sighed in order not to cry. “I never realized it would take everything from him...from us.”

“But would y' change what y' did?” Jaice asked. “If y'adn't tried to stop ‘im, ‘e'd been done in then an' there.”

“A quick death might have been more merciful.” She had let a tear escape anyway. “I do not believe he has long now. Regardless of anything you might say, it is a burden I will always carry in my heart.”

Jaice stopped her with his hand. “Y' talk like ‘tis too late. But tha's why I came back. I want to take y' to the Veil. I won't go in, but I can take y' there.”

Stunned, Catherine's lips parted. Then she shook her head. “You saw him. You know he would never survive the journey.”

“I know no such thing.”

“Jaice, he can barely walk,” Catherine said, her voice rising. “I want to help him. I want to believe there is a way he can be what he once was, but it has taken many tears to acknowledge the truth." She took his hand. "Your intentions are noble, but the idea is impossible."

Jaice bit his lip. "But don't y' think we should try? What's 'e 'ave to lose? I could 'ardly recognize the bloke. 'Tisn't right. 'Tisn't fair. I know I can do my part 'ere."

"I would rather he die in a comfortable place, where I can be there and care for him." Catherine turned to face the direction of the jungle, extending her hand. "I do not know what is out there. He could meet with any number of hazards." She looked at him again. "So could we."

"*I* know what's out there, luv," Jaice insisted. "An' for a lady 'oo came all the bloody way from Cerborath, I know y've risked more then than you'll face in that jungle. Y're the toughest lady I know. Risked y'r own life for 'im. Don't give up on 'im now, Catherine."

"I'm not giving up," she cried, frustrated. "I am not. It has been so difficult for me to accept this decline, and now I do not want to place faith in an unlikely destination."

"But 'twas where 'e wanted to go, no?" Jaice murmured. "After the mountain, 'e wanted to go to the Veil. 'E 'ad a purpose."

Catherine's head fell. "To save his friend. But he cannot even save himself."

"But we can."

She said nothing, hesitating for reasons she did not want to speak aloud. Reasons that seemed selfish. Excuses, really. She had found a way to live the rest of her life. She could be happy with Halgon as her husband. He treated her like a lady, but he also treated her with genuine kindness and love. They had been married a little more than a month; how could she leave him for some fragile chance? And what would she say? That she was taking Erik to see some immortals so that they could heal him with their magic? Oh, and that Erik was an immortal too, and he had the power to—

"Catherine?"

"How do I do this?" she said aloud. "How do I leave him?"

Jaice's face portrayed his sympathy. "I think y' know. If 'e really cares, 'e'll let y' go."

Catherine thought of her dream. She could be happy with Halgon. It would be a version of the life she had wanted to lead. But it was Erik she loved, and a future without him… "I would have to find a way to tell him," she said to herself. "I would need time to think. He has done so much for me *and* for Erik."

"But y' don't owe 'im for what 'e chose to do," Jaice said.

"Do I not? Do I not owe him for all his assistance, his kindness?"

"Not if 'e did it for love."

Catherine laughed in spite of her dilemma. "You are quite the romantic, Mr. Ginmon." She watched him blush. "It is a wonder you haven't married yet."

"I don't 'ave a finger for a ring," he said with a smile, lifting his handless arm.

They both fell silent for a while, walking the rest of the way toward the Thayliss manor. Catherine knew he was hoping for an answer. What she told him was not unexpected, but the security in knowing it was the right answer was a welcomed surprise. "We would have to leave soon," she said. "He doesn't have much longer."

Jaice nodded, his eyes bright. "I can 'ave everything ready by tomorrow."

"Tomorrow," she mused. "Tomorrow everything changes." She took a breath. "I will be ready."

The adventurer took his leave, and Catherine faced the place she had come to call home. Halgon had not returned yet, and she was grateful for the time she had to think about her approach. While it ate at her to leave her husband, she also felt strangely liberated in believing that she could still save Erik. Or maybe this was pure foolishness on her part. Jaice clearly believed in the mission; he had made the journey from Southern Secramore just to help them.

As she climbed the stairs to Erik's room, one of the servants stopped her in passing. She was carrying a tray with a half-eaten meal. "Milady, I tried to coax him, but he wasn't having it today."

Catherine was not surprised. For Erik to focus upon anything more than a few minutes was a challenge. She once had better success when she tried to feed him, but then one day he would not submit to it.

"Thank you for your efforts," she told the servant, and continued into his room. Like a wilted plant, he sat at the window. His face was down-turned, white hair drooping like petals in the rain. His neck and shoulders were bent, like a fragile stalk that bore too heavy a burden. Listless, his arms remained at his sides in the chair, leaves that no longer had the strength to reach for the sun. His feet were planted—it was too great a struggle to rise each day.

Catherine shrugged away the pain at the sight of him and strode to his side. She knelt and peered into his face, wondering where the color had gone. No matter. It would return. Gently she brushed his hair aside and touched his cheek. With all her will, she looked into his dull and clouded eyes. "Erik," she said, loud enough that he might hear her, "our friend has returned. Jaice will take us to the Veil. We are going to save you." Catherine tried to smile for him, and he lifted his head but a little.

"We have traveled so far together," she continued, heartened by the response. "But this will be the most important journey yet." She allowed her forehead to touch his. "I haven't forgotten you. My vision has been cleared. Tomorrow, we will go."

"We will go," he echoed. "Home?"

"Yes. Home." Catherine hugged him. He was so very frail. "Promise me you will endure. Promise me, Erik."

"To the light," he said. "Always."

"Tomorrow," she assured him. She helped him to his feet and to the bed. "You must rest now. Lay down. Close your eyes. Sleep." He did as she asked, and she pulled the blanket atop him, humming her song. She ran her fingers along his hand until his breathing slowed. Then she blew out the candles and quietly closed the door. She was startled to find Halgon waiting in the hall, his expression unreadable.

"Good evening, Catherine," he said. "How fares our guest?"

She did not answer the question, for he knew Erik's state. And she was certain he had heard much of what she had said to him as well.

"He is tired, isn't he? Weak. Worn," Halgon said for her. "Please tell me that you do not intend to take him anywhere."

"Halgon—"

"Because it is simply madness, and I won't allow it. I came upon Mr. Ginmon on my way home. I stopped him, knowing he was a friend of yours. He told me you were considering an excursion."

"I am," Catherine said, her words sturdy. "For Erik's sake, I need to take him to some people who might be able to help him."

"'Some people.'" Halgon frowned. "I know you have endured much in watching him deteriorate. But you and I both know that the finest medic could not save him. You accepted this, just as you accepted your role as my wife. We will make him as comfortable as we can, knowing that when Jedinom claims his spirit, you and I will have a future to embrace."

"You must believe me when I say there is more to his tale," Catherine said, trying to pull him away from the door. "He needs—"

Halgon slipped from her grasp and stood his ground. "We have made a commitment to each other. I care about you, and because I care about you, I have allowed Erik to stay here. I have no commitment to him, and his needs, at this point, are few. *I* need you—need you by my side."

"Do not think me ungrateful," Catherine said, keeping her voice low, "but this may be his only chance." She tried not to sound desperate, but she was, after all… "If I could just take him, I could return, and—"

"Listen to yourself. You have lost all reason. My responsibility to you is to keep you safe. I will not allow you to go, and I will not hear another word about this." He lifted her chin. "Do you understand me?"

Catherine felt a rise of indignation inside her. She wanted to assert her independence—to tell him that she would go whether he approved of her leaving or not. She wanted to strike him for treating her like a child. But she did neither. Instead she nodded. "I understand."

Halgon gave her a slight smile, as if that would suffice for closure. "It is late. You should prepare for bed."

Again she nodded and waited while he kissed her cheek. Too cross to move, she let him be the first to retreat. What he had not realized was that she was not asking his permission. She would leave with Erik and Jaice tomorrow, and that was her decision.

THE DOOR OPENED, and the torchlight was swallowed by the darkness, but still it burned his eyes. Arythan recognized Hunter and Dagger as they stood as silhouettes before the door. Hunter glanced at his partner before descending down the stairs, the torch directed at his footing. Dagger remained where he was.

"This was an order," Hunter reminded his partner. "You have a job you—"

Arythan lunged, and the torch fell. He clung to the giant's back as they tumbled down the last few steps. The rope was in place; all he had to do was hold it. It seemed a simple enough plan except that he had not eaten in a couple days, and Banen had smashed his hands. But this was his only chance, and he could not fail. The giant thrashed and grunted, but his sounds were choked by the rope that restricted his airway.

Dagger's voice emerged in the darkness. "Frostbite?"

Arythan's ragged breathing was further labored as Hunter rolled his back onto him, pinning him to the ground. The giant's weight bore down upon him; a full breath was impossible. *Keep it taut!* he told himself. Then Hunter sat forward, and Arythan braced himself for what was to come. The giant would smash him into the floor—probably breaking a few of Arythan's ribs in the process. *Keep it taut!*

There was a sound, and Hunter keeled over—not with deliberate force, but listlessly. Arythan was still pinned beneath the unconscious man, and he struggled to liberate himself before Dagger could resume the brawl. Arythan looked up to see Dagger was already standing over him; his hand was extended.

Wait. Did he—? He met Dagger's gaze, staring in disbelief.

"I've done some crazy shit," Dagger said. "But this takes it."

Arythan took his hand, and the brute pulled the mage to his feet with a swift motion. "This is it, Frosty. The end. For me, ennaway." Dagger bent down and plucked the short sword from Hunter's scabbard. He handed the weapon to Arythan and proceeded to drag the giant away from the stairwell. "Gimme the rope."

Arythan handed him the rope, and Dagger bound Hunter's wrists. Then the brute stood and wiped his hands upon his trousers. "'S gone sour, mate. I'm leaving 'afore they find me sorry carcass. If y' can keep up, y' can come."

There can be no more running. "No," Arythan said. "I 'ave business to finish."

Dagger studied him. "Y' gonna kill Mikey too, ain't y'? Two-king Killer," the brute said with approval. "Well, good luck. 'S y'r arse." He headed back up the stairs, and Arythan followed.

"Why?"

Dagger did not turn at the question. "'Cuz I know 'ow 'tiz, Frosty. The only honour, 's what's in 'ere." He thumped on his chest.

The sun never rises on black earth. Arythan watched him disappear down the hall, knowing he would never see him again. Dagger had provided him a final opportunity; he would not waste it. He had failed at all else, but there was one last matter to resolve. Revenge or justice—neither mattered, for there was nothing to gain. He merely wanted to end the circle of destruction that had started with the Crimson Dragon, sacrificed his wife and child, and ended with the wrongful death of Garriker II.

Whatever little strength he had saved, he would need it now. Adrenaline kept him upright, kept him in motion. He gripped Hunter's sword as he clung to the walls and the shadows and stopped halfway down the hall. Michael's study was at its end, and Michael would be inside, awaiting Arythan for an interrogation. He need not keep the king waiting any longer.

Except that Arythan had already lost everything. The dead were dead, and he could not change what had happened. But not everyone was dead; perhaps their fate could still be turned. And if not, well...he knew what fate awaited him regardless.

He set to the stairs without a sound and stopped at the top to catch his breath. Then he approached another door, one left partially ajar. His heart jolted when he peered inside and saw her there, in her bed. His wife. Victoria.

Her eyes were closed, and he could see the red and swollen burns upon her face. She would be forever scarred because of him. And in her arms should be their child, sleeping with her, swaddled in his blankets. Where would he be in this family portrait? He wondered if he had ever really had a place, or if he had been destined to fail in his role from the beginning. Failing his family had been his worst fear, and he had realized that fear completely.

His frozen heart climbed into his throat as he pushed the door open and walked inside. In silence he went to her bedside, took a place in the empty chair, and waited. He had loved to watch her sleep. The way she lay still and peaceful, the way her long hair fell across her face and body, the unassuming expression upon her face as she dreamed her dreams. It had been as though nothing could touch her.

Her expression suddenly changed as her features strained, and her brow furrowed. This was not a pleasant dream, and he felt he could envision what she was experiencing. Without realizing what he was doing, he reached out to comfort her.

Victoria's eyes snapped open, widening to their fullest when she saw him. She had started to scream, but he had covered her mouth, hating that he caused her pain.

"Shh! Tori, please," he begged in a whisper. "Please, let me speak." Arythan glanced nervously at the door, then back at her. "Please," he asked one more time, and slowly removed his broken hand.

"I hate you," she spat. "I hope they find you, and they—"

"I know," he interrupted, his voice laden with grief. "And I deserve it. I…I came to tell y' I'm sorry."

Her eyes cut into him. "You've already said that. Sorry won't bring him back to us."

"No, it won't," he whispered. He wiped his eyes. "I was wrong in so many ways. I wanted to save y'. I wanted to take y' an' Reiqo away. I was ready." He clenched his injured hands. "But it all fell apart too soon."

Victoria studied him, her mouth set in a firm line. At last she asked, "Why are you here, Arythan?"

He tried to meet her gaze. "Because I wanted to ask y'r forgiveness before I…" He faltered and took a breath.

She waited for him to finish.

"Before I leave," he said.

"You're running away from this," she assumed.

"Leaving before I do worse," he said weakly.

"You murdered the king. You killed him with your magic."

Arythan ran a hand through his hair, finding instead the bloody mess on his temple. "I was wrong. 'Twasn't 'im." He looked at her. "'Twas Michael. Michael 'ired those men to attack y'."

Her surprise turned to anger. "You're mad. Michael would never do such a thing. Just as his father would not."

"Michael did this," Arythan insisted. "'E blamed 'is father, 'oping I would seek revenge. I was a fool. I fell into 'is plan. Now 'e's king, an' 'e admitted all of it to me. I—"

"Stop it. Just stop it," Victoria said, shaking her head. "I cannot believe you would try to blame Michael..." she trailed, her eyes widening again. "You're going to kill him, aren't you? You got away, and now you're going to kill him."

"No. I'm leaving. I just wanted to—"

"To ask my forgiveness," Victoria finished flatly. "You cannot have it, Arythan. You destroyed my life—our life. My love for you died with Reiqo."

His head fell forward. There was nothing more he could say.

"Bloodrot." Banen stood in the doorway, his hand already upon the hilt of his sword.

Arythan stood, Hunter's weapon still in his grasp.

"I will see you dead!" Banen cried and charged him.

Arythan stepped aside at the last moment, but the tip of Banen's blade had caught his arm. The sting of the wound roused his senses, and he parried the next blow that came at him with both speed and fury. He had no desire to kill the prince, but he did have every intention of escape.

Banen came at Arythan with renewed vigor, but this time, his rage had blinded him. Arythan struck him in the leg—a dirty but effective move meant to incapacitate him. The prince stumbled and cursed, and Arythan bore down upon him. He struck at

Banen's other leg, but Banen took advantage of his proximity. He hacked at the mage's side, and while Arythan was quick to move, the bite was deep.

"Stop!" Victoria cried. "Please stop!"

Arythan was already on his way, clutching at his side as he fled past the injured prince and through the door. His strength—the little he had harbored—was failing. Dizzy and breathless, he stumbled and fell down the steps. A servant passing by screamed and ran the other way. Arythan managed to stagger to his feet. If he could make it to the stable... His logic was failing him, too, or he never would have tried to see Victoria. But then again, was there truly any hope of escape?

Nothing mattered or made much sense, but he headed for the stable anyway, envisioning his exit through the gates on Narga's back. The courtyard was busy with workers, and they all stopped to gawk as he passed them, unsteady on his feet, blood dripping through his fingers at his side. When he entered the stable, cold sweat was running down his face, and his ears were ringing. He collapsed against the door of Narga's stall, burying his face in the thick coat upon her neck, breathing heavily as his heart collided with his chest.

"I wondered if you might come here," Michael said, appearing in the doorway. He was flanked by several members of the garrison.

Arythan gripped Narga's mane for support as he peered from beneath her head to see his captors. None of them moved.

"Did you believe you would fly over the castle walls? Or merely charge through them?" Michael asked. He held out an arm when the garrison started to advance.

Arythan spat to keep from vomiting. Without knowing why, he tried to pull himself onto the mare's back.

"Help him," Michael ordered.

Arythan felt someone boost his leg, someone else pull him from the other side. The stall door opened, and Narga plodded down the aisle toward the door. She snapped at anyone who drew near, and so Michael and the garrison followed them in a wide circle.

"To the gate," the king announced. He waved at the guards there. "Raise the gate!"

The gate started to rise, and Arythan saw the open land before them. *"Narga, run,"* he urged, clinging low to her withers. She needed no urging. She cantered through the gate and onto the road. But Arythan was through. His fingers loosed their grip on her mane, and his body slumped forward. He fell from her back and did not stir, staring up at the blank winter sky.

Michael appeared over him, his face fuzzy, his voice muffled. "And so concludes our entertainment by the Dark Wizard, Arythan Crow." He nudged the mage with his boot. "Fetch Diana Sherralin, and bring her to my study. We can't have him making such a mess."

Arythan closed his eyes and waited for death, but it did not come.

CATHERINE HAD NOT KNOWN this excitement since Eraekryst, Manil-Galzur, and she had traveled Northern Secramore. She had spent the better part of a year in Brandeise, lost to growing sorrows, learning to be complacent, succumbing to a sense of helplessness. She had forgotten what freedom was truly like; Eraekryst had always been her reminder.

She glanced at the old man atop the mule. He had perked up since their escape, looking around him with renewed interest. Erik had said next to nothing, but he had followed her willingly enough when she packed their bags and slipped out of the manor and into the night. Jaice had been waiting for them with their mounts a short distance away, hidden amongst the trees and shadows.

Catherine had found the adventurer earlier that day to inform him that their excursion would have to begin in secrecy, and he had taken the time to retrieve the crystal rose from the cottage. There was still a part of her that felt guilty for leaving Halgon, but it was eclipsed in knowing that she had made the right choice.

So they set out beneath the stars, enjoying the first of what would be many nights in the Wild. There were chirps and trills of nocturnal insects surrounding them in a rhythmic concert. Jaice had explained that a fair stretch of their journey would not be through thick jungle at all. Rather, they would be crossing through a sandy stretch of open vegetation, keeping just far enough from the coast that they need not been seen in any of the colonies. However, if they should need additional provisions, they would not be too far from civilization. All this would change once they reached the interior of the continent, which was untamed, tropical forest. Jaice declined to say more until they had earned more distance from Brandeise.

When the sun crested the horizon, the adventurer turned a wary eye in the direction from which they had come. "What do y' think ol' Mr. Thayliss will do when 'e finds y' vanished?"

Catherine considered the question. "I left him a letter in which I explained the reason for my actions. I did not elaborate upon where we were headed or our exact intentions. I had hoped he would understand, but the difference is that his heart is not torn as mine is. I could not justify to him why I had to go. I could not tell him that I still love Eraekryst."

"'Ave y' considered," Jaice said, "what 'appens after y' take Mr. Sparrow to the Veil? I mean, say 'e gets back to 'is olde self, and 'e plans to go an' save 'Awkshadow. Will y' go with 'im, or will y' go back to Mr. Thayliss?"

Catherine looked at Erik. "I can't say, Jaice. It is not that I haven't thought about it, but so much depends on him. If he is healed, I would be tempted to travel with him again." She sighed.

"But he may not want me at his side. And I may not have the endurance for another great journey; I could not keep pace with a rejuvenated Ilangien."

Jaice frowned. "Now why would y' think 'e wouldn't want y'r company, luv?"

"Because the truth will be known to him. I am the one who did this to him. He may not forgive me."

"I find that 'ard to believe."

Catherine shrugged. "All the same, if I returned to Halgon, I could live the rest of my days in Brandeise. But he may not be willing to forgive me, either."

"Y're pretty 'ard on y'self. Y'd think y' were some evil witch, they way y' talk. All y' want to do is the right bloody thing, eh?"

Catherine's mouth set in a thin line. "I have learned it is all a matter of perspective. You must be willing to see beyond your own wishes and logic. It is not always an easy task."

Jaice brought the mule to a halt. "I think it is." He and Catherine helped Erik down from the saddle. "I think y' just can't be selfish. 'S all. Look at y'. Y' don't ever think o' y'self, Lady Catherine."

She smiled at him. "That is not true, Mr. Ginmon, but I appreciate that you think me so virtuous." They unpacked some provisions and started on a light breakfast. Catherine found Erik willing to accept some bread and dried fruit.

"'E looks better already," Jaice said, studying the old man.

Catherine nodded. "I never told you, but I wanted to thank you for coming back for us. You opened my eyes, gave me hope again."

Jaice did not smile. "We're not at the Veil yet, luv. Y' might curse me for this."

"I would never—"

He held up a hand. "Y' don't know what I know. I'll tell y' me story, but not yet. 'S too early. An' I want to enjoy me breakfast."

Catherine said nothing but listened as the adventurer chattered on about the plants and creatures they might encounter. She had never forgotten the fear in his eyes when they had first tried to enlist his help. She wondered how he struggled with it now, as they traveled to the very place he had cursed.

The sun rose steadily in a clear sky, no longer as gentle as it had been that morning. The travelers donned their hats and kept their costrels in-hand. The mules' tails swatted at flies and insects the size of a kingpiece, and at one point, Jaice had them smear the juice of the galingo plant upon their skin as a sort of repellant. Of course, it also smelled like curdled milk, but their noses eventually adjusted to the sour odor.

It was late afternoon when they took another break, and Catherine presented Erik's costrel to him. It felt strangely light, and when she inspected it, she found a small hole in the side that had leaked the precious water within.

"Rats," Jaice said. "I should've noticed it before." He chucked the empty vessel into the vegetation. "Can't fix 'em once they've been chewed." He scratched his chin. "I 'ave to make a detour, luv. 'E needs 'is water."

"Erik and I can share a costrel," Catherine said.

"'S not enough. If we can't refill, y' both go thirsty." The frustrated adventurer approached his mule. "Osenn 't'ain't far. I can be back by sundown if I go now."

"Is there anything I can do while you are gone?" Catherine asked.

"Nah. Jus' stay put," he said, and swung into the saddle.

She was amazed at how adept he was at managing tasks with only one hand. As he rode away, her focus turned to Erik. "Mr. Sparrow, this is not unlike our journey to the Nightwind Mountains. It seemed like we were the only ones on the road, swallowed by a vast wilderness." She looked around. "There is no road here, of course."

Erik followed her gaze.

"Just like then, I wish I knew what to expect from our destination. Will we be greeted with kindness or hostility? Will we be greeted at all? What are these immortals like, having been isolated for so long?" She took his hand in hers. "Will they be able to help you? If they cannot restore your Light, then…" She could not finish her thought.

At the mention of "Light," his eyes had returned to her. "To the Light. Always," he said.

"What is it you mean by that?" she mused. "Or do you merely say it because it is an idea you cling to?" Catherine smiled in spite of herself. "Listen to me. That was a question you would ask."

"A question for me." Erik looked at her expectantly.

"Would you answer one?" she asked him, hoping for another response. His words were so few anymore. She missed his voice. Missed his conversation, his humor, his wit.

At first Erik said nothing. He watched her, as if gauging her expression. Then he focused on a fly that had landed on his hand. "Yes."

Was there meaning behind his response? Catherine could not say. "I will ask you one question, then." She tried not to set herself up for disappointment, but she knew the truth in her heart. "Erik. Who am I?"

He was still focused upon the fly. "The Lady." He nodded slightly. "The One."

Catherine searched him, her heart in slow motion. The Lady. The One. Vague as his response was, he still knew her—even if just by sight. She sat down beside him. "Jaice will be a while yet. Let me tell you a story."

The sky was awash with color when Catherine spied the men approaching. Men. Her stomach knotted. As they came nearer, she could see Jaice in the lead, his face drawn with tension. He was flanked by Halgon and two others. When Halgon saw her, his pace quickened, and Catherine braced herself for the encounter to come.

Jaice kept his distance as husband and wife came face-to-face. Though there was no place for privacy, they stood apart from everyone else. Catherine glimpsed Erik's eyes upon them, and she drew strength from his attention.

"This foolish endeavor is at an end," Halgon said stiffly. His fingers locked around her arm. "We are going home."

Catherine held her ground. "No. I can't. I won't." She leveled her gaze at him, watching as he colored with anger.

"Stubborn woman, you are my wife. We discussed this ludicrous notion of yours, and I forbade you from going. Yet you threw yourself in harm's way to defy me. If not for spotting Mr. Ginmon, I never would have found you. I wonder if Mr. Sparrow is not the only one who has lost his mind."

Now it was Catherine who turned a shade of red. She squared her shoulders, but Halgon would not release her. "I understand why you are angry, but do not define me by some subservient role or dismiss me as some simple, frivolous girl. I have managed my own estate as Countess of Silvarn, and I have found my own prosperity, gained the respect of my servants. The decisions I make are weighted and careful, and they are *my* decisions."

"You think only of yourself," Halgon said, hurt creeping into his voice. "What of the commitment you made to me? What of our marriage, our life? How can I stand aside and allow you to journey into a dangerous jungle, knowing you will not likely return? I care too much for you, Catherine. I will not allow it."

"I have traveled as a peasant along unprotected roads, was threatened by bandits, held against my will, and nearly buried by a crumbling mountain. I have knowingly faced danger for one I believe in." Catherine lifted her chin. "And while I agreed to become your wife, I admit that I had lost sight of one commitment I made long before I met you."

Halgon followed her gaze to Erik, who was still watching them from where he sat. "I can respect your independence and your strength," he said slowly, "but I cannot support this cause. Whatever allegiance you have to your friend, it is at an end." He extended a hand in Erik's direction. "Look at him. He is an empty vessel. He has lost his mind." Halgon shook his head. "He knows nothing of where he is or what he is about. You cannot save him. It is too late." He gripped Catherine's arm tighter. "The man you respected and knew is gone. Accept it, Catherine."

While he spoke, she had been attentive to Erik's expression. No longer blank and unassuming, she could see something in his eyes —a glimmer that might have been a tear. But more telling was how his shoulders had slumped, how he had turned his face to the ground. Somewhere in that aged and dying body was the Ilangien, and whether or not he understood her mission, Halgon's words had reached him.

She swallowed the lump in her throat, fighting back the tears she never wanted to shed in front of Erik. "Respect? I did respect him. But that was not why I followed him all this way." She turned back to face Halgon. "I love him. I have loved him for a long time, and nothing that has happened has quelled those feelings."

"Are you saying, then, that you do not care for me?" Halgon asked. "Did you accept my proposal merely because I offered you stability? A place to reside, food on the table. Is that what I represent to you?"

"Of course not," Catherine said, her free hand upon his arm. "When you proposed to me, I was alone, my hope fading. I was lost, and you found me—vulnerable and uncertain." She searched him. "You cannot tell me that you had not seen opportunity at that time."

Halgon looked as though he would protest, but she continued.

"There is no shame in it. You came to help me, and you did. You have been very kind and generous. I saw a different future with you, and I found a different hope—a dream that I had come to believe impossible. And while I could be happy with you, I had blinded myself to the reason for my being here." She nodded toward Erik. "I came here with him, for him. I am not bound to him through marriage, but I am bound to him through love."

Catherine eased Halgon's fingers from her arm. "I care about you very much, and if fate is willing, I will return to you once I have seen him safe. But if you stop me now, you will never have my heart or my respect."

Halgon let his arm drop to his side. "That I could be what he is to you." He looked at Erik and sighed. "Whoever he was, whatever he did, I wish I knew. If only he knew how fortune smiles on him, to have you devotedly at his side."

Catherine took Halgon's hand and held it to her heart. "Hold a place for me," she said. "I feel that Eraekryst's journey will part from mine. The mission was always his—even from the start. I had no goal, and while I will carry him this stretch, he must continue where I have no place to go."

Halgon kissed her hand and pulled her close. "I will be waiting for you. Please return to me."

She drew away from him. "That is my hope."

"Is there nothing I can do for you?" he asked, desperate. "You are determined to find these 'jungle dwellers' in so savage a land. Let me send my men with you for protection."

Catherine shook her head. "I already have the best guide at my side. I have every bit of faith in Mr. Ginmon and his leadership."

Halgon gave Jaice a stern glance. "Then I will also have faith that he will return you to me unharmed."

"Farewell, Halgon," Catherine said, watching as he retreated to his waiting companions.

"Until I see you again," he vowed. Then they slowly departed, leaving the original trio in silence.

"I admit to feelin' a bit pressured now," Jaice muttered to himself.

"All will be well," Catherine assured him, still watching the now-empty landscape. "I have not come this far to submit to nameless fears." She moved to Erik's side to help him to his feet. Once he was standing, she embraced him and looked into his eyes. "You are still with me, and I will not fail you. To the Light. Always."

23

SECRAILOSS UNVEILED

"We made it, Erik. We found the Veil." Catherine knew this was the place, though she had not known what to expect. It was a dark and shadowy forest with massive spiderwebs stretched between tree limbs and the ground. There were sounds she could not describe, but they kept her ill at ease, her senses on edge. She took a step forward and felt Erik's hand slip from hers.

When she looked behind her, he was not alone. He was standing next to a woman garbed in the shades of night, with eyes stained like wine, and hair shining like the black waves of the ocean beneath the moon. The Huntress had found them.

Seranonde wrapped her arms around the old man, and he wilted in her grasp. Catherine gave a shout, but Erik's flesh shrank against his bones and flaked away like ash on the wind. The Huntress began to laugh, and Catherine had to cover her ears for fear of going deaf. But the sound persisted inside her head, haunting her as she realized her failure.

"Please, luv, open y'r eyes."

Catherine pried her hands from her ears and opened her eyes. Jaice was beside her, and the night sky reigned above them.

"I wasn't sure I'd be able to wake y'," Jaice said.

"It was only a nightmare," Catherine said, relieved. But she saw Jaice's concerned expression did not change. "What—"

"'E's gone. I didn't want to wake y', but I didn't want to leave y' to search for 'im. 'E can't 'ave gone far."

Catherine immediately sat upright. "How did—he can scarcely walk!"

"Tha's why I think 'e can't 'ave gotten far," Jaice repeated. "Weak as 'e is, we should find 'im easy." He scratched his chin. "Jus' don' know 'ow 'e left without us 'earing 'im."

Catherine stood and scanned the landscape, her heart pounding. "Where do we start?"

"The brush is trampled this way," Jaice said, stepping ahead of her.

They followed the trail for just under an hour, and Catherine was amazed that Erik would venture this far on his own accord. What had lured him from their camp? Surely her dream was not a glimpse of reality? She wished she could shake the ominous feeling that pricked her flesh and ate at her nerves.

"Oi," Jaice whispered and held out a hand behind him.

She stopped and gaped at the phenomenon a short distance from them. Translucent, luminous figures stirred amongst the vegetation. Dull, chalky light surrounded bipedal, amorphous forms, and it seemed they shed a powdery substance like dust as they moved. At times they looked almost Human, their shape shifting to recognizable features. Otherwise they had no faces at all. They reminded her slightly of the specters she had seen in the Nightwind Mountains. Erik was kneeling upon the ground a short distance from them, as if he was awaiting their approach.

"This is no good," Jaice said in an unfamiliar tone that nearly made Catherine shudder. He motioned for her to crouch down with him.

"What are they?" she breathed. "Ghosts? Spirits?"

"'Graylings', I call 'em." Jaice narrowed his eyes upon the scene. "I think they come from that place y' call the Veil. Whatever 'appens, don't lettem see y'. Stay quiet."

"Erik is right there," Catherine whispered back, panicked.

"We can't 'elp 'im," Jaice said, not looking at her.

"What will they do to him?" She waited for a response but received none. Catherine bit her lip and started to stand. "I won't abandon him."

Jaice pulled her back down with his one strong hand. His face was inches from hers, and all she could see were his wide, unblinking eyes. "Jedinom's Bloody Sword, listen to me!" he hissed. He released her, and she drew back in shock. It took her a moment to realize that for the first time, she was witnessing his terror.

Rattled by his change in demeanor, Catherine clenched her hands until her knuckles were white and her fingernails threatened to break the skin. She watched as the handful of Graylings advanced upon the old man, and he reached out toward them—toward their light. *Erik, no!* she screamed inside her head, but her lips remained tightly pressed. He was engulfed by their presence, and she could no longer see him.

Catherine found Jaice had not budged, and she hated her helplessness—hated that misfortune might once again take Erik from her. What more could she lose? Would it even matter if she ran at the creatures, shouting at the top of her lungs? What was her life without him?

Just as she tensed to stand a second time, the Graylings moved away from their victim. They drifted a distance before they vanished entirely. Erik was still kneeling, still reaching. But then his outstretched arm slowly lowered, and his shoulders slumped.

Jaice would not stop her now. Catherine was on her feet and racing for Erik before the adventurer could grab her again.

"Gone," the old man murmured, looking up at her mournfully.

"What did they do to you?" Catherine asked, searching every

part of him for some change. He did not respond, of course, but he did allow her to help him to his feet. Jaice came to join them, his face pale, his expression grim. "Explain the Graylings," she insisted, and Jaice hesitated.

"Jaice," Erik said. He held out his hand to the adventurer, his long fingers uncurling to reveal an object in his palm.

Jaice turned a shade paler as he reached for the item—a small wooden carving of a woman holding a book to her breast. It trembled in his hand until he gripped it tightly and pressed it to his forehead. He closed his eyes and gave a long, heavy sigh.

"What is the matter?" Catherine asked.

The adventurer took another breath. "I think it's time I told y' about the Veil." He opened his eyes and handed her the carving.

"There were five of us. Young blokes with nothin' better-a-do than roam around an' call ourselves adventurers. Tal, Rossen, Silver, Quick, an' me—all grew up together in an orphan 'ome in Fanorin. We didn't 'ave naught but the rags on our backs…and all o' Secramore t'explore. We wanted fame, riches, women—all the good things we never knew.

"So we traveled around the South a bit, learned the land, caused some drama where we weren't wanted. Drama's easy enough where beer an' women go. Author'ties told us to get lost, lest we wanted to end up downside o' the rope." He made a gesture to indicate a noose.

"We felt 'twas time we got serious about our business, an' we set our sights on the biggest mystery we knew: Secrailoss. Uncharted, wild, beautiful Secrailoss. At the least we could map it and sell our works to the kingdoms starting their colonies. We set sail and tried to learn what we could afore we set out.

"There was a rumor—more of a story, really—'bout a place o' paradise. Waterfalls o' gold, a river that made y' young again, so y'd live forever. Didn't even 'ave a name, this place, but we knew we 'ad to find it. We 'eard 'twas in the 'eart o' the continent, an' so we started on the adventure of our lives."

Jaice paused, lost in reminiscence. "Oh, we 'ad some good times. I miss those bastards like I miss me 'and." He held up his truncated appendage. "If I'd a'known what would've 'appened, I never would've come 'ere." He glanced at Catherine. "But I guess we can all say such a thing now and again."

Catherine said nothing but nodded in agreement. She gripped Erik's hand tighter and listened as Jaice continued.

"Started out beautifully, I'd say. No rain, plenty o' food, no worries. We'd sit around a fire each night an' tell stories, sing a song or two. We'd talk about what we'd do when we made our fortunes. We 'ad no idear 'twas all about to change.

"One night, Tal was all restless. Y'd 'ave thought 'e 'ad spiders crawling in 'is clothes. We turned in for sleep, but I kept an eye open—watched 'im while 'e fretted. 'E gets up and wanders off—jus' like Mr. Sparrow, 'ere. I nudge me mate Silver, an' we follow 'im at a distance. We spot this glowy shape, an' Tal 'eads straight for it. Can't really say what 'appened, but the shape disappeared, an' Tal wasn't 'imself.

"'E seemed a world away, mumbling to 'imself when 'e spoke at all. 'E din't sleep, an' 'e ate 'cuz we forced 'im to. 'Is eyes," Jaice pointed to his own, "were always set to the south an' the thick o' the jungle. That was where 'is feet took 'im, an' we 'ad to follow, 'cuz 'e wouldn't go any other way."

"Did you ever try to turn back?" Catherine asked.

"Ah, the idear was mentioned once or twice, but we thought 'e'd shape up once we got where we wanted to be. Turns out 'e was takin' us there." He looked at the carving longingly. "Made that for Tal as we went along. I 'oped it'd bring 'im 'round. 'Twas a girl 'e met, fancied 'e'd marry once 'e was rich."

Catherine handed the figure back to him, realizing it was a

talent he could no longer enjoy. "Do you believe the same Grayling gave it to Erik?"

"I don't know," Jaice said quietly. "I don't know, an' I don' much like it, luv. As much as I 'ate to say it, I think 'is state o' 'ealth may've saved 'im. 'E don't seem any diff'rent—not like Tal. Then again, Mr. Sparrow ain't 'ad much to say of late ennaway. Or maybe those bloody Graylings know where we're 'eaded, an' they're just lettin' us come." He shook his head. "Either way, s' no good."

"The Light," Erik murmured, and turned his head to the south.

"'E knows," Jaice said warily. "'E knows where we're going."

"Jaice," Catherine pressed, "what happened to Tal?"

"Tal—'e never got better, not even as we got closer to our destination. We took to the jungle an' came to a river. 'Twas strange—a feeling in the air I can't explain. An' 'struth, the river did sparkle o' gold. Shimmered. Even in the dark." Jaice frowned. "'Twas in the dark I tripped. Broke me leg, I did, an' I was in a bad way. Fever an' all, though I still remember it all clearly. I wasn't crossing any river, but the others decided to take Tal an' scout a'ead. They were too excited to wait for daybreak.

"So I stayed behind, an' Quick stayed with me. When the sun came rising, we saw death on the shore o' the river." He closed his eyes and shuddered. "Luv, there were skulls an' bones of all kinds. Animals I never seen. All dead around us. We wanted to leave, but we couldn't—not without our mates. So we waited all day, an' well into the next night. They never came back.

"Poor Quick, 'e didn't know what to do. The river was shallow enough to cross, an' 'e said 'ed come right back if 'e didn't see 'em on the other side. I waited 'til the sun was 'igh, an' I thought more'n once I was going to die in that jungle graveyard. Me eyes played tricks in me fever, but now I wonder if they were tricks at all. There were so many sounds, but I never sawr a thing. I 'aven't been a good friend to Jedinom, but I was talking to 'im a lot then.

Maybe 'e 'eard me, 'cuz Quick came back. Brought me water from wherever 'e'd been an' said 'twould 'elp me.

"I was too weak to argue, an' I sipped it. The pain in me leg disappeared. I drank a lil' more, and I swear on the golden sword if me leg wasn't 'ealed in an eyeblink, luv. Me fever was gone, and once in me right mind, I said we 'ad to go an' get our mates.

"Quick got real quiet an' said they were dead. 'E said the Graylings killed 'em. I didn't want to believe 'im, but 'e wouldn't let me go. 'E said we 'ad to get moving, because 'twas too dangerous to stay. So we left, and neither of us said a word 'til that night."

Jaice took a moment to compose himself as his eyes watered. "Quick, that bastard. Damn bastard saved me life. 'E never said what 'e found beyond the river. Never spoke a word of it. But whatever 'appened, 'e grew really sick. 'Twas like the life was draining from 'im. 'E grew weak an' pale, an' even that water didn't 'elp 'im. 'E was just wastin' away." The adventurer brushed his sleeve over his eyes. "'E died a couple days later, and I did me best to bury 'im. Last thing 'e 'ad said to me was, 'Don't go back.' I promised I wouldn't." He managed a weak smile. "Guess I'm not good for keeping me promises."

"You broke your promise to the dead so that you would save the living," Catherine said. "For that I am so very grateful."

"Y' say that now, luv, but I din't tell y' this to make me feel better," Jaice said. "When we get to the Veil, y' got to let Mr. Sparrow go in alone. If there are blokes like 'im in there, then they can 'elp 'im, an' 'e can decide what 'e wants to do. We," he gestured to her, "stop at the river. Then I'll bring y' back 'ome to Mr. Thayliss. That's the plan."

Catherine nodded. "I will heed your warning."

"We should 'ead back to camp an' try for a lil' sleep—even if 'twon't come easy."

~

Catherine found her strength tested in the following days. Jaice, try as nobly as he might to downplay his fears, slipped slowly from his chipper spirits. He would swear that he heard his name whispered in the wind or in the rustling of the leaves, but she wondered if it was not his sense of guilt that played upon his mind. He seemed to appreciate her attempt to assuage him, and she, in turn, appreciated his honesty about his concerns.

By contrast, she knew nothing of what Erik thought or felt. His few expressions had dissolved into an empty mask, and he had abandoned all verbal communication. He rode with them as his strength would allow, but Catherine had to admit that was fading faster than a spring blossom. He seemed to press onward by some subconscious necessity rather than by his own will. His movements were slow and labored, and she would swear by his appearance that he had aged another decade. Her own greatest fear was that he would not endure the final stretch to the Veil.

They did not see the Graylings again as they finally left the open land to penetrate the jungle. Catherine was reminded of the final moments when he had truly been Eraekryst of Celaedrion, when his mind was breaking under the haunting of the Black Mountain, Kirou-Mekus. He had been capable enough of leading her and Jaice astray so that he might achieve some notion of justice or vengeance for himself. She caught herself wondering how different a path it would have been had he never veered from his original mission. They would have gone straight to the Veil, she never would have employed the rose, and he would now be as he once was. To look at him now and know he had been the cause of his own descent, it filled her heart with pity. If the immortals of the Veil could help him, would he be doomed to repeat the mistakes of his past? Or would he emerge wizened and focused—enough to continue his mission? But perhaps Arythan Crow was already dead, slain by Seranonde in Eraekryst's extended absence.

Catherine would never know the truth; her journey would end at the river.

It pained her to think that the last she would see of him would be as he was now—a whisper of himself. She would never know his fate, never know if their journey to the Veil had met with any success. From the moment Eraekryst had appeared at Lorrelwood to this point in time, she had given everything to be with him. Her wealth, her title, her home, her time, her body—of all that she had sacrificed, it was her love for him that would be the most difficult to surrender. How could she leave him now, after all they had endured? She would have to leave a piece of her heart behind, knowing it would never heal. There was no alternative.

Twilight was falling when she stumbled across the first skeleton. Long, white, fleshless bones had been unscathed by rain or creature, a grim warning to whatever fate lay ahead. As the trio progressed, the ground much resembled a forest that had been felled, the trees strewn and splintered—only these were skulls, rib cages, vertebrae, and the bones of limbs. They could not walk without stepping on them, and the sound of crunching and cracking beneath hooves silenced any words they might have.

In the deepening hues of night, they heard a different sound: the pervasive din of flowing water. "We're close," Jaice said. "Maybe we ought to stop 'ere for the night."

"I don't know that I want to stop in a place like this," Catherine said, drawing her cloak tighter around her shoulders. Their mules echoed their sentiments, for they stomped and tossed their heads, the whites of their eyes apparent despite the intensifying shadows. "How can this be paradise when all we see is death? I'm afraid to leave Erik here."

"We don' know what's beyond the river," Jaice said. "It's 'is only chance, luv. Y'ave to take it."

"What if he doesn't have the strength to cross?" Catherine protested.

"'E's still riding, ain't 'e?" Jaice dismounted and tied his unwilling mount to a tree. He moved to help her down. "We'll 'ave to go on foot now if y' want to press on. Poor beasts 'ave better sense than we do."

They both helped Erik from the saddle, and Catherine tried to gauge him. Had he been Human, she would have guessed he was etched by the lines of eighty-some years. His legs were wobbly, his bones bearing little more flesh than what littered the ground around them. If he would last another night, it would be one more night she would have with him, but there was no cause in holding on. She would not base her decision on her own selfish needs. She had to let him go.

"Let's continue," she murmured, taking Erik's hand. "We will see him to the river, and then we can go."

"Alright," Jaice said, hesitation in his voice. He took the lead, and they picked their way over bones and around vegetation.

Catherine glanced at Erik frequently. She was not ready to let him go. Not into the unknown. It seemed cruel, condemning. Did he even know what they intended? Or would he stare at them, wondering why his companions were abandoning him to this land of death? What if there was no paradise beyond the bank? What horrors would await him if he did make it across?

Jaice gave a cry, and Catherine shifted her focus. "No," she mouthed, sighting the shapeless, glowing masses heading for them.

"Faster," Jaice said, trying to urge them on. Catherine pulled Erik along, and they nearly fell over a ribcage.

"He can't," she cried, and nearly lost her own footing. There was nothing to distinguish in the black landscape before them. Behind them, however, the Graylings drew nearer.

"Golden Sword, they're calling me," Jaice said, horrified. "They know me! They know me!"

"Do not look back!" Catherine told him. "Do not listen to them!" She thought she glimpsed a flicker of light in the distance.

"By the Sword, it's them," Jaice insisted, spinning around. "I know 'tis. Tal, Silver, Rossen. I can 'ear them calling me."

"There are only the Graylings," Catherine said, trying to sound calm as she tugged Erik forward.

"Maybe tha's what they are. An' I left 'em behind. They're 'ere for me!" Jaice plunged ahead of them.

"They're herding us toward the river," Catherine said aloud as the realization struck her. "This is a trap, Jaice!"

The Graylings were closing in, gaping eyes forming where none had been before. Skeletal, transparent arms reached in the trio's direction.

"We can't escape it," Jaice gasped. By now the shimmering light of the golden river appeared like a stream of embers cutting through the darkness. They stumbled onward until they reached the edge of the embankment. Broad but seemingly shallow, the water seemed the better alternative to the creatures pursuing them. But to cross the river would mean no return.

Catherine felt Erik's hand leave hers. She grasped at empty air, her eyes straining against the darkness to see where he had fallen down the embankment—to no avail. "Erik! *Erik!*" To lose him now was to lose everything.

She heard Jaice curse and looked up to see the Graylings were just yards away. Had they slowed? Or was her mind toying with her?

A shadow moved in front of her sight. A gaunt frame. Catherine gave a cry and lunged forward, but her foot caught, and she fell to the ground amidst the bones. The shadow lifted its arms, its hands raised as if to offer resistance to their pursuers. Catherine screamed, just as the Graylings bore down upon him. There was a flash of light bright enough to devour the whole of the night, and when it dimmed, the shadows moved back in like the rings of a fathomless pool. The Graylings were gone.

The sound of her own broken breathing was all she perceived until she heard the crunching of bones underfoot.

"Catherine? Catherine, luv?" Jaice's words reached out to her like a lonely candle. But she did not want to answer.

"Catherine?"

"Here," she managed, her voice caught in her throat. "I'm here."

Then he was beside her, and her eyes had adjusted enough to see his face. "Y'alright?" Jaice asked quietly.

She did not answer him but tried to rise. He steadied her with his one hand. The forest was so very quiet. Even the sound of the river fell short of her ears. She did not quite straighten as she slowly moved to where she had seen Erik a moment ago. He was there, upon the ground, and she did not want to look. She could not look.

"'E saved us, din't 'e?"

Catherine turned to him. "Jaice...I have to go back on my word. I will not return to Halgon." Without clearly seeing him, she could feel his eyes searching her.

"Don't go, luv—"

"That is my decision," she interrupted. "Please do not try to dissuade me."

"I—I won't," he said, resigned to her will.

Catherine embraced him. "Thank you for everything. I wish you the best." She pulled away from him, but he did not move. He took the bag from his back and handed it to her.

"The rose, luv—'s inside," Jaice said. "I don' know if it'll 'elp y'. I'm sorry."

She could not find the words to respond, so she did not. She waited until the sound of his footfalls vanished, and then she knelt beside Erik. "To the Light," she whispered, "always." She did not know if there was life yet in him, but she did know she had to complete his journey.

Catherine took his arm and secured it around her shoulders.

She had expected a struggle to lift him, but there was little weight to him at all. The only trait that hindered her was his height; she had forgotten how tall he was, for his posture had become bent over the past months. When she reached the embankment, her confidence ebbed. It was an awkward descent that was more of a stumble and a spill.

The golden water meandered around her calves, and Catherine hoped it would not grow any deeper. Despite how light he was, he was still dead weight, and her muscles were unaccustomed to such an awkward and persistent burden. The water dragged at her legs with every step, and the current pulled at Erik with relentless determination. Her shoulders began to ache, and she lowered her head so that her back would help support him.

There was no room in her mind for sadness, despair, or fear. Her sight was locked on the opposite bank, and once she reached it…well, that was the next step. With deep and steady breaths, she ignored her pain and weakness, trudging ahead because it was all she could do. The water was up to her waist, but the buoyancy aided her rather than hindered her. The river was surprisingly warm, and its light hinted at the features of the shore. She tried to determine the best place to climb, but the vegetation was thick—even on the steeper slopes.

Erik did not move at all, limply supported by her side. As the water level dropped, Catherine felt the added weight of their soaked clothes. She could not catch her breath, and once she reached the bank, she fell to her knees, gasping for air. She laid Erik on his back beside her, daring to assess his condition for the first time. His eyes were shut, and though the golden light of the river cast a warm tone to his skin, he felt cold and clammy. She touched his cheek, hardly aware that it was her tears and not the water that dampened her face. She was not ready to say goodbye.

"Please stay with me. We're nearly there," Catherine whispered. Awkwardly she tried to reposition him as he had been, and then she warily eyed her objective. There was no thinking about it, no consideration to be done. She simply had to move. She gave a cry as she thrust all her effort and strength to clawing her way up the slope. Rooted plants dislodged beneath her hands, and dirt wedged beneath her fingernails. Her limbs nearly gave out from the strain. For every inch she slipped, she hoped to recover two.

At the top she collapsed, Erik beside her. She wondered how much further she would have to go. Ahead of her was a thick tangle of vegetation—a veritable dark wall that could continue endlessly. Either the immortals of the Veil did not want to be discovered, or some other power had taken care to hide them. Whichever the case, Catherine had felt the same disconcertion at Kirou-Mekus and the Nightwind Mountains. Fortifying her uncertainty was the idea that this final venture was a mistake—that before them was a dark and evil place that would be their end.

But if she did not press onward, Erik's end was inevitable. And so, perhaps, was hers. At least she knew she would not recover her strength here, upon the jungle floor. Without knowing how, she found herself standing again, legs splayed ungracefully to support Erik as she plowed her way into the dense foliage. Catherine took a breath and started forward.

Branches struck her, leaves smeared against her face, and vines resisted her passage as she blindly struggled against them. She gasped at the silken snare of a large web across her face and hastened her pace. Perhaps her eyes deceived her, but she thought she glimpsed a flicker of blue light. Her first panicked thought was that the Graylings had returned, but as she drew nearer, she found the source of the luminescence was more constant and expansive. Like mist, it rose around her, growing thicker by the seconds. This mist, however, was warm, and it tickled her skin and fluttered in her lungs. Her head began to spin, and she tried to find a tree to lean upon. But the trees had disappeared. Everything, it seemed, had vanished in the wake of the rising cloud.

Unable to tell earth from sky, Catherine took a clumsy step and careened forward. Erik slipped from her shoulder, but she did not hear the impact of his fall. The bag with the rose also fell away, and then she was upon the ground again, too confused and disoriented to form any questions in her mind. From amidst the light, a tall silhouette manifested in its approach. Features materialized upon its body, and Catherine gawked up at the pale-skinned, white-haired, blue-eyed being. He looked down at her without expression, and she knew that she had made a grave error. She could not move—even as the Durangien reached for her with fingers outstretched. His cold touch upon her brow was the last sensation before she succumbed to darkness.

24

AWAKENING

Arythan awoke to a room full of candles and a ewer with three wine glasses upon the bedside table. His head ached fiercely, and his stomach was done up in knots. This was how he had felt each and every day since his great escape attempt—at least, it was how he felt on the days he could remember. Diana had told him he had been unconscious for some time, which really meant nothing to him. Time had never been so irrelevant.

"Doq e-sieqa?" he whispered, his throat dry enough to break open.

"Are you speaking to me?" Diana asked. She moved towards him from across the room. "You know I do not understand your language—whatever language that is."

"What is this shit?" Arythan translated. The healer had not been patient with him, and he was fairly certain she was angry with him. She probably felt betrayed, as did most everyone he knew. *Tough bones. She's not the one in chains.*

"The king seems to believe you are well enough for an interrogation," Diana said. "If I were you, I would tell him what he wants to know. He might spare you the dungeon." There was a knock upon the door, and she opened it to reveal two servants bearing platters and a tureen of whatever meal was at hand.

He intends to stuff his face in front of me. Fantastic. Arythan shifted uncomfortably upon the bed, and the chains further chafed where the skin had worn raw around his wrists and ankles. He grimaced at the burn, and this did not go unnoticed by his caretaker.

"I would wrap them if I could," Diana said. "The prince does not believe there is such a thing as 'infection.' He will not let me move the chains."

He is afraid of me. He should be. If I ever got free... It was wishful thinking, and Arythan knew it. There would be no more opportunities, and he had no other friends willing to chance helping him. He could not blame them. His chin started to itch, and he lifted his arms to try and rub it against his bindings.

"For the love of the sword," Diana muttered, walking over to scratch his bearded face.

"Say what y' want to say. Get it out," he told her.

"What would be the point?"

I could face the wrath of everyone then. He continued to watch her as she mixed the salve. *I could die knowing I had not one friend left to worry about.*

But the usually tight-lipped healer had accepted his invitation. "I told you that you were playing a dangerous game. You knew what you stood to lose. And even after you had lost, you had to dig your own grave."

"What does it matter?"

"Damn you, Arythan," she said, pausing to glare at him. "Some of us actually care—even if you don't." Then she turned away to add more herbs.

He was not sure how to digest her comment.

"For over a week I have been here, trying to keep you alive." She cut him short before he could interrupt. "Not because anyone asked it of me. It was because I was unwilling to let you die."

"Sorry to disappoint y'," Arythan said and turned away from all the flickering lights. Death was all that waited for him now, and it would come to him in one form or another.

As if on cue, Michael strode through the door, another familiar face at his heels. "How is our mage, Lady Sherralin?" he asked brightly.

"He is resting, Your Highness," Diana answered.

"Perhaps he has rested enough." Michael presented his guest to the healer. "I do not suppose you know Medoriate Alwin. He formerly worked for the Seroko and is now my royal medoriate."

"A pleasure to meet you," Brann Alwin said, giving a slight bow before Diana. Then his eyes roved to where Arythan lay.

The mage stared back.

"Oh yes, I do see the effects of the Ice," Alwin said with a vague gesture. "His eyes are the key, dark as they are. But it may soon be time to administer another dose."

"Nigqor-slet," Arythan said in his rocky voice.

"Yes," Michael said with a smile. "Medoriate Alwin will be administering the Enhancement to our mage, to keep him compliant."

"'E works for the Seroko," Arythan emphasized, dumbfounded by the wizard's presence.

"*Worked*, Crow." Michael held up a finger and approached the bedside. "The Seroko have since withdrawn from the Plains to gather more talent from Mystland. Medoriate Alwin could not very well process the Black Ice alone." He winked at Arythan. "You are, after all, dead. Or so I told them. You were executed for your crime."

"No one stops working for them," Arythan said. "'E's a slave for life."

"Allow me to interject," Alwin said. "I was merely a wizard for hire. My term is finished, and I am at liberty to pledge allegiance to whomever I choose."

Arythan turned his head and spat on the ground.

Michael sighed. "Medoriate Alwin is here to join us for dinner, Crow. Please be civil." He waved for the servants to position a couple chairs at the bedside table. Before he sat down, he glanced in irritation at the healer as she scraped the sides of her bowl. "Lady Sherralin, have you finished with him yet?"

"I need only apply the salve, Your Highness."

"Your haste is appreciated. I have business to conduct."

Diana came to the bedside and applied the mixture to Arythan's wounds. She looked at him only once, her lips set in that thin, hard line that told him she was upset. Then she took her leave, and he was forced to face his enemies in a "civil" dinner meeting.

Michael apportioned the food on three plates and poured the wine. He offered Arythan a sip, and the mage could feel his mouth water for how parched he was. Several gulps graced his throat before Michael pulled the glass away. "Easy, now. I need you coherent."

The king set the glass down and traded it for another item. Arythan's eyes fixed upon it in surprise. "This," Michael said, holding up the encrusted crystal, "has me quite intrigued. I see you recognize it."

Arythan said nothing, but his thoughts were a flurry. *That is why Othenis didn't know I was ready. You stole the rock...and likely the book as well.*

Michael passed the crystal to Alwin, who took his turn to speak. "It is amazing," the wizard said, turning the piece in his hand. "You actually managed to alter the crystal. I mean to say, I examined this before—tested it—and the residue is inert." He looked at Arythan. "How did you manage it?"

Arythan maintained his silence.

"Regardless," Michael said at last, "I think his intentions were clear. To thwart his enemies, he aimed to destroy the crystals. Is that not what you were doing when Tigress found you?"

No response.

Michael waved his hand. "Ah, it is not important." He took a sip from his own glass and began to eat.

"It is," Arythan said, riveted to the food.

Michael raised an eyebrow. He speared a piece of meat and offered it to him. "How so?"

Hunger overpowered his queasiness, and Arythan devoured the morsel. "Y' think the Seroko need the En'ancement?" he scoffed. "Y' think they're in it for the money?" He turned to Brann Alwin, awaiting a reaction.

Michael faced the wizard as well. "Is that not the case? This had been a partnership in business. A lucrative business."

Alwin's face remained blank. "I know nothing of their business, Sire. I was only given orders concerning the production of the Ice."

Liar, Arythan thought. *Bloody liar.* He considered Diana's words about cooperating—considered what awaited him in the dungeon.

As if reading his mind, Michael asked, "You like being in your old room, do you not? I regret that we must exercise such brutal precautions, but this—" He moved his arm around the room. "One cannot argue with this sort of prison." He gave Arythan another piece. "The Seroko. What did they want, do you think?"

"Immortality."

Alwin started to laugh. "You cannot be serious."

Michael smiled slightly but did not waiver from his focus. "Immortality. That is a rather grand concept. One I would be inclined to believe is impossible."

"The En'ancement is made from dead immortals," Arythan said, humorless. He restrained a shudder as he remembered what immortality had done to the Larini. "'S not impossible. I've seen it."

Michael gazed at him thoughtfully. "You've seen it," he echoed. "You are quite the mystery, aren't you?" He returned to his meal.

"I still say the notion is ludicrous," Alwin said, wine in-hand. "How can an immortal die? They don't even exist, for no one has ever seen them. At least, *I* haven't," he said, clearly amused.

"Erik," Arythan said quietly. "Erik was an immortal."

Michael paused to swallow his food. "Lord Sparrow?" he asked, incredulous. "Really?" He considered the idea. "He did recover from his poisoning...."

"He is concocting this," Alwin said.

"To what end?" Michael asked. "My entertainment? No, Medoriate. In my experience with him, Crow has never lied. Kept secrets, yes, but lied, never." He finished his glass. "If this is true, then I cannot help but feel I have been cheated in this arrangement. Who wouldn't want to live forever?"

Me, Arythan thought. *Just kill me, and be done with this.*

Michael apportioned him several more morsels. "There may be some renegotiations pending," he mused. "Now if only I had more leverage..." He allowed Arythan just a sip of wine before taking the glass away. "Oh, but wait. I *do*. I have you, dear Crow. But what is your value? Why do they want you?"

"I told y' I don' know," Arythan said.

"Perhaps I was wrong," Michael said, frowning. "Maybe you are capable of lies as well." He stabbed a large, juicy piece of meat and slowly chewed it before the mage. Once he had swallowed, he waved the empty knife at Arythan. "Of all the wizards and talented medori the Seroko can gather, they have set their sight upon you. *You*—this scrawny, foreign boy limited to elemental magic. *Why?*"

"Revenge," Arythan said quickly, "because I lost them their immortal."

"No, no." The king shook his head. "If they wanted Lord Sparrow, they would have followed Lord Sparrow, rest assured. There is something you possess, be it object or physical prowess. You should know they were most unhappy to learn of your demise."

"I 'ave nothing," Arythan insisted.

Michael stood. "Disappointing. Well, we have time to sort this out." He assessed the mage and turned to Alwin. "I would say Medoriate Crow is much improved. It is time to change his accommodations. If you would prepare him for his transition…."

"Certainly, Your Highness." The wizard stood as well.

"I told y' what I could!" Arythan's voice broke. He tried not to tremble at the thought of the dungeon.

"Which was not enough," Michael said and turned his back. "I will fetch one of the syndicate to return him to the dungeon."

"Y' think y're in control," Arythan seethed, anger surging past his fear. He strained against the chains. "I should've done it then."

"Done what, dear Crow?" Michael asked, humoring him with a glance over his shoulder.

"Burned y' from the inside out."

"Yet you chose to visit with poor Victoria. An opportunity missed, I am afraid."

"No."

Michael turned a little more. "No?"

"The Seroko 'ave y' now," Arythan said with a wicked grin. "Y're already dead." He watched the king walk away in silence until Alwin shoved his head back against the pillow and stuffed a wadded rag into one side of his mouth. Unable to close it, he squirmed and struggled as the wizard apportioned the dreaded black powder into the wine glass.

Alwin took a look at him. "You cannot keep your mouth shut, can you, Arythan?" He smiled at his own comedy. "No matter. The victor of this little game has already been decided." He raised the drink. "To you, Medoriate Crow." With one hand he gripped Arythan's hair; with the other he set the glass to the mage's open mouth. "Drink up."

Arythan could feel the Ice sizzle on its way down his throat, and though no sound could be heard, he began to scream.

~

He sat on the ground, staring up at the forest canopy. A chill wind raced through the treetops, tearing the browning leaves from the branches and sending them cascading down upon him. The trees were dying, and it made him sad, though he did not know why. How it was he had come to this place, where he was, he did not know. Even he had once borne a name, but it had gone—just as the life had ebbed from this withering forest. And so he sat there, waiting for whatever was to come.

The leaves stirred behind him, and he turned to see six figures there, their forms blurry even as they approached. *"Who are you?"* a voice asked.

"I do not know," he answered.

"How came you here?"

"I cannot remember," he said. *"But 'tis cold here. The sun is gone now."* He squinted at them. *"Have you come to stay?"*

"We do not belong here," another said.

"Do I belong here?" he asked.

"This is all that is left of you," came a female's voice. *"You cannot leave."*

"Oh." He looked around, and the sadness made him shudder.

"You must heal," she continued. *"You need to repair the damage done."*

He picked up a tattered leaf from the ground. *"That is fine and well, but I have no notion of what you mean."*

"If you do not heal, you wil die."

He looked up at the blurry apparitions. *"Die? Am I alive now? What must I do? Who are you?"*

They did not answer, but another cold gust swept by him, and he began to shiver. More leaves came down, and he watched them helplessly.

"Gather them! Catch them before they fall."

"But there are so many," he protested.

"You must try!"

He stood and waited for a stray leaf to spiral downward. He ran to it and clasped it in his hands. When he gazed down at it, he was lost in a vision of faces and voices. Names and words solidified from the fog in his mind, and he came to understand what it was he saw. *"I know this,"* he told them. *"This is part of me, is it not?"*

"This is you," one corrected. *"This place."*

"Why is it dying?" he asked, realizing the danger. *"What is happening to me?"*

"Catch them. Catch them, and heal." The apparitions began to fade. *"We will grant you the Light."*

He looked frantically around him. So many leaves were upon the ground. What had been lost? He gathered an armful and waited for an image to surface, but the leaves remained leaves—lifeless and brown. They dropped from his arms, and he looked to the sky. There was a thinning in the heavy, gray clouds, but the wind would not relent. The trees groaned and creaked, and they shed their foliage like tears.

He raced after each and every leaf, agonized that he would never be able to save them all. For those he did snare, he was bombarded by sights and sounds, people and names, places and feelings. It was almost too much to bear, but it was wonderful at the same time. Though the leaves vanished, the visions remained in his mind, filling it where the emptiness had grown.

For how long he continued, he could not say. Running back and forth amongst the trees, reaching for the sky, reeling at the new sensations. Somewhere in the midst of his maddened efforts, he was forced to pause. Warmth and light angled down upon him through breaks in the clouds. He reveled in it, holding his hands out as though he could catch the sun as well. He had forgotten what it was like, forgotten the life and the energy it brought. When he dared look up again, those fading leaves yet upon the branches had started to green. For the first time in a very, very long while, he smiled.

The expression was short-lived, however, for when his gaze fell back to the horizon, he saw a rising mist. Lazily it rolled toward him, until it was close enough that he could see the forms within it. There were many of them—undefined figures walking in obscurity—moving steadily in his direction. He shivered, knowing there was nowhere for him to go. A growing idea rose amongst his salvaged memories; he knew who they were, knew what they were. They had been lost; they belonged to him. He had destroyed them. And now they were waiting… waiting for him to remember.

CATHERINE WAS TOO exhausted to move, save the opening of her eyes. There was a pastel sky above her, muted by soft clouds and lit by a veiled, rosy sun. Branches stretched high above her, baiting her with leaves of blue and violet that twirled from a passing breeze. The air itself was cool but vibrant, and she would swear that it breathed—like a giant beast in slumber. A large, emerald butterfly with wings as big as a bird's dipped and lifted above her upon unseen waves. Was this a dream? How often had she wondered at her own reality? Her body did not seem a part of her, yet her eyes were dazzled by the strange palette above her, and every breath she took slowly infused her lungs and gave her strength.

It was the sound of broken breathing that urged her to turn her head, and she gasped at what she had forgotten. Erik was a short distance from her, on his hands and knees as though his back supported some great weight. His head was bent, but she could see that though he was alive, he was unchanged. Like an ancient and brittle tree, he seemed to endure some invisible force, straining just to stay upright. He trembled on those bony arms, and his sides heaved with effort as he fought for each breath.

Her weariness forgotten, Catherine tried to roll onto her side. She felt out of control, as if she was being physically restrained from reaching him. "Erik!" His name remained trapped inside her, and she could only watch his lonely struggle.

Strands of golden light lifted from the surrounding trees, earth, and the very air itself. Like spider silk in the wind, they wove their way toward him, dipping into his flesh like needles, and disappearing in small bursts of white light. His breathing quickened, and his posture grew rigid. The threads of light came to him faster, like hundreds of shooting stars converging in one destination.

In awe she felt her own breathing slow, immersed in the transformation of the old man. His form thickened, his back straightened, and he lifted his head. Light shone from his eyes, and the sags and creases of his added years faded as his skin drew taut. The white of his hair gleamed with gold as color returned to it, and the broken gasps became slow, deep intakes of air. He sat back and closed his luminous eyes, and the Light continued to fill him. His shoulders straightened, and his expression was the most placid she had ever seen upon his face.

His face—she had not seen this face in some time. Flawless and radiant, the immortal spirit that had for so long been starved now shone forth unhindered. This was not Erik Sparrow. This was not even the Minstrel. This was the Ilangien she had met the night of Summerfall. This was Eraekryst of Celaedrion.

In the midst of her joy and her amazement, she felt her thoughts darken. Would he remember her? Her, this dirty, shabby, older woman who was not without blame in what had been his steady decline. Would he know what she had done to him, having stolen his memories and rounded his edges so that he would fit into the life she had always wanted? Would he remember her commitment to another when it seemed like her only choice was to abandon him to his fate? The guilt and the doubt welled within her, and she suddenly wanted to run and hide from him—hide from those piercing, knowing eyes that would inevitably turn in her direction.

The forest was no longer ablaze, though a golden aura remained around the Ilangien's form. He sighed and did as she feared. For a moment, maybe several, he regarded her without any expression. But then a smile graced his thin lips, and he stood. Tall as he had once been, and more graceful than she could remember, he came to her side, kneeling next to her.

"Lady Catherine," he said in a voice as warm and gentle as a beam of sunlight.

She found she could not hold his gaze. She could not even think of one word to say. Those silver-blue eyes were searching her. She knew they were. And they would see—

Long fingers entwined in hers, and her skin tingled. Like water down a parched throat, the magic traveled along her arm and filled the whole of her. Her breath caught as she was immersed in the *Ilán*, and all her pain and weariness fled. The guilt did not.

"You are responsible for this," Eraekryst said. "For the leaves I have salvaged, your name persists in so many of them." He picked up a leaf and pressed it to his forehead. "I stumble upon the holes of the road of my recollection," he whispered to himself.

He let the leaf fall and helped her to sit upright. "This place…."

"The Veil," she supplied.

"Aye, the Veil." He brushed the dirt from her shoulder. "This is the Veil." His smile faded.

"Erik, I…" Catherine dabbed at her eyes with her sleeve. "I am so happy to have you back."

"Then I had strayed at some point," he mused, looking around them.

She brushed her shame aside and embraced him, wondering if it was wrong of her to do so to an immortal being. She could feel the magic surrounding him, and it was so very different from when she had embraced Erik Sparrow. He had been tangible then, but holding him now was like holding sunlight, kissing the ocean, or dancing with the wind. She could sense his uncertainty as he returned the gesture, and when she pulled away, it was not her reflection in his eyes but that of a wild forest.

There was something different about him other than his rejuvenation. It was something beyond the physical, but Catherine could not pinpoint the problem.

Already his attention upon her had wavered. "Life is within this land," he murmured, his fingers tracing in the earth. "Immortal life."

"You told me once of the immortals who are said to dwell here. The Forgotten," Catherine said. "I saw a Durangien once I crossed the river. He reached toward me, and that was the last I remember."

"Not truly forgotten then, was he?" Eraekryst asked. He stood and offered Catherine his hand. She felt energized enough that she did not need his assistance, but she took his hand anyway, and he pulled her to her feet. "Where are they now, I wonder. Here and yet not. 'Twas they who assisted me, in mind and in body."

"Would they hide from us?" Catherine asked. "It is not as though they should fear us."

"There is another explanation for their absence, I am certain. Shall we discover it?"

There was a glimmer in his eyes that made him impossible to refuse. She took his hand, and they moved into the vegetation. Leaves and branches shifted before them in so subtle a fashion that she might not have noticed but for their unhindered passage. To be with him again—to feel his Light, to watch his movements, to hear his voice—Catherine found she could have lost herself at his heels. It did not matter where they went or how they arrived; she was where she needed to be. And yet he asked nothing of his arrival to the Veil, how she had managed to bring him, where Jaice had gone. He had not questioned her at all, and while she told herself that he was intent upon his mission, she found it strange that he should neglect such details.

Stranger still was their environment. This section of jungle *felt* differently from what she had traveled with Jaice. The trees might have had eyes for the way she felt like a beetle under observation. When the wind passed by, she would swear it was like fingers pulling lightly at her clothes and hair. Even the earth beneath her feet was soft and warm, like flesh that lived with coursing blood beyond what she could see. For as much as Eraekryst's presence was a comfort, this place became increasingly unnerving the further they penetrated it.

He stopped before a massive tree garbed in soft layers of moss. The thick, lichen-encrusted branches arched upward to support a weeping crown of tiny golden leaves and fragrant white blossoms. Its foliage stirred, though the air remained still. Catherine took a step backward, but Eraekryst moved forward to place a hand upon its bark. His eyes widened, and his lips parted.

"Erik, what—" She fell silent when he lifted his other hand, commanding her patience.

"The lake," he said. "We must find the lake." He took a long and lasting look at the tree before they pressed on.

"Did it speak to you?" Catherine asked.

"She did," Eraekryst answered, distant. "To be so old, to know another life beyond one's own...."

"You had," Catherine reminded him, unsure if she should question him or not.

He glanced at her in surprise. "I was old for a mortal, was I not?" He paused to lift his hands and study them. "I remember feeling like my flesh was not my own. It was a prison in which the flame grew steadily dimmer...impending darkness as death waited, though I knew not what was beyond such an end."

"Is that what mortality was to you?" Catherine asked, saddened by his response.

"It was how I remembered feeling at one time," he answered. His hands fell to his side as he continued. "But I came to know more. I remember laughing. Laughing, of all actions, had once felt frivolous and completely unnecessary. As a mortal, it was compelling—nearly unavoidable when certain emotions could not be contained."

Catherine smiled. "You had a wonderful laugh. I should like to hear it again—a deep and heartfelt sound."

"I do not know that I can laugh again," he admitted.

"You mean to say that after all you experienced as an old man, you have forgotten how to feel? How could immortality rob you of such strong impressions, Erik?"

"Lady Catherine, I could not hope to explain this change to you," he said, dismissive.

"You avoid the truth because it makes you uncomfortable," she challenged. "You remember all that you felt, and for some strange reason, you equate emotion to insecurity. You do not want to be accused of being a sentient Human."

"I was never Human," he said.

"You were when you knew nothing but Humanity," Catherine countered. "Do not attempt to hide from me." She grabbed his hand and pulled him to a stop. "I know you remember. I know that you care."

Eraekryst lifted his chin stubbornly. "Then why persist in this subtle interrogation?"

"Do you not know?" she asked. Suddenly it seemed very important that he acknowledge her and her feelings. His denial was like a wall without a door, and he was trying to shut her out.

He merely stared at her with those discerning eyes.

"Please," Catherine said, taking both his hands. "It means everything to me." In the back of her mind was the truth Jaice had told her. This time of hers was all she had. She moved closer to him. "You must remember this," she said quietly, lifting on her toes to kiss him. His lips parted for her, but there was no heart behind them.

She moved back and looked away.

"For what were you hoping?" Eraekryst asked, his voice cool but softer.

"I don't know," she whispered, her heart broken.

He plucked a leaf and turned it between his fingers. "We are on the brink of the answers we seek. 'Tis not each other we should test—not now." He pressed the leaf into her hands. "Follow me, Catherine," he said in earnest. "Your name is with me."

She wanted to ask him what that meant, if it meant anything at all. But she remained silent and merely nodded, following suit behind him. The trees opened around a small lake with water so clear that one could see the rocky surface below even the deeper regions. Eraekryst did not hesitate to wade into the lake, ripples radiating around his knees. Catherine remained ashore, watching him with mixed emotions as he peered down past the surface.

He lifted his head and gestured for her to join him. Reluctantly she did, feeling the surprisingly warm water saturate her boots and trousers as she waded to where Eraekryst stood. He took her hand. "Gaze with me."

It was a strange request, but she complied. At first she saw only the rocks below the surface, but then the water darkened. She started to draw back, but Eraekryst held her fast. A different image took shape beneath the waves, and then Catherine blinked.

But it could not have been merely a blink, for though they were still standing in the lake, their environment had completely changed. They were in a cavern, dimly lit by the pale aura of the water itself. The rocky walls were white and glistening, as were the icicle-like stalactites and stalagmites that surrounded them like a forest. Eyes wide as she took in the new setting, she gripped his hand harder. There was a chill in the air that unnerved her despite the bath-warm water around her legs.

"We are on the other side," Eraekryst said.

"The other side of what? The lake?" Catherine murmured in awe. "That is impossible."

"You see it for yourself, Lady." He grazed the surface of the stone with his fingers. "You would ask me how it is we came here, and the answer is that he granted us passage—the same Durangien you had seen when you arrived in the Veil."

She did not bother to ask how he knew this. Magic surrounded them in a presence as unseen but as permeating as the air they breathed. "I do not much care for this place," she said quietly. "I should like to know how we will return."

"What is it you fear?" he asked, peering into her eyes.

"The unknown. Being trapped. The feeling that something terrible could happen." Catherine shivered.

"These fears exist in any setting," Eraekryst reasoned. "Their likelihood of affecting us has not increased with our change in environment."

"I am glad you are so brave," Catherine said wryly.

"Nay, I am merely unconcerned."

"I would think you *should* be concerned given why we are here," she returned. "Your mission is hardly a stroll in the countryside."

"My mission," he echoed to himself, his expression distant but thoughtful.

"Yes," Catherine said, now attentive to his reaction. "Your mission to defeat Seranonde."

He mouthed the name silently, and when he did the horrible truth struck her. "You had been aged," she began. "How was it that the Light was taken from you?"

"Only potent magic could accomplish such a feat," Eraekryst said easily.

"*Whose* magic?" Catherine pressed.

"The one of whom you spoke. Seranonde. The one I must defeat."

"You are only repeating what I told you," she said, shaking her head.

"Do not be absurd. You know that I detest repetition—even if by—"

"You don't remember, do you?" Catherine interrupted in a low voice.

Eraekryst's face tensed.

"You do not want me to know it, but you did not regain all you memories...did you?" She gently took hold of his arm to keep him from avoiding her, but he recoiled so suddenly that her fingers slipped from him.

"I have lost nothing!" he snapped, his voice rebounding off the walls of the cavern. "I will find the pieces. I will be whole again. For now there is nothing I cannot deduce from our environment." He spread his arms wide. "I gathered the leaves, and they are mine. And even those that fell, they are for me to recover. I *will* recover them."

"Erik—" Catherine reached for him, but she could sense his anxiety. He was a branch ready to snap, and the only other time she had seen him in such a state was at Kirou-Mekus—at Kirou-Mekus when he nearly killed them both as he razed an entire mountain. How could she hope to calm him if he traveled down this path again?

But for as quickly as his composure had broken, he regained it. His rigid posture eased, and he took a breath. "There is time," he assured her. "At present, we are meant to be here—to learn what we might from this place."

"It's rather like a prison," she admitted. "I only hope we can leave when we wish." She watched him wander away, knowing he would not respond. His mind was intent on solving mysteries; he had no desire to leave until he was completely satisfied. Catherine wondered just how he would find his answers in an empty cavern, but if anyone could pull secrets from stone, it would be Eraekryst. She was content to watch him—perhaps because she did not want to stumble upon any secrets. There was an underlying darkness to this place—much like a spider's web glistening in the morning dew. The beauty was there, but the purpose was only ever to snare and entangle, and somewhere the spider waited.

Restless but unwilling to move, Catherine peered at her reflection in the alabaster surface of a stalactite as thick as her waist. Distorted though her image was, she gazed on in interest, noticing how much she had aged since she had left Lorrelwood. She found it strange that she had only truly started living once her journey with Eraekryst began, but living so much in so short a time had taken its toll. "The brighter the candle burns..." she murmured. "You say we have time, but only you have that unending gift."

She turned to see what Eraekryst was about, but he had vanished from her sight. "Erik?"

There was no response.

"Erik?" she called, louder. "Oh, please—not now. Do not leave me alone in this place." Unhappily she waded a distance in the direction he had gone, but there was no telltale Ilangien glow to be seen. He made no sound when he moved through the water, but surely he would have answered her call. She tried his name again, but her voice trailed when she realized how lonely it sounded as it echoed off the stone walls.

He would find her when he was ready. That was how he worked. There was no need to panic. Yet she could not block her ears as they perceived the hard thudding of her heart. "I must be patient. I must wait." But how could he have disappeared so quickly?

A glint of golden light a short distance ahead caught her attention. Warmer than the glow of the water, she wondered if Eraekryst had found his clues after all. A wave of relief washed over her, and she approached the source of the illumination. Her heart dropped when she realized it was not the Ilangien; it froze when she discovered what the object was.

On a shelf in the rock sat the crystal rose. It still glimmered with his blood the way it had that terrible moment at Kirou-Mekus. It unearthed memories she would have rather left buried—seeing Eraekryst entangled and bleeding, his eyes upon her in realization of her betrayal. It had been the end of Eraekryst of Celaedrion and all that he was. And though he had miraculously been restored, it was apparent that the crystal rose still kept precious pieces of him. Could he ever regain all that was stolen?

She dared not touch the rose, else she would shatter it. It had been her weapon, used in desperation then, now haunting her in shame. She saw that it was not alone. There were true weapons beside it: two swords, two knives, and two bows with their quivers of arrows. Not knowing much of weaponry, she found them beautiful in their curves and ornate designs. The metal of the blades was bright and flawless—unstained and intact. The stone of the arrows was opaline and fiery, and the bows were wrought from a dark and polished wood. She felt compelled to touch them—specifically the knife with a handle as rich as the darkest ruby. When her fingers grazed it, she drew a sharp breath, for it was as cold as if it had been left in the snow for hours.

Catherine drew back so quickly that she lightly skimmed the knife's blade. A small red sphere welled upon her finger, and she bent to wash it away in the water. When she lifted her hand to inspect the cut, she found it was gone. A shadow crossed her vision, and she thought she heard a whisper in her ear. She spun to find Eraekryst was walking toward her, a look of irritation upon his fair face.

"Instruments of deceit and treachery," he said, his tone dark.

"Where have you been?" Catherine said, hurrying toward him. "I called to you—did you not hear me?"

"I met your rescuer," Eraekryst said. "The Durangien."

"Where?" Catherine asked again, her own frustration surfacing.

"Neither here nor there," he murmured, moving past her to see the shelf and the objects it bore.

She watched his eyes rove over the weapons and come to rest upon the rose. "What did he have to say?" she asked.

"The significance of what he imparted," Eraekryst began, his eyes still locked upon the crystal rose, "is difficult for me to extract. Two truths I now know."

Catherine waited, dreading his response.

"The name Seranonde the Huntress is as black as the frozen hearts of the ancient Durgoth. I have somehow earned myself the most deadly enemy known to my kind."

Catherine stared at his back. "More that you have earned her interest; it is your friend she wishes to destroy."

"None of that is a part of me!" he shouted, and she would believe the walls shook. She shrank away, unused to this demonstration of anger and frustration. He confronted her, his pale eyes glinting "How do I not remember?"

Catherine was speechless. Did he know the truth about the rose? Or did he truly have no idea what she had done to him?

"This *extraction*—this *rape*—of what was mine and mine alone —" Eraekryst tore at his hair in anguish. "*I cannot tolerate it!*"

His words slipped through her skin, drawing out her tears. She had done this. She was the cause of his misery. "I'm sorry!" Catherine blurted. "I am so sorry!" She dragged her sleeve across her eyes. "It's my fault that you cannot remember. The rose was from Baliden. He would have used it on Naeva, but he gave it to me instead. I was afraid—afraid for you and for me. You nearly brought the mountain down upon us—you would have if I hadn't acted. I wanted to save you, but I nearly destroyed you. The rose took the past away, but then it started to take everything. There was nothing I could do but watch!"

The guilt, the pain, and the sorrow that had built below the surface now erupted, and Catherine could not contain them. She gripped the wall of the cavern lest she collapse to her knees. What had been the Ilangien was now a blurry mass, standing perfectly still while she agonized over the exposed truth. She wanted comfort, but she knew she did not deserve it. Likely he would never forgive her for her betrayal. Worse, he would resent her, and that alone would be a fate comparable to death.

She wiped her eyes again and found he had turned away from her to face the rose once more. She held her breath while he stood there, silent, motionless, for what seemed a long while. If only he would say something—anything—to let her know his thoughts. At last he reached toward the crystal flower until his fingers just touched it.

"What had I done?" he asked, barely audible.

Catherine was not sure if she was expected to respond. She saw a glimmer of light move from his fingers to the crystal, and the flower darkened to a smoky color and began to dissolve. It took no more than a few seconds before nothing remained of the rose but a puddle. When she looked up from the remains, she saw Eraekryst was looking at her, bearing as solemn an expression as she had ever seen upon him. It renewed her tears.

He came up to her, gently took her arms, and gazed into her eyes. "What had I done..." he said quietly, and Catherine could hear a slight tremor to his voice, "...that you would find need to employ such a poison?"

She wanted to look away for all the pain she saw in those pale eyes. She wanted to look anywhere but at him, but she could not. She owed him that much. Catherine took a deep breath. "You wanted revenge for what had happened to you inside Kirou-Mekus. You were intent on destroying it."

"I would have taken our lives had I done so," he concluded.

Catherine nodded.

His head fell, and his shoulders dropped. He let go of her arms. "Madness, then. As I have so often been told."

"No," she said, gathering strength. "No, not madness. You were wronged—wronged by so many and in terrible ways I could not imagine." Catherine took a step toward him. "What I did was out of desperation. I wanted to save you. Erik, I...."

"'Twas given to you in the Nightwind," Eraekryst interrupted.

She knew what he implied. She had borne her burden in anticipation of what she believed he would do. There was nothing spontaneous in how she had acted. But for him, had it been madness? Obsession? Or a driving thirst for justice? "I had my fears," she confessed.

"Because I had given you cause to fear," Eraekryst said. "Now I suffer a consequence from an action I cannot remember." He sighed. "I was told that I cannot recover what was lost. I will never be whole, Catherine. So much of what I am is gone."

The despair was in his voice, and his words weighed upon her heavily. He was not angry with her, and the fact he understood her actions only deepened her sorrow for him. She took hold of him. "Erik... I want you to see it. I want you to know what happened."

He looked at her, his brow furrowed.

"See it through me," she insisted. She placed his hands upon her face.

"I would not." Eraekryst tried to pull away. "'Twould be an invasion of your mind, and I will not—"

"I ask it of you," Catherine said, holding him fast. "So it is not an invasion."

He frowned. "I respect you too much," he said. "I will not do it."

"Erik—" She cut herself short and released him when she saw his expression change to one of great displeasure. All at once he seemed removed from her, responding to stimuli she could not perceive. It was an expression she had witnessed often enough on their journey together, when he held conversations with those he had dubbed the, "Lost Ones." For whatever memories he had lost, his ghosts seemed to have returned to him.

"They scream," Eraekryst mumbled. "They scream because they know. I remember how they died, with minds torn open for me to read. Though I was but an instrument in the hands of my captors, the risk is the same." He gave her a hard look. "I will not be the cause of your death."

Catherine squared her shoulders. "I will die when we leave this place. It was the price of coming here, and it was a choice I made willingly."

The flicker of surprise in his eyes dimmed to his stubbornness. "I will not allow such a fate to come to pass," he said.

"This time it may not be in your hands," Catherine said gently. "You must do as I ask, or you will never know what was lost to you." The rigidity remained upon his face, and she pursued her argument. "You are not being manipulated now. You are in control. I know that you will not harm me."

Eraekryst began to pace before her, and when he spoke, his voice was louder. "What do you suppose 'tis like, to have one's past strewn about like a flower plucked, dismantled, and discarded?"

"You would never do such a thing," she answered calmly. "I have no secrets from you, and I would gladly share all my memories if it would undo the harm I've caused you. Please, let me help you." She reached up to touch his face, and he did not pull away.

His hands were actually trembling when he placed them upon her shoulders. She had never seen him scared, and there was a time when his fear would have unnerved her, but not now. Not anymore. She had nothing to lose.

Catherine could see that he was searching her for one last shred of doubt, but she would show him none. This was her final gift to him. She gave a nod and closed her eyes. A steady force began to build in her head, like an insistent change in pressure that made her slightly dizzy. Her mind was beyond her control as images sped by, like wind rushing through her consciousness. There was the night they met—at Summerfall—and her first glimpse of Seranonde. There was the snowy forest of Lorrelwood, the grim-faced Arythan Crow, and a dying nobleman whom she had known all her life. There was an aged Ilangien and his Jornoan companion, the melodies of a violin, the vibrant nights they spent in excess at the taverns and inns. She saw again the terrifying battle between Naeva and the Huntress, saw Baliden's eyeless corpse and the cursed crystal rose.

She wore a green dress at the mayor's daughter's wedding and danced with the Minstrel. She searched the jungle for him and beheld Kirou-Mekus as he razed it. He walked through her front door as an older man. He lay dying on a bed in a tavern, so very pale and weak. She read his note and learned that he had left her, embarking on his mission to the Nightwind Mountains without her. She stayed at his side when he had first been brought to Jaice's cottage, and she rushed to him when he knelt over the water and wondered who he was. There were strolls along the beach and stories shared between them in a life that was meant for mortals.

But then she was alone, hiding her tears in a journal. Another man held her hand in a ceremony that would bind them as husband and wife. Under the stars she journeyed to an unknown destination. There was a glowing river, frightening creatures, bones underfoot....

There was no order to her memories, no pattern to be followed. And they did not center solely around her acquaintance with the Ilangien. There were other faces: her father, old friends, family... She was a little girl one moment, a blossoming young woman the next. There were creatures in the forest that appeared throughout her life. With every memory came the feelings so strongly tied to it. Somewhere in the midst of this bombardment was a growing sadness that all these experiences would be left behind her, and this would be the last she would ever reflect upon them. This was the life of Catherine Lorrel, Countess of Silvarn, the eccentric woman who left her wealth behind to follow the immortal who she had grown to love.

The images faded.

The darkness submitted to the soft light of the cavern, and Catherine felt herself supported in Eraekryst's arms. He was holding her above the water, his own back braced against the cavern wall so that he could stand. His eyes were shut, his breathing slow. She gazed at his radiant face, wanting to touch it but being too weak to do so. Finally he opened his eyes, and one of the most powerful beings she had ever known suddenly seemed vulnerable and overwhelmed.

"I do not know what to feel," he said in a small voice.

"What a Human thing to say," she whispered with a smile.

"Your life—it is so full. There is meaning to all of it, and it never grows tired, never slows," he said, dazed. "My own purpose is empty, Catherine."

"My life *has* slowed," she told him. "And I once thought like you—that it was lacking and empty. We are fulfilled by our sense of purpose. You became mine." She took a breath, feeling the strength slowly return to her, feeling his Light renew her. "You still have purpose, Eraekryst."

He said nothing, but the dubious expression upon his face clearly spoke his thoughts.

"The second truth," Catherine said. "What was the second truth you learned?"

His gaze lifted from her and to their surroundings. "You were correct in what you had said. This place—river, cavern, forest, and all—is a prison."

25

THE SONG

Eraekryst lowered Catherine to her feet when it seemed she was capable of standing. He knew she was awaiting an explanation, so he led her back toward the weapons. "Veloria is but a name to me; precious little of the Great Forest remains in my mind," he said quietly. "My identity, in relation to my origin, has become irrelevant." He stopped her with a hand before she could interrupt. "I do, however, remember the name of the great war amongst the immortals: the War of Light and Shadow.

"The resolution of the war is the reason you have not met more of my kind. The Ilangiel, the Durangiel, and the Durgoth decided to retreat and allow the mortals to occupy the world. I am told there were those unwilling to fade into the Unseen; they were determined to keep the conflict alive."

"Seranonde," Catherine said.

"She and six followers," Eraekryst said. "They initiated a conflict that spilled the blood of Ilangiel and Durangiel alike. They desecrated the fallen in the darkest manner of corruption, drinking of their blood and assuming the life and soul of the victims."

Catherine visibly paled. "I saw her do the same to Baliden."

Eraekryst sifted through his memories. "At the tower," he said slowly. "When we fled the Nightwind."

"Yes," she said. "It was likely the most horrifying moment I have known."

"Alas, Naeva," Eraekryst mourned. "She now numbers amongst those fallen victim to the Huntress." He gazed absently into the cavern. "I expected I would feel a sense of justice served, but I feel only pity."

"You remember what Naeva had done to you," Catherine said.

"Aye," he replied, "as I remember many of the transgressions by my captors—all founded upon the intentions of usurping my abilities. As powerful as she is, I cannot help but wonder if this motive is also what drives Seranonde's interest in me."

"That may be true, Erik, but do not forget about Arythan."

He looked at her, confused. "The mage-boy I saw in your memories? What of him?" He watched her surprise turn to sorrow, and he felt his irritation stir. Clearly this was another he should remember.

There was not a chance for Catherine to elaborate, for a thickening mist rose around them with such rapidity that their next breath was full of the cool, damp air. Eraekryst felt her take his hand as their sight was obscured. But the phenomenon did not last long, and when the mist had dissipated, they were standing where they had been—knee-deep in the lake.

"The Forgotten," Eraekryst murmured thoughtfully, feeling their presence in the air. "They have been here so very long, living not as you or me, but as the heart that beats in this land…this prison."

"I'm not certain I understand," Catherine said, following him as he waded for the shore.

"Seven were chosen to hunt and vanquish the defectors. Six

succeeded, and one perished. The problem was that the offending Durangiel could not be destroyed—not unless Seranonde was destroyed with them. She, however, was not to be found, and the Forgotten were forcibly bound to their prisoners and brought here —where no further harm could be done. You saw their weaponry. Their only hope of freedom is the destruction of the Huntress."

"That was your mission," Catherine said, hopeful. "You had wanted to come here to learn how to defeat her."

He stopped and turned to her. "'Twas in vain, then, for she cannot be defeated."

She stared back.

"For the immortal lives she has stolen, no single being could hope to bring about her ending," he explained.

"Is that what the Forgotten told you, or is that what you believe?"

Eraekryst sighed. "'Tis the simple truth, Catherine. I am nothing in the scope of her power. She will take me too, given the opportunity, and then she will know what I know, see as I see."

She shook her head. "She has had plenty of opportunity to take your life, and instead she had chosen to save it. She has need of you, and if that is true, then there must be a way for you to succeed in her destruction. The immortals here were able to restore your youth and your life. They were able to undo the harm she had worked upon you. Seranonde is not omnipotent."

"You do not want to believe this effort was one of futility," Eraekryst argued. "Even the Forgotten do not believe she will face justice. They have accepted their fate." He could see the disbelief in her eyes—more than disbelief: disappointment. What, exactly, did she expect of him?

"Then you have given up," Catherine said flatly.

"There is nothing lost," he said, growing angry.

"Just the life of your friend." She held his gaze before turning away and walking past him. "For all you have learned to feel, it is your compassion that is still lacking."

Eraekryst lifted his head in indignation. "You refer again to the mage-boy." He saw her pause without turning back to regard him.

"I refer to Arythan Crow, your companion. The one who saved you from Kirou-Mekus."

"I do not rem—"

"You do not need to remember. I am telling you what you once told me." At last she looked at him. "Arythan Crow, the demon in Human form. The young man who could have easily left the mountain without you, but he turned back…out of compassion. He traveled with you to Norkindara, liberated you from the wizards of I.M.A.G.I.N.E. You watched the witches change him and nearly take his life. You joined the Crimson Dragon, becoming the sensational dueling duo, 'Sparrow and Crow.' You were with him when the troop was massacred by the hands of the Warriors of the Sword, and then you accompanied him to Crag's Crown, where he would become the king's royal medoriate.

"Somewhere in the midst of these changes, you became aware of another danger. Seranonde spoke to you of her intentions to kill him when he had caused enough chaos. You knew then that you could not defeat her, but still you tried to defend him. In your desperation, you tried to control him, and that betrayal cost you your friendship. Yet you were determined to save him, and after all that has happened to you, here we are." She lifted her arms and turned, showing him the landscape as though he could not see it.

"All for this 'mage-boy,'" she said bitterly. "Just because you have lost him in your memories does not mean he does not exist. It does not mean he never shared a friendship with you. It does not mean he does not face the danger of your enemy. The choice is yours to care or not. I came with you, because the Ilangien I know *did* care—even if he was reluctant to show it."

"What would you have me do?" Eraekryst asked, defensive.

"What you feel is right," Catherine responded. "I cannot tell you how to defeat her. I cannot direct you." She pointed to her head. "Your gift is here. You are brilliant, clever, and the possessor of gifts that are wonderful and frightening. Before you can worry about Seranonde, you need to ask yourself what you are willing to do."

He watched her move back into the forest. "To where do you go?" he called after her.

"I have a headache," Catherine answered. "I wish to lie down."

"I can help you," Eraekryst said and started in her direction.

"Thank you, but I need only close my eyes."

He let her go, his shoulders drooping. *She is cross with me. Disappointed. She does not know how difficult it is to feel passionate about a cause I cannot remember. This "Arythan Crow" is a stranger to me, yet I alone know of his waiting peril. I alone must save him.*

Eraekryst exhaled a long breath and skirted his own trail around the lake. *A better mission would be the recovery of the memories I have lost. I could return to Veloria, see into the minds of those who knew me. I could recreate the journey since my liberation from Kirou-Mekus, fitting the pieces together again.*

"The demon has shared that journey with you," said a woman's voice in his mind.

"I know that now," he grumbled.

"Maybe you don't need to face Seranonde. Maybe all you need do is find the demon—talk to him."

"If he yet lives," Eraekryst said. "I must assume an ancient Durangien is patient enough to wait for her prey to—to do whatever it is she expects him to do." He frowned. "Once again, I find myself drowning in speculation. What is logical and what is fiction? How can I distinguish—I, who cannot remember my homeland, let alone the grim promises of a murdering immortal."

He stopped in his tracks when he spied a glimmer of light not far from him. It was, in fact, growing in size and intensity, swallowing leaves and branches in its wake. And it was racing for him. He shielded his eyes and braced himself for the collision.

It was not light but darkness that choked him. He was where he had been standing before—the lake and the forest constituting his surroundings—but it was as though night had slammed into day, displacing it instantly. There was no moon, and there were no stars, but he could see around him as though they were present. He felt a pressure on his back—like a finger jabbing him lightly.

When he spun, he discovered that was indeed what it was. The finger belonged to a boy—an Ilangien boy whose head did not quite reach Eraekryst's chest. He knew the arrogant smile upon the child's face, just as he knew the glimmer of mischief in his pale eyes. It was himself.

"You wil want to see what I have found," the youth said, taking Eraekryst's hand and tugging on it.

"You are of the Veil. One of the Forgotten," he said. "You are making use of the memories you have glimpsed."

The youth smiled but did not answer. He led Eraekryst back down the path and turned into the jungle. They walked until they came upon a fallen tree, now painted with the vibrant greens of moss and gray and crusty lichens. The youth presented it to him and waited.

"Why has it decayed?" Eraekryst asked. "Unless we are no longer in the Veil."

"How astute of you," his younger self said. *"This does not belong here."*

"'Tis not what it seems," Eraekryst mused, enjoying the mystery. "So what would it be? An illusion? A trap?"

The youth motioned for him to continue.

"A disguise," he said, "concealing what should not be discovered."

"Should not?" The boy tapped the log with his toe. *"Secrets are for discovery. This one was created especially for you. I found it in your head, amongst the leaves that had fallen."*

Eraekryst stared at the youth, immediately suspicious.

"'Twas not my doing," the boy asserted. *"'Twas the product of those who knew you well. Your kindred."*

"My own kind sought to hide something in my mind. What logic is there in this?" Eraekryst asked.

The youth gave an impatient sigh. *"The reason may have been lost to you, but you have a spirit of discovery, and I offer you this opportunity. Crawl inside and learn what was concealed from you, or walk away now and be content with what you are."*

It hardly seemed a choice at all. Eraekryst crouched beside the log and peered into the darkness inside. "Why do you show me this? Do you believe it will help me defeat Seranonde?"

"How you use your gifts is not for me to predict. The others and I—we have been here a very long time. We know what 'tis like to be confined, and we know the meaning of justice." The youth looked at him directly. *"Consider this your justice for all the wrongs committed against you."* He raised a hand. *"I do bear a word of warning, Eraekryst. You cannot unlearn what you encounter. Within is power that might walk you to the brink of madness. 'Tis your power by right, but you will not be unmarked once 'tis tapped."*

Eraekryst looked darkly at his younger self. "Madness is a word undefined. I have been so described upon many an occasion. Why should I fear a state that already defines me?"

"The barriers—built by ourselves or by others—are intended for safety. If you have scathed insanity, you have not yet immersed yourself within it."

"Would I know the difference?" he asked.

The youth said nothing, and Eraekryst crawled into the darkness.

~

Catherine had eased into her nap without hindrance. While she could not fault Eraekryst for what he could not remember, she was frustrated that she had come so far with him to find they had gained nothing. Not only did he not see purpose to his mission, but he had seemingly closed the door and lost the key to the emotions he had learned to express when he was mortal. She had hoped she would glimpse the depths of his heart—the one she knew he possessed despite his assertion otherwise. It was too late now, and this he also refused to acknowledge.

Only now did she realize the truth to her own mission. She knew he cared about her. What she wanted was to know if he loved her. It may well have been a futile endeavor. Love in the way that mortals knew it could likely be impossible for immortals to experience. Never mind that he had, in fact, been mortal for a while. This was the pain of loving someone and knowing they did not love you back. Perhaps all this time, *she* had been the one in denial.

Too eager to leave these thoughts behind, she had nestled against the trunk of a tree, between the roots that jutted from the mossy earth. No sooner than her eyes had closed, she dreamed of singing flowers, golden clouds in the shapes of bunnies, and other frivolous, fanciful oddities. But then the dreams changed, the sky darkened, and the clouds turned into the luminous, chalky, amorphous forms Jaice had named, "Graylings." They gathered around her, and she choked on their dust. They suffocated her, moving closer and closer with their faceless heads, and when she extended her arms to ward them away, she found she was becoming as translucent as they were. She was becoming one of them.

Catherine's return from slumber was just as quick though not as pleasant. She awoke alone, in the silence, with a fading sky above her. "Erik?" It took her a moment to remember that *she* had left *him*. But how long had she been asleep, and just where was he? She did not want to be alone anymore, though he could find her more easily than she could find him.

All the same, Catherine stood and headed back to the lake. He was, surprisingly, where she had left him, though now he was sitting on the shore, skipping rocks across the surface of the water. Rather, skipping a rock... As soon as it sank, it rose from the depths of the water and sailed back to him through the air.

"You...you have been here the whole time?" she asked him, coming up to sit beside him.

He looked at her and smiled. "Now that is the question, is it not?"

Catherine turned away. "I did not mean to say much of what I told you. I should not try to stir guilt when you are the one struggling to remember. I'm sorry." She watched him toss the stone again, and it hopped nearly half the distance to the other shore. It made her strangely restless.

"That which is beyond my reach will not serve me in crossing the lake," he said.

"Is that poetry? A sort of metaphor?" she asked, confused by his odd behavior.

"One and the other but not both." The stone sailed back to his hand, and he caught it as one would an insect. Slowly he uncurled his fingers to gaze at it, and then he handed it to her. "You are troubled."

Catherine could not avoid those piercing eyes. "I...I need to leave here. Soon. I had a dream that I was surrounded by Graylings —that I was changing to become like them."

"Such being the fate of mortals who linger, I would imagine," Eraekryst said.

She clutched the rock tightly. "I would sooner leave and meet my fate."

"I will not let you perish, Catherine," he said. He stood and offered her his hand. "But if you wish to leave, then we will leave."

"Now?" she asked, incredulous. "The sun will be setting."

"I enjoy a pleasant sunset," he responded. "The night is nothing to fear, and I can be your personal moon."

She started to smile but then considered his words. "Are you... all right? You seem almost...carefree...as though you have no concerns at all."

"'Twould be the definition of 'carefree.'" He pulled her to her feet. "I have come to realize there is little need for worry."

"I wish I could say the same." She brushed off her clothes.

"All these moments, I have wanted to ask you," he started. "Who is Jaice?"

Catherine blinked. "He...is a friend—the one who led us here."

"Is he, then, expecting our return?"

"No," she said softly.

"Then 'twill be a surprise." He suddenly pivoted and headed into the forest.

Catherine followed him, unsure what to think. Something must have happened while she was asleep, but she doubted he would disclose anything, and if he did, she wondered if it would be too cryptic to decipher.

The sun had nearly set when they reached the golden river. Eraekryst helped her down the steep embankment and started to wade across. She did not follow him, and when he turned to question her, she felt her tears spill warm and salty down her face.

He immediately returned to her side.

"I'm afraid," she confessed in a whisper. "I am afraid to cross."

"No harm will come to you," he assured her.

She knew he did not understand. He would not understand until the moment had come.

"Come with me, Catherine," he coaxed. As before, he held out his hand.

She wanted to take it. She wanted to place her faith in him, but though he was immortal, he was not a deity. "I can't," she said, frozen. "Oh, I can't." She stared at the opposite side of the river in terror.

Eraekryst came closer. "Do not be afraid. I will protect you."

Catherine trembled beneath his touch, and he paused to study her, his face weighted with concern. Without another word, he lifted her into his arms and carried her. All the while she cried, because it was the end. She had carried him across to bring him life, but he was taking her to her death. She felt it immediately—as soon as he lowered her to ground on the other side. The power of the Veil left her, and she nearly collapsed from weakness.

Eraekryst touched her brow, and she felt the Light move into her. It was strength, and it was energy, but it would not be enough. She used his magic to climb to level ground, used it to pick her way across the bones that littered the ground. It faded like the waning day, faded like the last summer blossom, faded like water from the sand after the tide had gone out.

Her legs buckled, and Eraekryst lifted her again. He carried her a long while, until the stars spattered the deepest hues of the sky. He would have carried her to Brandeise, all the way to Secrailoss's shore, had she allowed it—had she the time. At her request, he set her down to rest, and he sat beside her.

"You are so far away," she told him, and he moved closer so that she could take his hand. It felt so warm that it tingled against her skin.

"When you are ready, I will carry you again," he said.

"I do not need you to carry me anymore." Catherine squeezed his hand and took a breath. "Just be here with me."

"A strange request, though I—"

"You need not act for me—nor for yourself," she said. "It's too late to pretend."

His mouth parted, but he said nothing.

"I have loved you for a long time, Eraekryst of Celaedrion."

"I know," he said—not in his customary arrogant tone, but in the softness of one admitting an obvious secret.

"My life did not begin until we met that night at Summerfall. Even now, I would not change it had I the power to go back." Weakly she pulled his hand to rest above her slowing heart.

"Catherine, I will heal you," he said, a hint of desperation in his voice. "I need you to stay with me—to come when I call to you."

"No. I have followed you to mountains, across the ocean, and through the jungle." She licked her lips. "But I cannot follow you anymore. You need to find Arythan. You need to save him from the Huntress."

"Catherine, please. I will do as you ask, but you must be at my side." His expression had changed completely to one of panic. "You are the only one who knows me."

"That is not true." She felt so weary, so tired. She knew if she closed her eyes, they would not open again.

"Stay with me," he repeated, pulling her to him so that she was cradled in his arms. "Do not leave me. Please. Catherine."

Then she heard him as his voice changed. Smooth and melodic, it shaped itself in the familiar rise and fall of a song—one to which she had forgotten the words long ago.

"The rose, it has faded
Like the hours, petals fall
One by one
'Til there are none left at all..."

He was singing for her. Soft and haunting, his voice gave her her song.

"The birds have gone silent
Beneath the darkening pall
No sound is uttered
There is no sound at all..."

She saw his tears, felt one drop—wet against her skin. It was all she had wanted, and now she knew.

"...All days have an ending
As do we all..."

He did love her.

"Give way to the shadows
That bring us Nightfall."

26

KINGDOM OF ICE

The night sky was white, smothered by the swarming mass of wind and icy snow pellets. They assailed the castle windows with a clatter, attacked any brave enough to venture in the storm. Crag's Crown had been silent for days, anyone with sense having confined himself to a warm shelter to wait for the heavens to relent. But even during the day, the sky never showed sign of lightening, and the blizzard never took a breath.

"It is remarkable," the king said, staring out at the indistinguishable landscape of the courtyard. "I can scarcely see the far tower." He took a sip of wine.

The unfortunate man who had been speaking—Medoriate Brann Alwin—realized King Michael Garriker III likely heard none of what he had been saying. Alwin glanced at Prince Banen, but the stone-faced young man showed no sympathy. "Your Highness...."

Michael turned to him abruptly. "Our supply of the Enhancement dwindles."

Alwin suppressed a sigh. "Yes, Your Highness. That is what I have come to address."

"What is the delay with the Merchants' Guild wizards?" Michael demanded. "The Guild has had ample time to gather medori and station them at the Plains."

Alwin shifted uncomfortably beneath his inebriated stare. "I cannot say, Sire. I have not had contact with the Guild since you have hired me as your medoriate." He turned away from Michael only to find himself beneath Banen's icy glare.

"If I cannot rely upon the Guild, then you will have to assume the production," Michael said.

"With respect, Your Majesty, I cannot produce the Enhancement alone. And I certainly could not do it here."

Michael threw his cup against the wall. "Then go to the Plains. And take Crow with you. I will send an escort."

The wizard frowned. "It is not so simple, Your Majesty. Medoriate Crow, you remember, is in the dungeon—"

"I know!" Michael snapped. "I put him there! We can force him to work. We need to keep production running."

"He cannot employ his magic," Alwin said, fighting to maintain his patience. "His current state is questionable at best. It is the reason for this never-ending storm. I had not foreseen such a consequence to his nullified magic."

Michael cupped a hand to his ear. "What is this I am hearing? Banen, doesn't this sound like a dung cart of excuses?"

"What is it you wish of me, Your Highness?" Alwin asked.

"Are you deaf as well as stupid?"

Banen cleared his throat. "In his defense, brother, we knew the Enhancement would render Crow useless. That was what we wanted—for the safety of everyone in the castle."

"So in short," Michael seethed, "I can do nothing but wait."

Banen shrugged.

"Meanwhile my kingdom grows steadily more impoverished." Michael waited for Brann Alwin to respond, but there was nothing for the wizard to say. He turned back toward the window and waved him away. "You may go about your business, Medoriate. Return to me when you have an idea to offer or a contribution to make."

The wizard colored. "I have done as you asked, keeping Medoriate Crow subdued. I had readied his dosage for tonight—"

"Do not bother with it," Michael said. "I would rather question him while he is somewhat coherent. You are dismissed." He waited until Alwin had stalked out before he left the window to pour another cup of wine.

"I do not pretend to understand you," Banen said, crossing his arms. "The wizard is an obvious traitor. We know he has been feeding the Merchants' Guild information. They know Crow is alive. Yet you lead Alwin to believe your ignorance of the situation."

Michael smiled and took a long drink. He dabbed his lips dry. "What would you have done, Banen?"

"I would see him punished like the treacherous dog he is," the prince said immediately.

"Medoriate Alwin has served his purpose well enough. I wanted the Guild to know Crow is yet alive. He is my bargaining piece."

"Then hand him over," Banen said. "The Guild will starve us. They have the advantage, not us."

"Then you, too, are fooled." Michael strolled to his brother's side. "I'll not give up my prize until I know its value. The Guild will not tell me why they want him, so I must extract the information from Crow himself."

Banen took a step back from Michael's wine-stained breath. "And if he doesn't talk?"

"He will talk," the king said, unconcerned.

"You are the fool to be so confident," Banen said. "You will raze Cerborath to the ground to learn the secret of one filthy bloodrot?"

"The Guild has more secrets than Crow's value, Banen," Michael said. "I have not shared with you their true intentions for this very reason: your lack of faith in me."

Banen scowled. "Perhaps I have just cause to doubt." He pulled a letter from his coat pocket and thrust it at his brother. "This is from Desnera. Her Majesty is outraged by our father's death. She demands justice, and she is calling to claim her rightful property."

"Deceitful bitch," Michael said, snatching the letter. "Cerborath is mine by right. If she believes I will serve her, then she will learn that we are independent. We will not subject ourselves to Desneran authority."

"You seek to undo all that Father has accomplished," Banen said, glaring at his brother.

"Our father gave her our kingdom on a silver platter!" Michael said, crushing the paper and throwing it to the floor.

"Or maybe he was trying to protect it by seeing the bigger picture." Banen held his ground. "The only one truly upset by the marriage was you, for the loss of your would-be throne."

"The throne *is* mine," Michael challenged. "I am disappointed how fickle you are, to side with that whore. Where is your pride? Oh—" He paused to regain his composure. "I had forgotten that you *are* the son of a whore. Your jealousy of my inheritance has clouded your vision." He took a drink. "Do not worry, Banen. I forgive you. And I will help you see the value in my cause."

The prince had turned a ripe shade of scarlet. "You truly are delusional," he seethed. He headed for the door and paused. "Try to remember that Cerborath is more than just you." The door slammed behind him.

"LADY SHERRALIN, I did not expect to see you here at this hour," Brann Alwin said. He paused to hold the door for her, though his eyes darted back down the corridor from which she had come.

The healer barely glanced at him. "The storm is the cause for my delay," she said without emotion. "The hour is late for you as well."

The wizard gave a phony smile. "I had a meeting with His Majesty." He took her arm. "I can tend to his meal, if you would like."

Diana raised an eyebrow in suspicion. "I have made the journey here, Medoriatc. I intend to complete my duty." She indicated the tray bearing Arythan's meal as well as her medical supplies. "Besides, someone must ease the effects of the poison you administer."

"Like you, I must do as directed, Lady," he said. He grabbed a torch and guided her down the abysmal stairwell. When they reached the bottom, he directed her onward. "It may be best you tend to him first."

Diana's stare was ice, though she did not object. Alwin kept the light at enough of a distance she could still see the contents of the tray as she approached the cell. She heard the chains shift, then the raspy breathing as a shrouded form crawled to her, dragging his bindings behind him. Two bony hands wrapped around the bars, but that was all she could see of him.

She crouched down and set the tray beside her. She never knew what to say to him. It was not as though she could strike casual conversation—not that she was one to do so anyway, even under ordinary circumstances. This time, however, her voice was not the first to break the silence.

"I've 'ad a lot o' time to think." He was barely audible, and it sounded as though each breath he took was an effort.

"Yes, I would imagine," Diana said.

"Othenis. I 'ad it planned with 'im. 'S diff'rent now, but 'e knew m' brother. 'E will 'elp them."

"Who will he help, Arythan?" She asked gently. She lifted the bowl of soup, which had not been warm for hours. She ladled some and started to reach toward him.

"'Tori an' Reiqo."

Diana stopped.

"'E'll find them a place—far away. They'd be safe."

Her thin veneer of control nearly shattered. "You need to eat," she said, forcing herself to extend the spoon again. He did not take it.

"Arythan, please." She bit her lip. "When you're released, you will need your strength for them. Victoria and Reiqo will be waiting."

There was a strange sound that alarmed her—a sound of gasping or coughing. "Arythan—" And then she realized it was laughter. "I don't believe it is funny," she said, her spirit plunging.

"Y' think I believe y'," he replied. "An' 'tis funny to me." Then he leaned closer, his raspy tone suddenly grave. "Find Othenis. Please. Take Reiqo an' Tori to 'im. Please. Dianar, please."

"I…I will," she whispered. "But I do wish you would eat—"

"Y' were always the best one," he said. He took his hands from the bars and sat back.

Diana heard him mumble in another language, then the sound of the chains dragging followed him back into the shadows. "Stay with me," she coaxed. "Talk to me."

There was no response.

"You can't give up," she said. "Please tell me you won't give up."

The only sound from within the cell was his labored breathing.

"Lady Sherralin," came the voice from behind her. "It is time."

"He hasn't eaten yet," Diana snapped. "How can he endure that poison when he has not taken his meal?"

"I am acting under the orders of King Garriker," Brann Alwin said. "I must do this."

She picked up the tray and heaved it at him. "So be it." She started for the stairs. "Curse your orders, and curse the king." There was only one idea left to her. One idea that could save Arythan, provided she would earn the support she needed. The support of another woman—a woman with authority.

He sat down in the chair and gazed out the window at the town below. People moved back and forth along the road—some faces familiar, others unknown to him. This was their life, the coming and going of a typical day. Working, talking, eating, sleeping, but also telling stories, catching the eye of another, holding the hand of a child... None of it had ever really been petty, not when so little meant so much to a finite existence.

Eraekryst had been one of them. He had worked and even sweated in a field, had shared stories from his imagination, tasted a hot meal, held the hand of one he cared about. One he had loved. He had never told her, but he remembered when she had first kissed him—what that kiss had come to mean once he understood its value. He remembered a lot about her: her hands working the needle through the fabric when he watched her at the tailor's shop, her voice when she hummed her melody, her trail of footprints on the beach, and best of all, her smile.

Where was she now? Where had she gone? Unlike the ghosts that never left his side, she was beyond his reach, alive only in the memories he guarded with his heart. How could such a spirit, such a life, simply vanish? And all the Humans who had known her—would they ever think of her? Or were her footprints as temporary as the ones she had left on the shore?

To not remember—it seemed a terrible fate to him now. Now

that there were names, places, and events that were simply gone from him. Gone—just like her spirit. He had her only in his mind, and there he would never let her fade from him. "Catherine Lorrel, Countess of Silvarn," he murmured. "I will do as you bid of me. I know not if I will be able to stop the Huntress, but I will find the demon, and learn the truth."

Eraekryst opened the case at his feet and cradled the violin in his arms. He ran his fingers along the strings, the polished surface of the wood, the contour of the tuning pegs. An old man's hands had only ever made it sing. He took up the bow and placed the instrument beneath his chin.

The gift Catherine had given him was alive once more, and it sang of her. Its melody was strong and clear—even when it shifted to be slow and gentle. But there was never a break, never a pause. It may have been lonely at times, but it never diminished or faded to obscurity. He would deem it the most beautiful of all the melodies he had ever played. He would also claim it unfinished, for in the midst of his playing, the door to the room opened.

Eraekryst recognized the servant standing there, though clearly he remained unfamiliar to her. She seemed alarmed and also curious—that this stranger saw fit to perform in an empty room of this cottage. "H-How did you get in here?" she asked. "Who are you?"

"My feet, the door, and the same route as you." He stood. "I am a passing thought, destined to leave without transgression."

"I should call for Master Thayliss," she said, turning to leave.

"Wait."

She waited.

"You need not trouble him. I came here to remember a lady… and to collect the gift she had given me." He placed the violin back in its case.

"You mean Lady Catherine, the mayor's wife."

"Aye."

"She went away, or I'd tell her you came to see her," the servant said.

"She will not be returning," Eraekryst said quietly. He gathered the case and approached her and the door. "I am sorry."

Dumbfounded, the servant could only nod and step aside as he made his exit.

Eraekryst said little to anyone he met on his way to the port. Brandeise had been the home of Erik Sparrow, but the old man was gone, and so, too, were his reasons for lingering. There was but one sight upon which he was set, and there was a long way to travel before he reached the kingdom of icc, thc Northern Kingdom of Cerborath. This journey, he would have to make alone…or so he thought.

27

TRAITORS AND SPIES

"He is Lord Kyrin, Duke of Si—"

Michael silenced the messenger with a sharp slice of his hand. "I do not care who he is. You said he is from Desnera. What is his business here?"

The servant shrank from the throne. "He did not say, Sire. He merely announced himself as an emissary from Queen Sabrina Jerian."

"I think we best entertain him," Ladonna said, coming over to touch her husband's shoulder.

"He best entertain *me,* lest I set him atop Crow's demon mare and take a whip to her," Michael said. "Dinner is nigh, and I will not be delayed by a Desneran high-collar."

Ladonna began to massage him. "He has come through the storm, Michael. He should join us for dinner. You must consider proper etiquette and set an example for your children."

He scoffed. "I am king. I determine proper etiquette." Then he looked at her and sighed. "Must you always make me feel a brute?"

"You are better mannered than you want others to believe,"

Ladonna said. "Your standards would not allow you to shame your blood with coarse behavior."

Michael sighed again and waved to the servant. "Allow him in."

"Now stand and greet your guest," his wife said, moving beside him.

The king narrowed his eyes at her and stood. His expression hardened when a well-dressed, older gentleman was escorted down the length of the hall. The man went to his knee, and Michael reluctantly gave him the signal to rise.

"Your Highness, I am here on behalf of Her Majesty, Queen Sabrina Jcrian of Desnera."

"So I was told," Michael said. He eased himself back into his throne. "What does she want of me?"

The old man seemed taken aback by the response. "It is my responsibility to direct you in the conduct of proper Desneran authority and business," he said.

"Why?"

"Your pardon, Your Highness?"

"Michael..." Ladonna whispered.

"I wish to know why you are directing me in my operation of this kingdom." Michael leaned forward in his chair and folded his hands. "As I understand it, Desnera has no further connection with Cerborath. We are an independent kingdom. My father is dead, Lord Byrin, and I have assumed his throne, as you see."

The nobleman's face paled with indignation. "With all respect, Your Highness, the alliances your father made with our queen are still viable. Cerborath is but a territory now, a property of Her Majesty. You may consider yourself a regent to your people, but in all formality, you are a steward.

"Furthermore, Her Majesty wishes a token of her late husband, and she demands assurance that justice has been served in his name."

The hall fell silent, and Michael rubbed his chin, staring down at the emissary. "We seem to be at a misunderstanding," he said pleasantly. "I do apologize." He left the throne and approached the great hearth, reaching for an ivory box adorned with gold and sapphires. The royal bear of Cerborath was carved into the lid.

"Michael, please," Ladonna begged, also rising. "Leave it alone."

Michael ignored her and descended the dais to meet the emissary face-to-face. He held out the box. "Here, my good man. You may take this to Queen Sabrina. It is only right she have it."

"What is this?" Lord Kyrin asked.

"My father, of course. What remains of him." Michael returned to his throne. "Do be careful on your way home. The weather has been frightful."

The emissary clutched the box in trembling hands, and his face tensed with fury. "This is an outrage! How dare you insult Her Majesty in this manner!"

"I mean no insult," Michael said, "though I cannot control how she chooses to view this gift. You may tell her that she need not concern herself with managing my kingdom. Cerborath stands on its own, guided by my hand. The only other guidance necessary is by my servant to see you to the door. Good day to you." He made a quick gesture, and the emissary was escorted from the hall—too incensed to speak another word.

"Michael," Ladonna said, horrified, "you risk war with such disrespect!"

"If Cerborath is but a territory, Sabrina would not waste her time with so extreme a measure."

"Do not be so certain," she warned. "Banen will be appalled to learn you have given away your father's ashes."

"He has little say about it," Michael told her. "And since I find my authority put to the flame of late, I think I will address another troublesome issue." He turned from her and called to the remaining attendants in the hall. "Someone bring me my royal medoriate."

"What are your intentions?" Ladonna asked warily.

"Do not fret, my dear queen, I will finish with business just in time for dinner." He patted his growling belly, which had become a true testament to his kingly lifestyle. They did not wait long before Brann Alwin appeared before them, his concern poorly concealed.

"Your Highness," the wizard greeted with a stiff bow.

"Do not pretend you serve me," Michael said, standing.

"I do not understa—"

"You understand perfectly. You are a spy. You kneel before me, but you disclose all to the powers of the Merchants' Guild."

"No, Your Highness, I—"

"The fact, for instance, that Medoriate Crow is alive in my dungeon. How would anyone outside this castle be privy to this?"

Brann Alwin turned as white as the blizzard outside. "I do not know, Your Highness."

"Now you lie to me." Michael began to pace. "The Guild wants poor Crow, and poor Crow will not tell me why. I had gone to ask him yet again, but strangely, he was unable to communicate."

Brann Alwin turned from white to gray.

Michael paused and bore into the wizard. "Perhaps you know why the Guild has an interest in him."

"I swear by Jedinom's Sword that I do not," Alwin said. "Please, Your Highness. Have mercy on me. You know how the Seroko tends its business. I could not leave them."

Michael smiled. "I do know, Medoriate. I do. And I know that they will not negotiate with me. Instead they offer me threats. They forget that I rule this kingdom, and I *will not* have them dictate *to me* what course of action I will take or what consequences will follow!" His voice had grown steadily until he was shouting. "This you can tell them when you return to them like the traitorous dog you are!"

Brann Alwin had fallen to his knees, his head bowed.

"You are worthless as a medoriate," Michael said, his voice quieter but not without an edge. "It seems you are only adequate as a messenger, so a messenger you will be. You can return to the Guild, and they can do with you what they will. But each time you return to me, you will be short one finger." He snapped his fingers, and Hunter appeared from the shadows. "We will start with your thumb."

"Your Highness, please, I beg of you!"

Michael turned his back. "Look away, my wife, for it will not be a sight for a lady to witness."

A sharp cry indicated the deed had been done. "Please have that cauterized," Michael told the giant, and Brann Alwin was dragged away.

"Do not look so stricken, Ladonna," Michael said, irritated. "If not dealt with a firm hand, all chaos would ensue. I must maintain control and respect, and if I learned anything from my father, I learned that a little fear and healthy intimidation can uphold one's authority." He spied a servant poke into the hall.

"The blood will be cleaned from the floor," Michael said to him. "You may tell the head cook that we are ready for the meal."

THE ICE PLAINS had been abandoned by all but one occupant. The bitter and relentless wind scraped across the raped and ravaged crater, shaping snow and ice into slick drifts to create a strange and foreign landscape. Tigress held her vigil, lonely and pointless though it was. She had come to question a great many decisions—those of authority and those of herself.

Her truest companion had abandoned Cerborath completely, and though she knew where he was, she had not yet found reason to join him. Dagger's traitorous actions had enraged her at first, but then she wondered if her loyalties held any integrity at all. She served her current king because she had served his father before him. Dagger served the symbol of the black sun—black earth—because he believed in what they were...what they had been, anyway. The syndicate was no more; it dissolved when Michael Garriker III ascended the throne.

She found she missed her comrades, and her anger at Dagger had become a longing sort of jealousy. He had done what she had been too afraid to do. But Dagger's gift was that he knew only right and wrong. The gray and muddied intricacies of politics never existed in his mind. Jealousy—that was the word.

Hunter had become Michael's hidden pawn—the man in the shadows who did the darker deeds dictated by the king. He was, perhaps, the only one of the syndicate who deemed that true authority rested with the one bearing the crown. Even Banen, who was unwillingly enlisted as his brother's personal protector, resented the collar placed around his neck, and she had no doubt he equally resented the one who placed it there.

Arythan Crow was the biggest mystery of all. When he had first joined the syndicate, she had pegged him for a brash and arrogant young man with a need to vent his youthful energy. As she had come to know him, however, pride had never been a driving force for the mage. He was more like a boy who had lost himself in a forest, trying to survive in a world he knew little about. He was smart enough to maneuver his way around, but then his past seemed to betray him. First his emotions took control, and then his guise collapsed. She knew little about him personally, but she did not need to understand his past to see how he had struggled, cracked, and finally shattered.

Therein was the true crime. He never really knew that he had been entangled in a high-collar game, and his naivety had made him the perfect pawn. In a world of royalty and power, there was no injustice. Arythan Crow, of all people, had learned the meaning of "black earth."

Tigress felt her horse paw the frozen ground impatiently. "You're right," she said. "This is shit." Talking to her horse was a habit she had picked up from the mage. It had only gotten worse now that she was doomed to this wasteland—"guarding" the king's precious Enhancement where it sat beneath feet of rock-solid earth and ice. She urged her mount toward the stable, only to find she had a guest.

"You cannot seriously patrol the entire basin," Banen said, watching her untack her horse.

"I prefer that to being bored," Tigress said. "What are you doing here?"

"Evading your watch, apparently," the prince said with a smirk.

"You can mock me all you like," she said. "As I see it, I have become worthless. Therefore there can be no degradation beneath this."

"Michael is afraid the Seroko will try to mine the Ice from under his nose," Banen said.

Tigress shrugged.

"He is breaking—losing his reason. You will not say it, so I will say it for you."

"It is not my place to question," she returned.

"No offense intended, Captain, but you can dispense with the bullshit."

Tigress blinked and faced him. "All right, Thorn. Your brother is a madman. He will destroy this entire kingdom, and the Seroko will help him do it."

Banen nodded. "He will ruin all that my father sought to accomplish."

"But you are merely a prince, and even that title grinds your teeth," Tigress said, folding her arms. "Why do you care?"

Banen looked away, and she could tell he was considering his answer. "Because..." he said slowly, "that is all I have left to care about. The syndicate is gone. All I have is my name and this kingdom."

"And Victoria Ambrin."

The prince spat on the ground. "Crow. Crow hurt her. If not for him, she would have been safe at my side. If not for him, my father would still be alive. That damn bloodrot took everything long before Michael lost his mind."

"Are you certain?"

Banen eyed her suspiciously as she finished untacking her horse. "What do you know?"

"You want to hate him, and so you will. But Crow was just a pawn."

"He murdered my father!" Banen cried.

Tigress stared at him. "Because your brother led him to believe your father was responsible for the death of his son and the near-death of his wife."

"What?"

"I saw the letter forged by your brother. It was, effectively, a contract with those who attacked Victoria and the child. I returned it to Michael myself; I saw his reaction to it, and I have no doubt he destroyed it so you would not see it. Michael hoped Crow would strike in revenge. After Crow was dismissed by your father in Desnera, he had every reason to believe your father was responsible for his loss.

"So yes, Crow killed your father, but Michael's hands also bear his blood."

Banen had turned away, trembling. "He wanted the crown, but I did not believe he would kill our father to achieve it."

"Power has a way of revealing darkness," Tigress said.

"I cannot serve him anymore. I cannot watch it all fall to ruin."

She knew what he would ask, and she answered before the words could leave his lips. “Yes. I will help you.”

He looked at her with surprise.

“What is your plan?” she asked.

“It is a simple one,” he said, his expression turning to the cold regard she knew so well. “We deliver Crow to the Seroko.”

28

TOO LATE

Morning stirred, dark and dreary and laden with snow—just as it had been for the past month. Diana fought the urge to stay in bed, just as she did every morning. There was little to rouse her these days, and the reason for her depression was also the reason she made the effort to leave her shop, face the storm, and walk the long road to Crag's Crown. She had watched people suffer, witnessed all manner of maladies and injuries, but never had she seen the deliberate destruction of someone's life. She was supposed to keep Arythan Crow alive—an impossible task when the king insisted upon poisoning him. How long could he endure? How long could she bear to watch?

Diana neglected to fix breakfast, for she lacked any semblance of an appetite. She half-heartedly packed her bag and glanced out the window, seeing only a wall of white beyond the glass. She bundled up as best she could, then headed out the door. She had not gone five steps before she was seized from behind, a hand stifling any sound she uttered. A strong set of arms wrenched her back inside her cottage before she could think to fight back.

There was not a chance to kick or swing at her attacker, for she was immediately released. "You can relax, Lady Sherralin," a man told her. His voice was familiar, and she spun to see a tall, middle-aged man removing his own winter layers, exposing his bearded face. "You might remember me from the cave," he said.

"You're an Ice Fly," Diana said, catching her breath and waiting for her heart to slow.

He nodded. "Othenis Strix, milady. Arythan's friend. I apologize for startling you."

"What are you doing here?" she asked.

"My eyes and ears do well outside the castle," he said, "but I am blind and deaf to what transpires inside." He took a step toward her. "Arythan—is he still alive?"

She gazed at her medical bag. "If you mean that he is still breathing inside that dungeon, then yes, he is alive. The king has a wizard administer the Enhancement to him, to keep his magic nullified. It is slowly killing him, and despite all my efforts, there is nothing I can do to save him."

"I would have thought he'd have been executed," Othenis said, slight relief upon his face.

"He is kept alive because the king would like to bargain with him. The Seroko have been threatening him to hand Arythan to them." She sighed and sat down. "His Majesty cannot seem to learn the nature of their interest in Arythan, but it has been his driving obsession."

Diana looked up to see him rubbing his chin in thought. He did not speak right away, choosing to take a seat across from her. "We cannot let the Seroko have him," he murmured.

"We? That request seems a little beyond my control," Diana said. "What do you know about this? Why do they want him?"

Othenis looked at her discerningly. "I can tell you only that he is the key to a hidden wealth of knowledge. Arythan himself does not know this, but if the Seroko take him, they will be able to corrupt all they touch. They will truly have Secramore as their empire."

"So Arythan is a pawn," Diana said, disgusted. "Everyone is using him, one way or another."

Othenis frowned. "Regretfully so, Lady Sherralin. Perhaps in your eyes, I look the same as they do. However, I do have other reasons for wanting Arythan safe. His brother served our cause well, and Arythan has sacrificed much to help us... I do consider him a friend as well as an ally."

Diana leaned forward and rubbed her brow. "He remains locked in the dungeon. I don't know what forces you have at your disposal, but it seems unlikely that you will storm the castle and break him out."

"Indeed not," he agreed. "But you have power that we do not. You are needed to keep Arythan alive. If his life is in danger, the king must listen to you."

"I have often thought of approaching His Majesty, but his reason has been called to doubt of late. Whether madness or obsession, he heeds no one—not even his... Well, I have considered speaking with the queen. She may or may not have the power to sway him, and he may or may not listen to her."

"I would say there is no harm in trying," Othenis said. "For my part, I must keep attentive to the Seroko's every move. If an opportunity opens for Arythan to escape, then we will be ready to take it." He stood. "But first I must know—before I involve you in this plot—that you are willing to take the risks before you. I cannot promise your safety inside the castle."

"I have always made my decisions with full knowledge of the consequences," Diana said. She rose to meet his gaze. "I will do what must be done...if it's not already too late."

THERE WAS laughter at the table that morning. Though the storm raged as fiercely as ever outside, her family was seated together around the high table in the Great Hall, a warm and blazing fire in the hearth behind them. The cupbearers stood by, ready to pour more drink as soon as vessels went dry. There was an elaborate spread upon the table that would feed twenty hungry mouths, though there were only six seated, including herself.

Ladonna gazed upon her plump and rosy-cheeked children—Cerborath's future. Mirabel was giggling at her brother's antics, and Riley was making faces at their father. It was hard for her to imagine what they would be like as adults, representing and leading an entire kingdom. Michael often boasted of the legacy they would inherit.

Michael....

Her attention migrated toward the center of the table where her husband sat, his eyes not upon his children but on his meal. She searched for any semblance to the man she had wed years ago. He had been in fine shape then, broad-shouldered and strong. He was as handsome as any man could be—black hair neat and preened as raven's feathers, a proud and noble face with alluring blue eyes. He was charming, witty, and so very clever. How the women had envied her!

She watched him now as he devoured his food as though on a mission, his thoughts somewhere beyond her reach. He was slouched in his chair, his hair in slight disarray, flecks of gray like the earliest few stars around his ears. That proud jaw line had softened and grown fleshy, and it was scruffy with neglect. He had once dedicated himself to upholding the latest trends in fashion, but now his attire was ill-fitted, hugging too tightly to a body that had expanded and rounded from overindulgence. He did not seem to mind, and in fact he would jest about the lavish life of a king.

If his children scarcely mattered, and his own upkeep did not matter, what did hold his attention? The easy answer was his throne. But even as the king of Cerborath, he could not be content. He wanted more, but what more was there? Ladonna hated to believe there was a secret Michael was keeping from her, but maybe she had allowed herself to be blind to his activities.

Her gaze shifted to Victoria, the scars upon her face. The young woman had ceased to smile, and she seldom spoke. Poor Victoria—the true victim in a dirty, bloody drama. She had lost her child, lost her husband, lost her pride. Banen came to her aid, and Ladonna knew it should have been her. It should have been her, because deep down, she knew Michael was responsible.

She had seen the letter—the contract—in Michael's possession. Yet even after she had heard the news about the attack on Arythan's family, she refused to believe her husband was capable of such wicked scheming. And when word arose how Arythan had murdered Michael's father, she had allowed herself to believe that sentencing him to the dungeon was a more lenient fate than execution.

Oh, she had become a weak and worthless queen! A deep-rooted and burning shame had risen like bile in her throat when Diana Sherralin had come to plead with her. The healer enlightened her to Arythan's condition, and if Michael could not see fit to remove the mage from the dungeon, he would lose his precious bargaining piece. That was politics and logic. There was another emotion that had surfaced upon the usually unreadable face of the healer. It was Diana's desperation that reached Ladonna's heart. The healer was not made of stone after all, and she did truly care for Arythan Crow. There was something different—something special about him. She had been drawn to it as well.

Now the mage was dying in Michael's prison, and it was time to discover if her husband still cared enough to heed her request. Ladonna cleared her throat. "I held an audience with Diana Sherralin today."

Three of the five heads lifted from their meals.

"She is concerned about Medoriate Crow's condition."

"Is she?" Michael asked, still chewing his food. "Rumor has it she is rather sentimental about him."

Ladonna glimpsed Victoria flush and look down again.

"Regardless," Ladonna said, "she labeled his condition as 'precarious.'"

"It is her duty to see that he is not 'precarious.'" Michael paused and looked at her. "I went down there myself to question him. Other than his nonsensical ramblings—courtesy of Medoriate Alwin—he did not give me any cause for alarm."

"That was also a month ago, my dear," Ladonna reminded. "Did you see him? Diana tells me he shrinks away from torchlight."

Michael shoveled another bite into his mouth. "The entire dungeon is dark. It is nigh impossible to see anything unless we light the walls afire. She could discern no more than me." He pointed his knife at her while he chewed. "What is it, exactly, you are trying to impart? You desire a demonstration of sympathy? Would you like me to place him in a cozy room, in a bed beside a hearth?"

"I am merely relaying Lady Sherralin's professional opinion," Ladonna said.

"Well," Michael continued, "it is no matter of opinion that he murdered my father. He deserves to be where he is. *That* is justice."

The children stopped talking, horror upon their faces.

Ladonna frowned at her husband.

"The situation was explained to them," he said casually.

"Let us be honest, Michael. This is not merely about justice," Ladonna said. "This is about politics. I know that Medoriate Crow is a man of secrets. You said yourself he was working against you with the Ice Flies. But your business associates—the Merchants' Guild—they want him alive, do they not?"

"You have been listening to my conversations with Banen," Michael said, his voice low.

Ladonna knew a dangerous tone when she heard it. She placed her hand atop his. "I am no spy, my dear. You know that I support you in every way, and I can only be strong by your side if I remain informed."

"I told her about the Guild," Banen said.

Ladonna tried to hide her surprise, but Michael did not question his brother. "Since this is a grand family affair," he said, "would anyone else like to contribute an interesting bit of knowledge?"

"I know how to make a dragon in my mashed potatoes," Riley announced.

"A useful skill," Michael said. "Well done, my son."

"We digress," Ladonna said, determined to make her point. "If Medoriate Crow has value to the Guild, it seems logical that we must keep him alive. Am I correct?"

"Of course," Michael said, growing bored of the conversation.

"Diana claims she cannot keep him alive while he is in the dungeon."

"That is questionable."

"But there is no harm done in relieving him of his current setting," Ladonna said. "Even if it is just long enough to see that he is in fair health. Consider it a protection of your investment."

Michael smiled. "You have borrowed one of my phrases." He took a drink and pushed his empty plate aside. "For argument's sake—from a logical standpoint—what if Crow decides to escape? What if he regains control of his magic?"

"Hunter," Banen said. "Hunter can guard his room. Crow should not be in any state to evade him, and magic is useless when you have been rendered unconscious."

Michael stared at his brother. "You loathe Crow, Banen. Why do you now fight for his comfort?"

"I do loathe him," Banen said, "but I care about this kingdom."

The king gazed around the table in thought. "I am heartened

that I have the support of my entire family in this venture. Either you are all more compassionate than I am, or you have little faith in my logic." He smirked. "Very well. Crow may have his relief. Hunter will be stationed with him at all times, and Lady Sherralin will continue to monitor his health. I hope I will not come to regret this."

"He is means to an end," Ladonna said. "Think on the future, Michael."

"Ah, my wife," he said, smiling, "what a grand future it will be."

DIANA TRIED NOT to be openly hopeful, but she had every desire to make this her last descent into the old dungeon. Hunter lurked behind her, the keys to Arythan's cell in his hand. For her part, she bore a blanket in her arms, to shield his eyes from the light and to hide him from the gathering crowd of onlookers who she knew was waiting in the keep. Her heart was racing as they approached the door, but just as they were ready to descend, the sound of rushing footfalls turned their heads.

Victoria hurried toward them, a look of determination upon her scarred face. "Please," she said, breathless, "let me come with you."

Diana frowned. "I don't think that would be a wise idea. We will bring him up soon enough."

"And everyone else will crowd around him," Victoria said. "I want to see him first. I want to talk to him."

"He has not spoken in over a month," Diana said. "Your words will be wasted." She had not forgotten how Victoria had treated her when last they spoke.

Victoria had not forgotten either, for she lowered her eyes. "I don't care if my words are wasted. There is something I must tell him—something he needs to hear. What he wanted to hear from me before." She squirmed beneath Diana's stare, but she did not retreat. "I apologize for how I treated you. I was upset, but I have had time to come to reason…and regret." She glanced upward. "Please, let me come with you."

Diana did not answer, but she motioned for Hunter to grab the torch and followed suit behind him. She could hear Victoria's quickened breathing over her shoulder, but otherwise the dungeon was silent. She approached the cell as Hunter bore the torch above her. The light caught the edge of the shrouded form, and she called to him softly. "Arythan." She did not expect a verbal response, but she had hoped he would at least turn in her direction.

"Arythan," she tried again, louder.

"Arythan?" Victoria's voice echoed in a question behind hers. Irritated, the healer motioned for her to stay back.

Diana crouched beside the cell. "We've come to take you out of here," she said.

The form did not move.

She ignored the volume of her own heartbeat, straining to hear his breathing. Faint and irregular, there was a grating sound that made her skin prickle. "Open the cell," she said, in a voice that quavered more than she liked.

"What's wrong?" Victoria asked, alarmed. "Why isn't he responding?"

"Hush," Diana ordered, waiting for Hunter to employ the key. The grille creaked open, and she hurried inside. She knelt beside him and gently touched his shoulder. He did not move. "Not now," she whispered. "Don't do this to me now."

She called to Hunter and set to opening the blanket. She wrapped it around his fragile form, covering his face. "We need to get him to the room straightaway. I can't tend to him down here."

"Is he dead?" Victoria asked in a small voice.

Diana ignored her and took the torch from Hunter. She

watched him lift the shrouded mage, uttering an astonished comment to Jedinom as he did so.

"Tell me he's not dead," Victoria said, panicked. "He can't be—"

"He's not," Diana snapped. "But he needs my attention. Stay out of the way."

Victoria said nothing more, and Diana focused on the path ahead of them. She replaced the torch at the top of the stairs and was close on Hunter's heels as they left for the keep. She could feel herself bristle as they passed the onlookers eager for a chance to glimpse the murderous mage. If only she had kept the torch to ward them away. The king's face was amongst them, of course, but it had paled with concern when he saw them hurry by. He deserved to be frightened.

It seemed an eternity until they reached the designated chamber. As soon as Hunter crossed the threshold, Diana closed the door—nearly upon Victoria. She had forgotten entirely about the young woman and did not consider that she might still be tailing them. With an impatient sigh she ordered her to shut the door behind them.

Diana took a deep breath and approached the bedside. Hunter had already uncovered the mage's face, and he stood there stupidly, gaping at what remained of Arythan Crow. Diana had never been one for tears, but they welled and fell anyway as she made her assessment. Victoria was surprisingly silent, but one glance at her grief-stricken face spoke for the one mutual sentiment they shared at this moment.

Diana's usually steady hands trembled as they brushed the hair away from Arythan's colorless face. He was skeletal, filthy, and covered in sores that leaked from infection. His emaciated chest strained to rise and fall, still rattling with the fluid that choked his lungs. When she pulled back his eyelids, she nearly recoiled, for his eyes were completely black—stained from the poison that still flooded his system.

Hunter looked as though he would vomit, and Diana sent him away to fetch a cloth and some warm water. Where could she start? Would anything she did matter? She would clean him, dress his wounds, and then... Then it would be time to hold her breath and wait to see if he would survive or not. Had he been left to the dungeon one more day, she was certain she would have discovered a corpse.

"You don't have to stay," she told Victoria, who had crept closer to the bed with her hand covering most of her face. "If he wakes, I can tell him what you were going to say."

"Do you...do you think he will?" she whispered.

"I don't know."

Victoria hesitated, looking from the bed to the door. "It's just that I...I can't look at him," she said, her voice breaking. "I can't bear to see him like this." She turned to Diana. "He asked if I'd forgive him, and I told him no. I meant it then, but now...."

"I will send for you if he wakes," Diana said, surprised by the touch of sympathy in her own voice. "I intend to stay here tonight."

Victoria nodded and slipped out the door. Diana half expected to see faces peering in before the door closed, but no one had followed them outside the room. If there were any curious loiterers, they could glean what they might from the expression on Victoria's face. Hunter reappeared not long after, bearing the supplies she requested. She noticed he kept his eyes from the bed and did not say a word—even after she dismissed him.

Once she was alone with the mage, the objective part of her mind seized control, allowing her to treat him without her emotions actively interfering. If she thought for one moment about who it was she was tending, she risked breaking down as Victoria had. With great tenderness, she wiped away the dirt and grime, cleaned and wrapped every wound. She only wished, when she had finished, that his appearance and his condition had improved.

She dragged a chair to the bedside and watched him in silence. There was nothing she had to say yet so much she wished to communicate to him. Like Victoria, however, she might have been too late. Diana reached toward the bed and took his hand in hers. She was determined to remain by his side, to be attentive to his every move. If there was a change, she would know it. If he needed her to respond, she would act in a heartbeat.

That was how Diana had intended her vigil to be. But there would come that unintentional moment—the one she would never be able to remember—when her exhaustion would defeat her. She would fall asleep....

She was jarred awake by sudden movement and a terrible sound. Though Arythan's eyes were yet closed, his body tensed and strained as his lungs sucked at the air. His hand parted from hers as it involuntarily clenched into a fist. His violent fit continued, and she could do nothing but watch through her tears as he fought his final battle. Then those black eyes opened wide as his body heaved upward. His mouth parted, but there was no sound. His gray and hollowed face tightened in the climax of his struggle, and then it was as though the taut strings that held him suddenly slackened. His body relaxed, his expression softened, and his eyes shut. It was over.

Diana stared at him in disbelief. He could not be dead. He simply could not be dead. She took his hand, and there was no resistance. She shook him, called to him—all with no response. Diana gave a cry of grief, and Hunter burst into the room. He never said a word but hovered near her while she wept.

When her eyes dried, a deepening emptiness began to swallow her emotions. Numbly she brushed the strands of hair from her tear-sticky face, straightened her attire, and stood. She took a last look at him and decided she did not want to remember him this way—that all his efforts to do what was right ended him here—a young life lost in an ugly and deceptive war.

She pulled the blanket over Arythan's face and walked out the door.

~

Michael Garriker III paced the length of the solar, his hands clenched behind his back. He was oblivious to his children, who fought a mock battle behind the couch. Nor did he notice how his wife's worried stare never left him. Banen also watched his brother, but through narrowed, searing eyes.

"This is absurd," Michael ranted. "She failed in her one duty. This cannot go unpunished."

"You are an idiot."

Everyone turned to face Banen. Michael stopped pacing. "What did you say to me?"

"You are an idiot, Michael," the prince said, his words stronger. "This is not Lady Sherralin's fault. It is yours."

"How dare you accuse me in such a way," Michael said. He took a step toward his brother.

"I have not yet begun my accusations," Banen muttered. He lifted his head. "You put Crow in the dungeon. You neglected to check on him. What did you expect?"

"He is a murderer!" Michael snapped. "He was fortunate I did not execute him!"

"Why didn't you?" Banen challenged, crossing his arms. "Crow's little secret? Your dealings with the Merchants' Guild—or should I say, 'the Seroko?'"

"You know nothing of my business," Michael said. "All that I do is for the best for this kingdom."

"All that you do is best for you," Banen countered. "I heard you insulted a Desneran emissary and sent him away with Father's ashes. One would think you are looking to start a war—all because of your pride and your delusions."

"When you speak your ignorance reeks from your lips," Michael said, taking another two steps toward his brother.

"Then enlighten me," Banen challenged, his eyes flashing.

"Michael, Banen, please," Ladonna said. "We need to support each other."

"The only support you've shown," Michael said, glancing in her direction, "is in blurting the happenings of a private affair!"

"They were your father's ashes," Ladonna stressed. "You think Banen would not have noticed them missing?"

"Father is dead, and his ashes are his ashes. To whom are you married, woman? Where do your loyalties rest?"

Ladonna's cheeks flushed. "Banen is your brother, not your enemy. I have only ever stood behind you, Michael."

"Her concerns are the same as mine," the prince said, "but she is too afraid to voice them."

"Afraid of what?" Michael demanded of both of them.

"Afraid to tell you that you have lost your mind," Banen said.

The king's round face reddened. "I cannot trust any of you," he seethed. "Not my own brother. Not my own wife." He bore into Ladonna until she turned away, tears in her eyes.

There was a knock upon the door, and one of the servants answered it. "Lord Hunter and Lady Sherralin wish to have an audience, Your Highness," the servant said.

Michael bit his lip, then said, "Let them in."

Hunter appeared first, grim-faced and slightly pale. Diana followed behind him, wearing her exhaustion like it was her last good attire. Both of them bowed, and silence ensued.

"What is it?" Michael asked at last.

Diana took a breath. "Arythan Crow is dead, Your Highness."

Her words shattered the moment, like a vase that had fallen to the floor. Everyone stared at her, and the truth of what she had said worked its way into their consciousness.

"No," Michael murmured. His own color fled, and he found a

chair. "No, he cannot be dead. I need him alive. I need his secret. Without him…."

"Without him, you have no way of bargaining with the Seroko," Banen finished. "You placed the future of this kingdom on the head of one dying bloodrot, didn't you? He was your game piece, and like the arrogant idiot you are, you believed yourself invincible with him in your grasp." Banen waved his hand. "Surprise, brother! The mage is dead. Now what?"

"Hold your tongue!" Michael shouted.

"I've held my tongue for too long. Desnera will be after us, the Seroko will be after us. Mighty king, what shall we do?" He held wide his arms. "Do we welcome war? Do we starve to death as the Guild cuts off our supplies? Or do you have a hidden secret—an army or—a *medoriate*—who will lead us from this darkening fate? What words of wisdom, Michael, now that you have done all in your power to destroy this kingdom?"

"Shut your mouth!" the king barked, standing in his fury.

"I will not! I will be heard, just as the truth will be heard." Banen's hard-eyed glare leveled at his brother. "Why *did* Crow murder our father?"

Michael started to speak, but Banen left no opening, speaking over him. "His son died. Victoria nearly died. Not because Father ordered the attack—because *you* did—in his name."

The king moved in on him, and Banen, lighter and nimbler, circled around, just out of reach. "Ladonna, take the children out," Michael growled.

The queen and dabbed at the tears from her eyes. "Perhaps they should know."

"Take them out!" he shouted.

Mirabel and Riley huddled under their mother's arms, cowering at the sight of their father's rage. "I know the truth," Ladonna said, holding her ground.

"You wanted the throne so badly that you had Crow do what you could not do yourself," Banen sneered.

Michael lunged at him, reaching for the sword at his brother's side. Banen felt the weapon slide from its sheath, and he acted instinctually, the knife slipping down his sleeve and into his hand. It was buried in Michael's chest before another word could be spoken. There was no sequence of events to follow; all ensuing action happened at once. The king fell to the floor with the knife still jutting from where it had pierced his heart. Mirabel screamed and Ladonna cried aloud. Diana and Hunter rushed to Michael's side, but Banen could only stand there, gaping at what he had done.

"He reached for my sword," the prince said, dazed. "I didn't realize what I—I didn't—"

The children were ushered past him quickly, coupled with Ladonna's order for Hunter to take them elsewhere. She was trembling when she knelt at Diana's side; Diana could only shake her head. The king of Cerborath was dead.

29

THE FALLEN

It was the beginning of what she had awaited: a flash fire of chaos initiated by the death of a demon. Seranonde moved slowly toward the bed, her red-violet eyes as luminous as the cold and distant stars in the abyss of night. With those eyes she peered into the body beneath the sheet. A trace of the fire remained, and it was enough. She held her hand above him, her fingers outstretched like a contorted spider. Without touching him, she began to pull. The sheet turned black above his face, where the poison forcibly exited his body from his eyes, ears, and nose. What started with a sluggish trickle began to stream like blood from severed veins, saturating the linens and running to the floor in growing puddles.

The Huntress did not cease with the extraction of the poison. She pulled harder, coaxing the stubborn flame that had been no more than a whisper of heat. And she wrenched at him further, allowing the darkness of the aura that had surrounded him to consume the empty vessel like the tide seizing the shore. All these forces amassed into one, and the momentum was unstoppable.

Then she herself withdrew and disappeared, for she had accomplished what she had come to do.

~

He lurched upright, forcibly immersed in a world he thought he had left behind. It was like slamming face-first onto a bed of shale. The warmth of the encompassing darkness had turned cold, and the cold was like solid stone, sending shockwaves through his body. There was no air. There was only blackness to be seen. And silence, and—

It poured from his mouth, thick and black and suffocating. It drained from his eyes, slowly returning his vision from dark blobs and masses of inky poison. It ran from his ears, the pressure dropping and the whirring sound quieting—as though he was surfacing from the depths of the ocean. It gushed from his nose, forcing him to taste it a second time as it ran past his mouth.

At last there was air—just a little—but enough for him to gasp and frantically try to feed his lungs... which resulted in a wretched, gurgling cough that rattled his bones and made his heart skip a beat —not that it beat so regularly anymore. He gasped for more air, and he coughed again. The cycle was endless, exhausting, and completely involuntary, but it became easier to breathe with each passing fit.

Finally he fell back onto the bed, drained of poison and of strength. He did not remember being here. His last recollection was of the darkness and the cold of his cell and knowing he was going to die. He was certain that he *had* died—again—but his reawakening this time was akin to be dragged by a runaway horse over the rocky and frozen plains of Cerborath.

Why was he here? Why? The confusion was the last to clear, and he knew not all of it would. His senses were returning to him, and as they did, he began to realize something was terribly wrong.

He stared at a hand resting across from his face upon the bed. It was connected to an arm—neither of which could possibly be his. But he moved the fingers, and with a bit of effort, he lifted the arm.

Panic seized him, and a surge of adrenaline had him drop from the bed. He crawled to the wardrobe, naked as he was, but refusing to look down at himself. He pried at the door with those foreign fingers and it opened to reveal a long, vertical mirror. His breath came in short gasps as he stared in horror. There was a skeleton staring back at him, eyes recessed somewhere in those shadowed sockets. His face was gray, and it looked as though it had been hollowed out where his cheeks and temples were. His hair was also a shade of gray, dull and stringy and thinned. A scraggly beard hung from his jaw, but the tattoo—that bloody black tattoo had not changed. It was the only trait that forced him to believe he was truly staring at an image of himself.

He did not have to open his mouth to know his teeth had rotted. The rest of him might well have rotted too, for there was nothing but bones held together by thin and pasty flesh. He was like a child's favorite stuff toy: abraded instead of threadbare, raw flesh exposed from unsightly sores instead of seams that popped with stuffing. Someone had taken the time to wrap his wounds, though the bandages were already soiled.

As he stared, he was overcome with the shamble that was himself, and he clutched at his head and cried a soundless cry that his raw throat would not grant a voice. He collapsed and wept, not knowing anymore who he was or what he was supposed to be. There were no answers for him as he lay there, completely shattered.

The thought occurred to him that he could take his own life. Smash the mirror and use the shard to... He pounded a weak fist against the grotesque image of himself, realizing he had not the physical strength or the strength of will to accomplish such an end. He lay there a long while, staring at nothing, thinking of nothing.

Echoes of his past and the lives he had led reached him from the depths of the void. None of it seemed real or even a part of him. All these faces he had worn had only been masks, and now he was stripped of them all, but there was nothing beneath. He was without a name, and to be unnamed was to be without a place, without a purpose. Empty.

But even as he lay there like a corpse upon the floor, he could sense a distant force—prodding, searching. He lifted his head, and the window shattered. Shards of red glass rained upon him, and the snow blew in like a white cloud of locusts, driven on black vapors that raced in with the wind of the ravenous storm. He braced stick-like arm before his face, but smoky tendrils enveloped him, filling his nose, his mouth, his eyes and ears—permeating his wounds like water tracing its way through loose stone.

Every breath seared his insides, making his eyes water. Hot coals burned in his stomach, the pressure and the heat welling inside him like magma and steam ready to forcibly escape. A surge of energy fed his limbs in sharp tremors that had him on his feet instantly. He staggered toward the door just as it burst open, an unfortunate servant in his path. The man was immediately engulfed in flame, his scream cut short by the intensity with which he was consumed.

Shrouded by Shadow and flame, he ran into the hallway, and smashed against the wall, his insides roiling and the flesh of his back ripping open with the emergence of two bony, leathery, dragonlike wings. Blood ran hot down his sides as he clutched at the stone in agony. His fingernails split and thickened as they grew into bone-white claws. His feet had changed as well, and his legs nearly buckled beneath him.

Another passerby skirted his blurry vision and fled from sight, crying at the top of her lungs. He rushed in her direction—only to be assailed by someone with a blunt object. He felt the weight of the weapon smash against his side, and in a fit of mad fury, lunged at his attacker. He bit into an arm, and the taste of salty blood filled his mouth as his rotten teeth shattered and gave way to sharper teeth that erupted through his gums. His attacker fell away, and he continued his flight down the darkened hall.

His sight sharpened despite the dim lighting, but so did his hearing. His own breathing was like a raging wind in his head, and when a couple children crossed his path, their shrieks were like knives twisting in his ears. He knocked both of them down but was flung back against the wall by a giant of a man.

A familiar voice bellowed at him, but he could not stop. He could not rest. The fire inside would devour him if he did. He raked at the giant's chest as the man bore into him, and ice crackled from his clawed fingertips. He could smell sweat and fear. He could smell blood and stone, hearth and food. He was dizzy and nauseated by his inundated senses, and he slipped away from the stunned giant to retch bile upon the floor. It froze and cracked, as did the bloody spatters left in his wake.

He made a panicked dash through the Great Hall and toward the massive double doors. They smoldered and caught fire with his touch, but he fled past them, clambering down the snow-laden steps and into the massive drifts of the courtyard. Shouts alerted him to his pursuers as he desperately melted his way through the thick obstruction of ground cover. The snow began to fall faster, half-frozen flakes the size of apples plummeting like rocks from the blackened sky. Carts, posts, doors, and other wooden structures combusted as he passed, and the sound of stone cracking resounded like exploding trees. The clouds whirled in a massive vortex that funneled downward—reaching for him.

He reached the inner wall and collapsed against it, the wind ripping the crumbling stone of the wall away as it spun around him with growing momentum. He was the eye of the storm, but any trace of calm vanished as torrents of violet lightning slammed down upon him in a pillar of blinding light. Strike after strike, like the pulsing of his heart, they came and dissolved what remained of Arythan Crow.

A SOLITARY FIGURE walked slowly down the road and to the gate of the royal city. She did not need to lower her hood for the guard to recognize her. "Another late night, Lady Sherralin?"

Diana merely nodded. "If you only knew..." she murmured. Of course, no one knew the king was dead—not yet. Tomorrow, perhaps, word would reach the city, and she hoped to be gone before it did. There was no reason for her to linger. Cerborath had treated her well, but she never acknowledged it as her home. The lies, the deceit, the violence—she would be eager to leave it all behind her.

The gate swung open, and she continued on her way. She felt as though Death marched behind her, spurring her recollection of the lives that had been lost that day. As if Arythan's passing had not been difficult enough to swallow, she had witnessed the demise of Cerborath's most recent king at the hands of his brother. The most horrific omen—if she had been a superstitious woman—would have been the appearance of the white-skinned creature that tore through the castle on a path of devastation. She placed all faith in the logic of her mind, but her own reason failed her when she sought to make sense of the phenomenon. She had seen it as it fled the castle—the monster made of fire and smoke. Amidst the darkened sky and blinding snow, she had seen its eyes—violet eyes that burned bright like embers. She had gone into the storm to watch it as it raced for the castle wall. It had been as though all the elements had unleashed their fury at the same time—fire, lightning, snow, wind, and ice—all relentless as they attacked the creature in its flight. She had lost sight of the monster until the lightning struck it and forced her to turn away, until the inner wall collapsed and razed part of the outer wall with it. The monster was buried beneath the debris, and only then did the sky clear for the first time in months.

Whatever the creature had been, it had left behind an aftermath of destruction. Claw marks were gouged in the stone, and what was not charred was cracked by ice. There was blood everywhere —from both the monster and its victims. One body was burned beyond recognition, two people had been mauled—one of whom was Hunter, trying to protect the queen's children. Stranger still was the state of the room in which she had left Arythan's body. The window had been broken from the outside, as though the creature had climbed the walls to force its way in. There was blood and black sludge upon the floor, upon the sheets and blanket, just about everywhere she had looked. But what was missing was the mage's body. Did the monster devour it? Hide it? From where had it come? There were no answers, and the queen forbade anyone from trying to uncover the creature's body. Ladonna Garriker, distraught with grief, readily believed that a curse was upon them all.

Too tired to trace the circles of her thoughts anymore, Diana focused upon returning to her bed. Whether or not sleep would clear her mind, she would pack her belongings and leave before the sun marked midday. With only the strength of determination to keep her upright, she did not immediately notice the dark silhouette standing in the shadows outside her shop. Only when it stepped toward her, did she freeze, her heart skipping a beat.

The figure stepped into the moonlight just far enough that she could distinguish some of his features: his tall and lanky build, his beard... Diana allowed her heart to slow before she approached the leader of the Ice Flies.

"I apologize for the late visit," Othenis said in a low voice.

She avoided his gaze. "Another night, and you would have

come to an empty shop." His silence spoke the question for him. She opened the door. "Come inside."

Diana lit a couple candles and gestured for him to sit at her table. She placed herself across from him. "You came to hear about Arythan."

He nodded.

"I was able to sway the queen, and she, in turn, swayed her husband," Diana said. "Arythan was moved from the dungeon to a secluded room where I could tend to him." She paused, feeling herself choke. "Despite my efforts, it was too late. Arythan is dead."

Othenis started to speak, but she was not finished. "The king is dead, too, as I'm sure you would have learned for yourself. If I were you, I would not waste my time lingering here. Cerborath will crumble."

The tall man rubbed his chin, his face darkened by concerns unnamed.

Diana took a breath and rubbed her brow. "You need not worry about the Seroko now. Your secret knowledge is beyond everyone's reach."

"Arythan's death is no small weight in my mind," Othenis said at last. "I feel I have failed him, and in turn, failed his brother." He took off his hat. "You may be right in your logic, but I regret that the safety of the Archives was achieved through his passing."

Diana looked up to find him studying her.

"Where will you go?" he asked.

"I have not decided, exactly," she confessed, "but I will start by heading south."

Othenis gave her a slight smile. "Everywhere is south of here."

"That is very perceptive of you."

"I am known for my astute observations," Othenis said. "And since I see that you have not firmed your destination, I might suggest that you travel with us."

Diana blinked. "What? To where?"

"To wherever we decide to go," he said. "In truth, we are in need of another skilled healer. We would offer you protection, shelter—all that you need."

"Just who are you?" Diana demanded. "Are you some dethroned king with riches at your disposal? Will I be immersed in some ageless grudge you carry against the Merchants' Guild? I will not leave one political entanglement for another. I would sooner fend for myself, as I have always done."

Othenis gave a short laugh. "I am no king, but I do lead my people as a regent should. We have our own means of funding, but we are nomads. We were once known as the Gray Watchers—a clandestine group of dedicated members who sought to record the growing history of Secramore. Above all, we value knowledge and the standing morality with which it should be wielded. The Watchers, however, had sworn neutrality—that they would not become involved or influence what they observed.

"There was a faction of the Watchers who wanted to use our resources to dominate Secramore. They became the Seroko, and much like an infection, they spread their influence quickly. They use the Merchants' Guild as a cover for their operation, but they seek access to the Archives of all we have collected. When the Watchers dissolved, I gathered those willing to oppose the Seroko in a less-than-neutral force. It is our duty to watch and meddle in their affairs, but we are small in number, and we choose our battles."

Diana traced the wood grain of the table. "So it is a war of sorts."

"We think of it as justice. A righteous cause," Othenis said. "You need become no more involved than you wish. As a healer, you would do as you have done for the people here."

"The Ice, then…."

"The Enhancement had become Cerborath's economic resource, but for the Seroko, it is a means to immortality. Arythan knew as much, and he had every intention of destroying the Ice Plains. Prince Michael had grown suspect to his alliances, thus Arythan's desperation to leave here once his son was able.

"The Seroko killed his brother, and his brother had once been a loyal Watcher. He had cause to help us as well as cause to sabotage their plans. He had not foreseen the treachery of the monarchy." Othenis looked away. "Neither had I."

Diana stared at him. "But what of his special knowledge of the Archives? Aren't you in as much danger?"

Othenis sighed. "There were only a few Watchers who knew its location. Arythan's brother was one of them, and when he died, we believed he passed that knowledge to Arythan."

"So you don't know where it is," Diana said.

"That secret may have died with him."

"For all that you've told me, what will you do if I refuse to come with you?" she asked.

"Nothing I have said is of any value," Othenis said. "I have given you the truth of who we are, and if you decide to go your own way, you will not hear from us again."

Diana stood, fighting a chill. "Arythan found reason to trust you." She headed for one of the cots to snatch a blanket, but she found both of them bare. She froze.

"We are loyal to our cause and each other," Othenis said. "I asked Arythan to join us. Had all worked according to plan, he would be with us now."

"They're missing," she murmured.

"Is something the matter?" He came to join her.

She held out an arm to keep him back. "The blankets are missing," she whispered. Her eyes swept the darkened room. They fell upon a bundle near the hearth.

"The embers," she said. "I had not lit a fire since the day before." How did she not notice them glowing when she walked in? She pointed to where she believed the intruder was hiding.

Othenis nodded, and his hand moved to the hilt of his sword. He walked soundlessly ahead of her until they stood just a couple feet from the bundle of blankets.

If a Seroko spy had broken into her shop, she would have thought there would be a sign of forced entry: a broken window, a tampered lock on the door...but there had been nothing telling. Blankets and embers? What sort of spy would jeopardize his location in an effort to keep warm?

Othenis drew his sword and used the tip to flip back the cover.

Diana gasped and took a step back. It was the creature from the castle. From what she could tell, its eyes were shut, and its naked, bony limbs—which included a pair of leathery wings—were folded protectively around its curled body. It did not stir—did not even seem to breathe. "Is it dead?" she whispered.

Othenis's eyes were affixed to the creature, staring in fascination rather than horror. He kept the sword poised at its body as he lightly grazed its arm with his boot. It remained motionless.

"Milady, a candle, please," he said.

Diana complied, her fear slowly shifting to intrigue. Still, she remained slightly behind the Ice Fly as he crouched beside the creature with the light. For a long while, Othenis said nothing. When he finally turned to her, he said, "He's still alive."

"*He*?" Diana asked.

"Arythan."

She gaped at him, then moved closer to see for herself. Gaunt as any creature she had ever seen and whiter than bleached bones, there were features she recognized as Arythan's and others that were not. Claws, pointed ears, and wings aside, it was *his* bare face—marked by the same black and jagged tattoo over his eye. There were fresh wounds, and there were the injuries she had dressed, already staining the bandages she had applied before he had died. *Before he had died....*

"It's not possible," she breathed, kneeling beside him, tears in her eyes. She watched the shallow rise and fall of his chest, watched the strength of his heartbeat reverberate through his battered body. "I saw him die. I *know* he died."

Othenis said nothing but reached out to gently nudge the mage's arm. When there was no response, he tried again with a little more force. "Arythan. Hawkshadow."

Diana brushed the white hair from his face and opened an eyelid. The same violet, feral eyes of the creature were there, but the gesture was not enough to rouse him. "I—I don't understand this," she said. "How is this Arythan?" She noticed the bumps on his skin, watched him shiver involuntarily. With pity, she re-covered him with the blanket.

Othenis went to stoke the fire in the hearth. "I had heard the stories, but I never interpreted them literally." He shook his head as he stirred the embers. "Hawkshadow, brother to Hawkwing of the Gray Watchers. His more notorious identity—which I know now is more a description than a name—is the White Demon."

"The bandit?" she asked, doubtful.

"The very one who served the Prophet in the desert outside Belorn," Othenis said. He placed a couple logs on the firedogs and watched the flames kindle and grow. Then he turned to her. "Wanted by Belorn's Crown as a notorious thief and for the murder of Duke Dinorthon. In Mystland, he is wanted for theft, assault, and the murder of the renown witches, the Larini. I have heard he also severed the hand of a prominent leader in the Thieves' Guild. Add the assassination of Queen Lucinda Jerian of Desnera and King Garriker II of Cerborath." Othenis glanced at the mage. "You would never imagine such a list of accomplishments from him, would you? Of course, only some of his accusations are just. I have done my share of research on our friend, and weeding truth from fiction is not the easiest task.

"My favorites are the legends from the desert. He was summoned by the Prophet to guard his stolen treasure, and any who opposed him were turned to sand. Himself, he could wear shadows like a cloak, call the lightning at will, set objects ablaze with a look. Some claimed he fed on the blood of virgins…."

Diana interrupted him with a hand. "Stories and rumors aside, I know the kind of person he is." She got up to gather some supplies for the mage's more recent wounds. "He may have been the only one in this kingdom with the heart to do what he knew was right, and all the while he was being manipulated. His child is dead, his wife lost to him. I watched him die from the poison that was fed to him."

Othenis approached her. "I know what you mean to say. 'Let him be.' He has answered for his crimes, perhaps. I would agree with you. He needs a chance to recover. He needs protection. In no way can he remain here." He placed a hand on her arm. "My offer. Come with us. We can help him and you."

Diana hesitated.

"I know you are not eager to trust me, but Arythan did." Othenis looked her in the eyes. "This is not a burden you should shoulder alone. If the Seroko believe he is alive, they will search for him until they find him."

She looked at the mage and sighed. "How do we proceed?"

30

UNFINISHED

The Demon awoke to a spoonful of cold sludge on the back of his tongue. He gagged and sprayed the substance upon his caretaker, lurching upright in an effort to catch his breath. Nothing around him was familiar, though he was not entirely sure what he should remember. The recent memories he did harbor were fuzzy, most of them horrific and altogether questionable as to whether they had happened in his life or in his head.

The interior of the cabin shifted until his dizzy spell abated, and he was left to face the stunned young woman sitting next to his cot. Eyes like moons, she gawked at him, his recent meal running down her face, dripping from her nose and chin. He stared back. She opened her mouth and proceeded to scream. The sound was enough to make his ears bleed, and he flung himself from the bed to escape it.

He hit the floor and scrambled for the door, his limbs shaky and unreliable. More people appeared, but none of them were stupid enough to get in his way. A potent blast of wind blew the door in, and freedom waited beyond. The Demon plunged head-first into a blinding world of white. The sun rebounded off the snow in a glare that inspired him to cry aloud—except that his voice did not work properly in his raw and swollen throat. What escaped him was a sound between a gasp and a gurgle, and he shut his eyes as tightly as he could, tears squeezing out the corners as the burning left impressions behind his eyelids. His clawed hands clutched at his face, undecided if they should shield eyes or ears.

He had forgotten about the claws—if he should have remembered in the first place. Accidental self-inflicted scratches began to run with blood. He collapsed in the snow, and the cold began to permeate whatever clothes had been placed upon his body. Instinctively, he curled in a ball and shivered violently, and while the screaming had stopped, there were voices all around him. And the smell of fire and people and food and animals—

Something touched his shoulder, and the Demon lashed out with his foot. He heard a cry and a curse, and the voices grew louder. There was one—a woman's—he could distinguish from the others. A familiar voice.

"Stay back," she said, and he heard her approach, her footsteps crunching over the snow. "Arythan." Gentle but firm. "Arythan, let me take your hand."

He did not want to uncurl—did not want to take his hands from his face at all.

"Arythan."

But he knew that voice. He trusted that voice. With great reluctance, the Demon lowered his hands, but he kept his eyes shut. He flinched when a warm set of fingers clasped his. "Breathe slowly," she commanded, and he tried to do as she asked. "I have a blanket for you." A light weight fell upon his shoulders, and it was dry and warm. "I'm going to help you inside." And she did. Blind as he was, she led him over the snow until he felt the wood of the floor beneath his feet. It grew warmer as he heard the crackle of the fire, smelled the smoke. He was eased to the floor.

"Open your eyes. It's darker in here, I promise."

Slowly he opened his eyes. The fire was to his back, and he was facing the wall of the cabin. There were people—lots of people—huddled in the periphery of the space—all of them watching him. But then her face came into focus, pale, lean, and creased with worry. Yet the corners of her mouth were slightly, subtly upturned. "I'm with you. You're amongst friends," she said.

But hers was the only face he knew. He could hear the others whisper, wondering what he was, if he would harm them, what sort of dark magic he harbored. They feared him, but he did not know why. The Demon turned away from the woman and the people. He started to pull at the rug beneath him, hoping for a place to hide from all their relentless eyes.

He watched his own trembling, clawed fingers grip the material, saw an arm of only flesh and bone... Had this happened before? There was only one person who would know. The one person who had been with him all those dark days when the chains weighted him down, and the silence roared in his ears. Emérion Aguilos, his brother.

"Em'ri? Are you there?" the Demon asked.

There was no reply.

"Em'ri...please...."

Another round of silence stirred panic from within. His brother would not abandon him, would he? He would not leave him alone. Not when he needed him so desperately.

"Em'ri!" the Demon called, his frail voice so lonely in the cabin. Everyone was watching him, waiting and wondering.

"It's all right," the woman next to him soothed.

But it was not all right. Where was his brother? Em'ri was gone—somewhere he could not reach him. The Demon buried his head in his hands, but still he felt the burden of their unforgiving stares. *"Stop it!"* he cried in his own tongue. *"Leave me alone!"* The fire flared and popped behind him.

Of course, he *was* alone. With his brother gone, he was alone in a world full of Humans—trapped beneath their sight, held prisoner by their fear. Fingers lighted upon his arm, and he scrambled away. *No more chains. No more darkness. No more. No more!* He would sooner die.

The Demon ignored the woman's voice when it called after him. He needed to escape and find his brother. And his family. Em'ri was likely looking after his son and Victoria. He would be waiting with them in the mountains, outside the desert.

There were people in front of the door now. Too many for him to contend with. He caught sight of a darker space—a passage that would lead him away from all their stares. But it was dark—dark as the prison to which they had condemned him. He hesitated, but the woman was advancing, and so were the others.

The Demon pulled the shadows around him and darted down the passage. His heart shook the whole of his body as it pounded inside him, and his ears started to ring. He knew this feeling—knew he would pass out if he did not rest, and if he passed out, they would catch him.

To the left there was an open door, the dim light of a candle flickering through the crack. He slipped inside, but now his vision was dimming, and his legs buckled from beneath him. *No. Not now.* He fell flat upon the floor, too numb to feel the full force of the impact. His shadows departed, and the door opened. The woman walked in, but it was only the woman. She knelt beside him, murmuring words he could not distinguish. Her fingers reached for him, but this time he did not move. They lightly grazed his forehead, nudging away stray hair that had fallen into his face.

The Demon trembled in spite of himself, but his heart began to slow. *A spell. She is casting a spell,* he thought, but he was utterly powerless to stop her. The soft touch of her hands upon his face, the words that overcame the ringing, the scent of mint and lavender... Like cool water her presence soothed him, calming the thoughts that raced like flames in his mind.

"I'm here, Collin."

"Em'ri?" The Demon tried to move, but his body was like stone.

"I know this is difficult for you. There is not much that makes any sense, is there?"

"I know Victoria and Reiqo are waiting for me. That's all I need to know. You can take me to them."

His brother stepped into view and knelt beside the woman. *"You have been very sick,"* he said. *"Even though the poison is gone, you need to heal—in body and in mind. You have to acknowledge the truth."*

"What truth? What have you come to tell me?" the Demon asked.

"Your wife is not waiting for you," he said sadly. *"And your son is dead."*

The Demon shook his head, feeling his eyes burn with welling tears. *"I won't believe you."*

"You must, or you'll never heal," Hawkwing said. *"I, I have been dead for years now, Collin. You see me because you believe you need me."*

"I do," the Demon said. *"I'm lost. I don't know what to do. I don't know what's real and what's not. I thought I died...."*

"You did," Hawkwing said, his golden eyes bright in the dim room. *"How it is you are alive now is not for me to say, but you are alive, and you need to continue."*

"All that I had is gone."

"Arythan Crow is dead, yes. The Demon has returned."

"Returned to what?" the Demon demanded. *"What is left for me?"*

"Perhaps one final act, if you wish it. One final role to play in this grand scheme of deceit."

"No. No, I'm done. I'm done with Humans, their kings, and their games. I'm done with feasts and dancing and courtship. I wanted a family, and you say it's gone. So let it be how it was, and I'll meet my fate as it comes."

Hawkwing frowned. *"It* is *how it was, Collin."* He gestured to the Demon's trembling hands. *"The question is, what will you do before your fate meets you?"*

The Demon regarded him defiantly.

"You had a mission you left unfinished, in the Ice Plains. Your Shadow has returned. You can achieve what was impossible before."

The Demon said nothing, his gaze returning to his quaking hands. When he looked back at his brother, he was gone. Only the woman remained, but her name had returned to him somehow. "Dianar," he whispered.

She smiled. "I didn't know if I would reach you."

He was not sure what she meant or if it even mattered. His breaths came slow and easy, and the remaining strength that kept him awake was waning. He found he had no desire to stave off sleep, and so he willingly closed his eyes.

When next he woke, the Demon was in the same small room, but he was now on a cot, covered with blankets. They could have been tree trunks atop him, for how pitifully weak he felt. There was no one in the room with him, but he did hear voices through the wall. He had not, initially, seen the second door beside the desk, but his hearing was acute enough that he need not leave the cot to press an ear against the barrier.

He recognized Diana's voice, and the man speaking to her also sounded familiar, though his mind was still too hazy to process any recollection. She had done something to him—brought clarity from amidst the chaos. He knew now that Hawkwing's appearance had been his own creation—his own reason reaching out to him in a form he had known well. Part of him lamented that the vision had not been real, because he still felt very much alone.

Death will do that to you, he thought sardonically. He still had no idea why he was alive. Perhaps Diana was more than a mere healer. He pulled free one of his shaking hands and sighed. *A wasted effort, bringing back a dying bloke. How many times can someone die? Third time's a charm, maybe. Mermaids and healers can't be everywhere.*

He tucked his arm away, disgusted by its appearance and realizing the rest of him could be no better. For as weak and as undernourished as he was, he had no semblance of an appetite. Diana must have fed him something to keep him alive, but for how long had he been beyond consciousness?

"With the king dead, there will be no one to contend with the Seroko."

The man's voice caught the Demon's attention. Was he speaking of Garriker II? Or....

"The kingdom will fall, as you said," the man continued. "My men report that Prince Banen or the queen has sent messengers beseeching the aid of the nobility. They are afraid of an attack, and rightly so. If the Seroko believe Arythan is yet alive and within those walls, they will come for him."

"How did you learn the content of the message?" Diana asked.

"That is the other unfortunate piece of news. The Seroko have cut off all communication and supplies to the castle. The messengers were intercepted. We found one yet alive, but we could not save him. The Seroko will wait patiently while Crag's Crown starves. It is only a matter of time.

"As it is, we suspect they have found an ally in Desnera. So long as there is Ice to be mined, there will be an interest in the land. What remains of the royal family is of no consequence. They are the final string to be tied, and the Seroko will search the castle from top to bottom for Arythan."

There was a pause before Diana spoke again. "Then the longer we stay here, the greater the danger we are in."

"I believe our site is secure, but I dare not move until he is well enough for travel. I would not risk losing him again."

Should I feel touched? the Demon wondered. *What do they want with me?*

"His will be a long recovery," Diana said in a low voice. "For all my efforts to give him nourishment, he seems little changed. It has been a week since we arrived… Maybe now that he is responsive, his condition will improve faster."

"Yes—you mentioned he came to while I was away. Has he said anything to you?"

The following pause was longer than the first.

"He is ill in more ways than one," Diana said. "He did speak—in a language I cannot begin to place. And it was not to me but to someone he thought was with me: 'Emry.'"

"His brother," the man said quietly. "Do you think his delusions will persist?"

"I can't say what the lasting effects of the Enhancement will have upon his mind, but he knew me. He said my name." There was the sound of a chair shifting upon the floor. "Do you think he is the same person? Or is he someone else entirely? This 'demon' razed a castle wall and was responsible for the injuries and deaths of several people in the castle. I want to believe this is the same Arythan I knew, but he would not knowingly commit such destruction."

Did I do all that? the Demon thought in disbelief and horror.

"I know little about who the White Demon was and nothing about how he became Arythan Crow," the man said. "He didn't attack you when he woke; that is a favorable sign."

The Demon shook his head.

"He didn't have the strength to lift a finger," Diana said.

I'm not a monster. You know me better. He had heard enough. With effort, the Demon pushed away the blankets and struggled to sit upright. He shifted his legs off the cot.

"So we approach him cautiously. Hopefully the dungeon has not damaged him to permanent madness."

The Demon tried to stand, bracing himself against the nearest wall for support. He approached the door slowly and unsteadily and gripped the handle.

"One with his power—I would dread the thought," Diana said

warily. "When I went after him, he turned as black as the shadows —as though he had pulled every trace of darkness from the hall around him as a cloak."

"I wonder what else he can do, what other stories about him are true."

I can hear better than you think I can, for one. He opened the door without a sound, but both occupants of the room gave a startled cry to see him standing there. The Demon almost smiled, but those days were long behind him.

Othenis Strix—the Demon recognized him now—was immediately upon his feet, while Diana held her hand to her breast. "Arythan!" the Ice Fly leader exclaimed. He took a step in the Demon's direction, then hesitated.

"I don' usually bite," the Demon said hoarsely.

Othenis mustered a smile. Diana remained quiet, and the Demon knew she was assessing him. Othenis came to assist him, but he sidestepped the tall man. The thought of anyone touching him made his skin crawl.

A flicker of confusion crossed over Othenis's face, but then it was gone. He pulled out a chair. "Please, sit with us."

"You shouldn't be up," Diana said. The Demon merely looked at her and accepted the chair.

Glances were exchanged in silence, but the Demon was the first to break it. "What else 'ave I done?"

"What is it that you remember?" Othenis asked, retaking his own chair.

"Dying. Darkness. Peace."

Silence again before Diana spoke quietly. "What you heard is what happened."

"Did I kill the king?" the Demon asked, bearing into her.

"Which one?" she asked, then apologized. "Michael—the prince —died at his brother's hands, not yours."

*I would be relieved if I cared. Reiqo's blood is on his hands...*was *on* *his hands. My son...* He had not realized that his expression had changed, but his audience had, and they were both watching him intently. "Why'm I 'ere?"

"To recover," Diana said. "We found you at my shop, and Othenis brought us here."

The Demon kept his eyes upon the Ice Fly. "Why'm I *really* 'ere?"

"We need to keep you safe, Arythan. I won't lie to you: you are of special interest to us. I'm certain you are the Key."

"Arythan is dead," the Demon said without emotion. Diana shifted uncomfortably, but he did not acknowledge her.

"Your brother held the Key to the Archives—the hidden wealth of knowledge that the Gray Watchers have amassed for centuries. I believe he passed the Key on to you, and that is why the Seroko want you. That is why they wanted Hawkwing."

"That's why 'e died," the Demon said. "I told y' I don' 'ave any bloody key."

"It's not a physical key," Othenis said. "The only way to know for certain would be to take you to the site, but you need time to recover from your ordeal."

"From death, y' mean." The Demon took a breath. "So that's why I'm 'ere. Y' need me."

Othenis turned away. "As selfish as it seems, the Archives are a Watcher legacy. I want to uphold that legacy—to protect it now that the Gray Watchers have dissolved."

If I had stayed dead, they'd be perfectly safe. He did not care about any archive—not when his brother had died trying to preserve that "legacy." But if Hawkwing had given him the Key, then... *What did you do to me, Em'ri?*

"In truth," Othenis said, "I know you would do your brother honor by joining us. You have served our cause without allegiance; why not belong to our family?"

Because I have no place with you. I have no place anywhere. I don't even have a name. The Demon said none of this, choosing to remain silent.

"Look, there is no need to weigh decisions or brood over the future," Othenis said, opening his hands upon the table. "Cerborath's worries are not ours. You are here, amongst friends, and we want to help you recover—starting with a warm meal."

"Yes," Diana said, returning to the conversation with new resolve. "I can get you some broth to start. I fear anything more would do more harm than good."

The Demon shrugged.

"After you eat," Othenis said, "I have something to show you."

The broth went through him like water—perhaps because it was mostly water. Diana gave him some dry bread for substance, and it was nice not to feel as though his insides had been hollowed out. He had never had a problem with his appetite—not until he had been practically starved to death—and then it seemed strange to him that he needed to be coaxed to eat. While he was far from good health, the little that he ate did give him a renewal in energy.

Othenis approached him with a bundle of clothes in his arms. "We're headed outside. You will need a few layers to keep warm."

"Are you certain this is a good idea?" Diana asked. "I think we're moving too fast."

"I'll go," the Demon said immediately. Nothing was "too fast" when there was not much time to be had. The healer frowned but then sighed in submission and helped him prepare to face the cold.

"This will cheer your spirits," Othenis said, waiting at the door. The three of them stepped outside, and it took the Demon a moment to allow his eyes to adjust. It was the faded light of the afternoon sun, and the snow was awash in a shade of amber, blue shadows settling in pockets where people had trodden. The mountains surrounded them like a crown of topaz and sapphire, a veil of clouds shrouding them like a sea of liquid gold. Diana and Othenis started down a worn path until they realized he was not on their heels.

The Demon stared at the world around him, orange plumes of his own breath rising like smoke before him. He thought of the Ilangien when they first stepped out of the mountain, onto the ledge that overlooked the Draebongaunt. It was one of his first impressions of the immortal, and though he could not understand then what had caused a timeless being to shed tears, the Demon understood it now. Eraekryst had been locked away for a century; the Demon had been left in darkness nearly half a year. The time was irrelevant, the sense of awe was not. This was beauty and life, and no one could appreciate it more than one deprived of both.

His companions let him gaze until he was satisfied, and then he followed them to a crudely fenced paddock. If either Diana or Othenis had said a word, he did not hear it. He pressed himself against the fence and stared across the snowy expanse to a black phantom that scarcely seemed to touch the ground. When it did, snow sprayed like sea foam as the mare bucked and reared and played like the untamed creature she was.

The Demon watched her, wondering if she would remember him, wondering if she would be frightened by his true form and the Shadow that surrounded him. Perhaps it was better not to test her. He would walk away, let her be.

"We had a terrible time coaxing her in there," Othenis said from behind him. "Apparently they could not manage her at the castle, and my scouts saw her running free near the forest. She won't let us near, so we feed her and water her here. She is truly a spirit of the Wild, and we would have let her go if…" He did not finish his thought, for as the Demon stepped away from the fence, the mare lifted her head in their direction. Her ears stood like turrets, and she was motionless for a heartbeat. Then she flicked her tail and charged the fence at a flat gallop.

Diana and Othenis stepped back, unsure if the horse would collide with or jump the fence. The Demon did not move—not even when they came to pull him away. Narga stopped inches from the Demon, great puffs of her breath leaving her flaring nostrils. She lifted her head and whinnied, then shoved her nose into the Demon's chest, nearly knocking him over.

He actually smiled, wrapping his arms around her neck, and burying his face into her tangled mass of mane. *"Narga. Dark One,"* he murmured. He pulled away to rub her nose, and she nipped at his fingers. *At least she has not changed. My Narga.*

"That is quite a reunion," Othenis said. He approached the mare to pat her neck, and she whirled away, galloping back to the opposite end of the paddock. "Hmph."

"Carved from the same stone," Diana said.

"Yes. The Dark Wizard and the steed he shaped from the blackest storm clouds." Othenis shook his head. "I think I will leave this moment alone," he said. "I have a few tasks to accomplish before nightfall."

The Demon watched him walk away, only to find Diana's eyes upon him. "Who are you?" she asked him. "Where do you come from?"

He shifted to his more Human form, watching her eyes widen as he did so. "A mistake," he said. "A curse. A bastard son 'oo left 'ome to find 'is brother. Nothing's gone quite right since then."

"Only you could answer a question without answering it at all," Diana said.

The Demon shrugged. "What's to know?"

"Your name. If you're not Arythan Crow, who are you?"

"I don' 'ave a name," he said. "When the witches took m' Shadow from me, I 'ad nothing. Miriar. Miriar gave me a name. An 'Uman name." He thought back upon that moment, and it seemed so long ago. Why did he feel so much older now? Four years in Cerborath… That would age him around twenty-three now. Middle-aged for an Ocrantilian. He looked at Diana. "*This* is me."

She nodded. "I see it now, but I knew you as Arythan. I wouldn't know what else to call you."

"Do as y' will," he said, looking back at Narga, who was now watching them. "Y' did something. Y'elped me—in m' mind."

"I did what I had to do," she said. "Your friend—Erik Sparrow. He knew about me—the trace magic I have. I wasn't sure I could help you."

"Y' did. An' I thank y'."

Diana blushed but did not reply. "I suppose the standing question is: what now?"

It was his turn to nod. "I don' know…yet."

"A fair answer, and one I share. I ask just one favor."

He turned to her, questioning.

"Don't leave me…" Her blush deepened, and she elaborated. "Don't disappear without a goodbye. Tell me before you go. Please."

"I will."

"Thank you." She gave him a slight smile and headed back to the cabin.

31

FINAL STAND

He was untouchable. The mare beneath him grazed over the snow as though she was sky-borne, dancing through clouds. She—she was merely an extension of himself—a wild spirit unbound and free of tangible concerns. Dusk alone was on their heels as they dipped and rose over the hilly landscape. Not unlike Narga when her saddle and bridle were lifted, the Demon guarded the compelling urge never to return. He was free from obligations, oaths, and Human laws. Arythan Crow was dead, and he was a demon reborn.

For the past couple weeks, he had exercised his best patience. For as weak and emaciated as he had been physically, a growing restlessness had fed his recovery—if it could be called a recovery. He would never regain his health, though he never saw a reason to enlighten Diana of the Quake and his inevitable end. Whatever strength he garnered from rest, her meals, and her herbs, it would have to be enough to fuel his escape...and his final act of vengeance. He would destroy the Ice Plains in his brother's memory, and then he would disappear. He could not imagine a better ending for the notorious White Demon.

Sweat ran down his fevered brow, but he dare not let go of Narga's mane. Diana would be quick to tell him that this stunt of his indicated he was not in his right mind. Perhaps he was not, or perhaps, for the first time in a long time, everything was just fine. It was she who had brought clarity back to him, and in doing so, she had unknowingly unearthed memories his consciousness had buried. Hers had not been an intrusion in the way Eraekryst's ability had trespassed upon his will. No, the Demon was fairly certain she could not have seen his thoughts or guided his actions. Her magic had been like a gentle hand upon his shoulder, guiding him from the darkness.

But it was darkness she had uncovered.

The labyrinth at the Cantalereum only existed in his dreams as blackened and fragmented nightmares that were little more than horrific images strung together by a sense of unnamed dread. Abysmal eyes, corpse-like faces, fire, stone... There had been more, though. He had forgotten the storm, the tall stone walls, the crumbling statues with vacant eyes. He had been running, frantic, desperate. Miria had been there with him, part of the time. But there were moments without her, when he was alone.

Narga stopped dead, nearly throwing the Demon from her back. She stood as still as the trees, her ears lifted to a dark shape several yards ahead of them. He wiped his bleary eyes and stared into the deepening shadows. Something or someone was there, watching them.

The longer the Demon waited, the more he believed he could discern a faint blue light—an aura—surrounding what looked like a hole in the shape of a woman. His mind jolted back the labyrinth, a vision of a woman in black. A woman with wine-red eyes and pale skin and such coldness—like the dead and stagnant mist that lingered over the ground. Not a woman. A—a—*creature*—a monster. She had reached for him and—

The Demon gasped for air, the wind knocked from his lungs.

He was upon the ground, and if not for the snow, he would have likely broken a few of his fragile bones. There were naked branches reaching over him before a bleeding sky. Was it her? Was she coming for him? He closed his eyes and waited.

Behind his eyelids he saw her reaching for him but never touching him. She had no need to touch him, for she was close enough to make him feel sicker than he had ever felt before. Sick enough that he could have met his end then and there....

He opened his eyes, and a shadow moved over him. Warm breath pulsed upon his face, and he weakly brushed Narga away. "Y' threw me," he murmured. Or did he fall? Did it matter? He forced himself upright, his eyes darting to the stand of trees ahead of them. There were only trees after all.

Slightly dizzy, the Demon took a deep breath. "She did exist, Narga," he told the mare. "I know she did. I felt the same cold when I woke...after I died." His observations did nothing to clarify the story he sought to assemble. If this monster-woman tried to kill him, then why would it bring him back from death? And— He looked up at the horse. "Erik. 'E knew. Erik was 'iding 'er from me. Tha's why 'e wanted to leave. Why 'e went inside my 'ead." He struggled to rise. "I'm sure of it." The mare lowered her head, allowing him to grip her mane to steady him on his feet. He caught his breath, and patted her on the side. "*Des,* Narga." She lay down so that he could climb upon her back. "Good girl."

There's nothing to be done about it now. I don't know who she is or what she wants, and Erik is gone. She can come and find me, but she doesn't have much time. Do I bother going back? It would be so easy to disappear right now. He could ride to the Ice Plains, destroy the Enhancement. Whatever happened after that would not matter.

Narga tossed her head and turned in the direction from which they had come. "Y' want to go back?" he asked, surprised. *Food, warm shelter, safety—why not?* The Demon sighed and blinked away the water from his burning eyes. "Alright, y'ave a point. An' I didn't say goodbye to Dianar." He pulled himself closer to the mare's warm, plush neck. *I hate goodbyes,* he thought bitterly and allowed his mount to find her way back to the hideout.

~

THE ICE FLY encampment was a flurry of activity. Arythan paused a distance away, confused to watch men and women scurry around like ants from a disturbed mound. He slid down from Narga's back and started for the cabin. Diana met him halfway, a look of disapproval upon her face. He was hardly in the mood for a scolding, but as he soon found out, her expression was not inspired by his brash ride.

"We're leaving," she said, her eyes sweeping over him discerningly.

The Demon's gaze moved past her to the people moving in the darkness. "Now?"

"Othenis has news. He believes this is the best time to go, while the Seroko are distracted."

He looked at her. *Distracted?* "Where is 'e?"

"He was addressing a few of the others in the cabin, last I saw him." Diana paused. "Are you all right?"

The Demon gave a slight nod, but she seemed unconvinced.

"I wasn't sure you would come back," she said, a strange look upon her face. Was she holding back a smile? Trying to hide behind the cool masque she had always worn so well? More and more lately he had noticed cracks in that exterior. Was it because she knew an ending was at hand? He did not respond to the comment as he patted Narga on the neck and let the mare wander. Diana, however, kept by his side as he directed his attention to finding Othenis. A few Ice Flies brushed past him as he slipped through the door.

The leader of the Ice Flies was alone beside the hearth, creases of deep thought upon his brow. He lifted his head when he saw them approaching, some of those lines easing from his face, though he did not smile. "Hawkshadow, I'm sure Diana has told you...."

"What 'appened?" the Demon asked.

"The Seroko have advanced upon the castle," Othenis said. "Over the course of a few days, we have seen servants and merchants evacuating the city and the castle. Those fleeing have been stopped and questioned. Anyone suspected to be nobility has been executed." He shook his head. "I have heard the royal family is locked in the castle keep...."

The Demon waited for him to continue.

"Mercenaries or assassins," Othenis said, his voice lower. "A band of riders was seen advancing up the hill to the Crown."

"They would still have defenses," Diana said. "The garrison."

"Most have deserted with news of the king's death," Othenis said. "There can't be enough food to keep a full garrison fed. Supplies have been cut off for weeks; the cooks have probably gone. The situation is bleak for the Garrikers." He turned to the Demon. "Their fate is our fortune. We must move now, while the Seroko believe you are still in the castle.

"There is but one loose string to tie, if you are able." Othenis leveled his gaze at him. "The Ice Plains. Can you destroy them? You are more valuable than the Enhancement; I will not have you risk your life needlessly."

The Demon remained expressionless. "'S not needless. I 'ave to destroy them."

Othenis frowned, searching him. "You need not go alone. I can give you an entourage."

"No. I'll go alone."

"Hawkshadow—"

"I'll go alone," he repeated, his words stronger. "I can't promise what m' magic will do."

Othenis shook his head again, this time with finality. "There must be a place we can rendezvous. I will not completely abandon you to this mission. What you seek to accomplish is no small task. We will wait for you at the pass. That should give you plenty of room to work."

The Demon was unwilling to argue with him. "I'm leaving now." He ignored Diana's frown.

"Give me a moment to gather some men. They can ride out with you." Othenis set to the task, and the Demon started for the door.

Diana started to reach for him, then hesitated. "Arythan, wait." She moved into his path. "You know you're not fooling me."

"Are y' going to stop me?" he asked softly.

"I wish that I could, but I know better," Diana said. She sighed, suppressing something more. "You don't intend to survive this."

"'S not up to me."

"What—where are you going?" she asked.

"I think y'already know." He held her gaze. "Thank y' for everything."

"This is it, then."

"I don' usually say g'bye."

Diana nodded. "If this is our farewell, then I..." Her face tensed, and she reached for his hand.

It was a gesture uncommon for both of them, but it was all that was left. The Demon clasped her hand and squeezed it with a nod. "Othenis will take care o' y'."

"I will take care of myself, thank you, Medoriate." She flashed a brief, sad smile. "I am glad to have met you."

He gave her a lasting look before his hand slipped from hers, and he went to find his mare. Without a glance from anyone, he mounted and rode into the deepening shadows, guiding Narga in the direction of Crag's Crown.

~

Another quiet night. From the silence emerged a handful of source-less sounds a castle had no right to make. Taps and creaks and groans and the scraping of stone—reaching her ears every time her eyes threatened to close. There had been no sleep—not for her, not for any of them—not in several nights. If it had been some wandering spirit—the ghost of either king or even her late husband—she would have found some relief. But every sound might just belong to one of the living—an assassin come to bring an end to them all.

Victoria drew the blanket tighter in an effort to stop shivering. It was the height of winter, and there was no wood in the hearth. Even if they had decided to sacrifice any of the furnishings in the solar, Banen would not allow it. He actually believed they might survive. Even now, he was prowling the castle, hunting for those who were hunting them. She wished he would return. She wished he would simply be there to hold her. But Banen had asked her to be strong, and that meant comfort was an unaffordable luxury. How long had it been since she had felt a tender but firm embrace? Not since Arythan....

She sighed, blinking back tears. A gentle pressure at her side forced her gaze downward. Riley had nestled closer to her, his eyes shut, his lips trembling. It was a hard lesson for the children, to lose their father, then the sanctity of their home. Did they know death awaited them? All because they were of royal blood. Victoria pulled him closer, knowing she would never be able to hold her own son in such a way.

She glanced at Ladonna, vacant-eyed and pale, occupying the adjacent corner of the room. Mirabel sat with her, the girl's face still smudged with dirt and tears. Though they sat together, the queen was not present. It seemed as though all heart and spirit had left her with Michael's death. Her children could have been shadows crossing her path, for Ladonna scarcely heeded them. If not for Hunter, both Mirabel and Riley might have perished at the hands of the monster that had attacked the castle the day their father died.

If Hunter felt any pain at all from his injuries, he did not show it. He stood tall and vigilant at the door, a stone giant with sharpened blade always in-hand. Victoria wanted to feel safe with him there, guarding them. She wanted to believe he could destroy any threat that dared venture through that doorway, but her faith was gone. It abandoned her the day the men came to the manor, and the most powerful person she had known had not been there to stop them.

This was their fourth day of confinement in the solar. Their fourth day of darkness and cold. Their fourth day of waiting. Banen and Tigress took turns patrolling the castle, searching for intruders and scrounging whatever food and drink they could from the cellar and the pantry. The cooks and servants left more than a week ago. The garrison had followed shortly thereafter. There had been no word from the nobles Banen had beseeched for help; the only letter that arrived had been from their enemies. A simple note saying they were coming for the mage. The very mage that had died after his reprieve from the dungeon.

When Victoria thought of him, she shuddered, and her skin prickled. That gray and skeletal form could not have been her husband. It had been more of a husk—a cold and lifeless form that might have been any forgotten prisoner. Any but Arythan. Arythan was too stubborn to die in such a way. Too spirited to simply relinquish his soul in the face of adversity.

But that had been her Arythan before he had broken—before he had been stripped of his son, faced her rejection, was forced to suffer in the king's dungeon. He had lost all hope, and he had died. With more than a twinge of guilt, Victoria wondered why she still lived. She felt like a coward, because she had hid her heart from him and shut him out. She doubted her forgiveness would have saved him, but it had been all he had asked of her in end, and she had denied him.

The truth was, she did not hate him. She did not even blame him—not anymore. If there had been anything left for her to give, she would have given it to have him with her now, in these final hours. She would hold his hand—hold it so tightly that no assassin's sword would part them. He had been her strength and her protector, but only now did she truly feel his absence.

A sound outside the door jolted them all to attention. Hunter waited, poised with his massive hand gripped upon the hilt of his sword. A pattern of tapping allowed them to relax but a little, and the giant allowed another hulking form inside the room. Tigress had returned, a bag hanging limply from her shoulder. Most of the food had already been stashed near the hearth, but it was disturbing how quickly they had consumed their rations.

Tigress dumped a handful of potatoes and turnips upon the table, and Victoria did not bother getting up. While her stomach burned, she did not feel the desire to eat. Riley stirred from her side and went to investigate the vegetables. His lips quivered some more, and Victoria wondered if he would whine or cry as he did the first couple days of their imprisonment. But then he wiped his eyes and sat down, his head bowed in silence. Mirabel went to join him, a comforting hand upon her brother's shoulder.

Victoria's eyes returned to the door. Where was Banen? She watched Hunter and Tigress ask each other the same question—silently and with only a shrug as a response. The former captain of the B.E.S.T. took a seat at the table, resting her head in her hand. She looked old and weary, but there was no fear. Victoria did not think it possible for her to be afraid, or maybe Tigress was merely too tired for fear.

"What if he does not return?"

Soft but pointed, the question pulled all heads in Ladonna's direction. The queen of Cerborath had been silent for so long that Victoria wondered if she would ever speak again. Clearly she was more attentive than she seemed, but her query merely added to the discomfort already thick inside the room.

"I believe he will return, milady," Tigress said.

"We cannot afford to be optimistic." Ladonna stood. "To remain here is certain death."

"What is it you suggest?" Tigress asked, rubbing her brow.

"We attempt to leave the castle."

Victoria bit her lip.

"Your Highness, with all respect, we have already considered that option," Hunter said. "Thorn has strong suspicions the Seroko are dispatching any nobility leaving the royal city. Our faces are too well known to conceal."

"Then there must be another way," Ladonna insisted. "Perhaps Banen has the romantic notion of defending this shell of castle, but I have every intention of saving the lives of my children. There is no hope of meeting that goal if we remain here."

"Where would we go?" Tigress asked. "If you're guarding knowledge of some secret passage, you best tell us now."

Victoria imagined the queen coloring in the darkness of the room.

"There is no such passage," Ladonna said tightly. "Our chances merely remain better on the move."

"They will pick us off in the dark," Tigress said. "In here we have the advantage of them coming to us. We have only one entrance."

"Only one exit, you mean." Ladonna approached the table. "You mistake my decision for a suggestion."

Tigress and Hunter merely stared at her.

"So long as this castle stands, I am still queen. You will serve me as you did my husband. You will protect my children, the heirs to the throne." Ladonna loomed over the table. "You will do this, because I know you still have honor."

Tigress scowled, but Hunter turned away. "Honor," the captain said, "is not a word that stretches far within these walls. But if it's honor you stress, then we'll do as you ask." She turned her attention toward the giant. "Hunter will lead you, Lady Ambrin, and the children out of the keep. I intend to look for Thorn."

Ladonna looked as though she might protest, but Tigress continued. "*That* is honor, milady. I'll not leave a member of my crew to the enemy if there is a chance he is still alive. I will find him and try to rendezvous with you at the forest's boundary...if either party makes it that far." The captain stood and straightened her shoulders. "No one stays behind."

"Very well," Ladonna said, lifting her chin. She gathered her children.

Victoria joined them. Her stomach twisted and turned, but she supposed fate would have the final say. Banen wanted her to be strong, so she would stand beside Ladonna and try to help the children. But nothing would stop her from hoping the prince would walk through the door at any moment.

Tigress approached the door first, listening for any noises outside. The only sound Victoria could hear was tense breathing and her own rapid heartbeat. Everyone watched as the captain slowly opened the door. She disappeared into the blackness beyond.

Riley began to whimper. "It's so dark," he said through his tears. "I can't see anything. I want to stay here, Mother. I want to stay *here.*"

"Hush," Ladonna soothed. "Your eyes will adjust. You hold your sister's hand, and she will hold mine. We will all stay together, and Hunter will protect us. It is not safe here."

Victoria touched the boy's shoulder. "You can hold my hand, too," she said in a voice more assuring than she felt. Riley immediately gripped her fingers, and she tried to smile for him. In another moment, they too were entering the voidlike hall beyond the solar. The way out of the keep was so very familiar, so very simple. Down the stairs, along the corridor to the Great Hall, then out the main doors. Or to the Great Hall and down the pantry stairs to the kitchen and the cellar, where they could leave out the cook's doors. It seemed either route was painfully obvious, and their enemies would be waiting for them no matter which exit they took. The distance never seemed so long.

Hunter's broad form was hard to miss, even in the dark. As a chain they followed him, their shuffled gait so loud without the usual bustle of castle workers. Victoria could almost trip on the giant's heels, and Riley did trip on hers—several times. Mirabel was behind them, and Ladonna brought up the rear. It seemed hours before they reached the stairs. Slowly they started downward, one step at a time.

The air was punctured by a sharp cry—Ladonna's—as chaos ensued. Victoria felt a shove from behind, and her feet lifted from under her. The children screamed, and Riley's hand slipped from hers. There was a grunt and a groan—Hunter's massive form heading up the stairs. The stone was unforgiving as Victoria tumbled down. Her ears rang, and a warm trickle ran down her forehead. Her nose throbbed, and a thick, sticky mess ran down and touched her lips. She dare not utter a sound, laying as still as she could at the bottom of the staircase. She could hear the ring of metal against metal, and in that instant, she knew she had to move. Her eyes clawed at the darkness, searching for the children. She scrambled across the floor until she found a wall and forced herself to her feet. The sound of quick breathing turned her head, and not far from her, she could barely see the smaller shapes of the children, pressed against the wall as she was.

Victoria hurried to them. "Don't let go," she whispered, taking their hands. She pulled at them, and they struggled to keep with her. She would not let them go, even if she had to drag them with her. But they would never make it to the doors. Instead, she headed for Michael's study, grateful to find the door gave way beneath her pressure. She shut the door behind them and gathered them behind his desk, hiding beneath it in the darkest shadows.

"Mother," Riley sobbed, and Victoria placed a hand over his mouth.

"Not a sound," she warned. "We can't make a sound."

BANEN KNEW he was being followed. There was no sound to betray his pursuer, but his instincts rang through his core, keeping his feet in quick and constant motion. He could not return to the solar, lest he betray the location of the others, but how long could he lead the assassin before it became obvious he was baiting him? He passed by Michael's study, wondering if he should duck inside and take his enemy by surprise. The library seemed a better choice. There would be more room to maneuver, more places to use as cover for a surprise attack. He walked past the study, hoping the next door would be ajar. To slip inside too quickly would alert his pursuer. Banen carefully took the handle and entered, closing the door behind him. He slid his blade from its sheath and waited against the wall.

The following thud nearly stopped his heart. A weighted object grazed against the door, and all was silent again. Banen stood there, his heart in his throat, his eyes wild. The handle clicked, and the door moved. It opened several inches and stopped. He waited.

After what could have been minutes, he took a step forward. A lump beneath his foot snatched his gaze downward, where a gloved hand lay still. Cautiously, he stepped beside the door and opened it farther with his free hand. He peeked around the barrier to find a body—one of the assassins—dead upon the floor. There was nothing but darkness in the hallway beyond. Hunter or Tigress would have entered the room, but then again, neither of them would be roaming the halls of the castle.

Without him pushing it, the door closed. Banen leapt backward, his sword clenched so tightly that his skin nearly broke.

"'S me," said a voice, barely audible.

Banen spun around, but there were only shadows to greet him.

"Who?" he hissed.

"Me," the voice said again. This time, the shadows solidified into a form—a slight form beneath a hood and cloak.

"No," Banen whispered, pointing his sword at the shape. "You're dead."

"Not anymore. I'm 'ere to 'elp."

"Whatever monster you are, we don't need you," Banen said.

"I know a way out."

The prince hesitated and lowered his sword. "This is a trick."

The figure shook its head. "Y'ave to trust me."

"Never," Banen muttered, but he relaxed his stance.

"The crumbled wall. I know a way to the forest."

"We're staying here," Banen said. "I won't run."

"Then y'll die," the voice said darkly. "They all will."

"We do not need—"

"There's no time," the shadow snapped. "Where are they?"

Banen hesitated. "The solar."

The shadow moved to the door and gestured for him to go first. Banen held his tongue and stepped into the corridor, over the body. He did not like the situation at all, but if the mage was ever right, he dare not question him now. He headed for the stairwell, wondering by the silence if Crow was on his heels at all.

Banen stumbled over something solid, his breath catching when he realized it was another body. Without knowing why, he bent closer, and his head began to spin. A woman. Ladonna. A gaping hole across her pale neck. An icy chill made him tremble, and he flew over the steps, several at a time. Another body was at the top of the stairs, this one foreign.

Banen finished his course to the solar, too anxious to be cautious. He pushed past the door to find the room empty. Empty but for the rattle of a dying breath. He turned to find Hunter beside the door, his massive hand clutching at his side. "The captain knew you would return," the giant whispered. "She went after you."

"No," Banen seethed. "I ordered everyone to stay."

"Her Majesty would not," Hunter said. He closed his eyes. "She is dead."

"I know. Where are the others?"

Hunter shook his head.

"Curse the Sword," Banen growled.

"Thorn…I am sorry…."

The prince shook his head.

"Go," Hunter urged.

Banen hesitated for a moment before bolting out the door. There was a sound from behind him, and a knife slid across the floor. A body fell after it. All reluctance gone, Banen headed back down the stairs. If Victoria and the children were hiding, there were not many choices at their disposal. But in the time it would take for him to find them, their enemies could reach them first.

He ran back down the corridor and past the library. As he approached the study, he swore he heard someone say his name. He ducked inside, only to be met by Tigress. "Crow's outside," he told her, but she had already shut the door.

"What?"

"Crow. He's here. He thinks he knows a way out." Banen fell silent when he saw Victoria and the children huddled against the wall.

"Are you mad?" she asked.

"He's alive," Banen insisted. "Out there." He pointed toward the door. Then his temper surged. "What is the meaning of this?" he hissed. "Why didn't you wait?"

"Does it really matter now?" Tigress countered.

Banen clenched his jaw.

"If we can't find a way out, we're all dead," she said.

"I know a way."

All eyes moved to the shadow in the corner of the room.

"Impossible," Tigress said.

Banen crossed his arms. "I told you."

"How?"

"Listen," the Demon interrupted. "Where the wall crumbled. 'S steep, but y' can scale down to the forest. Sneak away."

"Like a coward," Banen muttered.

"'S not about y'," the Demon said coldly.

"I know. It's about *you.* That's why the Seroko are here." Banen took a step toward him. "Give yourself up, and maybe they will spare us."

"You know it's too late for that," Tigress told him. "They will see the bloodline dead."

Banen gave a disgusted sigh and sat in Michael's chair. He turned to find Victoria's eyes upon the corner. "Your husband is the White Demon, in case he never thought to tell you." He watched her start toward the mage, then stop.

"Arythan?" she asked.

"No," came the quiet response. "Stay away."

"The White Demon," Tigress mused. "I thought it was a ridiculous title."

"But an 'onest one," the Demon said. A projection emerged from either side of him, unfurling as a pair of large, pale, leathery wings.

"Jedinom's Sword," Tigress breathed, then grinned. "All this time... You little shit."

They were interrupted by a new voice, one muffled from

outside the door. "You have no need to hide. We are here and ready to negotiate."

"Safir-Tamik," the Demon murmured.

"Release the medoriate to us, or we will unleash ours upon you."

The Demon stepped forward, crossing before the narrow window adjacent to Michael's desk. He remained a silhouette but for the violet shine that caught his foxlike eyes from beneath his hood.

"Trapped," Banen spat. "Just as we were before."

From beneath the Demon's cloak emerged a clawed, white hand that pressed itself against the window. Icy patterns formed over the glass, thickening into a sheet in seconds. "The wall," he repeated. "The break in the wall."

Brann Alwin's voice replaced that of the Jornoan's, uttering words in the language of magic. The door began to deteriorate.

The Demon tapped the ice with a clawed finger, and the glass shattered, allowing a blast of cold air to assail the study. Tigress shoved the desk beneath the window. "Let's go."

The Demon moved before the splintering wood of the door just as the children were helped atop the desk and pushed out the window. Tigress glanced at him, then followed them. Banen lifted Victoria, and the two of them were soon running over the snowy ground upon the other side, tailing Mirabel and Tigress, who carried Riley in her arms.

There was the sound of an explosion, and the refugees turned back to see the keep swathed in violet flame. Victoria gave a cry, and Banen grabbed her arm. "He'll find us," he said, boring into her eyes so that she could look nowhere else. She nodded and ran with him to the wall. They scrambled over the wreckage and into the wilderness beyond, leaving Crag's Crown to burn.

32

NIGHTFALL

O*ne night. One last, beautiful night to see it finished.* The Demon looked down from the mountain pass into the basin of the Ice Plains. The land glittered with a dusting of diamonds brushed away from the face of the waxing moon. Or maybe it sparkled with the frozen tears of the immortal spirits whose remains had been unearthed and exploited for greed. He alone had the power and the will to end it all.

The Demon slid from Narga's back. *"Stay,"* he told her. *"Don't follow me. Time for you to be free."* He rubbed her nose and walked away. With a glance he saw her watching him, her ears pricked in his direction. *"Stay,"* he repeated firmly, and disappeared down the trail. He had expected Othenis and his men to be there, but perhaps his detour at the castle had taken too long. *All the better. No more confrontations.*

It had been difficult enough to see Victoria again, to hear her voice, and sense her fear. He would never know if she made it to the forest, but at least he had given her a fighting chance. He could not say the same for the remaining Seroko assassins. Brann Alwin and several others had met their end in the burning castle. Regrettably, Safir-Tamik was not among them. The Demon had looked for his body specifically, but the Jornoan was a master of evasion. A coward like no other. He could not worry about Safir-Tamik now. His current mission was much greater.

A violent chill forced him to stop and grip the rocky wall to the side of him. He waited for the tremor to pass and took a deep breath. Perhaps he had less time than he thought. He stretched out his wings, took a running start, and lifted from the ground. The black trees and their snowy branches sped by, and the landscape slid under him. He had forgotten this feeling—the solitude and the rapture of being sky borne. For him, it felt appropriate, to be so removed from the world in which he lived. Now it was a final view —a summary of Cerborath, the dark kingdom, and the role he had played.

The Demon landed somewhere in the heart of the basin, his talon-like toes boring into snow and ice. More than ever he could feel the magic beneath the earth, but unlike before, he understood it completely. He had danced with the elements in the mountains, and now he would dance again with the ashes of the immortals. The raw energy that stirred flame, propelled the wind, rocked the waves, and split mountains—he would guide it, and that would be his final contribution to a greater cause.

As he had done once before, he knelt down and pressed his hands to the ground. *No, the more contact the better.* He lay down on his belly and closed his eyes. In his mind he pictured the Enhancement as he felt it. Like the roots of a tree, it spread in veins across the basin, broken in regions where the Humans had torn up the ground and extracted it. He took a deep breath and began to draw the potential energy around him. He coaxed it to live, enticed it into his body, and it filled him so that he nearly trembled from the growing pressure. Never had he channeled so much at once, and it left him on the verge of unconsciousness. He could no longer feel the physical form of his body; there was only the magic breathing through him, holding his being together.

Is this what an immortal feels? he wondered. The thought came and went, and then he began to shape the power and fuse it with the Shadow inherent in his being, reaching with it as an extension of his own arms, digging below the ground and coursing along every vein of Ice. He was vaguely aware of the earth quaking, the cracks and pops of rock and ice breaking around him. Where the magic could not escape, the pressure welled and erupted in a geyser of black and glittering shards, but the Demon saw none of it. He was the spider at the center of the web, feeling every silken line tremble until they began to grow still. One strand broke and fell away, then another. The web collapsed from beneath him, and he was falling....

The Demon opened his eyes and took a breath. A faint smile crossed his lips. *I did it, Em'ri. I destroyed the Black Ice. The Seroko will never know immortality. We won.*

He lifted himself on unsteady arms, just long enough to see how the landscape had changed around him. There were deep fissures and craters and massive rocks that jutted upward like broken teeth. It was a glorious sight, the result of unbridled chaos and power. He, the artist, was the only witness—the only one who would ever know the truth behind such an orchestration of elemental energy.

The Demon gave a weak laugh and fell back to the ground, spent. He closed his eyes again but maintained a satisfied smile as the cold began to move in around him. Eventually someone would discover his body, frozen and lifeless, but still he would bear his smile. It was a fanciful thought; he should have known better.

Much like how the earth had erupted, it felt as though his leg had exploded. The Demon cried, and stared at the black arrow jutting from his calf. Blue-white light flared and spat where the projectile met his skin, burning and slowly dissolving his flesh. He ground his teeth in misery, searching the darkness for the one responsible.

There were two glowing figures—one in the distance, pale and blue, the other golden and nearly at his side. The Demon gawked at him in utter disbelief—right until the Ilangien's proximity forced him to lean over and vomit.

Eraekryst knelt a few feet from him, his fair face bereft of expression. "You, then, are Arythan Crow, the demon-mage of Cerborath," he said. "You are not how my lady recalled you." Sharp silver-blue eyes swept over him discerningly, as though they had never seen him before. "The Huntress, she has restored you, as she told me."

The Demon looked from him to the arrow. "Why?" he gasped.

"I am told you were the cause of much death and destruction," Eraekryst said. He lifted his head and gestured toward the landscape. "A demon's work, indeed. The Huntress deems there is no need for you." He leaned closer, a slight twitch indicating his own discomfort at their proximity. "But my Lady Catherine, she had told me otherwise. I seek the truth."

"The truth?" The Demon reached for the arrow to pull it free, but his hands started to burn as they neared the shaft. He made a sound and fell back upon the ground. "Y're an idiot."

Eraekryst blinked, his brow furrowed.

"'S death!" the Demon yelled at him. He swore and closed his eyes, as if to shut out the pain.

"A consequence of what you have done," the Ilangien said calmly. "I cannot remember. What are you to me? Is there a reason I am here for you? Tell me, demon."

The Demon looked at him, searched those vacant eyes and found...nothing. "What 'appened to y'?" he whispered. Eraekryst frowned, but the Demon's attention shifted to the dark and malevolent creature who came to stand over the Ilangien's shoulder. It was her—the one from his visions of the past—the one who had brought him back from the dead...only to kill him again.

"I'm already dead," the Demon growled at her.

"Not so," she said, her eyes bleeding into him. "You will become mine." She bent down to touch the arrow with her fingertips, and the light blazed brighter.

"Bitch!" the Demon shouted, writhing to move away from them.

"To have so weak a creature carelessly destroy so much," the Huntress said, "is intolerable. It is for us, Eraekryst, to wield Light and Shadow, order and chaos. It is the sole purpose of an immortal."

"Nigor-slet." The Demon glared at them both, his eyes burning from rage and from his increasing agony. *Let it end, already.* He clutched at his leg, feeling soft and mushy tissue where solid flesh had been. He turned away from them and watched the snow steam around him. *Let it end.*

ERAEKRYST WATCHED the creature suffer with growing unease. He had left Secrailoss with such determination, but the closer he came to Cerborath, the more his resolve had faltered. Then she had found him, and she had shown him all she had witnessed. A regent was dead, a castle was burning, men and women were fleeing, and some were being executed—all because of one chaotic creature. He had witnessed for himself the final act of the demon: the destruction of immortal remains from beneath the earth. And the demon had laughed.

A persistent voice echoed Seranonde's words. A voice he could not seem to shake. A voice that he had not known before. There was logic there, in what the Huntress wanted. Immortals regaining control over a world immersed in ignorance and uncertainty.

Mortals without guidance, mortals who seemed intent on destroying each other. Eraekryst thought he had known his enemy, but now he was not so certain, and he had no memory to determine right from wrong.

He thought of Catherine and the Forgotten, and he wondered how their story was so very different from the one Seranonde imparted. Why was nothing clear? Why were the answers not obvious to him as they had always been before?

The demon's soul would be added to Seranonde's collection, and then he would never know the truth. Selfish as it seemed, the demon was the only one with answers for him. He had to know; he had to see it before it was too late.

Eraekryst ignored the voice that warned him against what he was about to do. He reached out to the demon with his mind, forcing his way inside. The reaction was unexpected.

A connection was made, and images blurred together like watercolors. Eraekryst's own memories sank from his consciousness as he lived the life of another. A white-skinned child born from a violent transgression, the death of his mother, the rejection of his father. Of wellings and beatings and isolation, there emerged a solitary hope of finding a lost brother. Flight from the island he had known as home, into the hard, calloused hands of slavery, and then welcomed by thieves. Faces he had come to care for were taken from him, and he was cast into the darkness of imprisonment. By a miracle he was liberated by the brother he so desperately sought, and for a short while, he was loved. His brother died for him, murdered by those driven by avarice. Alone he wandered, hiding, running, fearing his own inevitable end.

The Black Mountain, the glowing prisoner. A touch of compassion that prompted a daring escape. Two fates intertwined, and a horrific change that tore him in half. Hunger, cold, abuse, followed by acceptance and hope of a new life. Death struck again, robbing him of a family. A king called him to duty, and a woman called upon his heart. He shared in a new life, a part of himself—but the life was extinguished. Deceit and lies strangled the truth, and by his own hands, a death. In darkness he was locked away, poisoned, drowned in despair. Finally, his own death.

Not an ending. A resurrection, a decision made. A final mission as his body failed him. And then…betrayal.…

"Get out! GET OUT!" The sounds of the Demon's shrieks roused him from this other life. Eraekryst blinked and realized his vision had blurred. He wiped away the tears and tried to catch his breath, overwhelmed by the deluge of emotion flooding his senses. But he was not the only one.

The Demon cried and clutched at his head. *"I am not broken! I am not broken!"* he shouted until his words ran hoarse. Though spoken in another language, Eraekryst understood. And he knew the Demon had traded his own memories for Eraekryst's fragmented past.

This was his friend. The one who had saved him from Kirou-Mekus. The one who appeared time and time again, when he was in need or when he was needed. This was the friend he had betrayed—betrayed with the intention of saving him from Seranonde the Huntress.

Eraekryst looked up at her, only to find she was staring back at him with grim disappointment. "You could not trust me," she said.

He shook his head. "He is Shadow, but you are darkness."

"Because I chose to survive? Because I believe in the validity of our existence? I thought you were worthy of this mantle, Eraekryst, but for all you endured, you do not have the strength." Seranonde started toward the Demon.

"Leave him. He is nothing for you," Eraekryst said.

"He is mine, as are you." She crouched over the Demon.

Eraekryst bore into her with his eyes. *"Stop."* Whether he had uttered the words, or spoken in her mind, she did not heed him. He pushed all other thoughts aside and concentrated upon his enemy. The wall of her mind towered high into the night sky, and there were no cracks or holes in the stone. Seranonde was without weakness, impenetrable with power. But what she did not know was that her opponent was broken. He had been broken in order to reach the full potential of his abilities. Madness knew no limitation.

"Seranonde! You will heed me!" he cried to her. He placed both hands upon the face of a stone and pushed. It was so very solid. He pushed again, with more force, but the result was the same. *I am cleverer than this,* he thought, and he tapped his fingers on the stone in thought. Then he smiled.

With the tip of his fingernail, he traced jagged, imaginary lines across the smooth surface. Then he made a fist and slammed it into the stone. The wall trembled ever so slightly, and he curled in agony, clutching his throbbing hand. *Sweet pain,* Eraekryst muttered and took a breath before repeating the action. Again and again he smashed his hand against the stone until it was painted with his blood, and his hand was shattered in a discolored pulp. Tears streamed down his face, but there was a popping sound as the lines he had drawn materialized into cracks, and the cracks began to spread.

Eraekryst took a step back, watching as the stone fell away, leaving a neat little hole where it had been. *Were I the old man, I would not fit,* he thought, pulling himself to the other side. Such darkness he had never known. It dripped from the void, permeated the air, surged beneath his feet.

"What has happened to your heart, Huntress?" he asked. *"Or did you choose such a path? Why would anyone want this?"* His voice was swallowed by the blackness. *"You are here somewhere. I will find you."*

He took off his boots and started forward, the darkness sucking at his feet like mud. *"I once knew darkness too. In the mountain, for so many years. Is that why you chose me?"*

"She never chose you, Ilangien."

The intruder's voice in his head caused him to stop. *"You. You trespasser. You escaped from the Veil, did you not?"*

"I am her chosen."

Eraekryst shook his head. *"Jealousy does not flatter you. Is your heart so dark? Remember that she left you to your fate. She alone escaped justice, and she alone enjoyed freedom while you remained a bodiless spirit."*

When there was no response, he shrugged and ventured on. *This is hopeless and depressing. If there is no light to be found, then I should bring light to her.* From his hand he produced a leaf, and it began to glow. Trace outlines of barren trees formed before him. *This is Seranonde,* he mused sadly, thinking of the forest in his own mind. He crushed the leaf in his hand, forming a tight fist. Light streamed from between his fingers, and when he uncurled them, an acorn-like nut sat shining on his palm.

Just a suggestion. He knelt down and swept away some of the darkness as though it was dirt. He set the seed down, patted it, and covered it again. The ground-that-was-not quivered beneath his bare feet. *"Oh, what have I done,"* he wondered aloud, and walked away, back toward the wall from whence he intruded. He slipped back out the hole and waited.

Seranonde remained motionless over the Demon, as though someone had carved her from stone. Suddenly she turned toward the Ilangien, her eyes afire. She said nothing, but she rose to her feet and started toward him. From her hip she drew a black sword that was similar in adornment to those Eraekryst had seen in the Veil.

His journey into her mind had tired him more than he realized, for when he tried to stand, he nearly fell down again. There was no time to consider a strategy; he could only act. She swung at him so quickly that he was barely able to erect a wall of resistance between them. He could feel his strength ebbing, and the cursed blade cut through his resistance. He rolled away to evade her, but she struck again, piercing his side.

In shock of the pain, he gave a cry and pulled his hand away to stare at the golden blood upon it. Seranonde bore down upon him, digging her fingers into the wound. She licked them clean and reached to grab his throat.

"No!" Eraekryst shouted. He shoved her away with the force of his will, and she landed on her side a distance away, shock upon her face. "I am not a child! I will not be manipulated again!" With as much energy as he could muster, he got to his knees and glared at her. "Get up!" he commanded.

She fought him like a dog against its tether.

"UP!" he repeated, trembling with fury. He lifted his hand, and she slowly rose, as though her legs and arms were weighted with bags of rocks.

Eraekryst nodded toward the Demon, who had since ceased writhing but still twitched in his growing weakness. One labored step at a time, the Huntress approached him, her jaw set, her eyes bulging. Eraekryst's next commands were silent, the intensity of his gaze speaking where words could not. He forced her to kneel beside the Demon and grasp the shaft of the arrow.

"Draw the Light from him," he ordered. She fought him harder, and the pressure in his head felt as though it would shatter his skull. Still, he did not relent, watching as the luminous flames retreated from the Demon's leg and back into the projectile. Once the Light had subsided, only Shadow remained.

Eraekryst could have let her go. He could have forced her to leave, knowing that he had made a mortal enemy of her, and that she would return for vengeance. Even with the piece of himself that he had planted in her mind, he could not defeat her, but he had promised to try. He would keep his promise to honor Catherine, the Forgotten, and salvage what he could of his friend's remaining years.

"Take his pestilence," he ordered, and Seranonde asserted her greatest resistance yet. The Demon's Shadow would be her end. *"TAKE IT!"* Eraekryst demanded, his vision beginning to darken.

The inky black of the Demon's shadowy parasite enveloped the arrow and snaked up to Seranonde's arms. It infused into her pale flesh, and she shrieked, finally breaking the fragile hold Eraekryst had upon her. He fell back, blind as consciousness sought to abandon him to his fate. He could not allow it, could not succumb to the whim of the Huntress again. He blinked away the darkness, breathing fully and slowly until the landscape sharpened. Seranonde was gone.

Eraekryst crawled to the Demon's side, fearing he was too late. The creature lay there, his eyes closed, his breathing shallow. *"Durmorth,"* he said gently.

The Demon did not respond, and Eraekryst's eyes moved to where the shaft of the arrow still jutted from his friend's emaciated leg. Much of the white skin was gone from his ankle to his knee. Sticky, red pulp remained, and there were places where the white of bone emerged from the horrific mess. Eraekryst took hold of the arrow and it dissolved in his hands.

The sweat-lathered brow of the Demon furrowed, and a pair of foxlike eyes stared up at him. Eraekryst held his regard as though it was a physical contact, and there were no words to be said. They understood each other beyond the insight of any casual friendship. Each had gazed through the eyes of the other, lived with the breath of the past and felt the same emotions. And when the fire of that exchange had fizzled, there yet remained a bond where Light and Shadow could not divide them. Neither of them knew the depth or the true nature of that link—only that they were no longer alone in the turmoil they had lived. And it called to question just how they would face the future that awaited them.

Eraekryst turned at the sound of approaching footfalls. The Demon lifted his head as much as he could, waiting for the intruder. The dark shape separated from the night and loomed over them, a glint of moonlight in the pools of black that were her eyes. Narga nuzzled the Ilangien's shoulder and reached down to nibble upon her master's cloak. Eraekryst glimpsed it, though he would never make light of the rarity: the subtle smile that surfaced through the Demon's pain. Not all Shadow was darkness, and not all darkness was maligned. Until the end of days, for every dawn, a nightfall.

33

SOUTHWARD TRAIL

For the hundredth time, Victoria turned her focus to the north, searching amongst the snow-laden tree branches, boring into the shadows, squinting at the furthest stretch of the obscured trail she could see. Dawn had come, bright and cold, and with it was the truth she did not want to face.

"He is not coming, and you know it," Banen said. He sat beside her and the two children, handing her a bowl of hot stew.

She wrapped her hands around it, allowing the steam to warm her face. Mirabel and Riley were already busy with their own meals, or they might still have been clinging to her side. She had always wanted to be a mother, but she never thought she would inherit growing children. Her heart bled for the young heirs, robbed of their mother and their birthright. They would leave Cerborath and settle elsewhere, with new names and new lives.

Tigress had led them down the steep hill and to the forest, and there they discovered they were not alone. The Ice Flies were waiting for them, a man they called, "The Owl," at their helm. The group had escorted them through the darkness, but after a while it became clear that no one was following them. They had left the Seroko behind…left them behind with Arythan.

"I know," Victoria said quietly. "But I know he's alive. I know it."

The Owl—Othenis Strix—stepped up behind her. "Not to intrude, but my faith is with yours. He is, however, as slippery as the wind. When we didn't find him at the Ice Plains, there was only one other place he could be. I thought he would have escaped with you."

"He was never one to be trusted," Banen said.

"So how long did *you* know?" Tigress asked, suddenly voicing herself.

"Since my father's wedding." Banen kicked at a stick in the snow. "I heard his story when we were imprisoned by the madman of a wizard, but stories are stories, and I could not be sure…."

"If he was truly a demon?" Tigress asked wryly.

"His is an interesting past," Othenis said, "though I find it difficult to weed tale from truth. All I can speak for is his ability to disappear. If he is alive, I hope that he might see it fit to find us."

"Or not," Banen muttered. "Good riddance."

"Whether you liked him or not, he aided in our escape," Tigress said. "Give him a little merit."

Victoria listened as the conversation turned, but her thoughts lingered upon the mage named Arythan Crow—her husband. Yes, he was still her husband, regardless of what changes had come upon him. She understood now why he did not care to divulge his past, but he was somehow more a mystery now than ever before. Still he had shared with her an intimacy, and he had, with her, started a new life. It had ended tragically, but Victoria knew the blame was not for him. Diana Sherralin had been right: they had both lost so much. She set down her bowl and took Banen's hand. Arythan was gone, and she had to focus on what remained, what lay ahead in an uncertain future. She would never forget that he had come back for her, to see her safe, and in her heart she would guard the piece of her that loved him still.

~

NARGA SNATCHED a mouthful of greenery as they broke into the clearing. The mountains were pale and garbed in clouds where they rose above the trees, and the stream ran with vigor, fed by the remaining snow of an early thaw. The wildflowers the Demon remembered were not yet in bloom, but otherwise the setting was unchanged, remote and pristine. It had been a long winter…far longer than the Demon could ever have imagined. And still he wondered if it all had truly happened.

He glanced at his shaking hands, then back at the white monolith that stood like a foreign tree in the midst of the forest. Last he had seen it, he had been with his brother. It was not Emérion Aguilos who stood at the structure's base, however. Like a fragment of sunshine, Eraekryst stood tall and radiant, his gaze turned up in wonder at what he called an "Aryn."

The Demon tapped Narga on the rump, and the mare lowered to the ground so he could dismount. Even after a couple months, he would have thought his leg would have shown some sign of improvement. It still throbbed, still burned; he wondered if he would ever walk the same again. He pulled free the cane he had affixed to the saddle and slid from the mare's back. The blood rushed down to his feet, and he closed his eyes and clenched his teeth while the initial flood of pain came and abated. Then he limped his way to where the Ilangien waited.

"It's the Shadow in you," Eraekryst murmured, as if answering a question.

The Demon paused. It was a token phrase his brother had used. He doubted the Ilangien even realized the memory was not his.

Eraekryst was a patchwork of recollections—only some of them his own—and the lines had since blurred.

"'Tis why the status of your appendage but slowly changes. It *does* change, despite what you believe. The *Ilán* is as much as poison to you as your *Durós* is to me." Eraekryst turned to him and lifted his chin. "Why do you insist upon suffocating yourself?"

The Demon had produced a jack and took a deep hit. "I don' know," he said quietly. "Calms me down."

"Are you so agitated?"

He shrugged. "No. 'S an 'abit." He redirected his attention to the Aryn. "So 'ere we are. Is it all y'oped it would be?"

Eraekryst smiled but said nothing. He placed his hands upon the surface of the stone and closed his eyes.

The Demon waited, wondering if the Ilangien would have some kind of reaction. Eraekryst was certainly more expressive than when they first met, and his eccentricities had increased beyond what anyone else might deem sane. The Demon knew better. If Eraekryst was mad, then he would hardly be the one to judge him so. They were both marked by their experiences, and if others found them more than strange, so be it. He was through with trying to live a Human life. Unfortunately, Eraekryst seemed more intrigued by them than ever. The Demon wondered if he had cut his hair to better keep a mortal appearance, though oddly enough, his blond locks had not grown a sliver in the months they had traveled.

"The rumors abound, *Durmorth*," the Ilangien murmured. "Already I hear tales of the Dark Wizard who destroyed a kingdom, died, and was resurrected as a Demon."

"'S not a story, an' I don' really care."

"The peculiar and dark mark upon your visage runs deeper than your skin, perhaps. You still have not explained it."

"Something about me y' don' know, eh?" the Demon asked,

watching as Eraekryst pulled away from the Aryn and opened his eyes.

The bright, silver-blue eyes were suddenly upon him. "Ah, but what I *do* know..." He gestured to the Aryn. "Stand there, and set your colorless claws upon the stone."

"Why?" the Demon asked, defiant. He crossed his arms.

"To satiate my curiosity. I would venture you do not understand your role in this."

I would wipe that smug look off your face if I weren't just as curious, the Demon thought. He set the jack between his lips and placed his trembling hands upon the Aryn. *If only that immortal witch could have taken all my plague with her. She bought me a little time, but my end will be the same. It seems I have nothing to do other than follow Erik on his righteous mission to find and destroy her.*

"Clear your thoughts," Eraekryst's voice intruded in his mind. Yet another gift of the link they now shared. The Ilangien did not have to read his thoughts to be able to speak to him in his head. The Demon found it was not an altogether unwelcome form of communication. He could speak to his friend without having to open his mouth.

"Close your eyes. Imagine a door. Push your way through it."

"What?"

"Push!"

The Demon sighed and pushed. What had been solid beneath his hands gave way to emptiness. He nearly pitched forward, but his cane saved him from a fall. His eyes snapped open to see a black and undefined void where stone had been. *"Nigqora."*

"Such a filthy tongue," Eraekryst muttered, but then he drew up to the Aryn proudly and spun to see his companion's reaction. "Well?"

"'S a black 'ole," the Demon said, but his voice was not without wonder.

"A doorway. An opening. A passage. What had been locked is now open. *Durmorth,* you *are* the Key."

The Demon stood there, dumbfounded. *After all this Key nonsense, everyone was right. Sulinda Patrice, Othenis Strix... Em'ri, what did you do? Why entrust me with this responsibility and not tell me about it?* Then it occurred to him the absurdity of what he was witnessing. "Tell me again about the Aryn," he said to Eraekryst.

"Traditionally, it is a gateway to the knowledge and past experiences of the Durgoth. I have never, until now, seen one." The corner of his mouth twisted upward. "And this one is not entirely Durgoth-wrought. The *Ilán* is present here as well."

"Why would immortals care about the Gray Watcher Archives?" the Demon asked.

"Why indeed," Eraekryst mused, clearly delighted with the mystery. "Shall we venture yonder, oh Key?" He gestured grandly toward the void.

"Y'd like that, wouldn't y'?"

"It would entertain me, verily."

The Demon gave a nod toward the Aryn. "'S all that really matters. Y' first." He watched Eraekryst move forward without hesitation before following him into darkness.

The Adventure Continues...

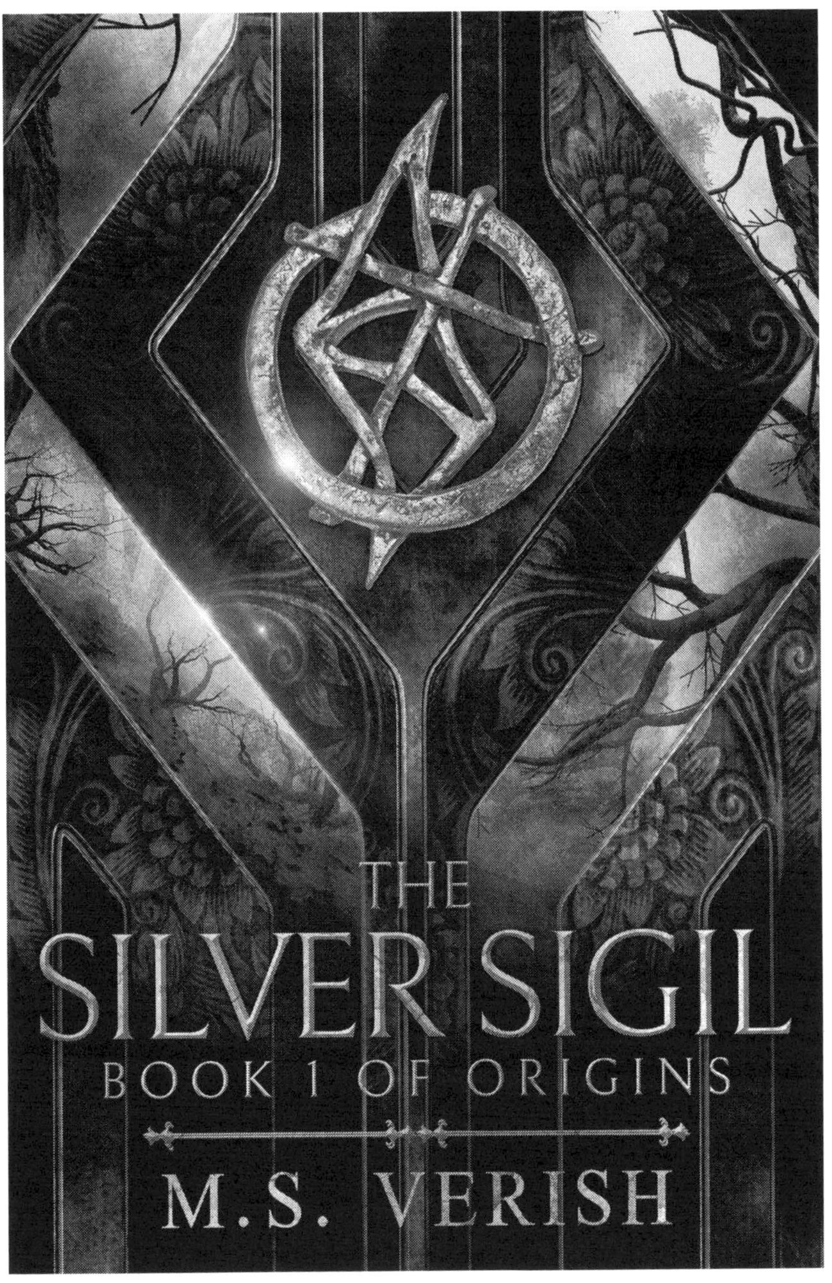

GLOSSARY AND PRONUNCIATION

Archives, the: the hidden wealth of knowledge accumulated by the Gray Watchers since the time of the Cataclysm

Aryn (AR-in): a monolith in which a Durgoth stores memories of ages past; may also serve as a gateway

Arythan Crow, Medoriate (AIR-ih-than): the alternate name applied to the Falquirian-mage who was once the Demon; also known as "the Dark Wizard of the North"

Banen Garriker: prince and second-born son of Michael Garriker II; half-brother to Michael Garriker III; his name in the B.E.S.T. is Thorn

B.E.S.T., the: Cerborath's royal, elite syndicate; the B.E.S.T. are: Tigress, Hunter, Dagger, Crow, and Thorn

Black Ice: a magical substance used as an enhancement

Black Mountain, the: see Kirou-Mekus

Bloodrot: vulgar, derogatory term for a Medoriate

Brandeise (BRAN-days): Southern Kingdom colony located on a peninsula in Secrailoss

Brann Alwin: lead medoriate for the Merchants' Guild in the production of Black Ice

Cantalere (kant-ah-LEER): a tool that aids a wizard in focusing and accessing magic; often magic is instilled within them to serve a purpose; cantalere may be a gesture, an object, or a spoken spell

Cantalereum (kant-ah-LEER-ee-um): a place where items of magical value---cantalere---are kept and maintained

Caster: a slang Human term for a magic-user or medoriate

Cataclysm, the: a catastrophic event in Secramorian history involving the battle between the being known as Jedinom and his nemesis Ocranthos

Catherine Lorrel: the Countess of Silvarn; cousin to King Garriker II

Celaedrion (sell-AY-dree-un): an Ilangien territory located within Veloria

Cerborath (SER-bōr-ath): the northernmost domain in the Northern Kingdoms

Crag's Crown: the castle residence of Cerborath's royal family

Crimson Dragon, the: a group of renowned traveling performers

Cyrul Frostmeyer, Medoriate: former royal wizard to King Michael Garriker II

Dagger: member of the B.E.S.T. whose expertise is tracking and wielding knives

Dark Elves: also known as the Durangiel

Demon, the (White): the half-Falquirian, half-Ocrantilian former mascot thief of the Prophet's clan; half-brother to Hawkwing

Desnera (dez-NAIR-uh): Northern Kingdom that rivals Cerborath

Diana Sherralin: medic and healer of the royal city of Cerborath

Durangiel (der-ANN-jee-el): Ilangiel who freely promote the *Durós* though they cannot wield it; singular, Durangien

Durgoth (DURE-goth): also known as Death Mages, they are an immortal race of beings who bear Shadow, the *Durós*

***Durmorth* (der-MORTH):** the Ilangien word for "demon"

***Durós*, the (dure-ŌS):** the energy of Shadow

Elves: a vague term applied by Humans to all Humanlike, magical creatures of Veloria; see Ilangiel

Emérion Aguilos (em-AIR-ee-un AG-ee-lōs): the birth name of Hawkwing

Enhancement: a manipulated substance that enhances the senses of its user; also see Black Ice

Eraekryst of Celaedrion (eh-RAY-eh-krist): first-born son of Alaeryn and Alethea of Celaedrion, brother of Atrion; he is an Ilangien whose status is similar to a Human prince

Erik Sparrow, Lord: alternate "Human" identity for Eraekryst of Celaedrion

Forgotten, the: the six immortals who vanquished the renegade Durangiel after the War of Light and Shadow

Gray Watchers: a clandestine group formed as a result of the Cataclysm; oath-bound observers who cannot interfere but record all they witness to contribute to a vast Archive kept by the Three

Grim: the Desneran royal medoriate, affiliated with the Seroko and the Warriors of the Sword

Halgon Thayliss: the mayor of Brandeise in Secrailoss

Hawkshadow: half-brother to Hawkwing

Hawkwing: a Falquirian of the eagle tribe who was reputed for his skill as a tracker and as a guide for travelers; half-brother of the White Demon; see Emérion Aguilos

House of Jedinom: the organized system of Human religion that is centralized around the deity Jedinom

Humans: a race of mostly non-magic-wielding people

Hunter: Blacksmith member of the B.E.S.T.

Ice Flies: former Gray Watchers who have undertaken the cause of hindering the production of Black Ice

Ice Plains: the vast basin in Cerborath where the Black Ice is excavated

***Ilán*, the (ill-AHN):** the energy of the Light

Ilangiel (ill-AN-jee-el): an immortal race of beings who bear Light, the *Ilán*; Humans refer to them as Elves

Ilangien (ill-AN-jee-en): singular form of Ilangiel or an adjective describing something of the Ilangiel culture

Jack: an object that is smoked, as in a habitual practice of people; traditionally, a jack is a redcorn husk rolled and stuffed with filler

Jaice Ginmon: an adventurer for hire

Jedinom: in Human religion, he is the deity who assumed physical form to save his followers by battling the Dark One known as Ocranthos

Jornoans, the: a Humanlike race bearing special magical abilities

Kirou-Mekus (KEER-oo MEK-us): the Black Mountain where Jornoans keep captive Mentrailyics in order to divine prophecy

Ladonna Garriker: wife of Michael Garriker III

Larini, Maevia and Neriene: the witches responsible for the Cantalereum

Light: *Ilán*

Links: Northern, Eastern, Southern, Western: the four main roads that comprise the Traders' Ring

Lorrelwood: the manor and residence of Catherine Lorrel, Countess of Silvarn; also the surrounding forest

Lorth: an abbreviation of Delorth; often used in Human slang, curses, and expressions

Lucinda Jerian: the former queen of Desnera; elder sister of Sabrina Jerian

Mage, Magess: a magic-wielding person or medoriate with a special aptitude for channeling natural energies, such as elemental magic; a mage does not need cantalere

Magic: a form of energy that can often be wielded or influenced by medori

Medori (meh-DOR-ee): the plural form of medoriate; a general grouping and proper term for magic-wielders: wizards, mages, and the like

Medoriate (meh-DOR-ee-at): singular form of medori

Mentrailyic (men-TRAY-lik): a "mind wizard" of varying abilities that involve the mind; some Mentrailyic abilities include telepathy, clairvoyance, telekinesis, and similar capacities

Merchants' Guild: the organization throughout Secramore that influences commerce; the front for the Seroko

Meridian: the point through which all possibilities exist

Metamorph: a person with the ability to change his form

Michael Garriker II: regent of Cerborath of the Northern Kingdoms

Michael Garriker III: first-born son of Michael Garriker II; half-brother to Banen Garriker

Minstrel, the: the reputed identity of Lord Erik Sparrow for his skill playing the violin

Mystland: medori territory consisting of Norkindara and Sorkindara

Naeva (nah-AY-vah): Durangien queen of the Nightwind Mountains

Narga: Arythan Crow's black mare

Nightwind Mountains: mountains in Northern Secramore to where the Durangiel retreated and now reside

Northern Kingdoms, the: a Human territory including the kingdoms of Cerborath, Caspernyanne, Desnera, Morwind, Damarus, and Sorvindale

Ocranthos (oh-CRAN-thōs): also known as "Oqrantos"; the being known as the Dark One worshiped by the Ocrantilians; the deity nemesis of Jedinom imprisoned during the Cataclysm

Ocrantilians (oh-cran-TILL-ee-ans): formerly exiled and

branded Nemeloreans, they were chosen by Ocranthos to be his followers; Ocranthos altered them into a demonic race that was banished to the Blackdust Islands after the Dark One was imprisoned

Old Magic: the natural, elemental magic of a mage

Othenis Strix (oh-TEN-us): former Gray Watcher and leader of the Ice Flies

Prophet, the: the alias of Nikolon Omarand, the former Mentrailyic noble who led a notorious band of thieves in the Carycos Desert

Qaidao Altyrix (kay-DAH-oh ALL-teer-icks): Ocrantilian priest-king and father of Quolonero Altyrix

Quake, the: a plague-like sickness first inflicted upon the Falquirian race by the Man of Ashes; the signature symptom of the sickness is constant, involuntary trembling

Quolonero Altyrix (kwoh-LO-ner-oh ALL-teer-icks): the son of Qaidao Altyrix; birth name of the "White Demon"

Reiqo (RYE-koh): the son of Victoria Ambrin and Arythan Crow

Sabrina Jerian: sister to Lucinda Jerian and wife of Michael Garriker II; the current queen of Desnera

Safir-Tamik (sa-FEER tah-MEEK): the Jornoan once known as Asmat

Sara: servant of the Countess of Silvarn who resides in Lorrelwood Manor

Secrailoss (SEK-ray-loss): the mysterious and largely unexplored continent adjacent to Northern and Southern Secramore

Secramore (SEK-rah-more): the world of the Northern and Southern continents

Seranonde the Huntress (sair-uh-NON-duh): the female Durangien who escaped retribution for her crimes against her people at the end of the War of Light and Shadow

Seroko, the (ser-OH-koh): the corrupt faction of the former Gray Watchers who use the Merchants' Guild as their front

Shadow: *Durós* or the dark, intangible form of the Demon

Stone of Prophecy, the: also known as the Immortal Prophet or the Seer of the Mountain, he is an Ilangien Mentrailyic with a special gift in foresight; he is employed to find the One Fate; see Eraekryst of Celaedrion

Sulinda Patrice: an agent of the Seroko

Summerfall: a Northern Kingdom festival celebrating the end of the harvest season

Thorn: member of the B.E.S.T. who is secretly the second-born prince, Banen Garriker

Tigress: captain of the B.E.S.T.

Traders' Ring: a prominent, well-traveled route connecting all parts of Northern Secramore; it is divided into four parts: the Northern, Eastern, Southern, and Western Links

Valestia: paradise in the afterlife

Veil, the: clandestine location in Secrailoss where the Forgotten are exiled

Veloria (vel-OR-ee-ah): the Ilangien forest territory; also known by Humans as the Great Forest or the Haunted Forest

Victoria Ambrin: wife of Medoriate Arythan Crow

War of Light and Shadow, the: war between the immortal races of the Ilangiel and the Durgoth to maintain a balance of order and chaos in the newly-created world

Warriors of the Sword: the radical religious faction of the House of Jedinom

Welling: an amassing of power that occurs when magic is restrained; the power is usually released in an eruptive reaction

Wizard: a magic-user or medoriate who generalizes in contrived magic but must summon his power by means of cantalere

Wizard's Sand: a solid form of Wizard's Fire

Wizard's Fire: artificially induced fire devised by wizards that burns longer and requires less fuel than natural flames; some Wizard's Fire may or may not generate heat in addition to light

ABOUT THE AUTHORS

M.S. Verish, better known as Matthew and Stefanie Verish, are co-authors as well as husband and wife. They knew they were destined for marriage when they could write together without killing each other. Their writing partnership has rewarded them with wonderful journeys into the realm of fantasy, culminating in their epic world, *Secramore*. The couple shares a love of nature and art and lives in Northeast Ohio with their shelties and large family of cavies.